Praise for Elin Hilderbrand's
The Hotel Nantucket

"Hilderbrand is the absolute queen of beach reads, and her latest offering is dishy and fun, as a classic Nantucket hotel attempts to reinvent itself with a new billionaire owner. It might look glamorous on the outside, but behind closed doors there's plenty of dysfunction among the staff, drama on the guest side, and a bad reputation the place can't shake from a tragic fire in 1922."
—Mackenzie Dawson, *New York Post*

"Hilderbrand, who has perfected the romantic beach read, returns with a summer scandal at a Nantucket hotel, where general manager Lizbet Keaton, fresh off a bad breakup, struggles to revive the storied but floundering business—and to write her own second act." —Barbara VanDenburgh, *USA Today*

"*The Hotel Nantucket* has lots to love: great food, juicy gossip, secrets and scandals, and that special something that Hilderbrand delivers novel after novel."
—Sarah Gelman, *Business Insider*

"It doesn't feel like summer unless I read an Elin Hilderbrand book, which I've done every year for almost a decade...Her stories are full of secrets and

The Hotel Nantucket

ALSO BY ELIN HILDERBRAND

The Hotel Nantucket

A Novel

Elin Hilderbrand

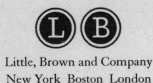

Little, Brown and Company
New York Boston London

Copyright © 2022 by Elin Hilderbrand
Excerpt from *The Five-Star Weekend* © 2023 by Elin Hilderbrand

Hachette Book Group supports the right to free expression and the value of copyright. The purpose of copyright is to encourage writers and artists to produce the creative works that enrich our culture.

The scanning, uploading, and distribution of this book without permission is a theft of the author's intellectual property. If you would like permission to use material from the book (other than for review purposes), please contact permissions@hbgusa.com. Thank you for your support of the author's rights.

Back Bay Books / Little, Brown and Company
Hachette Book Group
1290 Avenue of the Americas, New York, NY 10104
littlebrown.com

Little, Brown and Company is a division of Hachette Book Group, Inc. The Little, Brown name and logo are trademarks of Hachette Book Group, Inc.

The publisher is not responsible for websites (or their content) that are not owned by the publisher.

The Hachette Speakers Bureau provides a wide range of authors for speaking events. To find out more, go to hachettespeakersbureau.com or email hachettespeakers@hbgusa.com.

Little, Brown and Company books may be purchased in bulk for business, educational, or promotional use. For information, please contact your local bookseller or the Hachette Book Group Special Markets Department at special.markets@hbgusa.com.

Printed in the United States of America

Originally published in hardcover by Little, Brown and Company, June 2022

First Little, Brown and Company mass market edition, June 2023

10 9 8 7 6 5 4 3 2 1

*For Mark and Gwenn Snider
and the entire staff of the Nantucket Hotel
with my love and gratitude*

The Hotel Nantucket

1. The Cobblestone Telegraph

Nantucket Island is known for its cobblestone streets and red-brick sidewalks, cedar-shingled cottages and rose-covered arches, long stretches of golden beach and refreshing Atlantic breezes—and it's also known for residents who adore a juicy piece of gossip (which hot landscaper has been romancing which local real estate mogul's wife—that kind of thing). However, none of us are quite prepared for the tornado of rumors that rolls up Main Street, along Orange Street, and around the rotary out to Sconset when we learn that London-based billionaire Xavier Darling is investing thirty million dollars in the crumbling eyesore that is the Hotel Nantucket.

Half of us are intrigued. (We have long wondered if anyone would try to fix it up.)

The other half are skeptical. (The place, quite frankly, seems beyond saving.)

Xavier Darling is no stranger to the hospitality business. He has owned cruise lines, theme parks, racetracks, and even, for a brief time, his own airline. But to our knowledge, he has never owned a hotel—and he has never set foot on Nantucket.

With the help of a local real estate mogul, Eddie Pancik—aka "Fast Eddie" (who, for the record, has been happily reunited with his wife)—Xavier makes the savvy decision to hire Lizbet Keaton as his general manager. Lizbet is an island sweetheart. She moved to Nantucket in the mid-aughts from the Twin Cities, wearing her blond hair in two long braids like the younger princess in *Frozen,* and at the start of her first summer on island, she found a "prince" in JJ O'Malley. For fifteen seasons, Lizbet and JJ ran a wildly popular restaurant called the Deck; JJ was the owner/chef and Lizbet the marketing whiz. Lizbet was the one who came up with the idea for the rosé fountain and the signature stemless wine-glasses printed with the day's date that became a social media phenomenon. Not all of us cared about Instagram, but we did love spending long Sunday afternoons at the Deck drinking rosé, eating JJ's famous oyster pan roast, and gazing out over the shallow creeks of Monomoy, where we spied the occasional white egret fishing for dinner among the eelgrass.

We all believed that Lizbet and JJ had achieved what our millennials called #relationshipgoals. In the summer, they worked at the restaurant, and in the off-season, they could be found scalloping in Pocomo or sledding down the steep hill of Dead Horse Valley or shopping together at Nantucket Meat and Fish because they were planning to cure a side of salmon into gravlax or make a twelve-hour Bolognese. We'd see them holding hands in line at the post office and recycling their cardboard together at the dump.

We were all *shocked* when JJ and Lizbet broke up. We first heard the news from Blond Sharon. Sharon is the turbo engine behind Nantucket's rumor mill, so we were hesitant to believe it, but then Love Robbins at Flowers on Chestnut confirmed that Lizbet *sent back* a bouquet of roses that JJ had ordered.

Eventually the story came out: At the Deck's closing party back in September, Lizbet had discovered 187 sexually explicit texts that JJ had sent to their wine rep, Christina Cross.

Lizbet was, according to some, *desperate* to reinvent herself—and Xavier Darling provided a way. We wished her well, but the once-grand Hotel Nantucket had a tattered reputation to repair (along with the roof, windows, floors, walls, and sinking foundation).

Throughout the winter of 2021 and into the early spring of 2022, we watch local contractors, architects, and interior designer Jennifer Quinn entering and leaving the hotel—but every single employee has been sworn to secrecy about what's going on inside. There are whispers that our favorite fitness instructor, Yolanda Tolentino, has been hired to run the wellness center and that Xavier Darling is looking for someone with an "island pedigree" to operate the hotel's new bar. We see Lizbet Keaton come and go, but when Blond Sharon bumps into Lizbet in the vehicle-inspection line at Don Allen Ford—Lizbet in her Mini Cooper and Sharon in her G-Wagon—and asks how the hotel is coming along, Lizbet changes the subject to Sharon's children. (Sharon has no interest in talking about her children; they've just become teenagers.)

Jordan Randolph, the editor of the *Nantucket Standard,* ignores the first two calls he gets from Lizbet Keaton telling him the interior of the hotel is finished and asking if he would like a "behind-the-scenes first look." Jordan is one of the skeptics. He can't stand the idea of someone like Xavier Darling—a business titan from overseas—buying a historically significant property like the Hotel Nantucket. (Jordan is aware that Herman Melville wrote *Moby-Dick* before he ever visited the island. Does that make him feel any better? Not really.) But, Jordan reasons, if not Xavier Darling, then who? The place has been left to rot. Even the Nantucket Historical Association has deemed the hotel too big (and expensive) a project to take on.

When Lizbet calls the third time, Jordan answers the phone and reluctantly agrees to send a reporter.

Home and Lifestyle editor Jill Tananbaum is *obsessed* with interior design, as anyone who checks her Instagram will immediately realize (@ashleytstark, @elementstyle, @georgantas.design). Jill would love to use this job at the *Nantucket Standard* as a stepping-stone to a position at *Domino* or even *Architectural Digest*. Covering the renovation of the Hotel Nantucket could be just the way to do it. She's not going to leave out a single detail.

As soon as Jill steps through the grand front doors, her jaw drops. Hanging from the vaulted ceiling of the lobby is the skeleton of an antique whaling boat that has been ingeniously repurposed into a statement chandelier. The ceiling's beams, salvaged from the original structure, lend the room a sense of history. There are double-wide armchairs upholstered in hydrangea blue (which Jill soon learns is the hotel's signature color), suede tufted ottomans, and low tables that tastefully display books and games (backgammon, checkers, and four marble chess sets). The far corner of the room is anchored by a white baby grand piano. On the large wall next to the front desk hangs an enormous James Ogilvy photograph of the Atlantic off Sankaty Head that succeeds in bringing the ocean into the hotel.

Wow, Jill thinks. *Just...wow*. Her hand is itching to reach for her phone but Lizbet told her that, for the time being, photos are forbidden.

Lizbet gives Jill a tour of the guest rooms and suites. Local artist Tamela Cornejo has hand-painted the ceiling of each room with a mural of the Nantucket night sky. The light fixtures—glass spheres wrapped in brass chain link—evoke buoys and ropes. And the beds—*Excuse me, the beds!* Jill thinks. The beds have canopies fashioned from driftwood and thick nautical rope. They're a custom size—emperor—and they have ethereal white sheers hanging at the sides.

The bathrooms are the most spectacular Jill has ever seen in real life. Each one has a shower tiled with oyster shells, a hatbox toilet in a separate water closet, and a slipper tub, the base of which is painted the hotel's signature hydrangea blue.

"But the secret to success for any bathroom," Lizbet says to Jill, "isn't how *it* looks; it's how it makes the *guest* look." She flips a switch. Surrounding the long rectangular mirror over the double vanity is a soft halo light. "See how flattering?"

Jill and Lizbet gaze at themselves in the mirror like a couple of teenagers. *It's true,* Jill thinks; she has never looked dewier than she does standing in the bathroom of suite 217.

Then—then!—Lizbet tells Jill about the complimentary minibar. "I can't count the times I've been in a hotel room and just wanted a glass of wine and a salty snack, but being charged seventy dollars for a bottle of chardonnay and sixteen dollars for a pack of peanuts is offensive when I've already paid so much for the room. So our minibars will be stocked with a thoughtfully curated selection of Nantucket-sourced products"—she mentions Cisco beers, Triple

Eight vodka, and smoked bluefish pâté from 167 Raw—"and everything is free, replenished every three days."

Free minibar! Jill writes in her notes. *Nantucket products!* Jordan should give her article front-page placement for this announcement alone.

Lizbet leads Jill out back to see the pools. One is a sprawling family affair with cascading waterfalls. ("There will be lemonade and fresh-baked cookies served every day at three," Lizbet says.) The second pool is an adults-only sanctuary, a teal-blue lozenge surrounded by gray-shingled walls that will be covered with pale pink climbing roses in the height of summer. Around the pool are "the most comfortable chaise longues in the known world, extra-wide and easy to adjust," and stacks of custom-ordered Turkish cotton towels in hydrangea blue.

Next, it's off to the yoga studio. Jill has never been to Bali, but she *has* read *Eat, Pray, Love,* so she appreciates the aesthetic. The ceiling of the studio is an elaborate teak carving salvaged from a temple in Ubud. (Jill considers how much it must have cost to ship and install such a ceiling...*mind-exploding emoji!*) There's a gurgling stone fountain in the form of the somewhat terrifying face of the god Brahma that empties into a trough of river stones. The light from outside is diffused through rice-paper shades, and gamelan music plays over the sound system. *All in all,* Jill thinks, *the new yoga studio will be an idyllic place to find a child's pose.*

But as far as Jill is concerned, the ultimate reveal is the hotel's bar. It's a high-concept jewel box, a space painted Farrow and Ball's Pitch Blue (which falls on the spectrum between sapphire and amethyst) and a blue granite bar. There are domed pendant lights that look like upside-down copper bowls and an accent wall *sheathed in bright pennies!* There's also a copper disco ball that will drop from the ceiling every night at nine o'clock. There's nothing like it anywhere else on the island. Jill is gobsmacked. Can she make a reservation now, please?

Jill races back to her desk at the *Standard* office. Has she ever been so inspired to write a piece? She types like a fiend, getting all the details down—including the rainbow-hued Annie Selke rugs, the curated selection of novels on the bookshelves of the suites, the pin-tucked velvet stools in the new hotel bar—and then goes back over the piece one sentence at a time, making certain the language is as gracious and rich as the hotel itself.

When she finishes her final edit, she takes the piece to Jordan Randolph's office. He likes to read each feature article on paper and then mark it up with red pen like he's Maxwell Perkins editing Fitzgerald and Hemingway. Jill and her colleagues joke about this. Hasn't he ever heard of Google Docs?

Jill stands in the doorway as he reads, waiting for his usual "Outstanding." But when he finishes, he tosses the pages onto his desk and says, "Huh."

Huh? What is *huh?* Jill has never before heard her extremely articulate boss utter this syllable.

"Is it not okay?" Jill asks. "Is it...the writing?"

"The writing is fine," Jordan says. "Maybe it's *too* polished? This reads like one of those advertisement sections in the middle of *Travel and Leisure*."

"Oh," Jill says. "Okay, so..."

"I was hoping for more of a *story,*" Jordan says.

"I'm not sure there *is* more of a story," Jill tells him. "The hotel was falling to pieces and Xavier Darling bought it. He hired local—"

"Yes, you say that." Jordan sighs. "I wish there were another angle…" His voice trails off. "I'm not going to run it this week. Let me think on it for a little while." He smiles at Jill. "Thank you, though, for going to get a 'behind-the-scenes first look.'" He uses air quotes, which makes him seem like *such* a boomer. "I appreciate it."

Privately, Jordan Randolph suspects that the Hotel Nantucket will be like a work of art by Banksy—after it is unveiled, it will shine for one glorious moment and then self-destruct. One person who agrees is a ninety-four-year-old resident of Our Island Home named Mint Benedict. Mint is the only child of Jackson and Dahlia Benedict, the couple who owned the hotel from 1910 to 1922. Mint asks his favorite nurse, Charlene, to push him all the way to Easton Street in his wheelchair so that he can see the spiffy new facade of the hotel.

"They can fix it up but it won't succeed," Mint says. "Mark my words: The Hotel Nantucket is haunted, and it's all my father's fault."

Mint is talking nonsense, Charlene thinks, *and he definitely needs a nap.* She spins his chair toward home.

Haunted? we think.

Half of us are skeptical. (We don't believe in ghosts.)

Half of us are intrigued. (Just when we thought the story couldn't get any better!)

2. The Fifth Key

LIZBET KEATON'S BREAKUP PLAYLIST

"Good 4 U"—Olivia Rodrigo
"All Too Well" (Taylor's version)
—Taylor Swift
"If Looks Could Kill"—Heart
"You Oughta Know"—Alanis Morissette
"Far Behind"—Social Distortion
"Somebody That I Used to Know"
—Gotye
"Marvin's Room"—Drake
"Another You"—Elle King
"Gives You Hell"
—The All-American Rejects
"Kiss This"—The Struts
"Save It for a Rainy Day"
—Kenny Chesney
"I Don't Wanna Be in Love"
—Good Charlotte
"Best of You"—Foo Fighters
"Rehab"—Rihanna
"Better Now"—Post Malone
"Forget You"—CeeLo Green
"Salt"—Ava Max

"Go Your Own Way"—Fleetwood Mac
"Since U Been Gone"—Kelly Clarkson
"Praying"—Kesha

Ever since her devastating breakup with JJ O'Malley, Lizbet has been searching for an inspirational meme that will make her feel better. She spent seventy-seven dollars at Wayfair on a framed quote attributed to Socrates: *The secret of change is to focus all your energy not on fighting the old, but on building the new.* She hangs it on the wall at the end of her bed so that it's the first thing she sees when she wakes up and the last thing she sees before she turns off the light.

All your energy. Not on fighting the old. But on building the new. The secret of change.

Easier said than done, she thinks. She spends all her energy fighting the old.

Reliving September 30, the Last Night at the Deck.

Last Night at the Deck is a bittersweet tradition—it marks the end of the summer season. Lizbet and JJ have to say goodbye to the team they poured so much time and energy (and money) into building. Some of the staff will return next spring, but not everyone, so a summer can never be replicated. This, they've found, is both good and bad. Last Night is a time of bacchanalian revelry for the staff. Lizbet and JJ throw down an excellent party, opening tins of beluga caviar and bottle after bottle of Laurent-Perrier rosé.

One of the traditions is the staff photograph that Lizbet takes of them all leaning up against the railing with the Monomoy creeks behind them. She frames these photographs and hangs them in the hallway that leads to the restrooms. It's a record of sorts, an album, a history.

Tonight's picture will be the fifteenth. She can hardly believe it.

Lizbet calls for everyone to gather, and they configure themselves into a creative and cozy pose. Shorties up front! Goose, the sommelier, and Wavy, the head server, pick up Peyton, who is everyone's favorite (and quite petite besides), and hold her lengthwise. Christopher and Marcus reach for each other's hands, their first public acknowledgment that they've become a couple this summer. Ekash and Ibo and all the prep chefs, dishwashers, and food runners fill in, finding their places.

Lizbet uses JJ's phone to take the picture because it's sitting right there on table 10 in front of her. She punches in JJ's passcode—0311, her birthday—and his text messages pop up, all of them in an amusingly large font (JJ won't admit that he needs readers). Lizbet is about to click out of the texts when something catches her eye: I want you so badly. This is followed by Tell me what you want me to do to you. Lizbet freezes, but then she thinks, *Wait, this isn't JJ's phone after all.* It must be someone else's iPhone 13 Pro Max with an electric-blue cover and a photo of Anthony Bourdain on the back and her birthday as its passcode. A split second later—it's incredible how fast the brain processes even counterintuitive information—she understands that this *is* JJ's phone. These texts—she scrolls back until she finds pictures of a woman's breasts and what she knows to be JJ's erect penis—are being sent to and received from Christina Cross, their wine rep.

Goose calls out, "Take the picture already, Libby. This bitch is getting heavy!"

Lizbet's hands are shaking. What has she found? Is it real? Is this happening? Somehow she manages to play through (later, she will consider this a show of

14   *Elin Hilderbrand*

superhuman strength). She takes the pictures. They're
good. They're the best ever. Then Lizbet takes JJ's
phone and hurries to the ladies' room, where, sitting
in a stall, she reads through the pornographic text
messages—187 by Lizbet's count—that JJ and Christina have sent each other over the past three months,
the most recent of which was earlier that night. Lizbet
wants to flush the phone but she doesn't; she has the
wherewithal to take screenshots of the messages and
text them to herself.

Then Lizbet returns to the party. It's in full swing—
Polo G is singing "Martin and Gina" at top volume,
and Christopher, Marcus, and Peyton are dancing.
Lizbet finds JJ in the corner at table number 1, the
most sought-after in the restaurant, drinking a beer
with a couple of guys from the kitchen.

"There's my queen," JJ says when he sees her. He
places a hand on Lizbet's waist and tries to draw her
in for a kiss, but she stiff-arms him, pushing his phone
into his chest.

"I'm going home," she says.

"What?" JJ says. He takes his phone, and the texts
from Christina brighten on the screen. "Oh God, no.
Wait, Libby—"

Lizbet doesn't wait. She walks away, pushing past
Wavy, who senses something is wrong and tries to
stop her.

"It's not what it looks like!" JJ says.

Oh, but it is what it looks like, Lizbet thinks once
she gets back to the Bear Street cottage she owns with
JJ and reads through the texts one by one. *It's exactly
what it looks like.*

The Hotel Nantucket is perhaps the only place on
the island where Lizbet doesn't have any history or

memories with Jonathan James O'Malley, so when Lizbet hears that Xavier Darling has bought the hotel and is looking to hire a general manager, she drives straight to Bayberry Properties to see Fast Eddie.

"What can I do for you, Lizbet?" Eddie asks as she sits down across from him. She has caught him during a rare moment in the office. Eddie prefers to be out buzzing around the island in his Porsche Cayenne, wearing his panama hat, doing deals. "I hope you're not here to list your cottage? Though if you are, I can get you an excellent price—"

"What?" Lizbet says. "No!" She tilts her head. "Why? What have you heard?"

Eddie clears his throat and seems uncharacteristically reserved. "I heard that you and JJ parted ways…"

"And?"

"And that you're eager to put him in your rearview mirror," Eddie says. "For good. So I thought maybe you were leaving island."

"Absolutely not." *If anyone should leave island,* Lizbet thinks, *it's JJ!* But she won't drag Eddie into their drama; anything she says will be mangled by the Cobblestone Telegraph. "I'm here because I'd like Xavier Darling's contact information." She sits up straighter and flips her braids behind her. "I want to apply for the general-manager position at the new Hotel Nantucket."

"You must have heard about the salary," Eddie says.

"No. I haven't even thought about the salary."

"It's a hundred and twenty-five thousand a year," Eddie says. "Plus full benefits."

Lizbet pulls back a few inches. Her mind lands fancifully on a trip to the dentist when she wouldn't have to worry when Janice, the hygienist, tells her it's time for a full set of X-rays. "Wow."

"I'm happy to give you Xavier's e-mail." Eddie snaps his fingers. "Didn't you tell me your father owns a hotel in Wisconsin?"

Lizbet's father manages a retirement community in Minnetonka, Minnesota. As a teenager, Lizbet used to pull numbers for the bingo games and escort the residents to their hair appointments at the salon. One year, she judged the butter-sculpture contest.

"Something like that," Lizbet says.

Eddie nods slowly. "Xavier wants someone with a background in luxury hotels."

Lizbet blinks. There is no way she can make the Rising Sun Retirement Community sound like the Four Seasons.

"But he also wants someone who has dealt with the Historic District Commission and the Nantucket selectmen."

"Me," Lizbet says.

"And who can charm the chamber of commerce."

"Also me," Lizbet says.

"The hotel has quite a tattered reputation to repair."

"Agreed," Lizbet says. "I assume you've heard the rumors about the ghost?"

"I don't believe in ghosts," Eddie says. "And I *never* listen to rumors."

Ha-ha-ha! Lizbet thinks. At least one of those statements is a flat-out lie.

"Xavier has his work cut out for him," Eddie says. "There's a lot of competition at the high end—the Beach Club, the White Elephant, the Wauwinet. I told him I wasn't sure there was another seat at the table, but he was adamant, and he does have deep pockets. The hotel will open in June, and according to Xavier, it's going to be the finest lodging this island has ever seen. But he needs the right person at the helm."

Lizbet nearly leaps out of her chair, she wants this job so much. "I'll send Mr. Darling my résumé tonight. Do you think you might…put in a good word for me?"

Eddie presses his fingers together in a way that seems contemplative, and Lizbet hopes he's remembering all the times he called the Deck at the last minute and Lizbet found him a table, even when they were crazy full with a wait list. Eddie always requested table number 1 and Lizbet granted that wish when she could (that David Ortiz was sitting there one night and Ina Garten another wasn't Lizbet's fault!).

"I won't put in a good word," Eddie says. "I'll put in a *great* word."

The next week, Lizbet interviews with Xavier Darling over Zoom. Although she thought she *crushed it*— dropping the name of the chairman of the zoning board to underscore her *local connections*—Xavier's demeanor gave nothing away. Lizbet figured someone like Xavier Darling would have a short list for the position that included people like the GMs from Wynn Las Vegas and the XV Beacon Hotel in Boston. However, only two days later, Xavier Zoom-called Lizbet and offered her the job. She was calm and composed as she accepted, but the instant she pressed the Leave Meeting button, she jumped up and down, victorious fists raised over her head. Then she collapsed in her chair and wept tears of gratitude.

The secret of change is to focus all your energy not on fighting the old, but on building the new.

Lizbet had a proverbial clean slate.

She visualized a Hollywood production assistant snapping shut the clapper board as the director shouted: *Take two!*

* * *

On the morning of April 12, Lizbet is, unfortunately, back to *fighting the old*—specifically, she's remembering how it was *Christina* who called her to explain away the sexting (*Those texts are nothing, Libby, JJ and I were only kidding around*)—when she gets a message from Xavier Darling; he's requesting a meeting. It's six thirty a.m.—Xavier, in England, is oblivious to the time difference—and Lizbet sighs. She was planning to get on the Peloton. But she has agreed to be at Xavier's beck and call, so she pulls a blouse on over her workout tank, drapes her braids over her shoulders, and fluffs her bangs.

Join meeting with video.

"Good morning, Elizabeth." (Xavier refuses to call her Lizbet, even though she has asked him to twice, telling him that the only person who called her Elizabeth was her late grandmother.) Behind Xavier, Lizbet sees Big Ben and the Houses of Parliament, a view so iconically London, it might as well be a Zoom background.

"Good morning, sir." Lizbet tries not to worry about his stern tone of voice, though she briefly wonders if today is the day the hammer drops and the hopes she has invested in the hotel will collapse, the whole thing a belated April Fools' joke.

"I'm calling to shed some light on things that might have been unclear."

Lizbet steels herself. What is Xavier going to tell her?

"You've never asked me—in fact, no one has asked me—why I bought this hotel. After all, I live in London and I've never visited Nantucket." He pauses. "Have you wondered about this?"

Lizbet has, in fact, wondered, but she chalked it up

to her understanding of the very wealthy: They buy things because they can.

"I bought this particular hotel," Xavier says, "because I'm trying to impress two women."

Whoa! Lizbet pinches her thigh to keep from gasping. This is probably the only answer worth sacrificing her thirty-minute hip-hop ride with Alex Toussaint for.

"Two women?" Lizbet says. She checks her image on her laptop screen; she's maintaining a sort of straight face. Lizbet has, naturally, googled Xavier Darling. According to an article in the *Times* (London), he never married and has no children. The internet showed pictures of him at the Royal Ascot and the Cartier Queen's Cup with young, combatively beautiful women on his arm, but never the same one twice. Who are the lucky two, and will they both be coming to Nantucket? Because *that* will get the island talking! She would love to remark that buying each woman a private plane or a minor van Gogh might have been cheaper.

"Yes," Xavier says. "I'm going to share with you now who one of the women is."

"Wonderful, sir."

"One of the women I'm trying to impress is Shelly Carpenter."

Shelly Carpenter, Lizbet thinks. *Of course.*

"Do you know who Shelly Carpenter is?" Xavier asks.

"'Stay well, friends,'" Lizbet quotes. "'And do good.'"

"Precisely," Xavier says. "Elizabeth, I want a five-key review from *Hotel Confidential*."

Again, Lizbet checks her image. Does she look incredulous? Yes—yes, she does. Along with eighteen million other people, Lizbet follows Shelly Carpenter on Instagram. Her account @hotelconfidentialbySC has become a national obsession. Shelly Carpenter posts at noon eastern time on the last Friday of every month—a ten-picture carousel of each property (she's rumored to take these photos with her iPhone)—and the link in her bio takes you to her blog *Hotel Confidential,* where she awards properties anywhere from one to five keys. The secret to her success is her witty, brilliant writing, her razor-sharp intelligence, and her refined sense of what works and what doesn't where hotels are concerned—but there's also mystery involved. Nobody knows who she is. The internet agrees on only one thing: Shelly Carpenter is a pseudonym.

Whatever her real name is, she travels the globe, reviewing the Hampton Inn in Murrells Inlet, South Carolina, with the same critical eye that she does the Belmond Cap Juluca in Anguilla. (Both received four keys out of five.) It's well known that Shelly has never given a five-key review. She claims to be on a quest for that elusive five-key property, but Lizbet thinks this is a feint. Shelly will never give a five-key review; withholding it is her currency.

"Well, sir, we'll try our best," Lizbet says.

"That's not going to cut it, Elizabeth," Xavier says. "We are going to *do what it takes* to be the only hotel in the world that woman deems worthy of the fifth key. We are going to leave no doubt in her mind. Am I understood?"

"Yes, sir, you're understood."

"So we *will* get five keys from *Hotel Confidential* by summer's end?"

A competitive spirit that Lizbet hasn't felt since she raced her brothers swimming across Serpent Lake in Crosby, Minnesota, surfaces.

Building the new! she thinks. In that moment, Lizbet believes she can achieve the (highly) improbable—no matter what obstacles she encounters.

"We will get the fifth key," she says.

3. Ghost Story

For one hundred years, Grace has been trying to set the record straight: She was murdered!

In August 1922, the *Nantucket Standard* reported that nineteen-year-old chambermaid Grace Hadley had perished in the fire that consumed the third floor and attic of the grand Hotel Nantucket—a fire that had been started by an "errant cigarette of unknown origin." Technically, this was true, but the article left out secret, salacious details that only Grace knew. The hotel's owner, Jackson Benedict, had set up a cot for Grace in the attic's storage closet, directly above his quarters, so that he could sneak up and "visit" her whenever he was in residence. In addition to her job as a chambermaid, Grace served as lady's maid to Jack's wife, Dahlia, who called Grace "homely" (not at all true) and "a smart aleck" (occasionally—okay, often—true). On Grace's very first day of work, Dahlia spewed bathtub gin in Grace's face, temporarily blinding her. (After that, Grace always kept a safe distance between them.)

Before the fire started in the small hours of August 20, Jack and Dahlia hosted a dinner dance in the ballroom, as they did every summer weekend. These lavish events often ended with Dahlia getting drunk and throwing herself at other men. The Benedicts would then repair to the owner's suite and scream profanities at each other; one time, Dahlia threw a silver candlestick that missed Jack but hit their tabby cat, Mittens. (Afterward, the cat walked with a limp.) Grace could only too easily imagine Jack whipping out their secret during one of these feuds, like a dagger from a sheath: *I'm sleeping with your girl Grace.*

That would have been all Dahlia needed to hear.

Grace was woken by the sound of sirens (faint though they were in the attic) and she smelled the smoke and felt the searing heat of the floorboards—it was like standing on a griddle—but she couldn't get out of the storage closet. Her door was jammed. She pounded; she screamed, "Help me! Save me! Jack! Jack!" Nobody heard her. Jack was the only person who knew Grace was in the attic, and he hadn't come.

Ghosts are souls with unfinished business on earth, and such is the case with Grace. She has tried to just "let it go" and "move on" to her eternal rest—but she can't. She won't. She is going to haunt the damn hotel until she has an acknowledgment of the hideous truth: Dahlia Benedict started the fire *intentionally* and then locked the door to the storage closet from the outside. She *killed* Grace! And Dahlia wasn't the only one to blame. Jack had seduced Grace, and the vast difference in their social status left Grace with no choice but to comply. Jack hadn't saved her. He was ashamed about having a mistress, and so he let her burn.

After the fire, Jack sold the hotel for a song—but Grace became determined to let people know she was still there.

She started with the eight-foot-high mahogany doors—termites.

Then the silks that had been brought back from Asia by Nantucket whaleships and the hotel's velvets, brocades, and toiles—moths, mold, mildew.

Grace suffused the hotel with the smell of rotten eggs. Management suspected the cesspool and called the plumber, but nothing could eradicate the stench. *Sorry, not sorry!* Grace thought.

When the stock market crashed in 1929, the hotel closed. It remained shuttered throughout the Great Depression and during the war, too, of course. These were, Grace admits, dull years. It was just her, the rats, and an occasional owl. Anyone who had heard the story of the poor young chambermaid perishing in the hotel fire had bigger things to worry about.

In the 1950s, a new owner marketed the property as a "family-friendly budget hotel." This meant threadbare sheets that tore as easily as wet tissue and waxy coverlets in obnoxious prints that disguised stains. Grace hoped that wherever Jack was, he knew how common and low-rent his once elegant hotel had become.

In the 1980s, when movies like *Poltergeist* and *Ghostbusters* came out and everyone was suddenly an expert in paranormal activities, it became chic to say the hotel was haunted. *Finally!* Grace thought. Surely *someone* would do a little digging and figure out what had happened to her. Grace started properly haunting the hotel guests who deserved it: the philanderers and the casually cruel, the abusers and the loudmouths and the prejudiced. Stories accumulated—cold drafts, knocking noises, a bowl set spinning on the server in the third-floor hallway, water falling drip by drip onto the forehead of a slumbering man. (This man was handsy with the girls in his office.)

The hotel was sold again, this time to a young couple who set out to renovate it "on a shoestring." Do such endeavors ever succeed? This one didn't, though the hotel operated, sluggishly, into the new millennium. It next changed hands in 2007, sold to a man without taste (Grace had peered over the interior decorator's shoulder and saw plans for round beds and beveled mirrors). But the hotel never opened under this particular owner; he had invested with Bernard Madoff, and he lost everything.

After that, the hotel lay fallow and Grace again grew bored. During Hurricane José in 2017, she cracked a window, which caused a section of the roof to blow off and cartwheel down North Beach Street.

After the storm, the abandoned hotel's doors could easily be pried open, and the lobby became the site of many a high-school party. Grace received *quite* an education—she listened to the kids talk; she watched them pair off and head down the shadowy halls to find privacy in the guest rooms. She became a fan of their music (Dua Lipa, "Levitating"!). She learned about Instagram, Venmo, Tinder, Bumble, YouTube, TikTok—and the greatest platform of them all, Snapchat (the ghost!). Grace listened to debates about social justice and found herself growing impassioned. Every human being had dignity, even the maid/mistress kept in an attic closet!

Grace and the kids got along just fine until a girl named Esmé body-shamed a girl named Genevieve by posting a picture of Genevieve in her underwear in the gymnasium locker room. The next time Esmé entered the hotel, Grace's face appeared on the screen of her cell phone—her hair was still curly and dark under her white frilled cap, but her eyes were two infinite black holes, and when she opened her mouth, fire came out.

Esmé fainted dead away. When she came to, she swore to everyone that she'd seen a zombie on her phone; some real-life *Twilight* sh*t, she posted, a f**king ghost! A few kids googled *Hotel Nantucket* and *haunted*. But nothing came up; the digital records of the *Nantucket Standard* went back only to 1945. To get more information they would have to delve into the physical *archives*. The mere word evoked piles of dusty papers and more effort than they wanted to invest.

Grace had lost a chance to be recognized. And not only that, but the high-school parties came to an end and she was alone again.

Grace is, as the kids liked to say, hyped that a gentleman of tremendous wealth has bought the hotel and hired competent (and speedy) contractors and a decorator with impeccable taste. Grace zips around the first three floors trying to remain unobtrusive, though sometimes when she enters a room, an occupant will shiver and ask, "Did it just get cold in here?"

Grace is visible to certain people; she thinks of them as "the supernaturally sensitive." They can see Grace reflected in mirrors and glass, but most people see nothing at all. Grace can also pull off spooky-but-harmless manipulations. If she were to summon all her energy and strike out, she could probably hurt someone. (She fantasizes, of course, about walloping Dahlia Benedict, once on her own behalf and once for the cat, Mittens.)

In room 101, Grace catches a glimpse of herself in the full-length mirror that has just been mounted to the closet door and thinks, *No, this won't do.* Her long dove-gray dress and yellowing pinafore make her look like an extra in a Merchant Ivory film. She solves the problem of her dated outfit when she happens across an open box of the hotel's new bathrobes. They're white waffled cotton lined in a soft, absorbent terry cloth. Grace slips off her dress—naked, she still looks like a nineteen-year-old, full in both the chest and buttocks; she might even be considered "a dime"—and tries on the robe. It's as warm and delicious as a hug—and it has pockets! Grace decides to keep it. If someone caught sight of her in a mirror, what would that person see? Maybe a ghost wearing a bathrobe. Or maybe just a levitating robe wrapped around an invisible body.

Terrifying!

Grace is delighted by the thought.

When the new general manager, Lizbet Keaton, walks through the restored front doors of the hotel, holding a milk crate full of belongings, Grace thinks, *Finally, a woman in charge!* Lizbet is looking fit and sporty in yoga pants, a windbreaker, and a Minnesota Twins baseball cap that she wears over her blond braids. Although her face is as wholesome as a child's—she wears no makeup—Grace would place her age somewhere between thirty-five and forty.

Lizbet sets her crate on the new front desk and turns around, arms raised, as if to embrace the lobby. Grace sees bright sparks of grit and resolution flying off her. She is a person determined to succeed where so many others have failed—and Grace can't help but fall a little in love with her.

Hey there, Lizbet, Grace thinks. *I'm Grace. Welcome to the Hotel Nantucket.*

4. Help Wanted

Lizbet sets aside the third week of April to conduct her final round of staff interviews. She placed ads in the *Nantucket Standard,* the *Cape Cod Times,* and the *Boston Globe* and on Monster, ZipRecruiter, and Hcareers, but the pool of applicants wasn't as large as she'd hoped. Lizbet checked her junk folder but found nothing except e-mails from FarmersOnly.com (once, at a low point post-breakup from JJ, she'd made the mistake of visiting their website).

Lizbet doesn't mention the disappointing response to Xavier because day-to-day operations are her responsibility. She should be relieved she isn't inundated with college kids whose grandmothers will inevitably die the second Saturday in August. She doesn't need a *lot* of people; she needs the *right* people.

Grace is wearing her new robe and, to replace her frilled cap, the Minnesota Twins hat that she casually disappeared from Lizbet's gym bag a few days ago. She perches on the highest shelf in Lizbet's office, which gives her an excellent vantage point for seeing the candidates. Grace vividly remembers her own hiring in the spring of 1922. There were at least forty girls shepherded into the ballroom of the hotel, and each one was handed a rag. Mrs. Wilkes, head of housekeeping, had inspected each girl's technique as she dusted the wainscoting and the round oak banquet tables. Grace suspects Mrs. Wilkes had also been noting appearances, because it was mostly the pretty girls who were chosen; the ugly girls were sent home.

Lawsuits, Grace thinks now with a chuckle.

Grace peers over Lizbet's shoulder at the short stack of résumés on the desk. The first candidate is a twenty-two-year-old Nantucket resident named Edith Robbins who has applied for a front-desk position. Lizbet opens the door to her office and invites Edith—a young woman with luminous brown skin who's wearing a pencil skirt and kitten heels—to take a seat.

"Sweet Edie!" Lizbet says. "I can't get *over* how grown up you are! I remember your mom and dad bringing you to the Deck on your birthday."

Sweet Edie beams. "Every year."

"How's your mom doing? I haven't seen her since your dad's funeral."

"She's working full-time at Flowers on Chestnut and she took my dad's spot in the Rotary Club," Edie says. "So she's keeping busy."

"Please tell her I said hello. Now, I realize you're the child of two seasoned hospitality professionals, but I have to ask—didn't your mom want you to work at the Beach Club?"

"She did," Edie says. "But I thought this would be the more exciting opportunity. Everyone on the island is talking about this place."

"Oh, really? What are they saying?"

Edie gives Lizbet what might be called an uneasy smile. *What* are *they saying?* Grace wonders. Is anyone talking about *her*?

"Your résumé is *impressive!*" Lizbet says. "You

graduated from the school of hotel administration at Cornell, where you were a Statler Fellow. You were number one in your class!"

Of course she was! Grace thinks. *Look at her!*

"In your opinion," Lizbet says, "what's the most important aspect of hospitality?"

"Making a genuine connection with each guest from minute one," Edie says. "A warm greeting and a smile—'We're happy you're here. Let us help you have a wonderful stay.'"

"Great answer," Lizbet says. "It states here that you worked at the Statler Hotel on Cornell's campus and then, last summer, at Castle Hill in Newport?"

"Yes, my boyfriend and I worked at Castle Hill together. That property is a-*maze*-ing!"

Lizbet's eyebrows shoot up. "Is your boyfriend here for the summer? Because I'm still looking for—"

"We broke up right after graduation," Edie says.

Grace can't imagine what kind of fool would break up with this captivating young woman.

"We both got offers from the Ritz-Carlton management-training program," Edie says. "But I wanted to spend the summer on Nantucket with my mom. Graydon asked if he could come and I said no. I wanted to start my adult life as an independent woman."

Good for you, Grace thinks. She would have wanted to be an independent woman back in the day if that had been a thing.

"I'd love to offer you a spot on our front desk," Lizbet says. "Your starting wage will be twenty-five dollars an hour."

Grace understands inflation, but even so, this number is mind-boggling. In 1922, she made thirty-five cents an hour!

"We're paying well above industry standard,"

Lizbet says. "But then again, we expect more. It'll be a rigorous schedule."

"Not a problem," Edie says. "One of the things they drilled into us at Cornell was that we would have *no* personal life."

"At least you're prepared." Lizbet leans in. "I suppose you follow Shelly Carpenter on Instagram?"

"'Stay well, friends,'" Edie says. "'And do good.' Her reviews are fire!"

Fire, Grace thinks. Everything good these days is *fire*. She can't wait for this term to move along.

"Do you think she'll ever give five keys?" Lizbet asks.

"My friends and I used to debate what it would take for her to grant the fifth key. The woman is *so* nitpicky, and yet she's not unreasonable. If you ask for skim milk with your room-service coffee, you should get it. The blow-dryer should work without pushing the reset button. I'm of the opinion that, if you pay attention and have the resources, then yes, a fifth key is possible."

"Excellent. The hotel's owner, Mr. Darling, is determined to get the fifth key."

Sweet Edie beams. "I'm *so* here for it!"

The next interview is right in Grace's wheelhouse: head of housekeeping! Grace scans the résumé: Magda English, age fifty-nine. There are two addresses listed, one in St. Thomas, U.S. Virgin Islands, and one just around the corner on West Chester Street. Ms. English's experience includes thirty-two years as director of housekeeping on XD Cruise Lines. Ms. English retired in 2021, and yet here she is, the woman who might be the new Mrs. Wilkes.

Lizbet meets Ms. English ("Please," she says, "call

me Magda") in the lobby, and Grace trails them down the hall at a distance; she can tell nothing gets past this woman.

"We have thirty-six rooms," Lizbet says. "And twelve suites."

Magda has regal posture and barely a single line on her face. As she and Lizbet stroll the corridor, she admires the mahogany barrel ceiling and the brass portholes, salvaged from a French ocean liner, along the walls. "I used to run housekeeping on cruise ships, so I'll feel right at home," Magda says. Her voice has a delightful West Indian lilt (whereas Mrs. Wilkes's voice had been like a cheese grater on Grace's backside). "These portholes will need to be polished every week."

Lizbet opens the door to room 108. Grace slips in and settles on top of the canopy bed, adjusting her robe for modesty. She's chosen this spot because she can't be seen in the mirror or window.

Magda walks over to the emperor-size bed and runs a hand over the duvet cover. "Matouk sheets?"

"Good guess," Lizbet says.

"I know my linens." Magda picks up the hydrangea-blue cashmere throw at the foot of the bed. "This is lovely."

"All the rooms have them. They're woven at Nantucket Looms especially for the hotel."

"I hope they plan on weaving extras," Magda says, "because these will 'accidentally' find their way into the guests' luggage, I assure you." She pokes her head into the walk-in closet and then the bathroom. "How many people would be on my staff?"

"Four," Lizbet says.

Magda laughs. "That's a tenth of what I'm used to. But it should be enough."

"So what brought you to Nantucket?" Lizbet asks.

Magda sighs. "I spent the first half of my career on ships in the Mediterranean, then I requested a transfer back home to the Caribbean. When my brother's wife died in September, I took my retirement and moved here to take care of him and my nephew Ezekiel."

"Ezekiel English is your nephew? I'm interviewing him this afternoon."

"He's a lovely boy, as you'll see for yourself." She smiles. "Zeke and William have had a rough few months…but now that they're back on their feet, a little job will fill my days."

Lizbet raises her eyebrows. "This is more than just a little job."

"Well, it's not a cruise ship," Magda says. "My standards are impeccable, as my previous employer will attest. I promise you, the hotel will be cleaner than it's ever been in the past."

Well! Grace thinks indignantly. *I guess we'll see about that.*

After Magda departs, Lizbet considers going for a lunchtime run or grabbing one of the mountain bikes from the hotel's brand-new fleet and powering out a quick ride. This morning she finally felt a thaw in the air, but as tempting as it is to go outside, Lizbet decides to stay at her laptop. First, she checks the references of a married couple—Adam and Raoul Wasserman-Ramirez—who have both applied for bellman positions. They currently work at the Four Seasons in Punta Mita, Mexico, and want to come to New England for the summer. Lizbet has been putting off deciding about Adam and Raoul because she isn't sure hiring a married couple for the same job is a good idea, even though they both interviewed well over the phone. What if they bicker? What if one far outperforms the other?

The e-mail from the GM at the Four Seasons is glowing. It mentions that Adam has a "beautiful singing voice." (*How is this relevant?* Lizbet wonders. *He's going to be schlepping bags*.) The letter ends with *We at the Four Seasons Punta Mita have determined it's best if the Wasserman-Ramirezes are scheduled separately.*

Ha! Lizbet's instincts were correct—but the reality remains that she needs three bellmen, and her options are limited. She'll hire Adam and Raoul.

Next, although she has cautioned herself not to, she checks to see if there are any new reservations for opening week.

There's one, a booking for four nights made by a couple from Syracuse. This is heartening, but the fact that the hotel's overall occupancy is hovering at just above 25 percent a full week after the website went live is not. They placed banner ads on all the major travel websites, and Lizbet wrote what she felt was an excellent press release, but there have been very few takers. When Lizbet called Jill Tananbaum at the *Nantucket Standard* to see what had become of her piece, Jill said, "Jordan told me he might run it at some point but he can't say when."

Lizbet hung up, discouraged. The reputation of the hotel was, admittedly, abominable, and Xavier's interest in it was somewhat perplexing, but it had undergone a remarkable metamorphosis.

Building the new! she thinks. But only an instant later, she wonders if she's in over her head. It had been far easier to sell herself to Xavier than she'd anticipated (considering she had no actual hotel experience)—and only now does Lizbet wonder how much competition she had. Is it possible she was *the only person* who applied for this job?

Xavier has asked Lizbet to book him suite 317—historically, the hotel owner's suite—from August 24 to August 28. It feels a little strange that Xavier isn't coming until the end of August, but Lizbet is relieved. By then, she might know what she's doing.

Lizbet isn't sure where all this self-doubt is coming from; she's probably just hungry. She's tempted to run over to Born and Bread for a sandwich, but there isn't time. Her next interview is here.

The third résumé is quite impressive, Grace thinks. Alessandra Powell, age thirty-three, applying for a front-desk position. The very first line announces (in boldface) that Alessandra is fluent in Spanish, French, Italian, and English. She has worked at hotels in Ibiza, Monaco, and, most recently, Tremezzina, Italy. This draws Grace back in time. When Dahlia Benedict was being "nice" to Grace, she would gab about her and Jack's travels abroad. She told Grace that she and Jack had sailed to Europe aboard the *Mauretania,* and when Grace murmured sarcastically under her breath that it sure was a good thing the *Mauretania* hadn't hit an iceberg like the *Titanic,* Dahlia slapped her soundly.

It was a slap Grace deserved. By that point, Grace was so deep into the affair with Jack, she saw no way out. She very dearly wished the *Mauretania had* sunk with both Jack and Dahlia aboard.

Grace is yanked back to the present moment when a young woman with long, wavy apricot-colored hair steps into Lizbet's office.

No, Grace thinks. *No!* There's a stench coming off the woman that means only one thing: a rotten soul.

The woman, Alessandra, holds out a white paper bag. "I brought you an ABC grilled cheese from Born

and Bread on the off chance you've been so busy
interviewing that you skipped lunch."

Lizbet's blue eyes widen. "Thank you! That was
so…*intuitive*. I *did* skip lunch, and the ABC is my
favorite sandwich." She accepts the bag. "Please, sit.
So, Alessandra, your résumé is nothing short of
remarkable—Italy, Spain, Monaco. And you speak
so many languages! What brings you to our little
island?"

"It was time to come home. To the States, that
is, though I'm originally a West Coast girl. I studied
romance languages in Palo Alto—"

"Were you at Stanford?" Lizbet checks the résumé.
"It doesn't *say* that here—"

"And then I did the whole backpacking-through-
Europe thing—the train, the hostels—and I found
myself flat broke in Ravenna. I went there especially
to see the mosaics in the Basilica of St. Vitale."

"Mosaics?"

"They're the finest examples of Byzantine mosaics
outside of Istanbul. They're magnificent. Have you
seen them?"

Oh, please, Grace thinks. *How pretentious.*

"I haven't."

Alessandra says, "Well, when I say *flat broke,* I
mean I gave my last euro as a donation to enter the
church. Fortunately, I struck up a conversation with
a gentleman who was also viewing the mosaics, and
it turned out he owned a *pensione* in town. He let me
stay for free in exchange for working on the front
desk—and my career in hotels was born."

"So you were in Europe for…eight years, give or
take? I notice there are some gaps on this résumé—"

"I wanted to leave Italy while I still felt fondly
toward it. And I chose Nantucket because it seems

like the most exclusive of the New England summer-resort spots."

"I'm curious…did Shelly Carpenter from *Hotel Confidential* review any of the hotels on your résumé?"

Alessandra nods. "She apparently stayed at Aguas de Ibiza while I was working there. Her piece was positive, but she gave us only four keys. She had a couple of legitimate complaints. The first was that the bellman took fifteen minutes to deliver her luggage to her room, which was ten minutes too long by her standards—"

"Oh yes, I know."

"And there was no salt and pepper on her room-service tray even though she'd specifically requested it."

"Ouch."

"Yeah, people got fired. You know that she wears disguises and uses aliases and always shows up at the busiest times, when the staff can't pay as close attention to every guest as they might otherwise. And sometimes she creates extraordinary circumstances to see how the staff reacts. Rumor has it that when she visited the Pickering House Inn in Wolfeboro, she slashed the tire of her rental car to see how quickly the staff would change it."

"I did *not* know that," Lizbet says, slumping a little.

"My advice would be to train the bellmen in basic auto repair, because I'm sure once Shelly Carpenter gets wind of this place opening, she'll make an appearance."

"You think so?"

"I can almost guarantee it. She seems to like Nantucket. She reviewed the White Elephant—"

"She gave it four keys."

"And she reviewed the Nantucket Beach Club and Hotel, which is where I'm interviewing next."

"You're interviewing with Mack Petersen?"

"I...*am,* yes. Mack has basically offered me a position already, but I told him I wanted to keep my options open."

Oh, come on, Lizbet! Grace thinks. *She's bluffing!*

Lizbet runs her finger down the résumé. "These references have only the main numbers for the hotels. Can you provide any names or extensions?"

"As I'm sure you're aware, there's a lot of turnover in the hospitality business. My GM in Ibiza retired and bought an olive orchard. My GM in Monaco got throat cancer and died." She pauses, milking the moment for all its worth. "Alberto. He smoked a pipe."

When Lizbet makes a sympathetic face, Grace groans. She would bet her robe and hat that there had never been an Alberto!

"If you call the hotels directly, they can pull up my performance records."

"You have the experience I'm looking for," Lizbet says. "High-end luxury hotels with a discerning clientele."

"May I ask what kind of pay you're offering?"

"We pay twenty-five dollars an hour," Lizbet says. "Though, because of your experience, I can bump you to twenty-seven fifty and make you the front-desk manager."

No! Grace thinks. She needs to get this little witchy-witch out of here. Grace blows cold air down the back of Alessandra's neck.

Alessandra doesn't even blink. Figures.

"The hours are pretty brutal," Lizbet says. "One and a half days off every two weeks."

"A day off? What's that?"

"Ha!" Lizbet says. "You're too good to be true."

Grace has a feeling this is precisely the case.

***

Staff of five, Lizbet thinks as she takes a bite of the apple, bacon, and white cheddar grilled cheese on cranberry-studded sourdough that Alessandra brought her. Alessandra interviewed well, though her résumé has holes in it. There's a recent year-long period that's unaccounted for, but it's possible Alessandra was traveling between jobs; she seems cultured, into art and languages. And she said she'd studied romance languages in Palo Alto—"Palo Alto" is a wink-wink reference to Stanford, but if Alessandra went to Stanford, wouldn't that be plastered across the top of her résumé? Lizbet decides to overlook these things. Mack Petersen down at the Beach Club basically offered Alessandra a job, but Lizbet snapped her up!

Alessandra seemed to know a great deal about Shelly Carpenter. Alessandra could be their secret weapon.

What an improvement! Grace thinks when she sets eyes on the final candidate of the day. Ezekiel English, twenty-four years old, is, as the kids say, a smoke-show. (It's another piece of slang Grace doesn't love, though she can see how it applies now. She's feeling a little warm in her robe, and she pulls open the collar.)

Zeke gives Lizbet a dazzling smile and shakes her hand. "Hey, I'm Zeke English, what's good?"

"The sandwich I just finished was good," Lizbet says. "If that's what you mean?"

"Sorry, I'm a little nervous," Zeke says. "Thanks for having me in."

How adorable! Grace thinks. *He's nervous.*

"Please, have a seat," Lizbet says. "I met your aunt Magda this morning."

"Yeah," Zeke says. "Aunt Magda's the bomb. She

moved in with us last September..." Zeke bows his head, and when he raises it again, his eyes are bright with tears. He clears his throat. "My mom died of a brain aneurysm. Aunt Magda cooks for us and...just generally makes everything better." He wipes a tear with the back of his hand, and before Grace can stop herself, she flies down to give his broad shoulders a squeeze. She loves a man who isn't afraid to show his emotions. The hug seems to revive Zeke a bit (or maybe Grace is giving herself too much credit?), because he sits up straighter and laughs. "Am I blowing this interview or what?"

Lizbet leans forward. "I'm interested in hiring human beings," she says. "Not robots. You experienced a profound loss." She takes a breath. "Let's start over. Hi, Zeke, welcome! How long have you lived on Nantucket?"

"My whole life, born and raised."

"Where else have you worked on the island?" Lizbet asks.

"I've been teaching at the surf school out in Cisco since I was fifteen," Zeke says.

He's a surfer! Grace thinks. Well, it's official: Zeke is her crush. She wonders if he would be interested in a ghost with the figure of a nineteen-year-old but the wisdom of someone *much* older. (She's kidding! The scene in that nineties movie at the potter's wheel would—sadly—never happen in real life.)

"That's a fun job," Lizbet says. "Why make the switch to hospitality?"

Zeke laughs. "My dad told me it was time to grow up. He said I could either work here or work for him. He was the electrician on this renovation."

"Yes," Lizbet says. "William and his crew did a wonderful job."

Zeke says, "I couldn't believe it when I heard someone was fixing it up. It had always seemed like a lost cause. You know, my friends and I used to party here in high school."

O! M! G! Grace thinks. Zeke is one of her high-school partiers all grown up!

"Some strange stuff happened this one night," Zeke says. "A ghost's face appeared on this chick's phone." He pauses. "So then this place got a reputation for being haunted, and we stopped coming."

Lizbet gives him an indulgent smile. "Don't worry, we did an exorcism when we renovated."

Ha-ha, Grace thinks. She considers floating Zeke's résumé off the desk to prove just how wrong Lizbet is, but she doesn't want to show off. Yet.

Lizbet likes Zeke—he's a lovely boy, just as Magda promised—though Lizbet worries he might be a bit surfer-dude laid-back for the job. What if it takes him fifteen minutes to get bags to a room instead of Shelly Carpenter's prescribed five minutes? She sighs. Women will go crazy when they see him…he's a dead ringer for Regé-Jean Page. And she's already hired Magda, and his father *is* their electrical contractor, so she can't *not* hire him. Lizbet will just have to train him and Adam and Raoul that bags go directly to the room within five minutes! And she would like to train Zeke not to mention the ghost to anyone. Can she get away with that?

She sends him a text: You have the job!

Zeke texts back: Kk.

Lizbet closes her eyes. *Kk?*

A second text comes in: Thank you very much for the opportunity. I won't let you down!

Lizbet exhales. She can work with that.

The last person Lizbet has to hire is a night auditor, but the only application she's received for the job is from some guy named Victor Valerio (real name?) who sent a picture of himself wearing white face makeup, glow-in-the-dark fangs, and a long flowing black cape. When you ask for people to work the graveyard shift, Lizbet supposes, you end up with vampires.

Perfect company for their ghost, she thinks, laughing to herself. She'll have to handle the night auditing until someone suitable applies.

She sends Xavier an e-mail.

Dear Xavier—

I hired our core staff today. Onward toward the fifth key!

All best, Lizbet

5. Opening Day

June 6, 2022
From: Xavier Darling (xd@darlingent.co.uk)
To: Employees of the Hotel Nantucket

The day has come! We're finally opening our doors to the public to show them our living work of art. The thing that makes it "living" is all of you. What do hammered-silver basins in the bathroom matter if the staff is harried and distracted when you check in? What does the Swedish sauna in the wellness center matter if the bellman delivers the wrong bags to your room? Hotels are only as good as their staff.

I will be personally reading every review of our hotel on the TravelTattler website, and based on the content of that feedback, I'll be awarding a cash prize of one thousand dollars to the most outstanding employee each week. I hope each one of you wins, though be warned, this isn't a participation trophy. It's entirely possible, for example, that the same employee will win all eighteen weeks of the season.

It's my goal to make the Hotel Nantucket the undisputed best in the world. But I can't do it without you.

Thank you for your dedication and hard work.

XD

Lizbet pulls her cherry-red Mini Cooper into the space that says RESERVED FOR GENERAL MANAGER and throws back what's left of her double espresso. She's *livid* about the e-mail that Xavier sent out that morning. Xavier is going to award weekly cash prizes to her staff as though they're contestants on a reality show. Lizbet has spent the past two weeks training the front of the house, and she was crystal clear that putting forth one's best effort every single day should be *a matter of personal pride and integrity*. She also stressed teamwork, a concept that awarding individual cash prizes will unravel.

Two days ago, Lizbet stayed at the hotel as a guest. The staff was instructed to use Lizbet's visit as a full dress rehearsal. Front-desk manager Alessandra checked Lizbet in, and Alessandra presented her with the Blue Book, a compilation of Nantucket's best beaches, outings, museums, sights, restaurants, galleries, shopping, bars, and nightlife that Lizbet herself had spent countless hours curating, writing, and refining. Alessandra asked if she could make Lizbet any dinner reservations. No, thank you, Lizbet said, though she would like a Reuben from Walter's delivered to her room between seven fifteen and seven thirty. Alessandra said she'd take care of it, no problem. A few moments after Lizbet stepped into the room—only long enough for her to admire the view of Easton Street from the picture window—Zeke arrived with Lizbet's luggage.

Lizbet flung herself across the emperor-size bed. She wasn't at the Deck anymore, and she certainly wasn't at the Rising Sun Retirement Community in Minnetonka. She was the general manager of the new and improved Hotel Nantucket. The sheets were soft under Lizbet's cheek and they smelled vaguely, though not overwhelmingly, floral. The mattress was so comfortable that Lizbet closed her eyes and took one of the most delightful naps of her life.

The secret of change is to focus all your energy not on fighting the old, but on building the new.

She left a few tests for the housekeeping crew—a crumpled tissue kicked to the far back corner under the bed, a cake of the Nantucket Looms wildflower soap tucked incongruously behind the (complimentary) smoked bluefish pâté in the minibar. She even went so far as to empty the matches from the box by the bathtub into her suitcase. Would Magda's crew actually use their hundred-point checklist?

Yes, they would. When Lizbet investigated the room the following day, everything had been cleaned, replaced, refilled.

She had been eager to see what was happening down at the hotel bar—it was subcontracted out, so Lizbet had no say in how it was run—but she found the door locked and the glass front papered over. She could hear voices and movement inside but when she knocked, nobody answered. Lizbet had repeatedly asked Xavier who would be running the bar and he said he wanted it to be a "grand surprise." Apparently, he'd signed a "swoon-worthy" chef to prepare the bar menu, but he was keeping the announcement under wraps until opening day, which felt very cloak-and-dagger to Lizbet. She sneaked around to the outside door and noticed that orders had been delivered. A young woman popped out, startling Lizbet. She said her name was Beatriz, and when Lizbet asked who she worked for, Beatriz said, "Chef." And when Lizbet said, "Chef who?" Beatriz shook her head and said, *"No puedo decirte hasta mañana."*

Lizbet took a yoga class with Yolanda in the Balinese-inspired studio, and although it sounded trite, she emerged feeling centered and at peace...or as centered and at peace as she could feel with the hotel opening the next day.

When Lizbet checked out of her room, Zeke tucked her suitcase into the back of her Mini for the long drive home to her cottage on Bear Street, which was 1.2 miles away. Along with her bill, Lizbet was presented with a parting gift: a very cold bar of Nantucket Looms wildflower soap.

Lizbet knew it sounded ridiculous, but she wished

she could stay. It had been luxurious, even though she was technically working. And she was pleased to report that there had been no scary noises, no cold blasts, no ethereal visions, no signs of any ghost.

The hotel sparkles in the June sun with its fresh cedar shingles and crisp white trim. The hotel's landscaper, Anastasia, placed lavish pots overflowing with snapdragons, bluebells, lavender, and ivy on each step of the staircase leading up to the hotel entrance. The wide front porch of the hotel is set up with wide rockers with cushions in hydrangea blue and cocktail tables that can be turned into firepits. (The front desk sells a s'mores kit for eight dollars.) The porch will also be the site of the complimentary wine-and-cheese hour each evening. Lizbet has seen to it that they will serve excellent wine and a selection of imported cheeses garnished with ripe berries and plump, glistening olives.

Lizbet checks for mascara on her eyelids and lipstick on her teeth. She stayed up way too late last night trying on outfits. It's a new job and she wants a new style. At the Deck, she always wore muumuus because they were forgiving (she averaged eight glasses of rosé and fourteen pieces of bacon *daily*). Now her closet is filled with things that are fitted and a bit more professional. Today she's wearing a navy halter dress, nude stiletto sandals, and a Minnesota Golden Gophers charm on a chain around her neck.

She steps out of the car, so excited she could *levitate*. She feels like a living, breathing inspirational meme. She has stopped fighting the old and started building the new! She's weathered the storm by adjusting her sails! She is a pineapple: standing tall, wearing a crown, and sweet on the inside!

Lizbet slips her phone into her navy-and-white-striped clutch and looks up to find her ex-boyfriend JJ O'Malley standing in the white-shell-covered parking lot with his hands behind his back.

This is not *happening,* she thinks. Lizbet hasn't actually seen JJ since the awful day in late October when he moved the last of his belongings out of their cottage. He told Lizbet he was spending the off-season in upstate New York with his parents; he'd gotten a part-time gig cooking at the Hasbrouck House. By that time, Lizbet had already accepted the job at the hotel, but she didn't tell JJ that. But clearly he's heard the news. The Cobblestone Telegraph is real.

"What are you doing here, JJ?" Lizbet asks. He's wearing cargo shorts, his Black Dog T-shirt, chef's clogs, and a green bandanna around his neck. A thought occurs to Lizbet that's so horrible, she nearly drops her clutch: the chef of the new hotel bar has been kept "a grand surprise" because, in the world's most hideous twist, Xavier has hired JJ.

Lizbet will quit.

No, she won't quit. She'll make JJ quit. But one thing is for damn sure: she and JJ O'Malley are *not* working in the same building.

"Are *you* running the bar here?" she asks.

"What?" JJ says. "No. I wasn't even approached. Why?"

Sweet lightning, Lizbet thinks.

JJ brings his hands out from behind his back. He's holding a dozen long-stemmed pink roses wrapped in butcher paper. He gives her what she used to call his puppy-dog look—big eyes and protruding lower lip. In happier days, this would spur Lizbet to squeeze him tight and pepper his face with kisses, but now she thinks, *Wow, he looks awful.* It was normal for JJ to let his hair and beard grow out over the winter, but has it ever been *this* unruly? His beard straggles across his face like creeper vines on a brick wall.

"First of all, I came to wish you good luck for opening day."

A text would have sufficed (though Lizbet blocked his number months ago). "You betcha. And I'm not taking those flowers. What else?"

He drops the roses to the ground, reaches into the deep flapped pocket of his cargo shorts, and pulls out a ring box.

"Don't you dare," Lizbet says.

JJ sinks to one knee on the crushed shells and Lizbet winces—but no, sorry, she's finished empathizing with this guy's pain.

He opens the box.

Don't look at the ring! she thinks.

But come on, she's only human. She crunches through the shells in her stilettos and studies the ring; it's a dazzler. It's either fake or JJ took out an enormous line of credit on the restaurant—a move she would have absolutely vetoed if they were still together. It's over two carats, maybe even two and a half, and it's a marquise cut, which is what she's always wanted.

"I had a lot of time to think over the winter," JJ says. "I love you, Libby. Marry me. Be my wife."

Lizbet is standing close enough to see a hole in the shoulder of JJ's Black Dog T-shirt, a shirt she knows he's had since the summer of 2002. It was his first cooking job, over on the Vineyard.

"The answer is no. And you know why."

He gets to his feet; his knee is encrusted with shells. "You can't stay mad forever."

"I'm not mad," Lizbet says. "And I'm also not going to marry you. You cheated on me."

"I didn't touch Christina," JJ says. "Not once did I touch her."

"That may be so," Lizbet says. "But clearly there was enough *electricity* or *chemistry* between the two of you that the mere idea of her gave you a hard-on that you then went to the trouble of *photographing* and *sending* to her along with *one hundred and eighty-seven texts* describing what you would like to do with her if you ever got her alone in the wine cellar." The espresso Lizbet just finished asserts itself; it's liquid anger coursing through her bloodstream. "You're a *cheater,* JJ. I will not marry you and all the forgive-me flowers in the world won't change my mind. You're a jerk for showing up here."

"What do I have to do to get you to forgive me? I can't run the restaurant without you."

"Hire Christina."

"I don't want Christina. I want you."

"I'm guessing what you really mean is that Christina was blackballed by every restaurant on this island—as she should have been—so she moved to Jackson Hole." Lizbet can only hope this is true.

"Libby, please, I'm desperate. I'm lost. And look at you, baby, you're a hundred times hotter than you've ever been."

For one vainglorious second, JJ snags Lizbet's attention. She has spent the months since they split running and riding the damn Peloton and taking private barre classes with Yolanda. She has lost thirty-two pounds, carved out the sides of her thighs, and scooped out her ass cheeks. She can wall-sit for two and a half minutes and plank for three; she can hold a crow pose in yoga; she has triceps! And today, she has freed her hair from the usual braids; she's wearing it sleek and long, parted down the middle.

Lizbet has been chasing something, and that something is revenge. She has been waiting for the moment when JJ would acknowledge her change in appearance. *A hundred times hotter*. It's a start. Far more important than how Lizbet looks is how she feels, which is strong, healthy, motivated! She's not going to drink eight glasses of rosé every night this summer, she's not going to share JJ's cigarettes or stay up until three in the morning. She's finished with that lifestyle.

"I need to get to work," Lizbet says. "Please leave and take back the ring."

"So you're saying you don't love me?" JJ reaches into his pocket again, and Lizbet suddenly feels panicky, afraid that he's going to pull out a gun and…shoot her? Himself? Is he *that* unhinged? She takes a step back but then sees it's just his phone in his hand. "You're telling me you can listen to this and not feel anything?" He plays "White Flag" by Dido. *But I will go down with this ship*. How many times did Lizbet and JJ sing this at the top of their lungs in JJ's truck as they rode to the beach at two in the morning so they could see the moonlight on the ocean? How many times did they dance to the song in their kitchen? *I'm in love and always will be*.

Playing it now is unfair.

"What I feel is sad and disappointed," Lizbet says. "You betrayed my trust. You tossed fifteen years of my love down the drain because you couldn't stop yourself from telling Christina that you wanted to tongue her nipples."

JJ winces. "I never said that."

"Oh, but you did. Get out of here, JJ, before I have one of my bellmen physically remove you."

JJ puts the ring box in his pocket and straightens up to his full height. He's six foot five and weighs two hundred and eighty pounds. In the Land of Ten Thousand Lakes, where Lizbet was raised, that's called a Paul Bunyan.

"Or I'll get a restraining order," Lizbet says.

"Libby—" He grabs her arm and she wrenches it away.

"Is there a problem?" A man in a white jacket and houndstooth pants steps out of the entrance to the new hotel bar and strides over to JJ and Lizbet.

Who is this? Lizbet thinks. The script on his jacket reads CHEF MARIO SUBIACO.

Lizbet fights to keep her composure. Mario *Subiaco?* Almost involuntarily, Lizbet looks over at JJ. His mouth has fallen open a bit.

"I'm Mario Subiaco," Mario Subiaco says, offering Lizbet his hand. "The chef of the Blue Bar."

The Blue Bar. Of course—Mario Subiaco used to be the pastry chef at the Blue Bistro, which was Nantucket's best restaurant before it closed in 2005. Mario Subiaco is *the* OG Nantucket celebrity chef. JJ keeps Mario's picture—clipped from a profile of him in *Vanity Fair* that was written just after the Blue Bistro shut its doors—taped to his office wall! Lizbet thought Mario Subiaco was in Los Angeles working as a private chef for Dwayne Johnson. But apparently he's here now.

Holy buckets, Xavier, she thinks. *Good job.*

"Lizbet Keaton," Lizbet says, shaking his hand. "I'm the general manager of the hotel."

"Yes," he says. "I know."

"You're Mario *Subiaco!*" JJ sounds like a nine-year-old Pop Warner quarterback who's meeting Tom Brady. "You're a *legend,* man!"

Mario nods. "Thanks, that makes me feel really old. Who are you?"

"JJ O'Malley," he says. "I'm the chef/owner of the Deck."

Mario shrugs. "Never heard of it. But as a fellow chef, I'm going to ask you to let Lizbet here get to work." Mario checks with Lizbet. "If that's what you want?"

Suddenly, Lizbet is mortified that her messy personal life is on display in the parking lot like this, JJ with his serial-killer beard in his clogs, holding his phone (playing Dido), a dozen roses on the ground by his feet.

Lizbet smiles at JJ. "So good to see you again." Making a clean exit, she turns on her heel and follows Mario into the building. She hears the Dido song cut off. When she looks back, she catches a glimpse of JJ staring forlornly after her. *Revenge—check,* she thinks, and she feels a little sorry for him.

When Lizbet and Mario reach the service kitchen—which will be used for the complimentary continental breakfast and lunch by the pool—Lizbet says, "Thank you, but you didn't have to step in."

"I saw him grab you," Mario says. "I thought maybe you needed saving."

Immediately, Lizbet's starstruck awe diminishes. "I can take care of myself," Lizbet says. "And a lot of other people besides."

Mario has the gall to wink at her. "I'm guessing that was your ex-boyfriend, showing up to propose?"

It's none of Mario Subiaco's business who it was, but Lizbet doesn't need a feud between the hotel and the bar on the first day; there's plenty of time for that later.

"I should probably get upstairs," Lizbet says.

"I lied to him, you know," Mario says.

"Excuse me?"

"I told him I'd never heard of the Deck. I've been away from the island, sure, but I haven't been living on Mars. You two did some real stuff at that place, huh? A rosé fountain? Wish I'd thought of that seventeen years ago. And I heard the food was banging."

"'Those were the days, my friend, we thought they'd never end,'" Lizbet says. "Oh, but end they did. I left the Deck and I left him. We'll see what happens this summer."

Mario smirks. "This summer, I steal all his customers."

God, you're cocky, Lizbet thinks—or maybe in her caffeine mania she actually whispers it, because Mario bursts out laughing. "I know you need to be upstairs to start your very important general managing, but can I ask your quick opinion on something?" He waves her into the gleaming white-and-stainless-steel kitchen of the Blue Bar. Lizbet watches him for a second, thinking she'd like to put her stiletto right up his ass. It's only seven thirty in the morning and she's already had enough of chefs for one day.

But she follows him anyway.

"I was just back here doing a little mixology," Mario says. "Come see." He leads Lizbet over to a wide butcher block made of zebrawood—they spared no expense down here—that's crowded with fruit. There are tiny wild strawberries, kaffir limes, watermelons, blood oranges, kiwis, dragon fruits, rambutans, mangoes, two kinds of cherries (bing and golden Rainier), guavas, blackberries, coconuts, grapefruits, and something that looks like—yes, it is—a pink pineapple. It's a fruit festival, a fruit jamboree, a fruit *rave*. Down the counter is the alcohol, all top-shelf: Plymouth gin, Finlandia vodka, Casa Dragones tequila. Lizbet is impressed from a cost standpoint alone.

"I just need one more cocktail for my list. What do you think of this?" Mario reaches for a beaker filled with a liquid the color of a deep red sunset. He pours it into a stemless wineglass and tops it with champagne. It's Dom Pérignon, Lizbet realizes. Mario is doing his mixology experiments with *Dom*. That's quite a flex.

She shouldn't drink before eight a.m. on her first day of work, but Lizbet's focus is stretched out like a Slinky and she needs something to combat the aggressiveness of the espresso.

She takes a sip. *Gah!* So good. Another sip, in the interest of figuring out what's in the drink. Vodka. Strawberries. Ginger? Yes, there's a knob of ginger on the board. And some of the blood-orange juice.

She shrugs. "It's fine, I guess."

A slow smile crosses Mario's face and Lizbet takes a close look at him. In the magazine picture that hangs on JJ's office wall, Mario is much younger: smooth olive skin, thick dark hair, and a *Let me take you to bed* look in his eyes. He's older now; his hair and goatee are flecked with silver. He has lines cut deep into his forehead and radiating from the corners of his eyes. But he still has the swagger—and he knows this cocktail is the best thing Lizbet has ever tasted, that she would swim in it if she could.

"Well, then," he says. "We'll name that one for you. The Heartbreaker."

Magda English might be middle-aged, but her nephew Zeke has taught her some things. She knows that the rapper Pop Smoke is dead and that Wednesdays are called "Woo Back Wednesdays" in his honor. She knows about Polo G, House of Highlights, the Shade Room, and all things Barstool. She knows the modern meanings of *bet, sneaky link, bop, dip, bussin',* and *full send.* And Magda knows what a Chad is—it's a young man who embodies a certain stereotype of wealth and privilege: boarding school, college, trust fund, pastel polo shirts worn with the collar flipped up, golf, ski house, summer house, "vodka soda close it," and a river of money flowing from his adoring parents.

Therefore, Magda finds it amusing that the young man she's about to interview is actually named Chad. *Chadwick Winslow of Radnor, Pennsylvania,* the résumé on fine ivory stock announces. His appearance doesn't disappoint: He has shown up to the housekeeping office in khakis, pink shirt, a tie printed with starfish holding martinis, and a navy blazer. Boat shoes without socks. He has thick blond hair and the smooth cheeks of a child. His résumé also tells Magda that he's twenty-two, graduated from Bucknell with a major in "general humanities," and was in the Sigma Phi Epsilon fraternity. His previous work experience was as a counselor at a golf camp.

Although Magda has no idea what this child is doing in her office, she's not unhappy to see him. One of her four staff cleaners called to back out *yesterday,* the day before the hotel opened. When Magda informed Lizbet of this, Lizbet pulled young Master Winslow's résumé out of a folder that she jokingly (or maybe not) called "the Last Resort file."

"This kid stopped by the other day, insisting he wanted to clean. Honestly, I thought it was a prank. But feel free to call him and see if he was serious."

When Magda called, Chad sounded eager to come for an interview, and he showed up on time today—first hurdle cleared. But it could still be a prank, a bet, a dare, or a simple misunderstanding.

Magda says, "You realize, son, that I'm looking for *cleaning staff*?"

"Yes, ma'am."

"You're twenty-two, a college graduate. I could see you wanting to work the bell stand. But I don't understand why you'd want to clean hotel rooms."

Chad clears his throat. "I messed up. Badly."

"You won't get rich cleaning rooms," Magda says. "Have you asked about a job at the Blue Bar?"

"I want to clean rooms, ma'am."

But why? Magda thinks. *This makes no sense.* "Do you have any cleaning experience?" she asks.

"I help my mom around the house from time to time. And I was the social chair for my fraternity, so I was in charge of setting up for parties and cleaning up afterward."

Magda shakes her head, perplexed; she thought for sure he'd applied for the wrong job. From the looks of his clothes, he has plenty of money. And yet, she can see the earnestness on his face; for some reason, he wants *this* job. She studies the résumé. The local address he gave is Eel Point Road, which Magda has recently learned is high-roller real estate.

"Did your parents make you apply for this job? Are they trying to teach you some kind of lesson?"

"No, ma'am, it was my idea."

Young Chadwick Winslow sounds like he's telling the truth. Magda is intrigued.

"You would be the fourth and final member of our cleaning team, and as…the lacrosse coach at the Episcopal School might have informed you, there is no *I* in *team*. You won't get special treatment because you're male or because you have a college degree, and there will be no exceptions made because you went to the Chicken Box and are feeling too hungover to clean toilets. I need you here on time and ready to work. This isn't golf camp, Chadwick. It's stripping sheets and picking up wet towels and scrubbing shower stalls until they gleam. It's dealing with other people's excrement and urine and vomit and blood and semen and hair. I hope you have a strong stomach."

"I do."

Well, let's hope so, Magda thinks, *because I need someone today.* "I'm going to gamble and offer you the job," she says. She can't believe she's doing this. There's a 99 percent chance the kid won't last two weeks. He might not even last two days.

But Magda loves a long shot.

"Thank you," Chad says. "I won't let you down."

"You'll start right now," Magda says. "It's opening day, the rooms are all clean, and that will give me a chance to train you."

"Now is great!" Chad says. He has at least enough sense to take his blazer off and roll up his sleeves.

"So what did you do?" she asks. "When you messed up?"

"If you don't mind, I'd rather not say."

"It's none of my business," Magda says. "I was just curious. I happen to believe, Chadwick, that even the biggest disasters can be cleaned up, and I'll teach you to believe it too."

Edie Robbins wakes up on the morning of her first day of work on the front desk, checks her phone, and sees the e-mail from Xavier Darling. *Yes!* she thinks. *Yes-yes-yes!* Xavier is offering a thousand-dollar bonus per *week!* And it isn't a participation trophy! The same employee might win all eighteen weeks of the season!

Edie smells bacon frying. Just like every year on

Edie's first day of school, there will be bacon and eggs for breakfast and Tater Tot Hotdish for dinner. Edie's mother, Love, is trying to keep everything in their lives the same—even though nothing has been the same since Edie's father, Vance Robbins, died of a heart attack. Although Love says she's "doing okay"—she has taken a full-time job at Flowers on Chestnut to "keep busy"—Edie can sense she's still grieving. This is why Edie decided to spend the summer at home. Also, she had to get away from her ex-boyfriend Graydon.

Edie's plan is to save as much money as she can over the summer and apply for a job out in the "real world"—New York, São Paulo, London, Sydney, Shanghai—in the fall. She has a crippling student-loan payment (the Ivy League wasn't cheap), so although her hourly pay is more than she anticipated, an extra thousand dollars would really help.

She will win it, she decides. She'll win it every week. She is ready to slay!

Edie's fiercest competition for the prize money will be her partner on the front desk, Alessandra Powell. When Edie arrives at work—nearly ten minutes early—Alessandra is already there, and she has nabbed the more desirable computer, the one closest to the open end of the desk (Edie will have to scoot by Alessandra every time she comes or goes).

"Good morning, Alessandra!" Edie says brightly.

Alessandra does an oh-so-quick-but-still-noticeable up-and-down of Edie, presses her lips together, and says in a tone that is not cold but also not warm, "Good morning."

Edie wills herself not to take offense; from what Edie observed at training and during the first staff meeting, Alessandra is standoffish. (Maybe not a mean girl, but maybe not *not* a mean girl.) That, Edie can deal with. She has a harder time accepting that Alessandra is the front-desk manager. Edie doesn't understand why there has to be a front-desk manager when there are only two desk people hired so far. Edie realizes that Alessandra is older and has more practical job experience and speaks four languages. But something about Alessandra having the title feels wrong. She just walked in off the street; it's her first summer on Nantucket; Lizbet doesn't know her and neither does anyone else on this island.

The night before, at dinner, Edie complained about the situation to her mother. Love worked for years as the front-desk manager at the Nantucket Beach Club, and Edie's father, Vance, had been the night manager.

Love sipped her wine. "I bet the two of you will be best friends by the end of the summer."

"That's such a mom thing to say."

"Sorry," Love said. "I bet the two of you are going to have a tumultuous summer marked by incidents of envious backstabbing."

Envious, yes, Edie thinks now. Not only is Alessandra gorgeous and multilingual but she's a walking, talking Pinterest board. Edie and Alessandra are wearing the same uniform—white pants and a silky hydrangea-blue button-down blouse. Alessandra has accessorized her uniform with a Johnnie-O canvas color-block belt that probably belongs to her boyfriend (but looks *so cute!*), a pair of taupe wedge sandals, and a collection of gold bangles—among which is a Cartier love bracelet—that make bright jangly sounds every time Alessandra moves her left arm. Her reddish-blond hair is long, tousled, and beachy, yet not a strand is out of place (how is that possible?). She's wearing white eyeliner and has a tiny crystal pressed under her right eye. (At college, Edie thought eye crystals were trashy, but on Alessandra it looks chic. How is that possible?) Her name tag is upside down, which Edie thinks is a mistake but then realizes must be intentional—a conversation starter—because she can tell that Alessandra doesn't make mistakes.

Edie, by contrast, has her hair held back in a headband, no belt (she didn't think to wear a belt), and Skechers on her feet because she was worried about being comfortable. Her name tag is right side up.

"Thank you for setting up the coffee," Edie says as she logs onto the computer next to the wall. She tries not to feel hemmed in or trapped (she feels both). Alessandra's bracelets chatter in response and Edie thinks, *Fine, whatever.* The coffee smells rich and delicious and Edie wonders if she can pour herself a cup; Lizbet didn't say one way or the other.

But at that moment, Edie sees her mother's coworker Joan, from Flowers on Chestnut, rolling in a cart laden with the bouquets for the rooms. They have guests for eleven rooms checking in today and they've ordered a dozen Surfside Spring arrangements— enormous blue hydrangeas, pink starburst lilies, flame-orange snapdragons, and blush peonies curled up into tight little balls. Joan also has a supersize version of this arrangement for the pedestal table in the lobby.

"Sweet Edie!" Joan cries out. "Look at you on your *first day of work!* Your mom is so proud of you."

"Good morning, Joan," Edie says. She hears Alessandra murmur, "Sweet Edie?" and Edie feels herself flush. That's the thing about working on your home island, she thinks. Everyone knows you, and they all call you by your mortifying nickname. She has been Sweet Edie since she was small, her father's fault.

Edie moves the large arrangement to the lobby while Alessandra tasks the short, floppy-haired bellman named Adam with delivering eleven of the arrangements to the rooms. The twelfth arrangement goes back in Lizbet's office.

Joan reenters the lobby holding a planter of glorious deep purple vanda orchids.

"Those are stunning vandas," Edie says, showing off her orchid knowledge for Alessandra. "Are they for me?" She's kidding. That's at least four hundred dollars' worth of orchids, and although Edie's mother is proud of her, they don't have that kind of money to throw around.

"These are for Magda English," Joan says. "Seems she has an admirer."

Magda English! Edie thinks. That's Zeke English's aunt, the head of housekeeping.

"I'll take them to her." Edie carries the orchids down the hall to the housekeeping office, where she catches Magda just leaving with a blond guy about Edie's age who's wearing a pink oxford shirt and a needlepoint belt. He looks like one of the obnoxious summer kids who elbow other people out of the way to throw down their parents' credit cards at the Gazebo.

"Ms. English, these came for you," Edie says. "You have an admirer."

Magda stops in her tracks and stares at the flowers, then tsks and shakes her head. "Put them on my desk, please, dear," she says. "Chadwick and I have work to do."

Chadwick, Edie thinks, trying to hide her smile. *Chad!* She sets the orchids on Magda's desk and stares at the small envelope gripped in the prongs of the plastic stake. The envelope is sealed, and Edie can't very well open it, but she's tempted to hold it up to the sunlight streaming through the window so she can see who has sent Magda English these extravagant flowers.

Edie has successfully checked guests into two rooms and one suite when a family bursts into the lobby. It's a mother and two children, one girl, one boy. The mother is tall and supermodel-thin—she's all flat chest and protruding hip bones—and she has what Edie can only describe as "peacock hair," dyed ombré streaks of green and blue. She's either way cooler than your average mother, Edie thinks, or going through a midlife crisis.

Edie is on hold with Cru, attempting to secure a dinner reservation for the Katzens in room 103. She watches the little boy make a mad dash for one of the chess sets. When he picks up a knight and moves it, Edie hangs up.

"Louie!" the mother says. "Get back here this instant."

"They have chess!" Louie shouts. He goes to the opposite side of the board and moves a pawn.

Next to Edie, Alessandra snaps to attention and gives the family her radiant (and phony) smile. "Welcome—"

"Welcome to the Hotel Nantucket!" Edie calls out, stepping on Alessandra's words.

Without removing her sunglasses, the peacock-haired mother looks from Edie to Alessandra as though she's arrived at a fork in the road. She seems inclined to go to Alessandra, and Edie wonders if she will be forced to suffer this rejection check-in after check-in, day after day, all summer long. Given the choice between Edie and Alessandra, people will always choose Alessandra, either because she's beautiful or because she radiates the mesmerizing self-confidence of a Kardashian.

Edie waves the woman over so there can be no mistake. "I'll check you in!"

Alessandra's bracelets clinkety-clank. It's the passive-aggressive sound of her discontent. Thankfully, the phone rings and Alessandra answers it. Edie splinters her attention long enough to realize that it's the hostess from Cru calling back. Alessandra can handle the Katzens' dinner reservation.

"Okay?" the peacock-haired woman says. She approaches with her children now firmly in hand. Both have white-blond hair and are wearing little round spectacles with thick lenses that make their eyes look like pale blue fish swimming behind glass; they're so odd-looking, they're cute. "My name is Kimber Marsh and this is Wanda and Louie. We'd like to book a room."

"I can certainly help you with that," Edie says. Their first walk-in! Lizbet will be thrilled; she confided to Edie that she's concerned about their low occupancy. "What kind of room would best suit your needs?"

"I'd say we need a room with two queens. I can't very well get them their own room, they're too young."

"For how many nights?"

"I'd like to stay for the entire summer."

The entire summer? Edie thinks. She starts vibrating with excitement. This is what Lizbet has been hoping for: people hearing about the hotel and walking in off the street to book rooms.

"The rate on our deluxe guest room with two queen beds is three twenty-five," Edie says. "With tax and fees, that room is four hundred dollars."

"That's fine," Kimber says. "Please book us until…" She pulls up the calendar on her phone. "The kids have to be back in school then...add a few days to get ready...let's say August twenty-fifth."

Edie checks her availability, glances at Alessandra, who is just hanging up with Cru, and says, "Tell you what, I'm going to give you a free upgrade to one of our family suites." The hotel has twelve suites and only one of them has been booked, so Edie feels fine about upgrading Kimber Marsh. The suites are divine and, in Edie's opinion, should not be left languishing. Suite 114, which is the one Edie is giving the Marsh family, has a big living area with a full wall of brand-new hardcover books, all for the guests' reading pleasure, and there's a window seat overlooking Easton Street. This particular suite has a master bedroom and a whimsical room for kids with four wide bunk beds connected by tunnels and rope bridges; there are hidden reading nooks, and there's even a swing. It's very extra. Wanda and Louie will love it.

"You're upgrading us?" Kimber says. She raises her sunglasses to the top of her head so she can read Edie's name tag. "Edie Robbins, you're an angel fallen to earth."

Edie studies Kimber's face. She has bleary-looking blue eyes with brownish-purple rings beneath them; she reminds Edie of a beleaguered mom in a laundry-detergent commercial. Edie fills with joy at being able to offer this nice blue-and-green-haired woman an upgrade. "It's my enormous and whole-hearted pleasure," she says. She's overcome with a sense of professional pride and fulfillment. *This* is what hospitality is about—offering the guests something extra, something that makes them feel special, singled out and tended to. "I'll just need to run a credit card."

"Well, that's the thing," Kimber says. She glances

at the children, who are as still as sentinels beside her. "Kids, go play chess, please. But only *one* game."

"I don't want to play chess," Wanda says. "I want to read." She holds up a book that Edie recognizes—a vintage Nancy Drew mystery with the canary-yellow back cover. *The Secret of Shadow Ranch*. Edie read the same edition when she was Wanda's age.

"Please, Wanda?" Louie says. "I'll let you win."

Edie laughs and Kimber rolls her eyes. "He's *obsessed*. He brought a travel chess set with him, of course, but he accidentally left it at the Connecticut welcome center and it was a river of tears all the way up I-95. I hope you like children, because we'll never get him out of here. He'll sit at that chessboard all summer."

Edie laughs again, though a little less enthusiastically. Louie is able to drag Wanda over to the chessboard while Edie waits to hear what "thing" Kimber is talking about.

When the children are out of earshot, Kimber says, "I was hoping I could pay cash."

"Cash?" Edie says. The woman is booking a room for four hundred dollars a night for eighty-one nights and she wants to pay *cash*?

Kimber drops her voice to a whisper. "I'm in the midst of a divorce, so both of my cards have been frozen because they draw on joint accounts, yada-yada. I have cash, but I won't be able to give you a card, I'm afraid."

Edie blinks. Who in the year 2022 is crazy enough to think she could check into a luxury hotel without a credit card?

"The charge won't go through," Edie says. "We just put a minimum hold on it, fifty dollars per night."

Kimber Marsh says, "What I'm telling you is that

it's not going to work, the card will be declined."
She clears her throat. "We tried this already at the
Faraway."

"Ah," Edie says. The Faraway is a fairly new
boutique hotel in the center of town. If the Faraway
didn't let Kimber Marsh check in without a credit
card, then Edie obviously shouldn't either. But…she
knows it's the hotel's mission to *distinguish* itself from
the other luxury hotels on the island. Why shouldn't
they accept cash? Cash is money. But then Edie recalls the unspoken-but-understood reality of the hotel
business: Guests lie. Their relationship with you—
meaning the hotel staff—is temporary, so they feel
they can say whatever they want. How many case
studies did Edie read at Cornell about handling sticky
situations with guests? Dozens—and yet none exactly
like this. Her ex-boyfriend Graydon would probably
say that Kimber Marsh was trying to pull a con, using
her children as a smoke screen. She *says* she has cash,
but what if she doesn't? And even if she does, is she
just going to hand over a stack of bills?

Edie needs to speak to Lizbet.

"I'll just be one second," Edie says. She pops into the
back office and calls Lizbet's cell, but it goes straight to
voice mail. Ugh. She remembers that Lizbet is giving
a tour of the property to the couple from Syracuse
checking into room 303 and shouldn't be interrupted.
Every guest is a potential influencer.

Alessandra comes back into the office. "You're let-
ting those guests *wither*."

Wither, really? Edie thinks. She's been gone less
than sixty seconds. "I need to speak to Lizbet."

"Why don't you let me take over their check-in
since you're not comfortable doing it."

"I'm comfortable," Edie says. She brushes past

Alessandra, goes back out to the desk where Kimber Marsh waits. Edie hears Louie say, "Checkmate." He starts setting the board up again while Wanda sinks back into the armchair and opens her book. "I really need to speak to my GM before I okay this," Edie says.

Kimber Marsh leans in. "My soon-to-be-ex-husband left me for my nanny." She emits a short, bitter laugh. "It's such a cliché, but the reality is, I lost my spouse *and* my help. Craig and Jenny are spending the summer together in the Hamptons—Jenny just found out she's *pregnant*—so I wanted to take my kids away rather than let them stew in the cauldron that is New York City. But not having a functioning credit card *is* an issue, I realize this." She pauses. "What if I give you the first week in cash with an extra five hundred dollars thrown on top for incidentals?" She sighs. "Can you work with me? Please?"

Left her for the nanny? Edie thinks. *Who's pregnant?* Of course Edie can work with her. This poor woman needs her help. Kimber Marsh wants her kids to have a fun summer, and Edie is going to make that happen (and maybe win the thousand-dollar bonus for her superlative service!).

She hears Alessandra's bracelets but she doesn't look over. She slides two key cards across the desk. "I'll discuss your payment options with my GM, but for now, let's get you settled in your suite."

Alessandra clears her throat.

"Do you have luggage?" Edie asks.

"Yes, the gentlemen out front..." Kimber checks behind her. "There's quite a lot of stuff. I think they're just unpacking the car."

"And they have Doug!" Wanda reappears, though Louie has made himself comfortable over at the chessboard.

"Excellent," Edie says. She has no idea who Doug is; maybe a stuffed animal, maybe an imaginary friend. "I can't wait to meet him. Since the bellmen are busy with your luggage, I'll show you the way." At this point, Edie has no choice but to turn to Alessandra. "I'm just showing the Marsh family to their suite, I'll be back in a moment."

Alessandra's smile is glacial. "Of course." And then to Kimber: "Enjoy your stay and let us know if there's anything we can do for you."

No sooner does Edie emerge from behind the desk than Adam walks in with the luggage trolley, filled to the tippy-top with bags. Adam catches Edie's eye and says something under his breath that Edie doesn't hear and, based on his tone and facial expression, probably doesn't want to hear. A second later, Zeke English, who graduated from Nantucket High School two years ahead of Edie and who is so smoking hot he makes Edie feel kind of dizzy, comes into the lobby with a dog on a leash—a lean and muscled blue-brindled pit bull. Edie knows the breed because Graydon, her ex, had a pit bull named Portia. This dog, who is wearing a black muzzle, pulls Zeke along, its nails skating across the rare wormy chestnut floors of the lobby.

Edie's mouth drops open and she looks at Zeke and then Adam—but it's clear they're both expecting her to handle this. "Is this Doug?" Edie chirps.

Kimber's expression brightens. "Yes. I put the muzzle on him in the minivan, which he was *not* happy about. He's a sweet couch hippo, but he can act up around strangers."

He can act up around strangers, so why not bring him to a resort where there will be strangers around constantly? Edie starts to sweat. When you want to

spend the summer on Nantucket with your children
and your dog, you rent a house. Why didn't Kimber
Marsh rent a house? It's possible she couldn't find
a suitable rental at the last minute. Or maybe she
didn't want the upkeep. Maybe she wanted a pool,
a wellness center, and room service. There could be
lots of reasons, but one thing has become clear: Edie
needs to speak to Lizbet. She's too anxious to gauge
Alessandra's reaction. "Will you take Ms. Marsh and
the children to their suite?" Edie says to Adam. "I'm
going to call Lizbet."

"What about the dog?" Zeke asks. "Take him?"

All Edie can picture is Doug jumping up on the
sumptuous white bed, chewing on the rope and driftwood frame, clawing at the white sheers, peeing on
the Annie Selke rug. She gets the shivers. She figures
the Faraway turned the Marshes down not because
of the cash but because of the dog. "Would you and
Doug wait outside for two seconds until I speak to
Lizbet?"

Zeke looks put out; the dog quite obviously wants
to follow the rest of the family but Zeke shepherds
him back outside. Edie glances at Alessandra, who
offers ice-cap eyes. She's not going to help. Okay, fine.
Edie pops into the back office and tries Lizbet again,
and this time Lizbet answers.

"Lizbet?" Edie says. "We've had our first walk-
ins! It's a woman named Kimber Marsh and her two
children. They want to stay for the entire summer and
they're paying cash."

"Please tell me you got a credit card, Edie,"
Lizbet says.

"She's going through a divorce, so both her cards
are frozen. She said she'll give us the first week plus
five hundred for incidentals—"

"Oh no, Edie!"

Only now does Edie realize how absurd this sounds, and she's barely started. "I upgraded her to suite one fourteen because it was empty."

"You upgraded her," Lizbet says. "For the entire summer? Please tell me you're joking."

"Those family suites are just sitting vacant."

"They'll fill up," Lizbet says. "And when they do, we'll lose room revenue on your eleven-week upgrade."

Edie has messed this whole thing up. If this were role-playing back in college, she would get nothing but "feedback for improvement." Here in the real world, she might get fired, and she hasn't even told Lizbet the worst part.

"Also," Edie says, "she has a pit bull. His name is Doug."

"What?" Lizbet says.

Edie kisses her dream of this week's thousand-dollar bonus goodbye.

6. Staff Secrets

In her century as a ghost, Grace has developed and honed her EQ; her instincts about people are (nearly) always correct. Grace can sense trouble—it feels as though she's hearing a wrong note in a song or tasting a wine that has gone off. And while Grace is intrigued by the unexpected arrival of this family, she sees a flashing yellow light of warning when she looks at the mother. Kimber Marsh is lying about something. The children, however, are precious little angels, so cute and odd that Grace would like to cuddle them.

The children run, shouting, into the bunk-room wonderland of suite 114 with the dog following at a trot. The little boy, Louie, scales the ladder to the top bunk closest to the door, then clambers across a rope bridge to the other top bunk. The little girl, Wanda, tucks herself into the swing that looks like a wicker egg and opens her mystery book. Doug the dog stops just inside the threshold of the room and raises his bucket head. He starts to whine.

Oh, snap, Grace thinks. He senses her; animals nearly always do.

"What's wrong, Dougie?" Wanda says. "Come on."

Grace floats into the master bedroom, where Kimber Marsh runs a finger along the spines of the books lining the shelves. She's really quite lovely when she smiles, Grace thinks, though the green and blue hair is unsettling. And something else is off.

Kimber opens the small icebox and pulls out a package of crackers, a tub of smoked bluefish pâté, and—well, it is five o'clock in Greenland—a bottle of cranberry pinot gris from Nantucket Vineyards. She pours the glass of sparkling wine, then drags the cracker through the pâté and shoves it into her mouth. Grace forgives her table manners because she's so thin and needs to eat. Then Kimber slips over to the tablet by the bedside and suddenly the room fills with music. It's Mötley Crüe singing "Home Sweet Home." Grace hasn't heard this song since the early nineties.

Kimber goes into the bathroom with her toiletries and Grace follows cautiously; she has to avoid the mirrors just in case Kimber has, as it was popular to say in the late nineties, "a sixth sense." (*I see dead people.*) Kimber glances around, sniffs the Nest candle by the tub (Amalfi lemon and mint), turns on the soft halo light around the mirror, and winks at her reflection. *Okay?* Grace thinks. *Let's unpack this: Why would a person wink at herself? She's pulled something off? She doesn't have a penny to her name but now she and the children and the dog are ensconced in these glorious digs?*

Back in the bedroom, Kimber has another cracker and then, from the mess of luggage they brought, she fishes out a red duffel. She unzips it to reveal thick bricks of cash. *So she wasn't bluffing about the money,* Grace thinks. As she's stacking the cash in the safe in the walk-in closet, there's a knock at the door. Kimber tenses, then creeps out to the living room. She looks through the peephole and smiles.

It's Grace's crush Zeke (*sigh*) holding one of the marble chess sets from the lobby. "Edie said that Louie lost his travel chess set. She thought he might like to have a board of his own for the room."

"Thank you!" Kimber said. "How thoughtful." She holds up a finger. "Let me get you a little something."

"No need," Zeke says. "It's our pleasure."

Lizbet has just finished showing the couple from Syracuse around—the woman said she had a "nice" following on Instagram, and Lizbet thought she might help spread the word about the hotel—and she's been on her feet all day long (what possessed her to wear stilettos?), but when Edie tells her about the family in suite 114, she hustles back to the office. All she can think as she collapses into her chair is that Sweet Edie was duped on day one by some grifter.

She has to go to suite 114.

Lizbet limps down the hall and knocks on the door with a smile on her face that's so forced, it makes her head ache.

Kimber Marsh opens the door. Thank God Edie warned Lizbet about the hair, because it's startling. "Ms. Marsh, hello. I'm Lizbet Keaton, the general manager of the hotel."

"What a beautiful property you have here," she says. "The kids are in heaven."

Lizbet had meant to be firm but when the two little towheaded children in glasses tiptoe out of the bunk room, she relents immediately. The girl is holding a book, and the boy clutches a white chess queen. "I spoke with Edie, who checked you in. She told me you'd like to pay in cash, which is fine. I'll need the first week as a deposit."

"Yes, of course. One second." Kimber heads into the bedroom and reappears a moment later with a stack of bills. She counts it out: thirty-three hundred dollars. "The first week plus five hundred for incidentals. I can pay in advance every Monday if that's easiest?"

"In advance every Monday works," Lizbet says, relaxing a bit. If the woman pays in advance, there's no problem, is there? "We'll slip an invoice under the door and e-mail it to you as well."

Kimber Marsh opens her arms and hugs Lizbet, and the children run over and grab Lizbet around the legs. Over Kimber's shoulder, Lizbet sees the dog. He trots over to sniff Lizbet, then plops down at her aching feet.

At the end of the day, Lizbet calls the staff to her office. Raoul, who is working night bell, agrees to watch the desk.

Lizbet gathers Edie, Alessandra, Zeke, Adam, and

Magda, who is trailed by a preppy-looking kid wearing rumpled khakis and a pink oxford shirt rolled up above his elbows.

"Lizbet, let me introduce the newest member of my housekeeping staff, Chadwick Winslow," Magda says. "I trained him today. The other cleaners won't be in until the morning."

"Chad Winslow," the kid says, shaking Lizbet's hand.

"That's right, I remember when you dropped off your résumé. I'm glad this worked out. Welcome."

Chad dips his head. "Thank you for the chance. I'm grateful."

Chadwick Winslow sounds like a name straight off the *Mayflower* manifest, but Lizbet wants to foster diversity and inclusivity across the board. Why shouldn't a rich-looking dude named Chad be cleaning rooms?

Lizbet leads everyone into the break room, which has been decorated to resemble a 1950s diner; there's the signature turquoise and orange of a Howard Johnson's and a lot of chrome and Formica. It provides a complete psychological separation from the rest of the hotel, which is important when everyone is working six and a half days a week. There's a bar counter where the staff can sit and eat lunch, a low, curvy sofa with plenty of pillows for napping, a soft-serve ice cream machine, a vintage pinball machine—Hokus Pokus—and a jukebox that gives four plays for a dollar. Lizbet is seriously impressed by the break room, but for the most part, the staff seem nonplussed. Zeke stares at the pinball machine like it's a Martian spacecraft, and Lizbet can see him wishing there was a TV and a PS5 instead. Edie inspects the songs on the jukebox and says, "I've never heard of any of this music. Who's Joan Jett?"

Lizbet asks everyone to sit and then checks that the door is closed tight.

"First of all, I want to thank you all for your great work today." She brings her hands together in front of her chest. The incident with JJ and Mario Subiaco that morning in the parking lot feels like three days ago, and Lizbet has to stay to work the night desk. How is she ever going to make it through the summer?

She isn't, at this rate, and especially not in heels.

"We have guests in suite one fourteen who will be staying for the summer. I just want to remind everyone that although these guests may become very familiar to you over time, you should always treat them with the highest standards of service. And information about all our guests should be held in the strictest confidence."

"Of course," Edie says. Everyone else just nods.

Something about Kimber Marsh's cash felt fishy, and after the children and Doug retreated back to their room, Lizbet had wanted to ask Kimber a question—but she wasn't sure what that question should be. Was her ex-husband abusive? Was he in the Mob or a drug dealer? Was the family in hiding? In the end, Lizbet said to Kimber, "We're so glad you're here. I wrote a Nantucket recommendation guide, which I'm calling the Blue Book. I'll leave it for you at the desk." Then Lizbet zipped down to her computer and googled Kimber Marsh of East Seventy-Fourth Street, New York, New York. Nothing relevant came up. Lizbet checked Facebook, Twitter, and Instagram—nothing. She tried Kimberly Marsh, Kim Marsh, Kimmy Marsh—still nothing. As far as the internet was concerned, Kimber Marsh didn't exist. Was that suspicious? Lizbet reasoned that there were lots of people who didn't use social media.

Or maybe because of the divorce, she had deleted her accounts.

To the staff, Lizbet says, "I've advised Ms. Marsh to use the exit next to her suite to walk the dog. The last thing I want to see is that dog strolling through the lobby."

"I'll walk the dog for Ms. Marsh if she needs me," Zeke says.

Edie laughs. "Seriously? This afternoon, that dog was walking you."

"We bonded," Zeke says. "It'll be my pleasure to do that for Ms. Marsh."

"He just wants the thousand-dollar bonus," Adam says.

"About those bonuses," Lizbet says, and every pair of eyes snaps back to her. "In addition to reading the TravelTattler reviews, Mr. Darling will be hearing from *me* about staff performance. And what I'll be looking for is superlative guest service, of course, but also selflessness, sacrifice, promptness, consistency, kindness, and teamwork."

Alessandra, who has been sitting on the sofa with her arms crossed, raises a hand. "Will Mr. Darling be in residence this summer?"

"Not until August."

Alessandra frowns, but the rest of the staff look relieved. Adam raises his hand. "Can we get the piano in the lobby tuned?" he asks.

"Sure," Lizbet says. Until this second, she thought of the piano only as a piece of furniture. "Do you play?"

"I do," Adam says. He sings out "Welcome to the Hotel Na-antucket!" to the tune of "Hotel California," and everyone except Alessandra smiles. He has a great voice, a Broadway voice—just like his former GM said in the e-mail.

"I'll put that on my list," Lizbet says. She looks around the room. "Does anyone else have hidden talents?" She pauses. "Or perhaps a secret to share in this safe space?"

She watches every face in the room tense up.

Lizbet smiles. "Just kidding, guys. Thank you for a terrific first day."

Lizbet *isn't* kidding. She wants to nurture intimacy and trust. During her fifteen seasons at the Deck, Lizbet was a vault for all sorts of sensitive information. She was the first call when Goose's brother got arrested for a DUI; she sat with Juliette in the restaurant office while Juliette cried about accidentally getting pregnant. However, Lizbet kept boundaries in place—she was 90 percent boss, 10 percent big sister. Her staffers were a little afraid of her, but that meant she was doing a good job. She wants to create that same atmosphere here; it's her *strength*. She scrutinizes her staff. If they're hiding anything—as she suspects Kimber Marsh is—she wants to know about it now.

Chad Winslow leaves the staff meeting and drives his brand-new Range Rover back to his parents' summer house on Eel Point Road.

Secrets? he thinks. There's no way Lizbet could have heard what happened back in Pennsylvania, but the question made him uncomfortable.

He checks his phone only long enough to see that it's clogged with texts and snaps from his summer friends, but there's nothing from Paddy, which is both agonizing and a relief. Chad has texted Paddy every day since he arrived on the island but he's heard nothing back. Paddy is finished with Chad, hates his guts, will never speak to him again. And the thing is, Chad can't blame him. As Chad rumbles down the dirt road past the grandest beachfront homes on the island, he recalls Ms. English's words: *I happen to believe, Chadwick, that even the biggest disasters can be cleaned up, and I'll teach you to believe it too.* Chad wants to believe it. He wants to think that if he works hard and keeps his eyes straight ahead, he'll be able to scour the ugly stain from his life.

Ms. English and Chad spent all day in room 104, which was already impeccably clean. She stripped the sheets off the emperor-size bed and he started from scratch, pulling the fitted sheet tight around the corners. *Nothing worse than a rumpled bottom sheet,* Ms. English said. She showed him how to arrange the pillows; she made him take a picture of the finished product as though it were an art installation. They spent two hours in the bathroom alone, going over all the places on a toilet where bacteria hides, how to find and dispose of stray hairs and clipped nails, how to get water stains off the drinking glasses, and how to fold a towel, which was harder than it looked; Chad folded the same towel sixty-two times, starting over if the edges weren't straight. They ran through the one hundred points on the checklist, including the tiniest details that Chad never would have thought about—the number of hangers in the closets, whether all the light bulbs worked, and the temperature of the minifridge. Ms. English gave Chad strict instructions about which of the guests' belongings it was okay to touch; he was to fold discarded clothes and place them on the surface closest to where he found them. (The guests will always leave their underwear draped over the telephone, Ms. English told him, which made him laugh. He hoped she was kidding.) He was never to touch jewelry, watches, or cash unless it was a checkout and the cash had been left as a tip. He was never to go into the drawers, the closet, or a suitcase.

Obviously, Chad said, and Ms. English had given him a pointed look. Did she think he was a thief? He hadn't told her how he'd "messed up," so it was possible she thought he'd stolen something.

That was practically the only thing he hadn't done.

When Chad pulls into his driveway, he sees his friend Jasper's Porsche Cayenne parked there, and Jasper, Bryce, and Eric are standing on the front porch.

Chad aims the air-conditioning vents straight at his face and wishes he could disappear.

"Where you been, bruh, snapping you all day, we finally decided to storm the castle but your sister said you weren't home, and when we asked her where you were, she said she hoped you were bleeding in a ditch."

"Ouch," Chad says, though this comes as no surprise. Leith hates him now.

"She's cold," Bryce says.

"And yet so hot," Eric says.

Chad doesn't have the energy to flip Eric off for that. He's more concerned about the sweet green miasma hanging in the air above his friends.

"You guys smoked up on my porch?"

"We were *waiting* for you, man. We're hitting the brewery. You have to come."

"I can't."

"Whaaaaa?" Eric says. "Band is back together, bruh, come on. Didn't you miss us?"

The answer is no. Chad is still friends with these guys—the young princes of Greenwich, Connecticut; Mission Hills, Kansas; and Fisher Island, Florida— only because of their shared past. They threw sand at one another on Children's Beach, sneaked into R-rated movies at the Dreamland Theater, showed up late to steak night at the Sankaty Head Golf Club with their oxfords half untucked and their eyes bloodshot because they'd smoked out of an apple pipe at Altar Rock. But thanks to his friendship with Paddy, Chad has gained a modicum of self-awareness. He realizes that the Chad stereotype—passing out in public (like Jasper in front of the Gazebo on Figawi weekend) or stranding a car on the beach (like Eric in his father's Mercedes at Fisherman's)—is not only privileged and elitist but also ridiculous and pathetic.

What do you call a group of Chads? An inheritance.

However, this self-awareness, of which Chad is secretly proud, was tragically lacking on May 22.

Chad is amazed these guys haven't heard what happened back in Radnor; he half expected his sister, Leith, to spill the beans, even though their parents swore both children to silence "for the sake of the family name." Still, Chad knows that gossip flows fast along tributaries slicked by money and privilege. How did news of the party not reach these three?

Or maybe it did, and they just don't care.

The brewery sounds like fun. They can have a couple of cold Whale's Tales, get some lobster sliders from the food trucks, check out girls, listen to live music, pet other people's golden retrievers. (*No,* Chad thinks, *no dogs.*)

He'll go for an hour, he thinks, to appease them.

But then he recalls how an hour or two at the brewery can easily turn into drinks at the Gazebo, which will then become the four of them lined up in the front row of the Chicken Box, pumping their fists in the air to some cover band singing Coldplay before spilling out onto Dave Street and puking out the back of a cab.

Chad needs to be at work bright and early tomorrow. He will *not* show up hungover.

"Good seeing you guys," Chad says.

"Man, what's going on?" Bryce says. "You didn't open a single snap all day and now you won't go out with us?"

Chad knows his behavior must seem strange. He's never been the ringleader of this group—that has always been Jasper—but in summers past, he's gone along for a good time.

"Where were you all day?" Jasper asks.

"I…" Chad says. He could tell these guys he got a job, but there would be follow-up questions like "Where?" and "Why?" Chad is supposed to be having one last summer of carefree leisure before starting at his father's venture-capital firm, the Brandywine Group, in September. How can Chad explain that not only is he working this summer, he's a *chambermaid*? He spent today in rubber gloves, learning about disinfectants. "Maybe I'll meet you guys later." He reaches for the doorknob so there can be no mistake: he's not going anywhere with them.

Eric cracks a big, high smile. "Chad must have himself a lady friend. Look at his 'fit—did he even come *home* last night?"

Jasper and Bryce start catcalling—"Bros before hos, man, but no worries, we're gonna dip"; "We'll hit you up later"—as Chad slips into the cool air of the foyer and closes the door behind him. Leith is coming down the stairs; she flips him off and heads for the kitchen without a word. His sister has recently earned her doctorate in the silent treatment, which hurts because they used to be friends.

A second later, he hears his mother, Whitney. "Chaddy?"

If she's calling him the world's worst nickname—Chaddy—then she's already into the chardonnay.

Chad pokes his head into the kitchen and sees Whitney standing at the island with a large, uncorked bottle of Kendall-Jackson in front of her.

She flutters a piece of paper in his direction. "Pretty please," she says. "Market for Mom?"

He takes the list: *8 wagyu steaks, 3 lbs. bluefin tuna, 2 lbs. lobster salad, Comté cheese, truffled potato chips (6 bags).*

"This is a lot of food," he says. "Are we having company?"

Whitney shrugs and casts her eyes down into the golden promise of her wine. "Things for dinner."

Chad's father won't arrive on the island for another few weeks; he's busy closing a deal. Leith consumes only two things—hard-boiled eggs and Diet Dr Pepper—and Whitney eats even less than that. Yet his mother always stocks the fridge like the offensive line of the Philadelphia Eagles are coming for dinner. When she goes to the trouble of cooking, 90 percent of the food is pitched straight into the trash (neither of Chad's parents believes in leftovers). But most of the time, Whitney can't be bothered to cook. Instead, she pours wine, microwaves a bag of popcorn, and gets lost in Netflix or she meets "the girls" at the yacht club, and the groceries sit in the fridge until they grow a slimy film or greenish-gray fur. This never bothered Chad; he never even *noticed* until Paddy went on a tirade about the "conspicuous waste" of the Winslow household.

He'll buy three steaks, the cheese, and one bag of potato chips, he decides.

"I got a job today," he says.

"You did not." These are the first words Leith has spoken to him since May 22.

"At the Hotel Nantucket," Chad says. "Cleaning rooms."

His mother blinks.

"I wanted to do something," Chad says. "To make things right."

"Your father is handling it with the lawyers," his mother says.

"*I* wanted to do something. Get an honest job, make my own money to give to Paddy."

"Oh, sweetheart," Whitney says.

"Wait," Leith says. "You're serious? You're going to clean rooms at the hotel? You're going to be a…a…"

"Maid," Chad says. He watches his sister smile, which is nice because she has such a pretty smile and he hasn't seen it in a while. But then she dissolves into hysterical laughter that quickly becomes more hysteria than laughter and finishes as ugly sobs. She takes the closest thing she can find—a coffee mug with a picture of a dachshund on it—and throws it at him, hurling it like she's trying to get a lacrosse ball into the net for the game-winning goal against a long-time rival. She misses Chad; the mug smashes against the tile floor.

"You! Can't! Make! Things! Right!" she screams.

Chad leaves the kitchen and heads out the front door with the list clenched in his fist.

His sister is correct—he can't make things right. But he's going to die trying.

Since arriving on Nantucket last August and moving into the guest cottage behind her brother's house on West Chester Street, Magda English has established a tidy and modest routine. She attends the seven-thirty service at the Summer Street church every Sunday morning; she occasionally meets the church ladies (led by the sanctimonious and nearly unbearable Nancy

Twine) for afternoons of "crafting"; and she cooks—soups, stews, and rice dishes, all of them diabolically spicy.

When Magda leaves the staff meeting, she chuckles to herself. *Does anyone have a secret to share in this safe space?*

Magda has secrets but she isn't fool enough to divulge them to people she's just met, most of whom aren't old enough to remember the turn of the millennium. She finds it amusing that their new general manager, a woman well into her thirties, is naive enough to believe that any space is "safe."

If Magda were going to lead by example and share something, it might have been this: She's thrilled to be working again. Her tidy and modest routine had grown dull; she was bored and more than once she had checked flights back to St. Thomas. She'd retired from cruise ships for good but there was a new resort opening on Lovango Cay and she thought she might head up housekeeping there. But then she'd heard from Xavier, who told her what he'd done—bought a hotel, sight unseen, on the island where she now lives.

Xavier is like a schoolboy doing handstands and backflips to capture Magda's attention, only in his case, the acrobatics are displays of his wealth—the way he managed to get the renovation done so quickly, the thousand-dollar bonuses for the staff. And sending the orchids that morning! (Vandas are Magda's favorite flower, as Xavier well knows.) She'd left them on her desk; if she brought them home, she would be asked all kinds of questions that she had no intention of answering.

Magda slips out of the hotel and climbs into her brand-new Jeep Gladiator, which is part Jeep, part pickup truck, and a convertible to boot. Her brother, William, had given her *quite* a look when she drove it home from Don Allen Ford; he was certainly wondering how she'd paid for it. She said, "I've lived on ships for so long that all I ever dreamed about was a new car, so I splurged." If he wasn't exactly satisfied with her explanation, that was his problem.

Magda has errands to do. She stops first at Hatch's for a fresh bottle of Appleton Estate 21 rum—she constantly seeks out reminders of the Caribbean—and, because she can't help herself, she also buys a ten-dollar scratch ticket. When she gets back out to her car, she scrapes the silver coating off with a dime from her change purse.

Ha! She's won five hundred bucks! She'll go back in to collect it next time.

She considers stopping by Bayberry Properties to see if Fast Eddie has any more listings for her to check out. But she doesn't like the way Eddie's sister, Barbie, looks at her, so she decides to send Eddie a text.

Please don't forget about me, Mr. Pancik, she writes.

To his credit, Eddie responds right away: I could never forget you, Magda! I'll circle back later this week with a list, as we discussed.

Magda loves William and Ezekiel to pieces but it's time she got her own place, especially now that it looks like she's staying.

She has one more errand to run—the Nantucket Meat and Fish Market. Magda wants to get soft-shell crabs; she'll sauté them in brown butter and serve them with dirty rice and roasted asparagus. The market is pleasantly chilly and smells like coffee; it houses the only Starbucks concession on the island. Magda heads for the bounty of the long, refrigerated butcher case, where she finds impeccable trays of rib eyes, individual beef Wellingtons, steak tips in three different marinades, chicken breasts stuffed with spinach and cheese, plump rainbows of vegetable kebabs, baby back ribs, lamb chops, lobster tails, jumbo shrimp cocktails, cilantro-lime salmon, and swordfish steaks as thick as paperback books. The line at the case is four or five people long but Magda doesn't mind waiting. It's the first time she's stopped moving all day.

The hotel has turned out beautifully, she has to admit; but of course, Xavier never does anything halfway. *If you're not planning on being the best, why do anything at all?* Isn't that what Xavier said the night she met him a million years ago, back when he first bought the cruise line? He'd addressed the staff in the Tropicana theater; everyone had been thrilled, Magda included, because it was an hour of free drinks. Magda can still picture Xavier, upright and self-important in his bespoke suit. That was over thirty years ago now, the night her fortune changed.

Xavier is coming to the island in August. Magda will make sure his suite is spotless.

Just thinking these words makes Magda laugh—which attracts the attention of the young man standing in front of her. He turns around.

"Oh," he says. "Hey, Ms. English."

For the love of Pete, Magda thinks. It's her long shot. She has a hard time coming up with the boy's name even though she spent all day with him, showing him how to vacuum in neat rows, how to scrub the oyster-shell tiles with an electric toothbrush. They'd covered a surprising amount of ground, though it was immediately clear the child had never so much as cleared his plate from the dinner table. They still have the laundry to tackle—folding a fitted sheet; will he ever master it? They also need time to go over the sensitive things maids come across—sex toys and props for role-playing, birth control pills, condoms, diaphragms, tubes of lubricant, falsies, and drugs and drug paraphernalia. She doesn't want him to be shocked.

"Hello…" She can't for the life of her remember his name. Did she use it today? She must have. Her mind grapples for it the way her hand feels around on her nightstand for her glasses in the dark of the early morning.

"Chad," he says.

She starts giggling. She can't help it. She bows her head and chortles into her cleavage, her body rocking with laughter. It's so *funny,* not only her forgetting his name when she was *with him all day* but also the name itself, Chad, when he appears, outwardly anyway, to be precisely that Nantucket type. A Chad named Chad. Magda laughs so hard, her stomach muscles ache and tears leak out of the corners of her eyes. Chad is staring at her, as are a couple of other people in line, which begins to sober her, but then Magda catches a glimpse of Chad's expression and it's so *befuddled* that Magda doubles over again. She's making a ticking noise that doesn't even sound like laughter, but it's all she can eke out. She's probably thirty seconds away from someone calling an ambulance.

Now it's Chad's turn to step up to the counter and order. He asks for three Wagyu fillets, and although Magda has known the boy for less than twelve hours, this is exactly what she would have guessed his family eats for dinner. Magda is finally able to catch her breath and compose herself, though little bursts of laughter continue until Chad turns around with his wrapped parcel and smiles uncertainly at her. "See you tomorrow, Ms. English," he says.

"See you tomorrow, Long Shot," she says. His smile

widens; he can take a little ribbing, and Magda feels a pulse of optimism. She wonders if her gamble might work out after all.

Edie steps out of the meeting and thinks, *Is it just me or has this day been three weeks long?* She checks her phone.

There's a Venmo request for five hundred dollars from her ex-boyfriend.

No, Edie thinks.

This feels like a mistake or a joke, but a chill runs through her.

Graydon is out in the parched, cracked desert of Arizona; he accepted the job with Ritz-Carlton at its Dove Mountain property, the job they applied for together and planned to take together. But then things with Graydon got weird and awful and Edie changed her mind about the Ritz and decided to come home instead. Graydon, who by that point was *obsessed* with Edie, asked if he could come to Nantucket too—he said he would live with Edie and her mother, Love— but Edie said she didn't think that was a good idea. What she meant was that she didn't *want* Graydon on Nantucket. What she meant was that she wanted to break up. Edie had assumed she would work at the Beach Club like both her parents had, until her mother offhandedly mentioned that the Hotel Nantucket— which had been an eyesore and a blight throughout Edie's childhood—was undergoing a rumored thirty-million-dollar renovation. Edie wanted to be part of a team restoring a historic hotel to its former glory. And she would be safe; the waters surrounding the island would be nearly amniotic, protecting her from Graydon.

Except that now, here he is in her Venmo requests.

A couple walks across the lobby, dressed for dinner. Edie has nearly forgotten that there are guests in the hotel other than Kimber Marsh, her children, and their pit bull. It's the Katzens, Edie thinks, on their way to Cru; they wave as they head out the door. If Edie were playing her A-game, she would walk out with the Katzens, chat them up; after all, she had told Lizbet in her interview that the most important aspect of hospitality was making a connection with each and every guest at the hotel. But she does nothing and says nothing because she has a trash fire on her phone. *Five hundred dollars!*

She walks home to Sunset Hill, thinking there's no way she's going to let Graydon blackmail her. She deletes the Venmo request. He has some nerve!

A text comes in. Edie hopes it's her mother saying the Tater Tot Hotdish is ready. But when Edie checks, she sees the text is from Graydon: an emoji of a movie camera.

She has to pay him.

But she can't. She has a student-loan payment due on June 15 that's nearly half of her first paycheck.

She *won't* pay him! Who will he send the videos to? She's not famous; the *National Enquirer* doesn't care about her. And their mutual friends are woke enough that they'll realize Graydon is using his white-male privilege to get back at Edie for breaking up with him. They'll delete the videos without watching them (she hopes) and cancel Graydon.

But what if Graydon sends the videos to her *mother?* Can Edie risk *that?* Love had had Edie when she was forty. Now she's sixty-two years old, and although she tries to stay current—she knows who Billie Eilish and Doja Cat are—she doesn't quite understand the new sexual norms or the ways that Gen Z live their lives on their phones. Love probably doesn't think that Edie's still a virgin, but as close as they are, they never discuss sex. Nooooooo! (Edie binged the second season of *Euphoria* with her bedroom door not only closed but locked.) If Love saw Edie in the videos that Edie had allowed Graydon to take, she would die inside. Edie is Love's pride and joy, her prize and treasure, and her obsession with Edie has grown only more intense since Vance died. The worst thing would be if Love blamed *herself* for those videos, thinking that she didn't raise Edie right or set a good example.

Edie Venmos Graydon the five hundred dollars, which is most of what she has in her bank account—it's her graduation money. She wants to scream into the beautiful June afternoon, but she's afraid one of her neighbors on Sunset Hill will hear her.

She gets another text. From Graydon, of course. Ty! it says. With the thumbs-up emoji.

The last person to leave the break room is the one Grace most wants to see leave: Alessandra Powell. Grace hovers above as Alessandra drops four quarters into the jukebox (these are quarters that Grace watched Alessandra lift from petty cash) and picks songs—all of them the devil-worshipping heavy metal of the 1980s. Wow, Grace hasn't missed this music at all. She tries to spook Alessandra, positioning herself so that her figure in the white robe and Minnesota Twins cap might be reflected in the Plexiglas of the pinball machine that Alessandra has started playing. Grace does a little headbanging dance to amuse herself and get Alessandra's attention. Does Alessandra see her? No; she remains wholly focused on keeping the silver ball in play. Grace blows cold air down the back of Alessandra's neck, but she doesn't seem to notice that either. This can mean only one thing—the girl has demons inside her. Grace can practically hear their taunts: *You can't scare us! Nothing scares us!*

A second later, Grace realizes she's not the only one suspicious of Alessandra. There's someone else lurking just inside the door.

Lizbet isn't worried about the private life of Zeke or Adam or Chad or Edie, and she certainly isn't worried about Magda.

Alessandra is another story.

Right before the staff meeting, Mack Petersen from the Nantucket Beach Club called to congratulate Lizbet on opening day and ask how things were going. Mack did this in good faith despite the fact that they're direct competitors—Lizbet knows Mack from her days at the Deck. She couldn't keep herself from bragging, "I have Sweet Edie on my desk."

"You know I'm envious. She's my godchild."

"And I ended up hiring that woman Alessandra? The one who had been working in Italy?"

Mack said, "I'm not sure who you mean."

"Wasn't she supposed to interview with you? Alessandra Powell? For your front desk?"

Mack said, "I didn't have any front-desk positions open this year. The only position I hired someone for was night bell. I got lucky and nearly my entire staff from last year returned."

"Oh," Lizbet said. She was stymied for a second. Hadn't Alessandra said she was interviewing with Mack at the Beach Club? She had. She told Lizbet that Mack had basically offered her a position on the desk! "Well, let's hope I get that lucky next year."

Alessandra had lied, and that didn't feel great. Lizbet

should have been more guarded during their interview, but Alessandra had charmed her—bringing Lizbet a sandwich when she knew she was interviewing right before lunch. How canny! How clever! (How manipulative!) And then she'd dodged the questions about her references. This manager retired, this one died, there is no one in all of Europe who can vouch for my performance. Lizbet had called all four of the hotels listed on the résumé, and only at one hotel—the Grand Hotel Tremezzo—had she found someone who could verify that yes, Alessandra Powell had worked there for two years, but no, nobody was around at that moment who had known Alessandra personally. Lizbet left messages at the other three hotels and is waiting for them to call back—though what is she going to do now? Fire Alessandra? The woman is exceedingly professional on the desk, and she's stunning to look at. She's beautiful enough to get away with murder.

Lizbet is about to start her shift on the night desk (they *need* a night auditor!) when she realizes she saw everyone on her staff leave the hotel except Alessandra.

Lizbet cracks open the door to the break room. Alessandra is standing at the pinball machine gyrating her hips like she's making love to the thing, and the machine is dinging and flashing its lights like it's enjoying it. The jukebox is playing "Same Old Situation" by Mötley Crüe, which Lizbet hasn't heard since she listened to 92 KQRS back in the Twin Cities growing up.

When the game is over—Alessandra must be pretty good, because it lasts longer than half the men Lizbet has been with—and the song changes to "Highway to Hell" by AC/DC (nearly every song on the jukebox is from the previous century), Alessandra steps up to the soft-serve ice cream machine and swirls herself a gigantic bowl of chocolate. She digs in like she hasn't eaten in days.

"Hey," Lizbet says, stepping into the room.

Alessandra blinks. Her wavy apricot-colored hair falls over one shoulder.

"We haven't really had a chance to chat," Lizbet says.

"Chat?" Alessandra says. Her spoon hovers over the peak of ice cream.

Lizbet considers confronting Alessandra with her lie about Mack and the Beach Club, but she doesn't, because the fact is, she can't afford for Alessandra to get defensive and quit. "I thought maybe we could get to know each other a little?" Lizbet hears how hokey this sounds, even pandering, as though she's sucking up to the most popular girl at school. *Can we please be friends?* She changes tacks. "Would you like me to call you an Uber? Where are you living?"

"I don't need an Uber, I can walk. I'm living on Hulbert Avenue."

Hulbert Avenue? Lizbet thinks. That's the most exclusive address in town; all of those homes front the harbor. "Nice," Lizbet says. "Are you *renting* on Hulbert?"

"I have a friend with a house," Alessandra says.

"I didn't realize you knew anyone here."

"It's a new friend." Alessandra holds Lizbet's gaze and licks ice cream off the back of her spoon. "Someone I met on the boat over here."

Whaaaa? Lizbet thinks. Alessandra met someone *on the boat* and now has a place to live on Hulbert? "Wow, lucky you," Lizbet says. Her voice sounds a little arch, so she tries to soften it. "How was your first day?"

Alessandra gives Lizbet a pointed look that seems

to say, *Please go away and leave me to my ice cream*. "It was a day."

Lizbet changes into white jeans, a hydrangea-blue blouse, and—ahh—a pair of running shoes. She steps out to the desk and observes evening settling over the lobby. Golden, syrupy sunlight pours in through the open front doors, and guests head out to dinner—though, of course, not as many guests as Lizbet would like. The lobby feels a bit like a badly attended party. What can she do to increase occupancy? The hotel isn't cheap—it *shouldn't* be cheap—but it's slightly less expensive than their competitors are. Lizbet decides to reach out to every media outlet, all those places that fawningly covered the Deck. It would be nice to have some help from Xavier, but he doesn't seem concerned that their numbers are low. He cares only about the fifth key.

Kimber Marsh's son, Louie (the name completely suits the little dude; in his seersucker shorts and pressed white polo, he's both cute and formal, like a child king), wanders into the lobby alone, settles at one of the chessboards, and begins moving pieces. Lizbet watches him for a second, wondering if Kimber will appear. Mr. and Mrs. Stamm from room 303 stop by him on their way out the door.

"You really know what you're doing," Mr. Stamm says to Louie. "How old are you?"

Louie doesn't look up. "Six and a half."

Mr. Stamm chuckles and says to his wife, "A prodigy."

Louie moves his white rook and says, "Checkmate." He turns to Mr. Stamm. "Do you want to play?"

Mr. Stamm laughs. "I'm on my way out right now, but maybe tomorrow, how about that?"

Louie shrugs and the Stamms leave. Lizbet considers going over and offering to play with Louie, but then she sees the break-room door open and Alessandra slip out. Lizbet gets a nutty idea that she immediately dismisses. She's losing her mind; she's been at the hotel for nearly twelve hours and she has to last until midnight.

But...she deserves a quick break, and she's the boss, so there's no one to stop her.

Alessandra heads down the front stairs and pulls a bike off the rack—it's one of the hotel bikes; has she asked if she can use it? Lizbet approaches Raoul, who is posted by the front door and has the upright bearing of a guard at Buckingham Palace. "Do you mind watching the desk for twenty minutes or so while I get some air?"

"Not at all," Raoul says. Raoul has an old-school gallantry that Lizbet just adores and she briefly congratulates herself on a good hire.

"Little Louie is inside playing chess and I don't see his mother, so if you don't mind keeping an eye on him?" She winces. "I know you're not a babysitter."

"Happy to," Raoul says.

"Do you play chess?" Lizbet asks.

"I do, actually," Raoul says. "If it's quiet, maybe I'll let him beat me."

"Terrific! Thank you!" Lizbet watches Alessandra pedal off down Easton Street. "I'll be right back."

Lizbet also grabs a hotel bike—they're brand-new white Treks; Xavier bought a fleet of thirty-five—and takes off behind Alessandra. She savors the wind in her face, the softness of the air, and the gilded tone of the lowering sun, trying to ignore the fact that what she's doing is completely unhinged. She's following Alessandra home. If someone were filming this from above, they would see two women—in identical outfits!—one surreptitiously pursuing the other. The tail of Lizbet's blue blouse billows out behind her. She hums the Wicked Witch's theme music in her head.

Alessandra goes all the way down Easton, past Great Point Properties, past the entrance to Children's Beach, past the White Elephant, and Lizbet trails at a distance. She catches a whiff of garlic and butter coming from the Brant Point Grill and her stomach rumbles; she hasn't eaten a thing all day. Alessandra passes all the grand waterfront homes on the right and takes the curved left turn onto Hulbert before the Coast Guard Station and the Brant Point Light. Lizbet follows. A few cars pass, and Lizbet is afraid she'll see someone she knows. A bunch of customers from the Deck live on Hulbert; she and JJ used to be invited out here to private pool parties and croquet matches all the time. They'd become friends with two couples, the Bicks and the Laytons, both of whom live in this neighborhood. The Bicks' house, which has a tennis court, is up ahead and…Alessandra slows down.

There's no way that Alessandra is living at the Bicks' house, is there? Michael and Heidi are the quintessential golden couple—they're both tall, lean, and blond—and they have four young towheaded children. Maybe Alessandra has struck some kind of deal where she watches the kids in the evenings in exchange for housing? But that doesn't feel quite right. Heidi has a full-time nanny. And something about the way Alessandra said, *I have a friend with a house…a new friend. Someone I met on the boat* was sexual in nature. Lizbet *thought* Alessandra was intimating that she'd met a guy on the boat, the guy invited her back to his house, and now she's living there.

Alessandra stops, swings her leg off her bike, and turns around. "Are you *following* me?" she says.

Lizbet's foot slips off the pedal and the bike wobbles, but Lizbet pulls the handlebars straight, hits the brakes, and doesn't crash.

She has no idea what to say. She considers chastising Alessandra for taking a hotel bike without asking, but that seems petty. "I saw you head out and I decided I could use a ride as well. It's such a beautiful evening and I have to work the desk tonight." Lizbet glances at the Bicks' house. The gate to the tennis court is ajar and there's a racket lying on the bench, so the Bicks must be back on island. Lizbet dearly hopes they aren't watching this exchange from their window. She started out the day strong, but now she has devolved into some kind of psycho-boss who follows her employees home. With great awkwardness, Lizbet wheels her bike around. "See you tomorrow." She pedals away, fighting the urge to check where Alessandra is headed. She tells herself it's none of her business.

When she arrives back at the desk, she finds Raoul and Louie deeply involved in a chess match. Raoul looks up with wide eyes. "The kid is whupping my butt. Fair and square."

Lizbet nods, preoccupied with her embarrassment. What must Alessandra think of her? It's mortifying— and yet Lizbet still feels that something isn't right, something bigger than lying about an interview (that could be seen as strategic) and bigger than taking a bike without asking (who cares; she'll bring it back tomorrow). Once Lizbet assures herself that nothing pressing needs her attention, she retrieves her cell phone from her office and surreptitiously slides it next to her computer, even though this is, by her own decree, forbidden. She sends a text to Heidi Bick: Hey, girl, just thinking of you. Are you on island? Now that I'm not working at the Deck, we can actually go out to dinner this summer! Let me know when you're free so we can catch up.

She hits Send and takes a breath. Then she decides to place another ad for a night auditor in the *Nantucket Standard* classifieds—she won't be able to go anywhere or do anything until she hires someone. This time, she lists the pay: *$25 per hour, plus possible bonuses!* Hopefully, that will do the trick.

Suddenly, a young woman is at the desk, holding out a white cardboard box. It's Beatriz from the Blue Bar.

"Chef asked me to deliver this to you with his compliments," she says.

Chef, Lizbet thinks. *Mario Subiaco.* She recalls that morning, JJ's proposal, the fruit frenzy on the zebrawood cutting board, and the cocktail. She could really use that cocktail now.

"Thank you!" Lizbet says. She opens the top of the box and nearly swoons.

"It's called the bakery box," Beatriz says. "One of Chef's specialties. Clockwise, you have homemade pizza rolls, gougères filled with béchamel, and two favorites from the Blue Bistro—savory rosemary and onion doughnuts and pretzel bread served with his signature honey mustard."

Sweet lightning! Lizbet thinks. "This looks…amazing."

"Chef wanted to be sure you ate something delicious today," Beatriz says, and she vanishes through the door that leads back into the bar. Lizbet hears laughter and chatter and Nat King Cole singing "Unforgettable." It sounds…fun. And lively. Lizbet feels a pang; despite her bravado, she misses the restaurant business.

She isn't sure where to start—she wants to inhale the whole box of goodies, but she picks up one of the two glistening, golden-brown doughnuts because she has heard stories about them. *Gah!* The doughnut is so good that Lizbet's eyelids flutter closed and she has to keep herself from moaning. Next, she nibbles the end of one of the flaky triangular pizza rolls and finds it chock-full of crumbled sausage and pepperoni in a sauce that's slightly spicy. It's so *insanely delicious* that she feels guilty. She casts a glance at Raoul and Louie. Raoul stands up and announces, "I should get back to my post." Louie returns the pieces to their home squares. Raoul swings by the desk and says, "That kid is something else. I thought I would let him win and he *killed* me."

Oh so reluctantly, Lizbet offers Raoul the box. "Would you like a doughnut or some pretzel bread?" She dearly hopes he doesn't take a gougère, because there are only three.

Raoul waves the box away. "Thank you, but I don't eat carbs."

Ha! Brilliant! Raoul heads back to the bell stand and Lizbet absconds with her box of treasure to her office but keeps an eye on Louie through the doorway. He starts another game against himself, but then Wanda appears, holding a notebook and a pencil, and says, "Mom wants you back in the suite, Louie, come on."

"In a minute," Louie says. "I'm playing."

Wanda puts her hands on her hips like an aggrieved mother. "You have a board in the room." Louie sighs, then follows his sister down the hall.

Lizbet pops a gougère into her mouth and it

explodes with creamy béchamel. *Not bad, Subiaco,* she thinks. She remembers the night fifteen years earlier when JJ asked her to help him with some recipe development. He was trying to perfect an oyster pan roast, and Lizbet sat on a high stool in the kitchen at the Deck while JJ hand-fed her a plump, briny raw oyster, then a spoonful of the pan sauce (cream, bacon, thyme). This led to their first kiss, which led to them dating, then sleeping together, then, at the end of the summer, living together, and then to them buying the cottage on Bear Street and running the restaurant side by side until she discovered the pornographic texts on his phone. If anyone knows the dangers of being seduced by food, it's Lizbet Keaton.

And yet…she tears off a hunk of pretzel bread and swipes it lavishly through the honey mustard. She can't stop.

She decides to take a picture of the bakery box and send it to JJ; he'll be jealous and think she's gloating (she is). But when Lizbet picks up her phone, she sees a text from Heidi Bick.

Hey, girl, sorry, I was scooping Hayford from jiu-jitsu practice. I'm still in Greenwich, I leave for the island a week from Friday after the kids finish school. Michael has been up there for a couple months already working on a top secret project that requires complete silence, which cannot, of course, be found at home. I'm free any night after the eighteenth—it will def be Michael's turn to hang with the kids! Maybe you can get us into the Blue Bar? I heard it's going to be the new hot spot! Love u xoxo

Lizbet blinks. Heidi is back in Connecticut with the kids, and Michael has been on the island for a couple of months "working on a top secret project"? That doesn't mean he's sleeping with her front-desk manager, Lizbet tells herself. Being cheated on has destroyed Lizbet's faith in humanity; she automatically thinks the worst of everyone. It wasn't clear that Alessandra was pulling into the Bicks' house; that was just where she stopped to confront Lizbet. It was as if she had eyes in the back of her head. It was a little scary, to be honest.

Lizbet said she wanted to know everyone's secrets, but she understands now that she doesn't. She pops another gougère into her mouth. She doesn't at all.

7. Bad Reviews

June 15, 2022
From: Xavier Darling (xd@darlingent.co.uk)
To: Employees of the Hotel Nantucket

Good day, team. We have a sticky situation on our hands, I'm afraid. The reviews of our property on TravelTattler for the first week were primarily negative. Now, I understand that people are more likely to leave a review when they have a problem and that it's highly likely that all the guests who didn't leave a review left the hotel feeling perfectly content and satisfied with their stay. However, I will not be awarding the thousand-dollar bonus this week.

I hope you all realize that a satisfied guest isn't enough. I want you, please, to make every effort to see that our guests leave jubilant, energized, and inspired to tell the internet about their unparalleled stay at the Hotel Nantucket.

This is not meant as punishment or even a reprimand. Please think of this e-mail as an impetus to take your guest-service skills to the next level.

Thank you.
XD

TRAVELTATTLER REVIEWS

The Hotel Nantucket, Nantucket, Massachusetts
Dates of your stay: June 11–13
Number of people in your party: 3
Name (optional):
Please rate the following areas of the hotel on a scale of 1 to 10
Reception/check-in: 10
Room cleanliness: 10
Style/decor: 10
Concierge: 10
Wellness center: 10
Pools: 10
Room service/minibar: 10
Overall experience: 2
Please feel free to leave additional comments about your stay, singling out any staff members who made your visit memorable.
I wish you had a category for rating the bell

*staff because that would answer the riddle
of how my two gal pals and I could love
everything about this hotel and still give it a
two-star experience overall. The bellman who
was on duty during our stay was not only full
of himself but also incredibly rude, unfriendly,
and unaccommodating. He ruined what was
an otherwise wonderful experience. We also
suspect he was behind some inexplicable
phenomena that happened in our room on
the final night of our stay. He should be fired
promptly.*

Grace has been watching the day-to-day activity at the
hotel unfold with great interest, and although she's
biased, she happens to think her crush Zeke English
is doing a terrific job. He was a little awkward during
the first week while he was learning the ropes—and
admittedly, he's nowhere near as polished as Adam,
who works with Zeke during the day, or Raoul,
who works nights—but today is June 11, the start of
week two, and Zeke has clicked into gear like a fine
race car.

When Roger's Taxi pulls up to the front of the hotel
and disgorges three very exuberant-looking women
of a certain age, Adam nudges Zeke and says, "All
yours, stallion," and Zeke strides over with his winning smile, shoulders back, to welcome the ladies to
the hotel.

The ringleader of the three women introduces herself as Daniella, then turns to her two friends and says,
"Look at this hottie, gals!"

Gals? Grace thinks. That term is straight out of
1977. It makes Grace think of Farrah Fawcett Majors,

the Dallas Cowboy cheerleaders, and Charlie perfume (everyone staying in the hotel that year wore it).

The other two women are Claire (frumpy) and Alison (hippie-dippie). Claire tells Zeke that the three of them are from Florida and have come to the island to "whoop it up." (Again Grace wonders, *Who says that anymore?*) It's Daniella's fiftieth birthday—and they're also celebrating Daniella's shiny new divorce.

"I'm on the prowl!" Daniella crows. "Like only a woman who lost her orthodontist husband to one of his patients' mothers can be." Daniella is tall with ringlets of black hair down to her waist and a wide mouth. She's a not-quite Cher.

Oh, dear, Grace thinks. She sees trouble barreling down on Zeke like a freight train.

Zeke delivers the ladies' bags to suite 117 and displays its wonders—the sound system, the electric shades, the complimentary minibar. Daniella hands Zeke a hundred-dollar bill and asks him to stay for a beer.

"Thank you so much for the offer, ladies, but I'm on the clock for another five hours, so I'll have to take a rain check."

"We expect to see you later," Daniella says. She squeezes Zeke's biceps through his hydrangea-blue button-down. "Look at these *guns!*"

Alison, who has frizzled gray-blond hair and is wearing a tie-dyed sundress, shrieks, "Dani-*ella!*" Claire, who wears glasses and mom jeans, blinks at Zeke and says, "You are quite the snack," which actually makes Zeke laugh.

But he hightails it out of there.

Grace is relieved that Zeke gets off work before the ladies leave their room, buzzed from the bottle of Laurent-Perrier rosé they ordered from the Blue Bar, and head out to dinner at Lola. Claire briefly tries to flirt with Raoul, asking if he's taken, and Raoul deadpans perfectly that yes, he's married to Adam, the day bellman. That shuts them up!

The next morning, Grace sees Zeke arrive at the hotel not in his uniform, as usual, but in workout clothes. He heads down to the yoga studio…and Grace follows. There are eight or nine women stretching, in anticipation of Yolanda's barre class. When Yolanda takes her place at the front of the room, Grace sees Zeke melt a little.

Aha.

Grace can hardly blame him. Twenty-seven-year-old Yolanda Tolentino looks like Chrissy Teigen's little sister; she has tousled dark hair highlighted auburn, flawless skin, big brown eyes, and a deep dimple in her left cheek. Her body is trim, limber, flexible. Over the past few weeks, Grace has seen Yolanda sail through the lobby. Once, she stopped to talk to Lizbet and held a tree pose—foot tucked against opposite knee, hands held over her head like branches—which was unusual but also impressive. Another time, Yolanda was waiting for the elevator and executed a full-on backbend, which caused Mr. Goldfarb from room 202 to hiccup in surprise. Yolanda, Grace is happy to report, is as lovely on the inside as she is on the outside. And she must eat like a horse—she's back and forth between the yoga studio and the kitchen of the Blue Bar half a dozen times a day.

When Yolanda sees Zeke, she hurries over to get him set up at the barre with a ball, a looped resistance band, and two-pound hand weights.

"Um…" Zeke says, looking at the tiny lavender weights. "I've held burritos that weigh more than this."

"Feel free to switch them out for heavier ones," Yolanda says. "Just remember, I warned you. And unfortunately, I don't have any grippy socks that will fit you."

"Big feet," says a woman just walking in. It's Daniella; she's followed by Alison and Claire. "We know what *that* means, don't we, gals?"

No, this won't do, Grace thinks. She blows cold air down the back of Daniella's neck, and as she does so, she inhales the unmistakable scent of last night's tequila. Daniella doesn't notice the draft; possibly, she welcomes it. When Claire and Alison spot Zeke, they start furiously whispering.

Grace is embarrassed for them. She has seen fourteen-year-olds with more composure.

"Zeke is a barre virgin!" Daniella cries out. "Don't worry, I'll be right behind you, Zeke, admiring your form."

"Me too," Alison says. She's wearing leggings printed with rainbows and peace signs.

"I'm moving closer," Claire says. She has on a T-shirt that reads I DATE EVERYBODY.

Yolanda starts the music. "Ladies, let's try to focus." She lifts her leg while crossing her arms in front of her chest. Zeke follows suit; he can't lift his leg very high at all, or maybe he can but he's simply too enraptured by Yolanda, in her white leggings and her hydrangea-blue tank, with her hair in a thick braid hanging over one shoulder, to try very hard.

Leg lifts transition to planks on the yoga mats, followed by push-ups. Grace watches Zeke do all this with ease. When the class moves to the barre, Yolanda says, "Who's ready for a thigh party?"

Daniella hoots and raises her arms over her head, giving Zeke an unimpeded view of her chest; Grace notices that she has removed the pads from her yoga top so that Zeke can see her nipples protruding.

"Heels together, toes apart," Yolanda says. "Now sink down six inches and find your high diamond."

Zeke tries to approximate the position but his heels lift only an inch off the ground; when he sinks down, he winces. "Up an inch," Yolanda says, "and down an inch. Remember, an inch is the size of a paper clip." When they "press down to finish," Zeke's legs shake uncontrollably; it's the funniest thing Grace has seen in a long time.

"End of the first set," Yolanda says. "Two to go."

Zeke looks longingly at the door.

"Everyone grab your balls," Yolanda says.

Daniella rolls her tongue. "Now you're talking," she says.

When barre class ends, there's a standoff. Zeke seems to want to chat up Yolanda, but Daniella, Alison, and Claire are clearly lingering in order to talk to Zeke.

Yolanda says, "Thanks for coming, everyone. I'm going to run to the restaurant for an acai bowl before I teach yoga. Ta!"

Daniella, Alison, and Claire close in on Zeke, who has his back up against the barre.

"Tonight's my birthday dinner at Ventuno," Daniella says. "Then we're going to the Club Car to sing and hopefully to the Pearl for a nightcap."

"Guess what we're giving Daniella for a present?" Claire says.

Zeke tells the ladies he can't begin to guess.

"You!" Alison says. "Please join us. We'll pay for everything."

"Wish I could, ladies," Zeke says. "But I have to work tonight."

"That's okay," Daniella says. "There's always the after-party."

Zeke is a sitting duck when the ladies from suite 117 enter the lobby that evening in a flurry of high-pitched cackling and waves of perfume. The three of them are dressed in sequins and feathers and high heels with red soles. Daniella is wearing a tiara.

Zeke takes a visible breath. He's such a good sport, Grace thinks. "Here's my birthday queen!" Zeke says, taking Daniella's hand and allowing her to twirl. "Love the Louboutins."

The ladies scream. "He knows about Louboutins!"

Alison says, "Let's get a selfie. Daniella, you stand next to Zeke."

Daniella crushes herself against one side of Zeke, and Claire does the same on the other side while Alison, on the far side of Claire, holds her phone out in front of them. "Everyone say, 'Duck…duck…goose!'" She presses the button at the same time that both Daniella and Claire squeeze Zeke's butt cheeks.

"Whoa!" Zeke says, raising his arms and stepping back.

What? Grace thinks. It might be time for her to show her resting-bitch face on Claire's phone screen. These ladies are Out. Of. Line!

At that moment, Roger's Taxi pulls up and the ladies pile in; as the car pulls away, they wave at Zeke out the open window.

Grace dearly hopes that by the time Daniella, Alison, and Claire return, Zeke will be off work and safely home in bed. But at just a couple of minutes to midnight, Daniella stumbles up the stairs in her heels. Claire, behind her, is holding her shoes in her hand, and Alison is still down on the sidewalk doing some kind of psychedelic dance to music apparently only she can hear.

They're drunk, Grace thinks. *As blotto as Dahlia Benedict used to get, back in the good old days.*

"Hey, ladies," Zeke says. His voice is weary. "How was the birthday?"

Daniella snakes an arm around Zeke's waist and snuggles against him. "We have a proposition for you."

The church bells in town toll midnight. "All propositions will have to wait until tomorrow, ladies. I'm getting off my shift and I'm beat. I'll see you in the morning."

"Oh no, you don't!" Daniella says, her tone of voice serrated now. "We're calling in that rain check. Come upstairs and have champagne with us," she says, pulling him out of the lobby.

"Don't be afraid," Alison says. "We don't bite."

"Speak for yourself," Claire says.

Daniella pulls five hundred-dollar bills out of her purse. "We'll tip you for your excellent service."

Zeke holds up his palms. "I'm sorry, ladies." He takes careful steps backward into the lobby, which is deserted. *I'm here, Zeke,* Grace thinks. *I'm here.* "I have to get home now. You all have a good night, and happy birthday, Daniella."

"It's my fiftieth birthday," Daniella says. "Just come up for ten minutes."

Absolutely not, Grace thinks. She needs to get help. She widens her scope and sees the answer just on the other side of the door that leads to the Blue Bar. Grace ever so gently puts a hand on Yolanda's back.

"Hey, Zeke!" Yolanda steps into the lobby, holding a takeout box. She's wearing a stretchy black catsuit, a porkpie hat, and a pair of Chuck Taylors. She waves at the ladies and slips her arm through Zeke's. "Would you mind walking me out to my car?"

Zeke exhales. "Of course. I was just leaving myself. Good night, ladies."

"But…" Daniella says.

Zeke and Yolanda step out onto the front porch. Daniella, Alison, and Claire stare after him.

"Thank you," Zeke whispers to Yolanda.

"You don't have to walk me anywhere," Yolanda says, pointing across the street to a vintage metallic-green Bronco with a white top. She smiles up at him, revealing the cute dimple. "I had the most incredible meal at the Blue Bar tonight. Have you eaten there yet?"

"Uh…"

Yolanda sighs. "I'm madly in love with the chef."

"You are?" Zeke says.

She's in love with Mario Subiaco? Grace thinks. *Well, that explains why she spends so much time in the kitchen.*

Yolanda skips down the stairs with a wave. "Have a good night, Zeke." She drives off, and Zeke stares after her. He turns around to see the backlit figure of Daniella standing in the lobby. She crooks a finger at him, but Zeke runs for home. *Good night, sweet prince!* Grace thinks.

Then she follows the ladies to suite 117.

Claire passes out facedown on the bed in the second bedroom. *She's going to miss all the fun,* Grace thinks. Alison declares she's drawing herself a bath, and in a few moments the tub is filled with steaming water. She takes the box of matches from the little table next to the tub and tries to light the lemon-and-mint candle, but the match sputters and goes out. She tries a second match but it happens again. And again. She can't get a match to stay lit. She turns on the pearly light around the mirror, and this sets a similar mood, so she steps one foot into the tub.

She shrieks. The water is ice cold. And then the light goes out.

"Daniella!" she cries.

Daniella is in the master bedroom trying to make the electronic shade go down. Every time she pushes the button to lower the shade, the shade starts to go down, but then, as if it changed its mind, it travels back up. Grace is delighted! The petals of the lilies and peonies in the Surfside Spring bouquet wither and fall to the table, and while Daniella is gasping at this, Grace whips the shade all the way up. Daniella picks up the phone to call the front desk, but there isn't a dial tone. She flops on the bed, still in her red-soled shoes, and pulls a pillow over her face. Grace goes into the sound system, and an instant later music is blaring: Quiet Riot's "Cum on Feel the Noize." Daniella sits bolt upright in bed, and Grace laughs and laughs. She hasn't had this much fun since *girls* were *gals*.

TRAVELTATTLER REVIEWS

The Hotel Nantucket, Nantucket, Massachu-setts

Dates of your stay: June 12–15

Number of people in your party: 1

Name (optional): Franny Yates

Please rate the following areas of the hotel on a scale of 1 to 10

Reception/check-in: 1

Room cleanliness: 10

Style/decor: 10
Concierge: 10
Wellness center: 10
Pools: 10
Room service/minibar: 10
Overall experience: 5.5

Please feel free to leave additional comments about your stay, singling out any staff members who made your visit memorable.

I enjoyed my three-night stay at the Hotel Nantucket; however, I'm only giving it five and a half stars overall because the night of my check-in was an unmitigated disaster, and had the hour not been so late and had every other room on the island not already been booked, I would have left immediately. The front-desk clerk and the night bellman were harried and distracted, and the front-desk clerk was, at one point, snippy with me. Then it took the night bellman thirty minutes to deliver my bags to my room when all I wanted to do was put on my pajamas and go to sleep. Furthermore, when the bellman came, he neglected to explain any features of the room. I didn't realize until my final day, while chatting with a lovely couple at the adult pool, that everything in the minibar was complimentary.

The Blue Bar, however, was outstanding and the perfect place to eat as a party of one. I went all three evenings of my stay. My compliments to the chef!

This review, forwarded to her by Xavier, is waiting in Lizbet's in-box when she gets to work on June 16. (She could easily check their TravelTattler reviews herself, but she's too busy overseeing operations at the hotel, and Xavier has a five-hour jump on the day, which feels like an unfair advantage.)

The comments accompanying this survey read as follows:

Good morning, Elizabeth—

After reading this survey, I checked the schedule and discovered that the night-desk clerk was you and that the night bellman was Raoul Wasserman-Ramirez. I suppose I don't need to mention that, as the GM, you must uphold our rigorous hospitality standards. The hotel isn't anywhere near full, so I would urge you to pay close attention to the guests who are in residence. The woman who wrote this review could easily have been Shelly Carpenter. Keep your eye on the fifth key, Elizabeth! The fifth key!

XD

Lizbet is starting to resent Xavier Darling. How dare he judge her when he's in London and she's here, chest-deep in the trenches. He *checked the schedule,* as though he's Big Brother. Bah! He can send all the admonishing e-mails he wants, but he isn't going to impress Shelly Carpenter or the second woman, whoever she is, if he doesn't help her deal with their staffing shortages and low occupancy.

Even so, Lizbet's indignation (and why can he not call her Lizbet like she's asked him to?) is mixed with guilt and culpability. That woman—Franny Yates of Trappe, Pennsylvania—checked in three hours late (not her fault; Cape Air was delayed due to fog) during a moment of crisis.

The crisis involved Wanda Marsh. The Marsh children had made themselves quite at home at the hotel. Every morning and every evening, Louie would come down to the lobby in a polo shirt buttoned to the top, his hair wet and combed, wearing his funny little glasses, and he would sit at a chessboard playing against himself, waiting for one of the guests to notice him and offer to play a game. Louie always won, and he became something of a curiosity, a six-and-a-half-year-old chess genius right there in the lobby of the Hotel Nantucket! One of the guests (Mr. Brandon, room 301) had written about Louie in his TravelTattler review, saying how much he'd enjoyed playing chess every morning with Louie while he drank his cup of percolated Jamaica Blue Mountain coffee. Lizbet was just waiting for Xavier to award Louie the thousand-dollar bonus.

Wanda wandered the hotel freely as well. She always had a Nancy Drew mystery in her hand—she was working her way through them in chronological order, though her mother had only bought her up to number twelve, *The Message in the Hollow Oak,* and she was already on number nine, *The Sign of the Twisted Candles,* so she would soon be out of books. Wanda had also started carrying a spiral notebook and a number-two pencil because she wanted to write her own mystery novel starring girl sleuth Wanda Marsh. She was constantly asking people, staff and guests alike, if they had noticed anything strange or secret around the hotel, but the only mystery she'd learned of was the Case of the Disappearing Almond Croissants. It *was* unusual how rapidly Beatriz's croissants, filled with almond-flavored marzipan, vanished from the continental breakfast, and why didn't the kitchen ever make a second batch?

Unlike her children, Kimber Marsh was having a difficult time settling in. Back on the third night of their stay, Kimber had wandered down to the lobby at one in the morning. Lizbet was on the night desk.

"I suffer from chronic insomnia," Kimber said.

Lizbet nearly asked if they could switch places: Kimber could watch the desk and Lizbet would go to suite 114 and sleep in the emperor-size bed.

Kimber poured herself a giant cup of coffee—coffee?—and leaned against the desk to have a chat. *Fine, good,* Lizbet thought. It would keep her awake for her remaining hour.

Kimber said, "My husband left me for our nanny, whom he has now impregnated—and let me tell you, that was a wake-up call."

Yes, you told me, Lizbet thought. She'd had a wake-up call of her own, though she didn't want to tell Kimber Marsh about her breakup with JJ. She was so tired, she was sure she'd start to cry.

"I'm going to use this summer to reconnect with my kids," Kimber said. "I traveled so often for work, I barely saw them. They were always with Jenny, our nanny. Honestly, it's no wonder Craig left me for her. I was never around, so she slotted herself right into my vacant place and became not only a substitute mom but a substitute wife." Kimber leaned in. "That's why the kids are so consumed with the reading and the chess—something was missing from their little lives, and that something was me." Kimber sipped her coffee and reached for a copy of the Blue Book sitting on the desk. "Starting tomorrow, I'm going to do better. I'm going to do all the suggested itineraries in this guidebook."

The following day, Thursday, Kimber and the kids took Doug to Tupancy Links for a long walk, then they went to Barnaby's Place to do an art project, had lunch at Something Natural, and spent the afternoon on Children's Beach. But on Friday, Kimber plopped herself under an umbrella by the pool and read while Louie played chess in the lobby and Wanda inter-viewed hotel guests and Zeke took Doug out to do his business. On Saturday, Kimber didn't come down from her room until late afternoon. When she did, she had her laptop with her; she announced she was going to sit in the lobby and write her memoirs. *Okay?* Lizbet thought. At least Kimber could keep an eye on Wanda, who was finishing the last Nancy Drew mystery she had, and Louie, who was playing chess against himself. But Lizbet felt dismayed that the Marsh family had spent the entire day inside. Late-June days on Nantucket were the gold standard for the season—blue skies, plentiful sunshine, lilacs and cherry blossoms, and without the overbearing heat and humidity of July and August. But Sunday morn-ing, Kimber rebounded and took the kids strawberry picking at Bartlett's Farm. When they came back, Wanda walked into the lobby proudly holding an overflowing quart of luridly red fruit. While Lizbet was pleased they had gotten out, she couldn't help thinking about the pristine white linens on the beds and the Annie Selke rug, so she offered to wash the strawberries and let the children eat them over soft-serve vanilla ice cream in the break room.

Both Wanda and Louie had been gobsmacked by the ice cream machine.

"I want to work here when I grow up," Wanda announced.

Then, at a quarter past ten on Sunday evening—

when Lizbet was fading fast; she'd worked double shifts for seven straight days—Kimber Marsh came flying into the lobby in what Lizbet's mother would have called "a dither."

Wanda wasn't in her bed, she said. "Have you seen Wanda?" Kimber practically screamed. *"Have you seen her?"*

"I haven't," Lizbet said. She did a sweep of the lobby, checking Wanda's favorite reading chair and under the piano, where (inexplicably) Wanda sometimes liked to read, then said, "Let me look in the break room." (The allure of the soft-serve machine was strong; Lizbet had to fight it herself each and every day.)

But the break room was empty.

Lizbet enlisted Raoul's help—he would search the hotel, floor by floor. Kimber asked if it might be possible for her to let Doug out of their suite. She was certain he would lead them right to Wanda. Lizbet hesitated; the last thing she wanted was a pit bull roaming the halls of the hotel. But Lizbet sensed the urgency—an eight-year-old child was missing at ten fifteen at night—so she okayed it.

Raoul called up from the wellness center: no Wanda. "I thought she might be in the yoga room," Raoul said. "That fountain is mesmerizing." He was now moving to the first floor.

"Check all the unoccupied rooms, please," Lizbet said. There were twenty-one empty rooms and six empty suites (Lizbet felt each vacancy like a pinhole in her heart). "Maybe she found a way in."

Lizbet tried to think like Wanda. She seemed fascinated by the other guests, so Lizbet poked her head into the only populated area of the hotel, the Blue Bar—and wow! The place was popping. The bar was three-deep, every seat was occupied, the copper disco ball had dropped, and a group of people were dancing to "Tainted Love" in the space in front of the penny wall. Lizbet surveyed the crowd at hip level and tried to peer under tables. There was no sign of Wanda anywhere, though Lizbet spied plenty of people drinking flame-red cocktails, the Heartbreaker.

When Lizbet got back to the desk, a round, middle-aged woman wearing glasses with dark, square frames and a fanny pack around her waist—she looked like an aging version of Velma from *Scooby-Doo*—was standing at the desk.

"Finally!" she huffed.

"I'm so sorry," Lizbet said. "You must be Ms. Yates?"

"I arrived over five minutes ago and you're the first person I've seen!"

Lizbet returned to her spot behind her computer just as Raoul came rushing down the corridor, saying, "I'm headed up to the second floor."

Lizbet gave Raoul the thumbs-up; she was afraid if she spoke, she would lose her cool. A child missing in the hotel, she thought. Or *not* in the hotel. When was the right time to call the police?

"I'll need a form of ID and your credit card, please, Ms. Yates."

Franny Yates pulled both a Pennsylvania driver's license and a Mastercard out of her fanny pack.

"You're certainly traveling light," Lizbet said.

"My luggage is down on the sidewalk!" Franny said. "It's far too heavy for me to carry up the stairs. Silly me, I thought a hotel that costs as much as this one does might actually have a bellman!"

"We do have a bellman," Lizbet said. "Right now, he's assisting another guest. I'm happy to fetch your luggage."

"You won't be able to get it up the stairs," Franny said.

Lizbet winked at Franny. "You haven't seen me with kettlebells." But when Lizbet went to the hotel's entrance and looked down the staircase, she saw three black suitcases that were each big enough to contain a dead body. Franny Yates was staying at the hotel for only three nights. What could she possibly have packed?

Lizbet returned to the desk. "My apologies—you were absolutely correct. We'll have to wait for Raoul."

"How long will he be?" Franny asked, checking her phone. "I'd like to get to bed."

"Of course," Lizbet said. Just then, Raoul called. "She's not on the second floor, and Kimber says she and Doug checked the third floor and she's not there either. I'll sweep the fourth floor. You've checked the pools, yes?"

"Pools?" Lizbet said. She started to tremble. "No…"

"Oh, man," Raoul said.

Lizbet hung up. She held prayer hands up to Franny. "I'll be back in just a minute."

"But my room number? My key? My luggage is still on the sidewalk. What if someone takes it?"

"This is Nantucket," Lizbet said. "No one is going to touch it and it's too big for anyone to walk away with. I'll get your keys as soon as…" But Lizbet didn't finish the sentence. She hurried out the pool door, praying she wasn't going to see the small form of Wanda Marsh floating facedown. Both children could swim, she reminded herself. She hit the pool lights. No Wanda. She exhaled—but there was still the adult pool on the lower level and the hot tub. She recalled that Wanda was intensely curious about the Mystery of the Hot Tub, because it was restricted to people fourteen and older. Lizbet raced back through the lobby, passing Franny Yates, who had plopped herself cross-legged *on the floor* in front of the desk, which Lizbet understood was some kind of statement or protest, because there were armchairs and ottomans less than five feet away. "Be right—" Lizbet said. She ran down the stairs, through the wellness center, and out the door. The adult pool was dark and quiet.

"Wanda?" Lizbet whispered. She peered into the hot tub, feeling very much like the doomed heroine in a horror film.

It was empty.

Lizbet headed back upstairs, thinking she had dodged a huge bullet—Wanda hadn't drowned in the pools. Though Lizbet was growing more and more agitated. Where *was* she?

"Let me get your keys," Lizbet said to Franny Yates. "I'll upgrade you to a suite because you've been so patient. Here you go. Suite two fourteen. You can take either the stairs or the elevator to the second floor, and then it's all the way down the hall to the left."

"What about my *luggage*?" Franny Yates said.

"As soon as the bellman is free, I'll have him bring it to you."

"I want to go to sleep!"

"Ms. Yates, I need to ask for your indulgence. We have a situation here—"

"Your situation is that your hotel stinks," Franny Yates said. She marched off down the hall.

Lizbet wasn't sure what to do. Should she try to schlep Franny Yates's luggage up the stairs herself? Should she go up to the fourth floor to help look for Wanda? Should she call the police? *A child is lost.* Lizbet wasn't a mother but she understood how serious this was. Lizbet went down the stairs to the street and looked both ways. No Wanda.

She heard the phone ringing back in the lobby and she hustled up the stairs, taking them two at a time, so when she reached the top, her heart was pounding in her ears. "Hello?"

"We found her," Raoul said. "She was wandering around the fourth floor."

"Oh, thank God." Lizbet paused. "What was she doing *there?*" The fourth floor had odd roof angles and very small windows, and the Historic District Commission would have had to approve any structural changes that would be visible from the street, so Xavier had opted not to renovate it just yet. Lizbet had ventured up to the fourth floor only once; it was, essentially, a cavernous and dusty attic.

Raoul said, "She said she was looking for the ghost."

The ghost! Lizbet thought. She had been very careful never to mention the supposed ghost to anyone, and especially not Wanda, but Zeke might have let it slip.

"We have a check-in to suite two fourteen who is very anxious for her bags. There are three of them, and I would deliver them myself but they're each the size of a small home."

"I'll be down as soon as I'm finished cleaning up here."

"Cleaning up?" Lizbet said.

"Doug was so excited to see Wanda that he had an accident."

Lizbet closed her eyes. The other line of the hotel phone rang. It was suite 214. "You *have* to get suite two fourteen her luggage. Please, Raoul. Right now."

"But the dog—"

"Raoul, please!"

"Yes, boss," Raoul said.

Lizbet answered the other line. "Your luggage is on its way, Ms. Yates."

"You're a liar!" Franny Yates yelled. "I can see my luggage from my window. It's still on the sidewalk!"

Franny Yates's review is factually correct—it took Raoul a full thirty minutes to deliver her luggage, both Lizbet and Raoul were harried and distracted, and Lizbet was, perhaps, a bit snippy. But was the check-in an "unmitigated disaster"? No, an unmitigated disaster would have been Wanda staying missing or found dead.

Lizbet had comped Franny Yates's entire bill at the Blue Bar (three nights, two hundred and sixty dollars). Why didn't her review mention the comped meals?

Lizbet clicks out of the e-mail from Xavier and rests her head, ever so briefly, on her desk. It's seven thirty in the morning and she's so tired, she could sleep until seven thirty tomorrow morning. She's so demoralized, she feels like crying. Or crying uncle.

She needs a night auditor.

8. Lie, Cheat, and Steal

Grace tightens the belt of her robe and does her usual nocturnal sweep through the hotel, beginning with the room where Louie and Wanda are sleeping. They've been taking turns in each of the four bunks;

tonight, they're both in uppers. Wanda has her notepad tucked under her pillow, and Louie has fallen
asleep in his glasses, clutching the white queen piece.
Grace can hear Doug the dog snoring in the other
room. He always lies in front of the door of the suite;
if Grace goes anywhere near him, he'll wake up and
snarl. Kimber, the mother, sleeps with her arms and
legs in an X; she looks like a blue-and-green-haired
angel fallen from the sky.

Grace floats out of suite 114 and pops in to
check on the Bellefleurs in room 306—*Oops, sorry to
interrupt!*—then to suite 216, where Mrs. Reginella is
scrolling through the text messages on her husband's
cell phone, and then down to room 111, where Arnold
Dash sleeps with the urn of his wife's ashes on the
nightstand. Grace wishes there were more action. She
hopes that as July gets closer, occupancy will increase.
The hotel is so welcoming, the staff so attuned to
every detail. What's keeping the guests away? Maybe
there's too much competition or maybe it's too expensive. After all, when this was a "family-friendly
budget hotel," it was jam-packed. Maybe the hotel's
reputation is too damaged to rehabilitate. (Is that
her fault?) She wonders what ever happened to the
article that that lovely young woman, Jill Tananbaum,
came to write. As far as Grace knows, it hasn't been
printed.

Suddenly, Grace catches a whiff of something that
smells like a passing garbage truck, and she realizes
a new threat is about to enter the hotel. She swoops
down to the lobby, which is warmly lit, with Norah
Jones playing over the sound system. Lizbet is at her
post at the desk, perusing summer dresses on the
Alice and Olivia website. Grace can hear people in the
Blue Bar, chanting "Don't! Stop! Believin'!," which

is par for the course. The disco ball dropped over an hour ago.

Everything seems to be in order, but nevertheless, Grace's hackles are up. There's a predator approaching.

She hears footsteps on the stairs. A figure walks through the doors of the hotel.

Really? Grace thinks. *This guy?*

Lizbet is so tired when she interviews Richard Decameron—a fifty-four-year-old father of three from Avon, Connecticut, who has answered her prayers and applied for the job of night auditor—that the exchange has a dreamlike quality. He arrives at the hotel at ten thirty at night, fresh off the late ferry, but he's as ebullient and chipper as a QVC host trying to sell you the leaf blower that will change your life. He's dressed like it's casual Friday at the hedge-fund office, in a navy-blue spring suit, a navy-and-yellow-checked shirt, and chocolate suede Gucci loafers without socks. He has a dad bod—a bit of a paunch—and gray hair thinning on top, but his smile and his twinkling eyes are appealing. He gives Lizbet strong vibes of guys she knew in college, the fun, good-natured best friends of the hot-jock jerks everyone was in love with. Richard Decameron—he asks her to call him Richie—was the guy who actually stuck around to make sure you got in a cab after you did that last, ill-advised shot of tequila.

Lizbet prints out his résumé. He was an executive in the insurance business in Hartford for thirty years, and for the past two years, he's been working for something called Kick City.

"This…Kick City? I'm not familiar with it," Lizbet says.

"It's a sneaker-broker website," Richie says. "When athletes or rappers drop a limited-edition shoe, our brokers snap them up and resell them. I'm sure it sounds like kid stuff, but trust me, it's big business."

"What inspired you to make the switch?" Lizbet asks.

"I wanted a change from insurance, something with a little more sex appeal."

"And what brings you to Nantucket?"

Richie sighs. "I'm divorced, my ex-wife has recently started dating again, the new guy lives in the same town that I do, and it got claustrophobic, so I decided to treat myself to a summer at the beach. I'm a night owl by nature, so when I saw you advertising for a night auditor, I thought I'd reach out."

"Do you have housing?" Lizbet asks. *Please say yes,* she thinks. She wants a night auditor so badly, she might let Richie sleep in one of the empty rooms. (The rest of the staff would, no doubt, mutiny.)

"I'm staying at the hotel out by the airport tonight," he says. "Tomorrow I have an appointment with a woman who's renting a room in her home on Cliff Road."

"Ah, wonderful. And you're familiar with Fresh-Books? You'll be fully responsible for preparing guest invoices..."

"I have all kinds of systems-software experience," Richie says. "I'm a numbers guy. I was a math major at UConn back in the day." He pumps a fist. "Go Huskies!"

She likes his energy, especially so late at night. "How comfortable are you with guest interaction?"

"I talk to everyone. My kids find it embarrassing."

"How old are your kids?" Lizbet is asking just to be polite. She's going to hire this guy.

"Kingsley is thirteen, Crenshaw is eleven, and Millbrook is eight." He pulls out his phone. "Here's a picture of our family in happier times."

Grace hovers above so that she can scrutinize the photo. There's a slightly younger version of Richie posing next to a pretty brunette with three smiling children arranged in front of them. There's a river, a waterwheel, trees aflame with color—it's autumn. The youngest child is holding a basket of apples.

This family looks happy. Grace notices Richie's hand trembling ever so slightly as he gives the phone to Lizbet, who beams at the photo. Is she, like Grace, wondering what happened to the marriage?

"Will your children get a chance to visit Nantucket this summer?" Lizbet asks.

"Haven't gotten that far yet," Richie says. "I'm just trying to get a viable situation in place."

"Well, if this helps, I'm happy to offer you the position of night auditor. It'll be six nights a week, I'm afraid. I can only cover one night and still keep my sanity."

"I'm happy to work seven nights," Richie says. "I'd prefer it. It'll keep me out of trouble. It's best that I keep busy so I don't miss my kids as much."

Lizbet exhales with obvious relief and looks right at the space that Grace is occupying. For the first time, Grace wonders if maybe Lizbet is supernaturally sensitive and can see a stolen hotel bathrobe and her missing Minnesota Twins cap floating in the air. *Definitely not,* Grace thinks. The poor woman is merely exhausted. But even so, Grace rises a bit.

Lizbet says, "We have a family in suite one fourteen, a mother with two children. They're paying their bill in cash. You'll invoice them every week, and then Kimber, that's the mother, will bring down cash, which you can just keep in the safe until I find time to go to the bank to deposit it." She smiles. "I can trust you with the safe combination?"

Richie laughs. "My references will all vouch that I'm a perfectly average good-enough guy."

"Have you ever done any marketing?" Lizbet asks.

"I sat in on all the meetings at Kick City."

Lizbet frowns. "Occupancy at the hotel is below fifty percent, and I just don't understand why. The hotel was, admittedly, mediocre for a long time. I'm not sure if it's the lackluster reputation we're grappling with or..."

"Or?"

"Well, some people say there's a ghost."

Richie hoots. "The hotel is haunted? That's fantastic! I would think that would draw people to the hotel rather than keep them away. You should be promoting the ghost story."

"We should?" Lizbet says.

"Absolutely yes," Richie says. "Advertise the ghost! Market the ghost!"

Hmm, Grace thinks. There's still a stench coming off Richie Decameron—something's wrong; she can't say what—but she's willing to plug her nose and ignore it because it sounds like Richie is interested in her story. *Hello, Richie!* she calls out nasally, though of course he can't hear her. *I'm here! I was murdered!*

Everything Alessandra Powell owns fits into two (knockoff) Louis Vuitton duffels that she bought at the Mercato di Sant'Ambrogio in Florence.

Michael told Alessandra that his wife and children were due on island on June 18—but Alessandra had wormed her way so deeply into Michael's psyche that she thought, just maybe, he would decide to leave his wife. It would be quite a coup, though not her biggest (that would be Giacomo, who gave up both his runway-model mistress and his heiress wife for Alessandra). From what Alessandra can tell, Heidi Bick is the kind of wife and mother who meets her besties for yoga every morning after dropping the children off at their progressive and obscenely expensive private schools, then swings by the organic grocery on her way home so she can whip up whatever eclectic dish Sam Sifton has recommended that day in his *New York Times* cooking column. (*On Wednesday, maybe a tahdig…*) Heidi not only takes care of the four Bick children, she's also the point person for Michael's father, who has Parkinson's.

Alessandra met Michael Bick on the fast ferry back in early April. Alessandra had feared it would be slim pickings as far as male prospects were concerned—nearly all the men were sporting Carhartt's and work boots and dropping their *r*'s—but then Alessandra spied Michael with the Vacheron watch and his master-of-the-universe posture. At the ferry snack bar, he ordered a Sam Adams and a clam chowder, and Alessandra popped behind him in line and ordered the same. She took a seat one row over facing him and pulled out her well-worn copy of *The Sun Also Rises*. She drank her beer, let her chowder cool, and—surprise, surprise!—caught Michael staring at her.

"I'm sorry," he said. "It's not every day I see a beautiful woman drinking a beer and reading Hemingway."

By the end of the ride, Michael had moved into the seat across from Alessandra and bought them another round of beers; their respective chowders had gone untouched, and Alessandra's book lay facedown, forgotten. They had both stretched the truth about their situations. Michael said he was "taking some time apart from his wife," who was "back in Greenwich with the kids." Alessandra said she had been living in Europe for the past eight years and was "treating herself" to an American summer.

"The Riviera gets old after a while," she said, making them both laugh.

He invited her over to his place for a drink. She told him she had to check into her Airbnb (she didn't have one booked). He insisted, spinning her Cartier love bracelet and saying, "Unless your heart belongs to the person who gave you this?"

"Uh, *no,*" she said, regarding the bracelet as she might a handcuff. (Giacomo had given it to her a few weeks before he was sent to prison.)

"Great!" Michael said. "Then come for a drink."

"I really can't."

"Just one. Please?"

The house was more than Alessandra could have hoped for. It was one of the huge old family "cottages" right on the harbor that they'd passed on the ferry. It had a long, elegant pool that fronted their tiny private beach and a tennis court in the side yard. ("Do you play?" Michael asked. "A little," Alessandra said.) The inside of the house was tasteful and fresh, magazine-worthy—lots of white wainscoting and exposed blond beams and a massive stone fireplace and a table laden with silver-framed photographs (the wife he was supposedly taking some time apart from and the four children) behind the wide, deep sofa.

Michael kissed her outside on the deck, right away biting her lower lip. He wrapped his hand in a length of her hair, tugging a little to let her know who was in charge. (He, erroneously, thought this was him.)

He slid his mouth down to her neck, lingering in the kill spot just below her ear; good boy, he'd been well trained by wifey, though Alessandra would bet a schmillion dollars he no longer kissed Heidi Bick this way. He unbuttoned Alessandra's blouse slowly, his pinkie just barely grazing her nipple, and Alessandra felt a pulsing between her legs that was replicated by the ruby beacon of Brant Point Light in the distance.

He had her panting—shirt open, breasts exposed, jeans unzipped—when he turned and walked back into the house.

Alessandra waited a second, wondering if he was having a crisis of conscience. She chastised herself; she had made a poor choice.

When she finally followed him inside, she had to let her eyes adjust to the dark. There was milky moonlight through a window, blue numbers on a cable box—and then hands grabbed her waist and she screamed, genuinely frightened, and realized she wasn't in charge at all. She also realized Michael Bick had, very likely, brought home women he didn't know before. Possibly he did it all the time.

But in the pearl-gray light of morning—fog covered the harbor like a layer of dust on an antique mirror—Michael traced one of her eyebrows and said, "Where did you come from, Alessandra Powell?"

That was the question, wasn't it? Alessandra was originally from San Francisco, where her mother, Valerie, waited tables at the storied Tosca Café in North Beach. Valerie and Alessandra lived in a building down the street from the restaurant. Valerie kept their apartment clean, didn't drink too much (wine occasionally), and didn't do drugs (weed occasionally); there was always enough money for groceries and for Alessandra to get ice cream down on the pier or go to the movies or, when she was older, take the bus to Oakland and thrift-shop. But there was something a little off about Alessandra's upbringing. While Alessandra's friends were opening presents around the tree on Christmas morning, then sitting down to a rib roast, Alessandra was home alone watching R-rated movies on cable while her mother worked a double. She and her mother opened their Christmas presents on the twenty-sixth with eggs and a tin of osetra caviar and Springsteen singing "Santa Claus Is Coming to Town." On Easter, while Alessandra's friends were going to church and hunting for eggs and slicing into honey-baked ham, Alessandra was watching R-rated movies on cable and eating straight from a bag of jelly beans that her mother bought as a nod to the holiday even though she didn't celebrate Easter at all.

And then there were the men. Every week, Valerie would bring home married men who frequented the Tosca bar while they were in the city on business. These men would arrive after Alessandra went to bed, but she heard them in the shower the next morning while Alessandra's mother ransacked their wallets in the bedroom. Every once in a while, one of the men would stay for breakfast and listen as Valerie played her favorite CD and sang along: *Torn between two lovers, feeling like a fool.*

Alessandra knew better than to follow in her mother's footsteps but it was the only example she had. When Alessandra was eighteen, she seduced Dr. Andrew Beecham, the father of her best friend, Duffy. After Alessandra and Drew had been sleeping together for a few weeks, Alessandra realized she could cash in on the power she had—the power to tell Duffy and Drew's wife, Mary Lou—and get something valuable in return. Drew was the chair of the romance languages department at Stanford. Alessandra audited a full year of classes—Italian, Spanish, French literature, art history—and then demanded a one-way plane ticket to Rome, which Drew Beecham was only too happy to buy for her.

Where did you come from, Alessandra Powell?

Alessandra answered Michael in her prettiest Italian. *"Poiché la tua domanda cerca un significato profondo, risponderò con parole semplici."* She smiled; she had no intention of translating. "That's Dante."

Michael Bick kissed her tenderly. She was making progress. She stayed the next night and the next.

She made Michael milk-braised pork with hand-rolled gnocchi in sage and butter and a salad of bitter greens. She made coq au vin. She made scrambled eggs the way her mother used to make them for other women's husbands—with double the yolks (double-the-yolk scrambled eggs after a night of whiskey, Valerie used to say, felt a lot like love). Alessandra beat Michael soundly in tennis. (In Ibiza, she had taken lessons with Nadal's first coach.) When they made love, she screamed out in Italian. She didn't complain that they never went anywhere together—not to dinner or coffee, not for walks on the beach or in the state forest, not for drives to Great Point or Sconset. When the guy came to fix the internet, she greeted him in French and told him she was the au pair.

Secretly, Alessandra secured a job at the Hotel Nantucket that would start in June, though she hoped by then Michael would have fallen so deeply in love with her that he would tell Heidi their marriage was over and Alessandra could simply slip into Heidi's place. She would go to Surfside all day while Michael worked at home on his laptop (while he was sleeping, Alessandra had hacked into his computer and learned that he traded petroleum futures and in 2021 had reported $10,793,000 in income), and she would accompany him to Cisco Brewers to hear live music and to his standing Thursday-night reservation at Ventuno. She would become best friends with the Laytons next door; the families were so close that they had a set of keys to each other's house. She would bewitch everyone in Michael's life exactly the way she had bewitched him.

But this didn't quite happen. A few days before Alessandra started work, she overheard Michael on the phone with Heidi and his kids, his voice sweet and upbeat and guileless. "How was the game, Colby, did you hit the ball, did you swing? Hey, buddy, did you see Dustin Johnson sink that putt on the ninth?...I love you, I love you, I love you more, kisses, can't wait to see you all, only two more weeks! I'm getting the boat ready; Coatue, here we come!"

Alessandra felt most affronted by this last bit. She hadn't realized Michael had a boat.

She went to work at the hotel on opening day, disappearing from the house while Michael was on the phone, and she ignored all his calls. Let him wonder. When she walked in the door that evening, he was visibly shaken. "Where were you?" he said.

She narrowed her eyes and tried to read his face. Why did he care? How much did he care? She shrugged. "Out."

A tirade followed; it was the first time she'd seen him angry (other than when the Wi-Fi went down, but that was different), and it interested her. *Worried sick, went driving around looking for you, you just left without a word, the only way I knew you were coming back was your luggage was still here.*

Do you love me? she wondered. She thought the answer might be yes, but it wouldn't be enough.

"I got a job," she said. "Working the front desk at the Hotel Nantucket."

Michael's face turned pill white. "What?"

Alessandra stared him down.

Michael said, "Our...my friend Lizbet Keaton is working there. She's the GM, I heard. Is she the one who hired you?"

"Yes."

Michael nodded slowly, then backed away half a step, as though Alessandra were holding a gun. "You didn't tell her where you were living, did you?"

"Obviously not." Alessandra didn't tell Michael that Lizbet had followed her home. Thankfully, Alessandra had spied her in the bike's mirror before she'd turned into the driveway.

Relief softened his face. "Okay, good. I wouldn't want people to get the wrong idea."

"What you mean," Alessandra said, "is that you wouldn't want people to get the *right* idea. Which is that you're keeping a lover even though you are still fully married. Your wife has no idea you needed space. She thinks you came up here to switch out the storm windows for screens and tackle a 'top secret project' for work, which seems outrageous, but she doesn't question it because she trusts you and she's probably enjoying the time apart—she feeds the kids pizza three nights a week and goes out with her girlfriends to the new wine bar and flirts with the cute bartender and then goes home and curls up with her vibrator." Alessandra stopped to breathe. "You're a liar and a cheat."

Michael cleared his throat. "They're coming up on the eighteenth, so you'll need to go."

"Will I?" Alessandra said.

There was fear in his eyes. *He* was the one who had chosen poorly. "Baby, please."

"I'm not your baby, Michael. I'm a grown woman whom you've treated like a concubine."

"You knew what you were getting into," Michael said. "You can't tell me you didn't understand what this was."

He got everything backward. *He* was the one who didn't understand what this was.

"I'll go quietly the day before your family arrives," Alessandra said. "On one condition."

Alessandra walks from Michael's house to the hotel with a knockoff Louis Vuitton bag in each hand. It's a stylish walk of shame—or it would be if Alessandra felt any shame. What she feels most is regret. Michael Bick is the complete package. He has looks, money, intelligence, humor, and even a basic decency (if you ignore the obvious). He asks questions; he listens to the answers; he's generous and curious and thoughtful. The sex was mind-blowing; Michael is the only man Alessandra ever met who didn't need to learn a thing or two in bed. And they are so compatible. Oh, well. It has been Alessandra's experience that men like Michael Bick get scooped up early, in college or the first years of living as an adult in the city.

She also feels triumphant. In her suede Bruno Magli clutch is a cashier's check for fifty thousand dollars. Michael asked her to name her price and she did so judiciously, unsure of what she could get away with, but now she wonders if she could have asked for double. She won't worry about it. During their first week of sinful bliss, Alessandra watched Michael punch in the passcode to his phone, and later, while he was sleeping, Alessandra copied Heidi Bick's number. She also took pictures of herself in different spots throughout the house—in the pool, weighing herself on Heidi's scale (a trim 105), cooking in the kitchen, even sprawled across the master bed (although they'd never had sex in that room, Michael's one nod to fidelity).

If Alessandra doesn't find another situation, she'll simply text Michael the pictures and ask for more money.

As Heidi Bick is checking things off her packing list in Greenwich—Colby's inhaler, Hayford's putter, her Wüsthof tomato knife—Alessandra will be paying for a 1980 CJ-7 in "mint condition" that she found listed in the *Nantucket Standard* classifieds. The Jeep costs twenty grand; Alessandra will pay cash, then she'll write the bellman Adam a check for twelve grand, which is her share of the summer's rent now that she's moving in with him and Raoul on Hooper Farm Road. She'll throw ten grand at her credit card bills and still have a bit of a financial cushion.

Alessandra is growing weary of seducing men, then extorting them; she would far prefer to find a permanent provider.

She marches up the front steps of the hotel, trying to carry herself like a hotel guest checking in. Except she's wearing her uniform, and Adam says, from his spot behind the lectern, "You look like a high-class hobo."

Alessandra doesn't respond. She pictures Michael frantically cleaning the house, sweeping up every strand of her hair, wiping her fingerprints off the wineglasses, checking the drawers for an errant pair of panties. But will he notice the Chanel eye shadow that Alessandra left in Heidi's makeup drawer in the bathroom? (Heidi wears Bobbi Brown.) Will he check the shoe tree in Heidi's closet, where Alessandra has left a pair of size 6 crystal-studded René Caovilla stilettos winking coyly among the size 8 Jack Rogers sandals and Tory Burch ballet flats? Will he find the positive pregnancy test that Alessandra tucked into the copy of Jennifer Weiner's *Good in Bed* that sits atop the stack of novels on Heidi Bick's nightstand?

He will not, Alessandra guesses, because men don't pay attention to the way women live, not really. Michael will suffer for this, and for his hubris. He thought he was making a clean (if somewhat costly) getaway.

She wonders if Michael misses her. After handing over the check, he kissed her deeply, and when she pulled away, she saw tears glittering in the corners of his eyes. *Torn between two lovers,* she sang in her head, *feeling like a fool.*

"Raoul says he'll swing by around noon to get your bags," Adam says now.

"Kind of him, thank you," Alessandra says, though she wishes Raoul would come right away so she could avoid the inevitable questions.

Alessandra steps into the lobby and smells the deep roast of the Jamaica Blue Mountain coffee that Edie has percolating (they use a vintage percolator and the guests rave about the flavor). She hears Mandy Patinkin singing a Gershwin song: "They Can't Take That Away from Me."

She's late due to the check, the kiss, the walk with the bags. She likes to arrive before Edie because she feels it gives her the upper hand, and now, when Edie looks up and sees Alessandra and notices the luggage, she looks confused and just a bit superior.

"Good morning, Alessandra," she says. "Taking a trip?" Edie's voice is light and easy despite the fact that Alessandra is always chilly with her.

"Good morning, Edie." It's not that Alessandra

doesn't *like* Edie; she does. Edie is smart, self-effacing, and excellent with the Marsh children. (Both Wanda and Louie are terrified of Alessandra.)

But Edie is also young, and the last thing Alessandra wants is for Edie to look up to her. Alessandra doesn't want to lie to Edie about her past or her present, and hence, friendship between them is impossible. Alessandra has to push Edie away.

It's for your own good! Alessandra wants to say, because she can see her brusqueness hurts Edie.

Alessandra drops the bags behind the desk and logs on to her computer.

Lizbet pops out of the back office for what's probably her fourth cup of coffee; she drinks so much caffeine, Alessandra is surprised she doesn't flap her arms and fly away.

Lizbet notices the bags because she notices everything. "What's going on here?" she asks with an arched eyebrow.

Alessandra meets Lizbet's gaze. "My housing fell through, so I'm moving in with Adam and Raoul."

Lizbet moves for the percolator. "What happened to the place on Hulbert?"

Alessandra tries not to care if Lizbet has figured it out. Lizbet can't fire her for what goes on in her personal life, though it might invite scrutiny later on, something Alessandra wants to avoid. She smiles despite the bitter, nearly chemical taste in her mouth. "Oh," she says, "that was just temporary."

Chad has been assigned a cleaning partner named Bibi Evans who treats every room like it's a crime scene. This might be because Bibi aspires to be a forensic scientist, or it might be because Bibi is what Chad's mother would call a "nosy parker," or it might be because Bibi is a thief. Chad doesn't like thinking this last thing, but that's what his gut tells him, because Bibi touches every single item in any room that might be worth stealing. She touches the things that Ms. English has expressly asked them *not* to touch, such as watches, jewelry, cash, and pills.

They've been working together for two weeks when Bibi lifts a diamond tennis bracelet out of a travel jewelry case and *tries it on*. Chad is freaked out (and also somewhat impressed) at Bibi's moxie; she doesn't seem to be intimidated by Ms. English or the rules. Bibi holds her hand out so that the diamonds catch the sunlight coming in through the picture window overlooking Easton Street. "I was meant for the finer things."

"You should probably put that back," Chad says.

"You're such a *rule follower*." She says this like she's calling him a pedophile.

It would be easy for Chad to shock Bibi with the ways that he's broken the rules, but it's nothing to be proud of. "The guest could walk in any second, Bibi," he says. "Or Ms. English."

Bibi waves her arm around as though showing off the bracelet to a roomful of admirers. It looks wrong on her pale, knobby wrist. Bibi wears heavy black eyeliner and has a tattoo of a skull on the back of her neck, which Chad noticed when Ms. English insisted that Bibi gather her stringy dark hair into a ponytail. She's nothing like the girls Chad went to high school or college with; Chad understands that she's from a different "socioeconomic class." Bibi is the mother of a nine-month-old girl, Smoky (that's her actual name; it's not short for anything). She told Chad that she took this "crappy job" because she wants to go to college, study forensics, and join the homicide unit of the Massachusetts State Police so that she can give Smoky a better life than the one she had growing up. Bibi's life involved a drunk for a mother (Chad can commiserate with her there, though he's not sure his own mother and Bibi's mother have much else in common). Bibi often lamented that paying for child care and the ferry tickets from the Cape took more than half her paycheck. Chad made what he hoped sounded like sympathetic noises. He told her the baby was cute.

"You're a complete squid, Long Shot," Bibi said that first day. "Long Shot" was the nickname Ms. English had given him and he's secretly pleased because, on Nantucket, any name is better than Chad. "But I'd rather be paired with you than with those other bitches."

She meant Octavia and Neves. They speak Portuguese and wear thick gold crosses around their necks. Ms. English refers to Octavia and Neves as the A-team and Chad and Bibi as the B-team, which is probably not a random designation. This might be what fuels Bibi's dislike of the other girls (Chad doesn't care; he knows he belongs on the B-team), although Bibi's vitriol is so intense that Chad wonders if the sisters are mean to Bibi on the ferry. (He can't imagine this.) By her own admission, Bibi hates people. It's the one thing, she says, that brings her joy.

Chad announces that he'll clean the bathroom and deal with the floral bouquets if Bibi wants to vacuum and get started on the bed. She grunts in the affirmative, though Chad was hoping for a thank-you, since he's taking the more onerous tasks. The flowers are a surprisingly tedious job—he has to wipe up the blue hydrangea dust, trim the stamens of the lilies because pollen stains everything a bloody rust color, and change the smelly brown water in the vase. But the flowers are a picnic compared to cleaning the bathroom. In the two weeks that Chad has been working at the hotel, he's dealt with bloody pads and tampons in the trash (he appreciates anew that he and his sister never had to share a bathroom), and he cleaned up the puke of some bachelor-party dude who didn't make it anywhere close to the toilet bowl. Only slightly less repulsive are the globs of toothpaste and stray hairs he has to scrub from the sink.

By dealing with the flowers and the bathroom, he achieves the dual purpose of punishing himself and sucking up to Bibi. Her approval matters, even though she's not pretty and not sophisticated and not particularly well educated; despite her claim that she is "meant for the finer things," everything about her demeanor suggests otherwise. She's a twenty-one-year-old single mother (she hasn't mentioned the father of the baby and Chad isn't brave enough to ask), and Chad is both in awe of and afraid of her.

When Chad finishes scrubbing the shower and the tub—he does the tub conscientiously even though it's clear it hasn't been used—he pokes his head into the bedroom. The bed has been stripped and remade, the pillows artfully arranged; Bibi always does a really good job with the beds. Chad doesn't see Bibi, but instead of calling her name, he tiptoes around. He finds her in the walk-in closet, sifting through a suitcase. She holds up a belt first, then an amethyst silk negligée. He notices she still has the tennis bracelet on her wrist.

"Bibi?" he says.

She jumps. "Jeez, Long Shot, you scared me. What the hell?"

"What are you doing?" he asks. "You know we're not supposed to go through personal stuff. And you need to take that bracelet off."

"Who are you, the cleaning police?"

"I just don't want you to get in trouble."

"Why would I get in trouble? I'm just looking around. I'm not going to *take* anything. You probably think I'm a thief because I'm not rich like you, Mr. Eel Point Road. Mr. Range Rover."

Chad blinks. He's not sure how Bibi discovered what he drives or where he lives. He's been careful to present himself as a normal-ish summer kid. He parks way up on Cliff Road and told her only that he lived on a "dirt road, out of town."

"I don't think you're a thief, Bibi," he says. He's tempted in that moment to offer her part of this week's paycheck because he knows she has to buy things like diapers and formula, but he's afraid she'll find it patronizing. "Do you want me to do the vacuuming?"

The next morning, Ms. English sends Octavia and Neves to clean suite 114—Chad is grateful they're doing it, because being around Doug the pit bull makes him uncomfortable—but instead of giving Chad and Bibi a roster of rooms and sending them out too, Ms. English closes her office door and turns to them.

"The guests in room one oh five reported something missing," she says. "A black-and-gold Fendi scarf."

Chad closes his eyes. Room 105 was the last room they cleaned yesterday; it was a checkout. In room 105, Bibi had been suspiciously on task and Chad thought this was because the guests had left a forty-dollar tip, which Chad told Bibi she could take. Bibi had asked if he wanted to go down to

the service kitchen to replenish the items that went
in the minibar—the wine, the Cisco beers, the bluefish pâté and crackers—which was the best job of
all. The service kitchen was adjacent to the Blue
Bar kitchen, where Beatriz was usually pulling a
tray out of the oven—gougères or homemade pigs
in a blanket or the pretzel bread—and she always
offered some of whatever it was to the cleaning staff.
Yesterday afternoon, Chad hit the jackpot because
Beatriz was prepping lobster-roll sliders on homemade milk buns. Chad had eaten lobster growing
up the way other kids ate peanut butter and jelly
but he had never eaten anything like this slider
before. The outside of the milk bun was crisply
toasted while the inside was fragrant and pillowy;
the lobster meat had been mixed with lemon zest,
herbs, crunchy pieces of celery, and just enough
tangy mayo. The lobster slider was so...*elevated*
that Chad went back to room 105 feeling inspired.
He wanted to do his job as well as Beatriz did
hers. He wanted to clean the *hell* out of room
105!

But when he returned, the room was finished and
Bibi was gone. Chad peered out the window to see Bibi
heading down North Beach Street toward the ferry
with her backpack slung over her shoulder. He was
sorry she'd left—he'd brought a slider up for her—but
also relieved that he'd survived another day with her.

"Did either of you see a black-and-gold scarf?"
Ms. English asks. "Because Mrs. Daley is sure she left
one behind. She sent a picture of herself wearing it at
Ventuno and she says it's not in her luggage. Did you
find it and put it in the lost and found?" Ms. English
pauses. "Did you perhaps *mean* to put it in the lost and
found and forget to?"

She's giving Bibi a way out, Chad thinks. Because Bibi definitely lifted that scarf.

"I didn't see any scarves," Bibi says in a clear, steady voice that sounds so genuine, Chad believes her. "Did you, Long Shot?"

"No," he says. "And we checked all the drawers like we were supposed to."

"Yes, I double-checked as well," Ms. English says. She studies their faces. Ms. English is a handsome woman who has never been anything but nice to Chad; even when she made him fold a hand towel for the sixtieth time, he felt like she was doing it for his own good. She has high standards and a dignity that Chad respects. He does *not* want to disappoint her.

"Did you look in the laundry?" Bibi asks. "Maybe Mr. and Mrs. Daley were using the scarf in bed—you know, to tie each other up—and it got mixed in with the sheets."

"Of course I've checked the laundry," Ms. English says. She clears her throat. "I understand how tempting it is when you see something you covet and you think the guest has so many things that she might not miss something like a scarf…"

"It sounds like you're accusing us of taking it," Bibi says. "Which is not only insulting, it's absurd. Chadwick has family money, plus a dude would have no use for a woman's scarf. And I would never take it, because scarves like that are for boomers. Sorry, for older women. Plus I wouldn't be able to tell a Fendi scarf from a Walmart scarf."

That's a lie, Chad thinks. Bibi *loves* designer stuff. She makes a game of identifying the designers of bags, belts, and shoes without checking the labels—Chloé, Balenciaga, Louboutin—and she's always right.

Bibi says, "Besides, I would never steal from a guest.

I have a baby at home. I'm a *mother*." She pauses. "Did you ask Octavia and Neves if *they've* seen it?"

Chad lowers his gaze to the floor. He can't believe she's going there.

"The scarf was missing from room one oh five," Ms. English says. "That was your room to clean."

"But they each have a master key," Bibi says. "It's not impossible that they took it and tried to make it look like it was us. They have some kind of weird grudge against me that you should be aware of."

Ms. English is quiet. Chad is quiet. Bibi isn't speaking but there's a lot of disruption emanating from her. Or maybe Chad is projecting.

"I'll let Mrs. Daley know that we haven't found it but that we'll keep looking," Ms. English says. "Maybe it's in Mr. Daley's luggage or perhaps she took it off while she was out and left it somewhere. But I do hope nothing else goes missing."

Chad and Bibi take their cart up to room 307 in silence. Bibi doesn't touch anything in the room, and she offers to clean the bathroom and do the flowers, which, Chad realizes, is as close to an admission of guilt as he's going to get.

9. The Cobblestone Telegraph

The summer season is under way on the island and most of us are too busy with our own lives—tracking down the window washer, mulching our gardens, pulling our beach chairs out of storage—to pay attention to the happenings at the Hotel Nantucket. But every once in a while, we'll drive past and see Zeke English standing on the sidewalk in front of the hotel with a pit bull on a leash sniffing the dandelions, and we'll wonder how things are going.

Blond Sharon is having dinner at the Deck one evening when JJ O'Malley himself pops out to say hello. Blond Sharon does the intrepid thing and asks if he's heard how Lizbet likes her new job.

"No, I haven't," JJ says. "We don't speak."

"Well, I'm sure she's busy," Blond Sharon says. "Have you eaten at the Blue Bar yet? Everyone's raving about it. They have a copper disco ball that drops—"

"Out of the ceiling at nine o'clock," JJ says. "Yes, I know. But from what I've heard, you can't have a proper dinner there, right? He isn't serving a chop or a rib eye or even a pan roast."

"Right," Blond Sharon says. "It's more like great cocktail-party food, heavy apps that you can share, and then after you've finished grazing, someone comes around with shot glasses of whipped cream in flavors like Kahlúa and passion fruit. It's called the whipped cream concierge! Have you ever heard of anything so fabulous? And then everyone starts dancing. We went last week and, honestly, I've never had more fun in my life."

JJ O'Malley squares up to his full height and gazes across the creeks, perhaps to remind Blond Sharon that although the Deck doesn't have a *whipped cream concierge,* it does have a magnificent view. "The reviews of the hotel on TravelTattler have been underwhelming," he says.

"Oh," Blond Sharon says. "Have you been checking?"

Officer Dixon gets a call at four o'clock in the afternoon about a man asleep in his car at Dionis Beach.

"So what?" Dixon says to Sheila in dispatch.

"I guess he's been sleeping in his car in the parking lot the past three days," Sheila says. "Some mommy noticed him and thinks he's a potential predator."

Dixon takes a breath. A man sleeping in his car is what passes for crime on Nantucket; he supposes he should be glad. He climbs into his cruiser.

When he arrives at Dionis, he sees the man and the car in question—some guy in his early fifties in a 2010 Honda Pilot with Connecticut plates and a WHAT WOULD JIM CALHOUN DO? bumper sticker. The back window sports a decal that says PARENT OF AN AVON MIDDLE SCHOOL HONOR STUDENT.

Threatening stuff. Dixon wonders if he'll need to call for backup.

He approaches the open car window and sees the guy in the driver's seat, head slumped back, snoring away. He's wearing a white polo shirt and swim trunks; his bifocals have slid down to the end of his nose, and there's a copy of Lee Child's *Blue Moon* splayed open in the console next to an open Red Bull. Dixon backs away because he feels like he's intruding on the guy in his bedroom—and then he notices the open shaving kit on the passenger seat and a hand towel drying on the dashboard. A peek into the back seat reveals a gaping suitcase.

Is this guy…Dixon glances over at the public bathrooms. Dionis is the only beach on Nantucket that has showers. Is this guy *living* in his car?

"Excuse me, sir," Dixon says, jostling the guy's shoulder. "May I see your license and registration, please?"

Richard Decameron, age fifty-four, of Avon, Connecticut, here on the island to work for the summer at the Hotel Nantucket.

"So you're not…living in this car?" Dixon asks. "Because that's what it looks like."

Decameron tries to laugh this off, but it isn't quite convincing. "No, no, I live at the hotel."

"Why are you sleeping here in the parking lot? We've had reports that you've been here the past three days."

"I'm enjoying the beach," Decameron says. "I take an early swim, get a shower, read my book, and sometimes I conk out." He offers Dixon a friendly smile. "Is that against the law?"

He's "enjoying the beach" by sleeping in the parking lot? Something doesn't add up. "What's your position at the hotel?" Dixon asks.

"I work the front desk," Decameron says.

Dixon nods. Nothing about this guy screams predator or even vagrant. He seems like a regular guy—a Huskies basketball fan, the father of an honor student.

"So tell me something," Dixon says. "Have you seen the ghost?"

"Not yet," Decameron says. "She's playing hard to get."

Dixon chuckles and slaps the roof of the car. "All right, I'm not going to issue a ticket. Tomorrow, though, you'd better find a different beach."

"Will do, Officer," Decameron says. "Thank you."

Lyric Layton is in her kitchen at seven a.m. making a beet-and-blueberry smoothie after doing yoga on her private beach when she hears a light rapping on her front door. Anne Boleyn, Lyric's chocolate British shorthair, rises and places her paws on Lyric's shin, which is something she does only when she's anxious. Lyric scoops up the cat and goes to see who on earth is knocking at this hour.

It's Heidi Bick from next door. The Laytons and the Bicks have plans to go to Galley Beach for dinner that night. Lyric wonders if Heidi has somehow heard her news; Lyric was planning on telling Heidi at dinner if Heidi didn't guess when Lyric ordered sparkling water instead of champagne. But then she sees the stricken look on Heidi's face.

"Are you the only one up?" Heidi whispers. "I need to talk."

"Yes, of course," Lyric says. Her husband, Ari, and the three boys would sleep until noon every day of the summer if she'd let them. "Come on in."

Lyric leads Heidi into the kitchen, offers her a smoothie—no, thank you, she can't manage any—and then Lyric opens the slider so they can sit out on the deck. The rising sun spangles the water of Nantucket Sound; the early-morning ferry is gliding past Brant Point Light and out of the harbor.

"I think Michael is having an affair," Heidi says. She gives a strangled little laugh. "I can't believe I just said those words. I sound like someone on Netflix. I mean, it's *Michael*. We're Michael and Heidi *Bick*. This isn't supposed to happen."

Well, well, well, Lyric thinks. "Whoa, honey, start at the beginning. What gives you this idea?"

"I'm so stupid!" Heidi says. "Michael has been living up here since April. He told me he and his coworker Rafe were making moves to splinter off and start their own company. He chose to work remotely so he had the necessary privacy. Did I ask any questions? No! I took him at his word—and I was happy for some time to myself. Meanwhile, he was up here with someone else!"

To anyone other than Lyric Layton, this news about Michael might have come as a jaw-dropping surprise. Michael and Heidi Bick were widely considered to be "the perfect couple"—everyone said it here on Nantucket and back in Greenwich as well. But Lyric has gotten certain...vibes from Michael. Last summer when Lyric and Ari and Michael and Heidi were at dinner at the Deck, Lyric caught Michael staring at her from across the table. She thought she was imagining it—a lot of rosé had been consumed—but then he touched her leg with his foot. Lyric had quickly tucked her legs under her chair. She said nothing to Ari or to Heidi because she was sure Michael was just being a naughty drunk. Lyric considers herself an excellent friend—she remembers birthdays, she takes extra carpool shifts, she polishes other queens' crowns—so she would never, *ever* entertain the notion of an affair with Michael. But...if she's painfully honest, she would admit that there have been times when she was practicing yoga on the beach and wondered if

Michael Bick was in his master bathroom, fresh out of the shower, watching her from the window.

Lyric arranges her facial expression into one of both skepticism and concern. "Oh, Heidi, I doubt that."

"So you haven't heard any rumors about Michael running around the island with some other woman?" Heidi presses the heels of her palms into her eye sockets. "I had this horrible idea that everyone knew but me and everyone was talking about it…"

"I've heard nothing," Lyric says. "And I had lunch with Blond Sharon at the Field and Oar Club yesterday. She didn't say a word. What makes you *think* this?"

Heidi pulls a Chanel eye shadow out of the pocket of her jeans jacket. It's a half-used cream shadow in Pourpre Brun. "This was in my makeup drawer."

Lyric takes the eye shadow. "Not your color," she says. She's trying to make a joke, but inside, Lyric is shrieking. It's not *Heidi's* color, but it *is* *Lyric's* color—and Lyric wears only Chanel eye shadow, as Heidi well knows. Lyric wonders if Heidi is accusing Lyric of having an affair with Michael. This is getting extremely sticky. Has Michael been sleeping with someone who wears Chanel eye shadow in one of Lyric's go-to shades? He must be. Why else would the shadow be in Heidi's makeup drawer? Lyric feels a little jealous herself—which is insane, of course. She's happily married and pregnant with her fourth child. "Have you asked Michael about it?" Lyric says.

"No," Heidi says. "I'm going to wait and see if I find anything else."

Lyric agrees this is a good idea. It's probably nothing; maybe it was the cleaning lady's (this makes no sense) or it belongs to Colby, Heidi's daughter (she's only eleven, but kids are precocious these days). She says she's certain there's a reasonable explanation. Lyric shepherds Heidi to the door in something of a rush because she feels morning sickness wash over her (the beet-and-blueberry smoothie, ick; what had made her think that would be a good combo?). "Try to relax, Michael loves you, see you tonight at dinner." Lyric might not tell Heidi she's pregnant tonight, because how awful to share happy news when her friend is suffering.

Lyric shuts the door behind Heidi and runs down the hall to the bathroom, where she vomits up the smoothie. After rinsing her mouth, she goes hunting for her own Chanel cream eye shadow in Pourpre Brun.

The funny thing is, she can't find it.

Jasper Monroe of Fisher Island, Florida, wakes up in suite 115 of the Hotel Nantucket to a text from his mother: Where are you??? Did you not come home last night??? You know the rules, Jasper!!!

Jasper groans and rolls over. He kisses Winston on the shoulder and says, "I have to get out of here, man. My mom is kerking."

"Your *mom?*" Winston says.

"Yeah," Jasper says. He feels like he's twelve years old, and he senses that Winston, who was Jasper's teaching assistant at Trinity, wants to remind him that he's twenty-two, a grown man, and that he can stay out all night if he wants. But the fact remains that Jasper lives under his parents' roof and he did break a house rule by not telling his mother that he'd be out all night, and beyond that, his parents don't know he's gay. Nobody does.

Jasper puts on his Nantucket Reds and his polo, both rumpled and beer-soaked after a late night at the Chicken Box. He decides to get his mother half a dozen of the infamous morning buns from Wicked Island Bakery as an apology.

"Catch you later, man," Jasper says.

"When?" Winston asks.

Jasper isn't sure. Winston came to Nantucket specifically to see Jasper, but Jasper has to be careful. "I'll snap."

Winston gets out of bed to see Jasper out, so he can't be that mad. They do some pretty heavy-duty kissing in the doorway.

"Come back to bed," Winston murmurs into Jasper's mouth.

Jasper is actually considering it—his mom isn't going to be any madder in an hour than she is now—but then he hears a rattling and turns to see the house-keeping cart rounding the corner, and pushing that cart is...Chad Winslow.

What? Chad is wearing khakis and a blue polo, and he's with some beaten-down-looking chick who smirks at Jasper and shirtless Winston and says, "You gentlemen ready for service?"

"Jasper?" Chad says.

Jasper feels like a coyote with his leg in a trap. "Chad? Are you...*working* here, man?" Jasper and his buddies Eric and Bryce have all been wondering what's up with Chad, but him having a *job* never crossed their minds. A job cleaning rooms at a *hotel*? It makes no sense.

Chad shrugs and casts his eyes over Jasper's shoulder at Winston. "Yeah, I'm a maid," Chad says. "What are you doing here?"

I'm a maid. It must be a joke, right? Except Jasper can tell it isn't and Chad doesn't seem the least bit embarrassed. It's like Winston is always saying: There is nothing shameful about who we really are.

"Stayed over with my boyfriend, Winston," Jasper

says. And just like that, he's out. He grins. He can't believe how easy that was.

Chad nods. "Cool. Nice to meet you, Winston."

"Nice to meet you," Winston says.

"Nice, nice, nice," the chick with Chad says. "So, are you ready for service or what?"

Nancy Twine passes around the offering basket at the Summer Street Church. She tries not to notice how much a person gives; three dollars for some is as much of a sacrifice as thirty dollars for others. But it does catch her attention when Magda English drops several folded hundred-dollar bills into the basket. (*Five* hundred-dollar bills, Nancy would come to find out when she counts the money after the service.)

Now, where does Magda English, who moved here back in September to care for her poor bereaved brother, William, and her nephew Ezekiel and who is working as head of housekeeping at the haunted hotel on the other side of town, come up with that kind of money? Nancy can't begin to guess.

10. Last Friday of the Month: June

Lizbet, Edie, Adam, and Alessandra are crowded into Lizbet's office at 11:55 a.m. on June 24 so they can refresh their Instagram feeds right at noon.

Adam is the first one to see Shelly Carpenter's post. "It's the Isthmus in New York City. Four keys."

"Kind of boring?" Alessandra says. "Although she hasn't done New York in a while."

"She reviewed the William Vale in March of last year," Edie says.

"It's scary that you know that," Adam says. He swipes through the pictures while Lizbet, Edie, and Alessandra click on the link. Frankly, Lizbet is relieved that the Hotel Nantucket wasn't chosen; they're nowhere near ready.

Hotel Confidential by Shelly Carpenter
June 24, 2022
The Isthmus Hotel, New York, New York—4
KEYS 🔑

Hello again, friends!

The Isthmus Hotel chain has been synonymous with luxury and sophisticated service since the flagship opened in Panama City in 1904 to cater to visitors coming to view the man-made wonder of the canal. The Manhattan outpost, located on the very desirable southeast corner of Fifty-Fifth and Fifth, has long been a top choice for discerning travelers, especially those from Central and South America, who appreciate the bilingual staff.

The hotel underwent a soup-to-nuts renovation in 2019 with all rooms given a much-needed makeover. They've opted for a clean, modern look—the rooms feature a lot of ivory and pearl gray and may be the teensiest bit generic. The lights of each room are all on a master panel inside the door and offer three choices: Festival (every light in the room on), Romance (low mood lighting), and Nighty-Night (every light in the room off). I tried to figure out how to beat the system and turn some lights off and some on (the one next to my bed, for example). It seemingly can't be done without a degree in electrical engineering.

I wanted to check the concierge's knowledge of the area, so I requested the name of a salon where I could get an inexpensive pedicure within ten blocks on a Sunday. The concierge found me a place right away, but when I went to write down the address on the notepad next to the phone, I found the hotel pen was dry. Readers of this column may feel this is a tiny detail—and make no mistake, it is—but if a hotel is providing an amenity such as a pen, it should work.

The other aspects of my stay at the Isthmus were top-notch. The bedding was delicious, the comforter as fluffy as a mound of whipped cream; the toiletries in the sleek marble-and-chrome bathroom (which was massive by New York standards) were scented with sandalwood, and the water pressure in the shower was strong but not painful. My bags were delivered only two minutes after I arrived, and when ice was requested, it came within five minutes. Room service exceeded all expectations. The Isthmus in-room-dining menu includes some Panamanian flair with the additions of sancocho de gallina and chicheme, both of which I ordered and both of which were better and more reasonably priced than standard room-service fare.

Overall, I award the Isthmus Hotel in New York a solid four keys with a plea to any hoteliers reading this review: Put an individual switch on each lamp, one that's easy to find and preferably with a dimmer. Thank you!

Stay well, friends. And do good.

—SC

"Our lights all have individual switches, and the table and floor lamps have dimmers!" Edie says.

"I can't believe she complained about the *pens,*" Adam says. "I would never have thought to check the pens."

"Ms. English has the staff check every pen," Alessandra says.

"Yes," Lizbet says. The Hotel Nantucket pens are Uni-Ball Jetstream—the best—and they write smooth and dark. She's proud of their pen game. But the fact remains that no detail escapes Shelly Carpenter's notice. Their lighting and pens are up to snuff, but there might be a dozen other things Shelly could find fault with.

When—if—she comes.

11. The Blue Book

June 27, 2022
From: Xavier Darling (xd@darlingent.co.uk)

To: Employees of the Hotel Nantucket

Good morning, staff! I'm pleased to finally
be able to announce a winner of the weekly
bonus that I promised you all back on opening day. The winner for the week of June 20
was front-desk manager Alessandra Powell.
Alessandra received a glowing review from
one of our guests on TravelTattler for her outstanding customer service. Congratulations,
Alessandra! Keep up the good work!

XD

As they enter the final week of June, hotel operations
lose their new-shoe stiffness and start to feel fluid
and organic. (Speaking of shoes, Lizbet has traded
in her stilettos for wedges, an idea she stole from
Alessandra, and she's far more comfortable.) There
was one complaint on TravelTattler, about a missing
Fendi scarf, that did some damage—a mystery that
remains unsolved, according to Magda—but the rest
of the reviews have been positive and Xavier finally
relented and granted the first thousand-dollar bonus,
to Alessandra because some anonymous reviewer
raved about her. (If Lizbet had to guess, she would
say it was Mr. Brownlee from room 309; he made no
secret of the fact that he found Alessandra to be the
most beautiful creature he'd ever laid eyes on.) Lizbet
would rather have seen the bonus go to anyone else—
Raoul, for example, the unsung hero of the evening
bell desk, or Sweet Edie—but it went to Alessandra
and no one has expressed any resentment. They're
probably intimidated.

Lizbet's outlook has improved since Richie started

working nights. Lizbet now leaves the hotel at five thirty, fits in a run or a ride on her Peloton, makes herself some dinner (she's so tired, she can usually only manage a tuna fish sandwich or ramen noodles), then takes her laptop to bed with the intention of catching up on current events or bingeing a show so that she has something to chat with the guests about, but most nights, she falls asleep within five minutes of getting in bed.

Lizbet hasn't been out anywhere socially since she and JJ broke up, and now that she's finally ready, invitations are lacking. She'd thought that she and Heidi Bick had semi-confirmed plans on the eighteenth, but when Lizbet texted to definitively confirm, Heidi canceled. She said she needed "couple time" with Michael. Being ditched for someone else's couple time made Lizbet feel like a lonesome loser. Lizbet has other friends, but unfortunately, they're all tethered in one way or another to the Deck, and Lizbet doesn't feel she can reach out lest it seem like she's poaching from JJ's territory or, worse still, desperate. Again, she's hurt that Goose and Wavy and Peyton all seem to have abandoned her or "chosen" JJ like they're children in a divorce. Not only does Lizbet miss them but she would like to know how things are going without her. Who has JJ put on the reservation book? Probably Peyton—she's the most capable and would have been Lizbet's choice if anyone had asked, which of course no one did.

It's bright and early on the first of July—there's something fresh and optimistic about the first of the month, and Lizbet has high hopes for occupancy at the hotel picking up. Edie pokes her head into Lizbet's office and says, "There's a woman out front who would like to speak with you."

Lizbet jumps to her feet, ever mindful that Shelly Carpenter could appear at any moment. It's the Fourth of July week, which is traditionally crazy busy, and it's common knowledge that Shelly Carpenter tends to show up at hotels during stressful or extraordinary times.

But Lizbet's spirits flag when she sees it's Mrs. Amesbury. There is no universe where Mrs. Amesbury is actually Shelly Carpenter. Mrs. Amesbury came to complain to Lizbet the day before because cute Mrs. Damiani was breastfeeding her infant son in the lobby and Mrs. Amesbury found it distasteful.

"How can I help you, Mrs. Amesbury?" Lizbet asks. It nearly hurts, but Lizbet manages to smile. Mr. Amesbury—he's the kind of husband who carries his wife's handbag—is standing behind Mrs. Amesbury just as he was yesterday when Mrs. Amesbury complained about the breastfeeding.

Mrs. Amesbury holds out the Blue Book; it's open to the restaurant section. "This has a glaring error."

"Error?" Lizbet says, growing warm with panic. The Blue Book is her pet project. She double-checked all addresses, phone numbers, hours of operation, websites, and other pertinent details such as dress code, price range, and reservation protocol. She's very proud of the book and has actually considered submitting it to a mainstream publisher. The world needs a Nantucket guidebook written by an island insider. "What kind of error?"

"The Deck isn't in here!" Mrs. Amesbury says. "It's the most important and successful restaurant on the entire island and you *forgot* to include it!"

Lizbet blinks. She can't pretend to feel surprised, because she knew this moment would come. Lizbet didn't *forget* the Deck; she purposely left it out.

It might seem like a startling omission, but Lizbet doesn't care. There was no way she was putting JJ's restaurant in the Blue Book.

Lizbet says, "I'm aware it's not included, Mrs. Amesbury. I wanted to showcase the island's *other* restaurants, ones you might not be familiar with. Have you ever eaten at Or, The Whale? What about Straight Wharf?"

"We'd like to eat at the Deck," Mrs. Amesbury says. "On the evening of the Fourth."

"Ah," Lizbet says. The Deck *is* magical on the Fourth of July. Not only does JJ throw down a pig roast with family-style sides of baked beans, pickled chowchow, corn bread, and potato salad, but guests can enjoy a view of the fireworks across the harbor. Last year, Lizbet hired a bluegrass band and people danced until midnight. "The Deck probably sold out for that evening weeks ago."

"I'd like you to check for me, please," Mrs. Amesbury says.

"Have you ever eaten at the Tap Room?" Lizbet lowers her voice. "They have a secret Big Mac that's not on the menu."

"I've never eaten a Big Mac in my life," Mrs. Amesbury says. "We'd like to go to the Deck."

Lizbet nods robotically. "Their phone lines open at three. I'll have Edie call."

"I'd prefer *you* to call," Mrs. Amesbury says. "You're the general manager; you'll have the most clout. If it's as difficult to get a reservation as you claim, we'll need every advantage."

Ha-ha-ha-ha! Lizbet thinks. "I'd be happy to call myself, Mrs. Amesbury. I'll call at three o'clock on the nose."

* * *

But at three o'clock on the nose, Lizbet is up on the fourth floor testing out the ladder that leads to the hotel's widow's walk. The walk is quite large, probably big enough to hold thirty people, and Lizbet is thinking of offering a viewing platform to guests for the fireworks. Something to rival the Deck?

The ladder is rickety and steep. Lizbet manages to climb up, but not without effort. This won't work for the Fourth, but even so, she unhooks the hatch door and pulls herself up so she can take in the dazzling panorama. Lizbet can see all the way down to the yellow, green, and blue umbrellas of the Beach Club; she can see Brant Point Light and the streets of town in a neat four-block grid.

"What are you doing?"

Lizbet gasps. Wanda, holding her notebook and pencil, is standing at the bottom of the ladder.

"What are *you* doing?" Lizbet asks. "I thought we made it clear this floor is off-limits."

Wanda nods seriously. "I know. But this is where the ghost lives."

Lizbet nearly snaps, *There is no ghost, why isn't your mother keeping a closer eye on you? This hotel isn't your playhouse,* but Wanda, with her white-blond hair and her thick glasses, is too adorable to scold. She's wearing a red gingham dress with strawberries embroidered on the rickrack in front. Other eight-year-old girls, Lizbet suspects, are waltzing around in cutoffs and crop tops, checking their Instagram accounts.

Lizbet closes the trapdoor tight and takes Wanda by the hand. "Let's go."

When they reach the desk, Mrs. Amesbury is waiting. "Did you secure my reservation at the Deck?"

Lizbet considers saying, *Yes, I called at three and*

they're booked solid. But she can't bring herself to lie. "I'm so sorry, Mrs. Amesbury, I completely spaced about it. I'll call now."

Mrs. Amesbury nods with her lips pressed tight, as though she expected this kind of dropped ball. "I'll wait."

What can Lizbet do but pick up the phone and call the Deck?

"Good afternoon, the Deck." The female voice that answers is familiar, but it's not Peyton. Lizbet runs through her former staff, trying to put a name to the voice. Or maybe JJ hired someone new?

"Good afternoon, this is Lizbet Keaton calling from the Hotel Nantucket?" She waits for a response but is met with silence. "We have a party of two here at the hotel who would like a reservation on Monday evening at"—Lizbet looks at Mrs. Amesbury, who holds up seven fingers—"seven o'clock." There's no way Mrs. Amesbury is going to get seven. Five thirty or nine thirty maybe, *maybe,* if there's been a last-minute cancellation.

"By Monday, you mean the Fourth?" the voice says.

"Yes, the Fourth of July. At seven o'clock. For two people." Lizbet might as well be asking for the moon to be shot out of the sky or for the ocean to be dyed purple.

"Very good," the voice says. "What's the name?"

Lizbet is rendered temporarily speechless. Is it possible Mrs. Amesbury *will* get a seven o'clock reservation on the Fourth of July? Have things at the Deck gotten so bad that they have a table *available?* Lizbet isn't sure how to feel about this. She wants to gloat—the restaurant is failing without her—but she also feels sad that the place she invested so much energy in has fallen like a sloppy Jenga tower.

"Amesbury," she says. "And again, they're staying with us here at the Hotel Nantucket."

Mrs. Amesbury flashes Lizbet a smug smile. Lizbet can hear the words *I told you so.*

"Please let the Amesburys know they're number fifty-seven on the wait list for that date and time. Should a table become available, we'll let you know."

"Ah," Lizbet says. She'll be able to volley the *I told you so* right back to Mrs. Amesbury, but she's not happy about it. "We'll keep our fingers crossed, I guess. Thank you so much."

"Anything for you, Lizbet," the voice says.

"I'm sorry, I know I recognize your voice, but I can't quite place it," Lizbet says. "Who is this?"

There's a beat of silence before the voice speaks again. "It's Christina."

Lizbet hangs up and somehow finds the ability to smile at Mrs. Amesbury. "You're number fifty-seven on the wait list," she says. "Shall we try the Tap Room?"

This is why nobody from the Deck has reached out, Lizbet thinks. They didn't want to tell her, or they assumed she already knew: Christina is managing the front of the house. Christina is the new Lizbet.

When Lizbet gets off work, she heads straight into the Blue Bar like a woman possessed. Service for the evening has just begun, so the place has the feel of a Broadway show before the curtain lifts. The copper dome lights over the bar gleam; the stools are perfectly aligned and set at an inviting angle: *Come sit on me!* The stereo is playing Tony Bennett singing "The Best Is Yet to Come." Lizbet has wanted to stop in for a cocktail since day one, but she was too tired and too embarrassed about being alone. But tonight, she needs

a drink and a chance to quietly process JJ's newest
betrayal.

The bartender appears, her blue button-down
pressed, cuffs turned back neatly at the wrists. She
grins. "Hey, Lizbet."

"Hey, Petey," Lizbet says. Patricia "Petey"
Casstevens is a Nantucket superstar; for ten years, she
lit up the front bar at Cru. She's in her fifties, weighs a
hundred pounds with a pocketful of change, and she's
fiercely loyal to all Nantucket locals.

"I'll have the Heartbroken, please," Lizbet says.

Petey furrows her brow. "The…oh, you mean the
Heartbreaker? The drink Chef named for you?"

That's right—Lizbet is the breaker, not the broken.
This is as good an affirmation as any; she'll write it in
her phone. "He told you that?"

"It's the best drink on the menu." Petey goes about
mixing the various juices like an alchemist and she
includes an eye-popping pour of Belvedere vodka.
"Strong drink for a strong woman," she says. "Word
on the cobblestones is the Deck's not half as good
without you there." This is nice to hear, though Lizbet
suspects Petey is fluffing her.

Lizbet revisits the last time she saw JJ, when he'd
gotten down on one knee in the crushed shells of
the parking lot and, unless she's misremembering,
proposed. Now, only three and a half weeks later,
Christina is back, swirling her oaky chardonnays in
JJ's emotional life. JJ is such a skunk. Such a dis-
ingenuous jerk. Why doesn't knowing this make the
hurt go away? Why does finding out that Christina
is now working—and, who is she kidding, *sleeping*—
with JJ make him seem more desirable? It's a false
construct, Lizbet tells herself. We all want what we
can't have.

But this doesn't make her feel any better.

Anything for you, Lizbet, Christina said while she stuck Mrs. Amesbury in reservation Siberia.

Petey slides the Heartbreaker across the bar. Its deep red-orange color is even more mesmerizing than Lizbet remembers and she knows she should savor every sip—but she downs it in three long swallows. JJ and Christina are not only living rent-free in Lizbet's head, they've moved in their new Crate and Barrel furniture. How does she evict them? With all the advances in medicine and technology, why has someone not created a pill that cures heartbreak? Emotional penicillin. Why has someone not invented software that will sweep all traces of your ex out of your brain or an app that eliminates unrequited love?

"I'm going to tell Chef you're here," Petey says.

"Please don't," Lizbet says.

Petey clears the glass and winks. "He made me promise to tell him immediately if you ever came in. I'll be back in a few seconds to make you another cocktail. I assume you'd like another?"

"You betcha," Lizbet says.

Petey vanishes into the back for just an instant, then returns to shake up the second Heartbreaker. (*Breaker, not broken!* Lizbet thinks.) Tony Bennett is replaced by Elvis Costello singing "Alison." *I know this world is killing you.* Lizbet focuses on being present. She is, finally, *out.* It's a hurdle cleared. And not only is she out, but she's at the Blue Bar! She runs her hands over the blue granite and admires how the late-afternoon sun catches the bright penny-sheathed wall; she looks for the ceiling panel that conceals the disco ball. The curved banquette upholstered in sapphire velvet would be a wonderful place to curl up and cry.

Maybe JJ and Christina will get married and have

six kids and two Labradoodles, and JJ will coach football at the Boys and Girls Club and win citizenship awards, while Lizbet…what will Lizbet do? Work the front desk at a hotel that will receive a three- or possibly even two-key rating from Shelly Carpenter because the hotel is cursed or haunted or both—and that's only if Shelly deigns to show up.

No, Lizbet won't mope. She won't engage in negative thinking. She tries to recall an inspirational meme, but the only one that comes to mind is the quote attributed to Socrates, and she's sick of it.

Lizbet is careful to just sip her second cocktail. The strawberry and ginger and blood orange square-dance on her palate—spiraling out, reeling back in. She closes her eyes.

"It's good, right?" Petey says. "Those strawberries were picked at Bartlett's Farm this morning."

"Did you tell Chef I was here?" Lizbet asks.

"I sure did."

"Is he coming out?"

"Coming out here?" Petey says.

Yes, Lizbet thinks. That's what chefs do when there's a VIP—they come out to the dining room to say hello. It's only a quarter past five, so there's no way Mario is in the weeds yet.

"He doesn't believe in it," Petey says.

Lizbet feels stung; it's another rejection—not that she cares one whit about Mario Subiaco. He's full of himself.

She should probably leave. Even in 2022, there's something a little pathetic about a woman sitting at a bar alone. Lizbet has a bottle of Krug champagne at home, languishing in the back of her fridge. She'll drink the whole thing by herself. She was saving it for a monumental occasion, either good or bad. She had hoped, of course, for the former and gotten the latter, but there's no denying that Christina taking over Lizbet's job at the Deck is monumental.

Petey disappears into the back again and Lizbet can't blame her for wanting to escape; Lizbet isn't exactly a fountain of scintillating conversation. When Petey returns, she's holding a silver julep cup lined with parchment and filled with golden, crispy, paper-thin potato chips. Alongside these, she sets a dipping sauce that looks like creamy Thousand Island flecked with herbs.

"Our amnesia sauce," she says. "It's so good, it makes you forget everything else."

Oh, but that this were true, Lizbet thinks. Then she tastes it—and for one sublime moment, she can't remember her own name, much less the name of her ex-boyfriend or the wine rep he was sexting. For the next few minutes, she exists in a bubble where it's only her, the Heartbreaker, the blue granite, and the world's best chips and dip.

Elvis Costello yields to Van Morrison, "Crazy Love." The playlist isn't helping her, but what does help is Petey appearing with a trio of deviled eggs, one topped with bacon, one sprinkled with snipped chives, the third crowned with diced sweet red pepper. Lizbet takes a bite of each. They're perfection. If Lizbet closes her eyes, she could swear she was back in Minnetonka at the annual First Lutheran...

"Chef calls these his church-picnic eggs," Petey says.

Yes, precisely.

"Another Heartbreaker?" Petey asks.

"You betcha!" When Lizbet drinks, she starts sounding *very* Minnesota. "Please and thank you." She'll Uber home if she has to. Other people have entered the bar and are tucked into the banquettes.

Lizbet doesn't know anyone—yet. The second she sees a familiar face, she'll leave.

The third Heartbreaker arrives along with three chilled soup shooters—curried zucchini, cream of Vidalia onion, and a spicy watermelon gazpacho. Behind that are two hot chicken sliders with house-made pickles and cafeteria tacos, which are like the ones Lizbet remembers from Clear Springs Elementary except the shells are crispier, the ground beef richer, the shredded cheese smokier, the tomatoes riper, and the iceberg crunchier. Lizbet takes a bite of this, a nibble of that. She watches sausages wrapped in puff pastry with some kind of mustard sauce go past her and she feels a pang of envy. She'll get that next time, along with the painterly array of miniature vegetables from Pumpkin Pond Farm, served with buttermilk ranch. The food is so fresh and so fun and so flawlessly presented that Lizbet decides Mario Subiaco can have all the bragging rights he wants. The music picks up energy—Counting Crows, Eric Clapton. Lizbet bobs her head along. She hasn't looked at her phone even once; she is not unproud of that. She's a woman having fun at a bar alone. What was she afraid of?

Beatriz appears behind the bar, holding a tray of chilled shot glasses.

"Here's our whipped cream concierge," Petey says.

Whipped cream concierge! The third Heartbreaker has gone to Lizbet's head and she gives a little shriek. What a gifted idea!

"Our flavors tonight are coconut and caramel apple," Beatriz says. "Would you like one?"

"You *betcha!*" Lizbet says. "One of each, please and thank you!"

Beatriz arranges the shot glasses in front of her and hands her a demitasse spoon. Lizbet starts with the coconut, which tastes like a mouthful of coconut cloud, then moves to the caramel apple.

A man takes a seat two over from Lizbet. "Hey, hot stuff," he says to her, extending a hand. "I'm Brad Dover from Everett."

"Hi?" Lizbet says. Brad Dover has a thick Southie accent and a meaty face and, no doubt, a closet filled with Bruins jerseys and a bone to pick with Tom Brady.

He turns to Petey. "I'd like an Irish car bomb, please, dollface."

The only problem with the Blue Bar, Lizbet decides, is that it's open to the public, including people like Brad Dover from Everett, men who order Irish car bombs and call complete strangers "dollface" and "hot stuff." It's definitely time for her to go.

"I'll take my check, please and thank you," she says.

Petey raises her palms. "Everything is on the house."

"You're kidding," Lizbet says. "Well, thank you, it was extraordinary."

"You can't leave yet," says Brad Everett from Dover—or is it Brad Dover from Everett? She neither knows nor cares. "I just got here."

Exactly, she thinks. She pulls out two twenties to leave for Petey as a tip, swivels away from Brad Dover, and comes face-to-face with the person who has taken the seat on the other side of her, and that person is Mario Subiaco. He's in a white chef's jacket and a White Sox cap, and he's a little sweaty, which only serves to make him even hotter than she remembers.

"Hey there, Heartbreaker," he says.

She reels back in surprise. "I thought you didn't come out of the kitchen."

"There's an exception to every rule," he says. "How was your food?"

"It was…it was…"

"That good?" he says.

"Better than that good," she says—and to her mortification, she feels tears gathering. It's the vodka, obviously; she's had three Heartbreakers in just over an hour—who does that? A woman who is eating out for the first time in months, a woman who has had her shoddily stitched-up heart ripped apart at the seams *again*. It's not Christina's gloating that's making her cry. It's kindness—the food itself and someone caring what she thought of it.

Mario smiles into his lap. "Well, thank you. I know you have high standards, so I was trying my hardest. I wasn't sure about the cafeteria tacos."

Lizbet laughs and discreetly wipes under her eyes. "They were a hell of a lot better than the ones our lunch lady Mrs. MacArthur used to serve up."

"Good, good," Mario says. He clears his throat. "So, listen, I have the night of the fifth off and I was hoping I could take you to dinner."

"Hey, buddy boy," Brad Dover from Everett says. "Buzz off. I'm taking her out."

"No," Lizbet says to Mario. "He's not. And yes, I'd love to have dinner." She grins. There's no point trying to keep her cool, if she ever even had any, because Mario Subiaco is *asking her out,* which is a sentence that should be punctuated by ten exclamation points. "Where shall we go?"

"I was thinking about the Deck," Mario says. "How does that sound to you?"

Ha-ha-ha-ha! Lizbet thinks. Is this happening? Is this *happening*?

"Sounds perfect," she says.

"That's what I wanted to hear," Mario says. "We have a reservation at eight."

12. Graveyard Shift

Grace can't believe it. She can't *believe it!*

It has taken an entire century, but someone is finally doing the digging necessary to arrive at the truth about Grace's death.

This someone isn't Lizbet Keaton, and it isn't Richie Decameron, who showed such enthusiasm about a ghost in his interview and then promptly forgot about it. This someone is eight-year-old Wanda Marsh. Wanda has become, in modern parlance, *obsessed* with the hotel's ghost. Zeke mentioned the ghost in an offhand remark while Wanda was searching for a mystery to solve, and Wanda seized on the topic. She begged Kimber to take her to the Nantucket Atheneum, where she and librarian Jessica Olson dug into the archives of the *Nantucket Standard* and found the article published on August 31, 1922. Jessica made a photocopy for Wanda, who tucked it into the back of her notebook.

CHAMBERMAID DIES IN HOTEL FIRE

Island coroner Wilbur Freeman reported on Monday that there was one fatality in the fire that engulfed the third floor and attic of the Hotel Nantucket. Grace Hadley, age nineteen, a chambermaid at the hotel, perished in her bed, a death that went previously unnoticed because no one—not even the hotel's general manager, Leroy Noonan—realized that Hadley was living in the attic.

"The room she was occupying was an overflow storage closet that she'd managed to outfit with one of the hotel's cots and was using as a bedroom, unbeknownst to anyone on the staff," Noonan said. "Had we known Grace was living up there, we would have informed the Nantucket Fire Department immediately so that they might have tried to rescue her. Grace was known for her quick sense of humor, her willingness to take on even the most arduous tasks, and her dedication. We will mourn her loss."

As reported in our pages last week, the hotel caught fire at two a.m. on Sunday, August 20, following a spirited dinner dance held in the hotel's ballroom. We have now learned that the cause of the blaze was an "errant cigarette of unknown origin." Hotel owner Jackson Benedict and his wife, Dahlia, were asleep in their suite at the hotel; however, both the Benedicts escaped without injury.

Miss Hadley was predeceased by both of her parents and her brother, George Hadley, a commercial fisherman.

Wanda shows the article to her mother (who finds Wanda's interest in Grace's untimely death a bit disquieting), then to Louie (who doesn't understand or care to), then to Zeke (who indulges Wanda and listens to her read the entire article aloud), then to Adam (who doesn't indulge Wanda), and finally to Edie (who suggests that Wanda write an article that Edie will help her submit to the *Nantucket Standard*).

The truth is right there *between the lines!* Grace thinks. No one realized Grace was living in the attic. *(Jack hid her up there!)* Grace was known for taking on the most arduous tasks. *(Working as Dahlia Benedict's lady's maid!)* The Benedicts had escaped without injury. *(Dahlia set the fire, then ran out of the building!)*

Grace is flattered that Mr. Noonan mentioned her sense of humor. And her dedication. She's dedicated, all right. It's a hundred years later, and she's still here.

On July 2, in the darkest hour of the night, the door to the fourth-floor storage closet creaks open, and Grace—who isn't asleep, who never sleeps, never rests, though it's all she wants, please, someday—sees Wanda poke her little blond head in.

"Grace?" she whispers.

Oh, for heaven's sake, Grace thinks. *Be careful what you wish for.*

"Are you here, Grace?" Wanda asks.

Yes, sweet child, Grace thinks. *Now go back to bed.*

"Can you give me a sign?" Wanda asks. "Can you...knock?"

Grace considers this. She *can* knock—but what if this leads to trouble? What if it makes Lizbet *actually* hire an exorcist? Wanda might *think* she wants Grace to knock, but when Grace *does* knock, Wanda might scream, faint, or be scarred for life.

There is, apparently, no one more persistent than an eight-year-old.

"Please, Grace?"

Fine, Grace thinks. She knocks, three short, matter-of-fact raps that cannot be mistaken for anything other than the supernatural.

Wanda drops her pad and pencil and claps her hand over her mouth.

Now I've gone and done it, Grace thinks.

Wanda whispers, "I knew it. Thank you, Grace!"

Grace follows Wanda back to her room. Wanda takes the elevator all the way down to the level where the wellness center is and creeps up the back stairs. So *this* is how she avoids the lobby! Wanda opens the door to suite 114 with the key card she has tucked into her notebook and returns quietly to bed. Tonight she has chosen the lower bunk closest to the door, and Louie is on the upper bunk farthest from the door. Clever girl.

Grace is tempted to pull the covers up over Wanda's shoulders and tuck her in, but she's done enough for one night. She whisks out of the suite and down the corridor. In the lobby—oh, hello!—she finds Wanda's mother, Kimber, leaning over the desk, deep in conversation with Richie. It's so late that Raoul, the night bellman, has gone home. Richie and Kimber are the only two people awake in the entire hotel; this, Grace can sense. They're eating bowls of soft-serve ice cream that Richie has obviously brought from the break room.

"Craig told me I was too critical," Kimber says. "He claimed I was always harping on things that other people—such as my nanny—let ride. Do you know what happens when you let things ride? Mediocrity." She draws a spoon over the melting ridge of chocolate, then holds the spoon in the air before her mouth. "What about you? Is there a Mrs. Richie?"

"I'm divorced," Richie says. "Three kids. Unfortunately, we split while I was still at the insurance company, so my alimony and child-support payments are calculated on an income I no longer make. I worked for a start-up sneaker concern when I left insurance, but my CEO was a twenty-two-year-old kid out of West Hartford whose parents were bankrolling him. He mismanaged the business and it went under."

"Ugh," Kimber says.

"Big ugh," Richie says. "I've tried to go back to court but I still owe my attorney money from the first go-round, so he's not exactly eager to take my calls. I'm way behind in paying Amanda and she refuses to let me see the kids until I catch up."

"Oh no," Kimber says. "I'm so sorry."

"Hearing my sad story probably isn't helping your insomnia," Richie says. "Anyway, I try to be grateful for what I do have. I'm gainfully employed and I'm healthy."

"And handsome and charming!" Kimber says.

Well! Grace thinks. *That's forward!*

"Thank you," Richie says. "You're good for my ego."

"I mean it," Kimber says. She licks the ice cream from the spoon like it's performance art. "You're quite the catch. You could easily find a woman to date on this island."

Richie laughs. "During the *day,*" he says. "I work every single night."

"*I'm* here every single night," Kimber says.

Audacious! Grace thinks. She's making it very clear that Richie is her crush. How will he respond?

He clears his throat, blushes, stares into his bowl of vanilla.

"Wanda told me there's a ladder to the widow's walk up on the fourth floor," Kimber says. "Want to check it out?"

"I shouldn't," Richie says. "I'm on the clock."

"It's one thirty in the morning," Kimber says. "Nobody will need you."

"Mr. Yamaguchi is checking out tomorrow," Richie

says. "He's been here all week and I need to pull his bill together. Guy's a big spender—and a big drinker. He's ordered two bottles of Dom Pérignon every night, and as far as I know, he's by himself."

"Do his bill later," Kimber says. "Come on."

There's no way Grace is missing this. She trails Richie and Kimber up to the fourth floor and watches as first Kimber and then, reluctantly, Richie clamber up the ship's ladder to the widow's walk. Grace is confined to the inside of the building, but that's okay because she knows what the view looks like. She used to ascend that very same ship's ladder with Jack; they were standing together on the walk overlooking the harbor when he told Grace he loved her and that, in a few short weeks, he would divorce Dahlia and marry Grace. (Lies, all of it.) Back then, Grace hadn't seen how she was being used, and she certainly didn't know she would be murdered, and so the time on the widow's walk looking over the water and the streets of sleeping Nantucket had seemed...magical, transcendent. She had believed, in those stolen moments, that everything would turn out okay.

Ha.

From what Grace can see, it's a clear night. A crescent moon hangs just west of the white spire of the Congregational church. Grace sees Kimber shiver— she's wearing only shorty pajamas, a thin cardigan, and a pair of the hotel slippers, which is silly because Grace knows she has a perfectly good robe hanging on the back of her bathroom door. She may be exaggerating about how cold she is so that Richie will put an arm around her, but he's a good foot or two away, gripping the railing with both hands. His eyes are squeezed shut even though there is a sky full of stars. Then Grace realizes that Richie is afraid of heights.

"It's breathtaking up here," Kimber says.

"I should get back to the desk," Richie says. He steps down the ladder and Kimber follows, looking dejected. Her romantic rendezvous was a bust. Grace thinks she might have better luck playing hard to get.

As if reading Grace's mind, when Richie pushes the elevator button, Kimber says, "I think I'll take the stairs. Good night, Richie." She disappears down the stairwell and both Grace and Richie can hear her slippers slapping against the concrete steps. Now Richie is the one who looks forlorn. *Good move, Kimber!* Grace thinks. She's about to follow Richie back to the desk—something about him still bothers her— but then she feels a tug that lures her to the second floor. Grace arrives just in time to see the door to suite 215 open. Mr. Yamaguchi's room. A woman with long apricot-colored hair slips out, holding her shoes in her hand.

It's Alessandra.

13. Affirmations

July 4, 2022
From: Xavier Darling (xd@darlingent.co.uk)
To: Employees of the Hotel Nantucket

Happy American Independence Day, staff!
I'm delighted to announce that front-desk

manager Alessandra Powell has once again won the week's bonus. She received a rave review from a hotel guest who said she went above and beyond on his behalf during his stay. Great job, Alessandra, you're setting a wonderful example.

XD

On the fifth of July, Lizbet calls Edie into the office to say she's leaving fifteen minutes early.

"No problem," Edie says. "I can cover things." Edie gives Lizbet a valiant attempt at a smile but Lizbet knows she must be bitter that Alessandra won the thousand-dollar prize for the second straight week, and as soon as they all got the e-mail from Xavier, Alessandra said she had cramps and would be going home for the day. Later, when Lizbet checked TravelTattler, she saw a glowing review from David Yamaguchi from suite 215, who specifically stated that Alessandra had made his stay "sublime."

"You're doing a good job here, Edie," Lizbet says. "I hope you know that."

These words, which Lizbet meant to be reassuring, cause a lone tear to drip down Edie's face. She swipes it away. "Thank you," she says. "I love the job."

"But?" Lizbet says.

"No but," Edie says. "Though I did apply for a position at Annie and the Tees a few nights a week. I need the extra money."

Lizbet frowns. Edie is already working over fifty hours a week at the hotel. How is she going to handle another job? "Isn't that taking on a lot?"

"It is," Edie says. "But I have student loans and…other expenses."

Lizbet thinks for a moment about intervening with Xavier on Edie's behalf. An extra thousand dollars would help. But somehow, Lizbet knows Xavier won't go for it. *(This isn't a participation trophy.)* Next, Lizbet thinks about posting a review on TravelTattler under a made-up name, extolling the virtues of a certain Edith Robbins. *Fraud,* Lizbet thinks. Finally, her mind rests on the four thousand dollars in cash that Kimber Marsh handed over earlier that week. It's still sitting in the safe because Lizbet hasn't had a single second to get to the bank. *Embezzlement,* she thinks.

"You're so young, Edie," Lizbet says. "Don't you want a social life?"

"Not right now," Edie says. "I told you in my interview, I broke up with my college boyfriend…"

"And you're taking time alone, which is so…*important*." Lizbet leans forward. Here, finally, is one of the bonding moments she's been waiting for. "I'm not sure if you know this or not, but JJ and I broke up last fall." She pauses. "We were together fifteen years and it ended…badly." Lizbet wants to say more, but she won't. "I did exactly what you're doing. I got in shape, I found this job, I took the time alone to process and rebuild. I haven't gone out with anyone socially since we split." She pauses again. Should she tell Edie? Yes, she thinks. "But tonight, I have a date."

This brings a smile to Edie's face—because she is the kind of sweet, generous soul who wants other people to be happy even when she isn't so happy. "Really?" she says. "With whom?"

"I'll tell you tomorrow," Lizbet says. "If it goes well."

* * *

If it goes well. Lizbet is going on a date with an extremely hot famous chef who is taking her to the restaurant that is owned by her former boyfriend and managed by the woman he betrayed her with. Some might say this can do nothing but backfire, but Lizbet has other ideas.

She's wearing a white crocheted sundress that she bought at the ERF boutique on lower Main Street and that she knew looked good on her even before she stepped out of the dressing room and the sales manager, Caylee, whom Lizbet has known forever, shrieked, "Girl, yes!"

Girl, yes! Right after her conversation with Edie, Lizbet leaves the hotel both physically and—maybe for the first time since the place opened—mentally. She heads to the R. J. Miller Salon for a blowout. Lorna, her stylist, makes her hair look like blond silk; it hangs in straight shiny sheets. At home, Lizbet puts on mascara, shimmering face powder, and red lipstick. She wants to wear stilettos but she has witnessed dozens of women catch their heels between the deck boards (one time, in July 2016, it resulted in a gruesomely broken ankle), so she slips on wedges.

Looking in the mirror she thinks: *Breaker, not broken.*

She thinks: *A hundred times hotter than you've ever been.*

She thinks: *Girl, yes!*

Mario knocks on her door at quarter to eight, his silver pickup idling in the driveway. He's wearing jeans, a white linen shirt, a slate-blue blazer, and flip-flops, which in Lizbet's opinion is the perfect outfit on any man. His smile when he sees Lizbet is so…*naughty* that Lizbet flushes.

He whistles. "Do I need to say it?"

"Yes."

"You look…wow. Just wow."

Lizbet's flirting skills were dormant during her years with JJ, and she needs to wake them up now. She winks at him. "I brought something for later." She hands him a cooler bag and hopes he doesn't think she's being presumptuous.

He peeks inside and grins. "I like where your head is at." He reaches for her hand. "Let's go make people jealous."

When Mario pulls into the parking lot of the Deck, Lizbet panics.

She's back.

She sees JJ's big black Dodge parked in its usual spot, and next to it is the juicy orange Jeep that belongs to Christina. Lizbet can recall dozens of times when that Jeep would pull into the Deck and Lizbet's spirits would lift. Lizbet had *liked* Christina; she was charming, funny, modest. She and Lizbet would talk about wine, of course, but also about trips they wanted to take to Italy and South Africa, restaurants they wanted to try the next time they went to New York, and they both loved celebrity scandals (they were *verklempt* when JLo and A-Rod broke up, and Christina called Lizbet, *screaming,* when JLo was spotted with Ben Affleck).

Lizbet's eye is drawn beyond the restaurant itself to the Monomoy creeks. She misses this view—the meandering paths of shallow water through the reeds and cattails, the dinghies tied up to colorful buoys, the distinctive cupola of the Nantucket lifesaving museum in the distance. There are a few kayakers out tonight, paddling through the creeks as the sunset turns the sky a soft pink. Lizbet can hear the laughter, the clinking of glasses and silverware, the happy chatter that was the soundtrack of her former life. It's surreal being an observer, being an *outsider*. This isn't her place any longer. What is she *doing* here?

Well, it's too late to back out now. Mario reaches for her hand again; he must understand how difficult this is for her.

He stops right before the door. "You ready, Heartbreaker?"

She nods and they step inside.

Everything is the same. Off to the left is the arched entryway to the airy, rustic dining room. Other people might notice the cathedral ceilings, the exposed beams, the huge stained-glass window salvaged from a church in Salem, Massachusetts, at one end of the room, the plate glass on the other side offering unimpeded views across the water. What Lizbet sees is tables 25 through 40, including a twelve-top in front of the cobblestone fireplace that the staff fondly calls "the Bitch" because, well, that's what it is. Peyton is taking orders at the Bitch and Lizbet wonders if it was a mistake not to warn her former staff that she was coming in.

Mario leads Lizbet past the dining-room entrance to the hostess station and Lizbet feels herself hanging back like a child who doesn't want to start kindergarten. She sees the Robert Stark painting that greets every guest of the Deck—a wide canvas of bottle-green sea with one red-sailed boat on the horizon. They're at command central, Lizbet's former cockpit, her Oval Office, a place as familiar to her as her own bedroom. When Lizbet started working at the Deck as a server, they had a standard-issue lectern, straight out of a high-school auditorium, but Lizbet replaced it with an antique drafting table that she found at Brimfield.

"Good evening," Lizbet hears Mario say. "Subiaco, party of two?"

Lizbet is hiding behind him, trying to summon her affirmations. What are they? She can't remember a single one, not even the silly one about the pineapple. She hears Christina's voice, and while she's too addled to listen to the exact words, she can tell Christina is fawning: *My name is Christina … so honored to … I'll tell Chef … please let me show you …*

Mario ushers Lizbet forward. *Girl, yes!* Lizbet thinks. She smiles at Christina and says, "Hey there, how's it going?"

Never underestimate the element of surprise. Christina doesn't seem to recognize Lizbet at first (ha-ha—no braids), but then it lands, and Christina's eyes ricochet between Mario and Lizbet. She fumbles the menus, and one drops to the floor. Lizbet watches as Christina crouches to retrieve it while trying to make sure her very short, very tight black skirt doesn't hike up her ass.

Christina leads them to the corner table closest to the water, table number 1, also known as "Dirty Harry." It's not surprising that this is where they're sitting, considering that, for JJ, Mario Subiaco ranks right up there with God, Santa Claus, and Clint Eastwood— though now Christina is probably wishing she could pivot and put them at table 24 in the opposite corner or even inside.

Mario pulls out Lizbet's chair and Christina hands them menus and says, "We have a Whispering Angel rosé fountain here at the Deck. We sell our signature wineglasses for fifty dollars apiece. They're yours to take home and you may have as many glasses of the rosé as you'd like."

Lizbet stares at Christina. Is she *actually* giving Lizbet the spiel when Lizbet was the one who dreamed up the idea for the rosé fountain in the first place, when Lizbet was the one who repurposed a salvaged garden fountain that she bought from Marty McGowan, the Sconset Gardener? That fountain is *hers,* not Christina's. How *dare* Christina do this; she's either clueless or being catty.

Mario waits until Christina's finished, then reaches across the table and squeezes Lizbet's hand. "Thanks for that, Tina. Would you mind giving us a second?"

Christina blinks. "I'm also the sommelier here…"

Lizbet nearly squawks. What happened to Goose? Did JJ *fire* him so that Christina could take over the sommelier job? She realizes she's crushing Mario's fingers and she eases up a bit. She reminds herself it's no longer any of her business.

"So let me bring by the wine list—"

"Not just yet, Tina, thanks," Mario says.

Take the hint, Tina, Lizbet thinks. *Scram.*

Christina lingers and then very distinctly addresses only Mario. She touches the sleeve of his beautiful blue blazer with her French-manicured fingers. Lizbet realizes that it's not beyond Christina to throw herself at Mario. "I know Chef will want to come out and say hello."

Mario keeps his eyes locked on Lizbet's. "Thank you."

Another few beats pass while Christina tries to figure out what's going on.

Finally, Lizbet gives Christina a look like a harpoon through the lungs. "Thank you, Christina."

Christina takes a stutter-step back and Lizbet's eyes

follow, thinking she's going to fall into table 3, which is occupied by…Ari and Lyric Layton. Ari and Lyric are deep in conversation, and Lyric is upset, wiping at her eyes, so they don't notice Christina, who rights herself at the last minute, nor do they appear to see Lizbet.

When Christina finally heads back to her station, Mario says, "Should we get out of here?"

"Yes," Lizbet says, and they go.

Back in Mario's truck, Lizbet isn't sure whether to laugh or cry. *Laugh,* she thinks—and she does. They walked out of the Deck holding hands, Mario leading the way, Lizbet ignoring all the people calling after her. When they reached the front, they encountered Christina and JJ having a whisper-fight, Christina no doubt saying something to the effect of *Mario Subiaco showed up with Lizbet! They were rude to me!* Christina's back was to Mario and Lizbet, but JJ saw them and said, "Whoa, hey…are you leaving, Chef?"

Mario stopped. "We're going someplace where the service is a bit more polished." He saluted JJ. "Good to see you again."

JJ followed them out the door. "Wait," he said. "Lizbet, come on, don't be like this."

Mario held the passenger door of his truck open and Lizbet climbed in. She waved at JJ as they pulled out.

She doesn't know where they're going; she doesn't care. Mario heads into town, where people are out and about in full July revelry. There's a group of young women having a bachelorette party; families; happy couples and one couple arguing, which reminds Lizbet of seeing the Laytons. Lyric Layton, who is one of the calmest, most Zen people Lizbet knows, was *crying at the Deck*. Something must have been very wrong.

Lizbet suspects Mario is taking her to the Club Car, but they bump over the cobblestones of Main Street, so then she thinks they must be going to Nautilus. Then they pass Nautilus and Lizbet thinks, *Lola?* She's with Mario Subiaco, the former king of the Nantucket restaurant world. They'll be able to walk in anywhere.

Mario pulls down the white-shell lane behind Old North Wharf and parks in a spot marked RESIDENTS ONLY. He says, "I probably should have checked with you. Is it okay if I cook for you at my place?" He smiles. *He's so fine,* Lizbet thinks. Now that JJ and Christina have been properly humiliated, she feels energized—and nervous—for another reason. She's on a date with Mario flipping Subiaco! He's going to cook for her!

He leads her past the cute cottages of Old North Wharf, past the famed Wharf Rat Club, past Provisions and the Straight Wharf restaurant on the right— where are they going?—and out a rickety dock over the water. Lizbet watches where she puts her feet on the old, uneven boards, thinking in her emotionally heightened state that she could easily topple into the harbor, where her wedges would anchor her right to the bottom.

The dock leads out to a lone cottage, and Lizbet looks around. How in fifteen years has she never realized this little place was here, floating on pillars in the middle of the harbor? To the left are the grand homes of Easton Street and Brant Point Light and to the right she can see and hear the people eating on the porch at Straight Wharf.

Mario opens the door and they step back in time.

The cottage feels like something out of what Lizbet vaguely thinks of as "the good old days," that era in the 1950s and 1960s when properties were both loved and neglected, when summer homes were passed down through families and not purchased online for eight figures thanks to the dazzling 360-degree photo gallery. The cottage features a boxy, wood-paneled room that smells of the sea. There's a gray tweed sofa and two upright armchairs, a braided rug, a dinged-up dining-room table with mismatched chairs, a kitchen with brown cabinets, Formica countertops, a four-burner electric stove and a white icebox with a long pull-handle. There are some truly atrocious oil paintings hanging on the walls. Lizbet squints—they're landscapes of Nantucket, no doubt the efforts of one of the former owners who took a summer's interest in rendering the island *en plein air.* She can tell without checking that in the cabinets she will find Junior League and Congregational church cookbooks stained with cranberry sauce and clam juice, as well as a speckled black lobster pot and a box of frilled toothpicks purchased sometime during the Kennedy administration.

Off to the left is a door that leads to a bedroom (low bed, covered with a patchwork quilt) and another door that leads to a bathroom tiled in iridescent pink (it must have been renovated in the seventies). "This is fabulous," Lizbet says.

Mario sheds his blazer and kicks off his flip-flops. "I'm glad you like it. Some people wouldn't understand. They wouldn't…get it." He has brought Lizbet's cooler bag from the truck and he pulls out the bottle of Krug. "Let me show you the best part." He grabs two jelly jars from the cabinet, hands them to Lizbet (they're painted with cartoon scenes from *Tom*

and Jerry), and opens a door that leads out to his—
well, Lizbet supposes it's his front porch. It's a covered
deck that overlooks Nantucket harbor; water laps up
against the pilings beneath their feet. A ladder hangs
off the railing.

"How," she says, "did you get this?"

"Xavier," Mario says. "I was on the fence about
working at the bar, but then he dangled this place
and I caved." He expertly takes the cage off the Krug
and gently pulls the cork. He pours the champagne
into the jelly jars, then he and Lizbet face each other
and touch glasses. "This is more like it," Mario says.
"Here's to you, Heartbreaker."

By their second glass, they're sitting next to each
other on a wicker love seat on the deck, bare feet up
on a wrought-iron table, gazing out at the darkening
sky. The red beacon of Brant Point Light glows,
then dims.

"How did you get to Nantucket from Minnesota?"
Mario says. "I don't think you've told me."

"Well," Lizbet says. "When I was at the University
of Minnesota, there was a girl in my dorm who
showed up to school a week late. All we knew about
her was that her name was Elyse Perryvale and she
was from out east. None of us could understand why
anyone would miss the first week of freshman year."
Lizbet sips her champagne. "She was tan and had this
sun-bleached hair, and she was wearing faded jean
shorts and boat shoes that looked like they'd been
repeatedly run over by a vintage Jeep Wagoneer. And
she said, 'Sorry I'm late. My parents wanted to eke out
one more week at our house on Nantucket.'"

"Did you hate her?" Mario asks.

"I *worshipped* her," Lizbet says. "I thought that was
the most seductive sentence I'd ever heard. We were

from Minnesota—summertime for us was going to our lake cabins and waiting in line for Sweet Martha's at the state fair. And here was this...mermaid among us. I asked her all about Nantucket and she lent me a Nancy Thayer novel, which I devoured. The summer after I graduated, I moved out here and got a job waiting tables at the Deck, which was brand-new that year. I started dating JJ and fifteen years passed."

"You never wanted to get married?"

"When I met JJ, I was too young to get married. Then we became sort of anti-establishment. We wanted to be like Goldie Hawn and Kurt Russell. We thought getting married would kill the romance. But JJ killed it a different way."

"I take it Tina is the new girlfriend?" Mario says.

"Christina, yes, our former wine rep. A woman I used to like." Lizbet tells Mario about Last Night at the Deck, finding the texts, their subsequent breakup.

"Ouch," Mario says. "I'll point out that he's not good enough for you."

"He was, though," Lizbet says. She has a hard enough time understanding this herself, much less explaining it to someone else. What she had with JJ was real. Every minute together felt like an investment in their future—breakfast, lunch, dinner, drives, walks, cocktail parties, meetings with food vendors, trips to the post office, ferry rides, the vacations to Bermuda and Napa and Jackson Hole, holidays with her family in Minnetonka and his parents in Binghamton, every movie they watched, every show they binged, every song they heard on the radio, every cookbook they tried a recipe from, every funeral they attended (there had been three), every wedding (six), every baptism (five), every beach day, every text and call, every trip to the Stop and Shop, every house they toured before buying the cottage on Bear Street, the fights and quarrels, the flat tires and dead batteries, the leaks in the ceiling and the power outages and the day the fridge died, the football games, the concerts (Kenny Chesney, the Foo Fighters, Zac Brown), the burns and cuts in the restaurant kitchen and the head colds and stomach bugs at home—all of these things had been like bricks in a fortress that was supposed to keep Lizbet safe and happy for the rest of her life. She and JJ had inside jokes, secret code words, routines and rituals. Lizbet scratched JJ's back every morning; she knew where his spot was, southeast of the shamrock tattoo in the center of his back that was always extra-itchy. On Sunday mornings in the winter, JJ would draw Lizbet a bath, light her scented candles, and leave her a pile of food magazines. While she was in the tub, he would go to Nautilus to pick up Caleb's bagels with sriracha schmear and they would eat in the kitchen— Lizbet still in her bathrobe—while they listened to old Springsteen concerts. Those Sunday mornings were sacred, their version of church.

Lizbet had actually thought they *would* get married someday, despite their cool posturing. She wanted a marquise-cut diamond, she wanted a ceremony on the beach at Miacomet followed by a clambake; she wanted to dance in her wedding dress at the Chicken Box. They had talked about children—they wanted two—and when Lizbet missed her period in January of 2021, they were both giddy and nervous. It wasn't exactly what they had planned—a baby arriving in September, Lizbet hugely pregnant all through the summer season—but they both grinned like crazy, calling each other Maw and Paw, naming the baby "Bubby"—and when Lizbet started to bleed at nine weeks, they cried in each other's arms.

The sexting with Christina had started that summer. JJ had bulldozed the fortress. Worse, he'd allowed Lizbet to think that the fortress had existed only in her mind.

The ending, rather than creating a stronger place that Lizbet could launch from into a new, different, better-quality life, was an obliteration, as though fifteen years of Lizbet's life—her prime years, twenty-three to thirty-eight—had vaporized. She couldn't salvage anything from them except the knowledge that she had, technically, survived.

Lizbet drinks what's left in her jelly jar and turns to Mario. "You're how old? Forty...?"

"Forty-six."

"Have you ever had your heart broken?"

Mario sighs. "Not like that. Not by a woman, romantically. But when Fiona died..."

Fiona Kemp, Lizbet thinks. Chef of the Blue Bistro. She died of cystic fibrosis at the end of the 2005 season. It's Nantucket restaurant-world legend.

"...and when the Blue Bistro closed, my heart broke. It's going to sound pompous as hell, but it was the dismantling of a dynasty. The bistro was the best, not because of the food or the location...it was the best because of the people. It was like a winning football team before the quarterback declares free agency and goes to a different team or like that string of golden summers at sleepaway camp before you get your driver's license and a job making subs at Jersey Mike's. We all knew Fiona was terminally ill and that we were living on God's grace. But even so, when it ended, we were shell-shocked. The dream died with Fiona, a piece of all of us died with Fiona. So yes, I've had my heart broken by this island. So badly that I left for seventeen years." Mario takes Lizbet's hand and leads her back to the railing. They watch the Steamship ferry glide majestically out of the dock; it's all lit up, as big as a floating building.

Mario puts his hands on either side of Lizbet's face. "I'm going to kiss you now, but I think we should both be careful."

Lizbet laughs. "I'm never falling in love again, don't worry."

"Okay, then," he says and he leans in. The first kiss is just a brushing of lips, warm and soft. Then Mario pulls Lizbet close enough that their hips lock. He kisses her again, and his lips linger on hers but it's still tentative, like he's making a decision. With the third kiss, Mario's lips part and their tongues touch and a second later, they're kissing like a couple who are destined to fall in love despite their best intentions.

Eventually Mario leads Lizbet to his bed, which is pleasingly (and surprisingly) firm. He takes his time undressing her. His fingertips graze her nipples, back and forth, back and forth, until she moans into his mouth. He kisses her under her ear, sucking a little, then whispering, "You are so beautiful to me, Lizbet." She soon realizes there is no comparison between Mario and JJ in bed. JJ made love like a bull in a china shop—all power and bluster, no finesse; he liked to get it done as noisily and raucously as possible. Mario tends to her; he makes her ache. She wants him inside her and just when she thinks she can't wait another second—she's a dish on the stove that's going to burn—he makes the next move. They rock together on the firm bed and Lizbet squeezes her newly powerful thighs around him and he cries out. The surrender in his voice is something

Lizbet knows she'll replay in her head over and over again.

He rolls off her, breathless. She's dazzled.

"Why do we have to be careful, again?" she says.

He laughs. "I was just wondering that myself." He stares at the ceiling for a second, then he pushes himself up and kisses her. "I said that because I have only a one-season contract. And, as I'm sure you're aware, there are no guarantees the hotel is going to make it."

Lizbet pulls back like he's run vinegar under her nose. "The hotel is going to make it." She realizes she has no idea if this is true. Their occupancy, a month after opening, is right around 40 percent. Lizbet is too busy with the day-to-day operations to fret about this like she did at the beginning. Is the hotel losing money? Yes. But will Xavier pull the plug after only one year? Would he spend all that money just to abandon it? He said he was trying to impress two women, and one of them is Shelly Carpenter. Who is the second woman? Lizbet hasn't wondered about this for a while. (She dearly hopes it's not Alessandra.) "The hotel is going to be in business next year if I have anything to say about it. The hotel is going to be just fine."

Mario kisses the tip of her nose in a way that feels patronizing, and suddenly Lizbet wants to swat him. "Okay, Heartbreaker," he says. He pulls on his boxers and a T-shirt from Cisco Brewers. "Come to the kitchen with me, please. I'm feeding you."

14. A Desk Thing

It's the second Saturday of July and the hotel has three checkouts and four check-ins. (Alessandra can't believe the hotel isn't busier. If she'd known it was going to be this dead, she would have worked at the White Elephant.)

One of the check-ins is, thankfully, a man traveling solo named Dr. Romano; he has the chiseled good looks of a doctor on a soap opera. Dr. Romano is staying in a room, not a suite, and he's wearing a black titanium wedding band, but Alessandra chooses to overlook these two unfortunate circumstances and slips him her number. He tilts his head at her upside-down name tag and says, "Thank you *very* much, Alessandra."

Outstanding, she thinks. He'll text her the second he gets to the room, she's sure of it.

Edie, meanwhile, is trying to get the woman in room 110 a blowout at R. J. Miller. *Forget it, they're booked solid,* Alessandra thinks; she hasn't been able to squeeze anyone in there all summer. But then she overhears Lindsay at the salon granting a favor because it's "Sweet Edie Robbins" calling. When Edie hangs up, Zeke wanders over to the desk and says, "How do you make room keys, anyway? Is it like magic or something?"

Edie takes a breath, no doubt to explain that it's

magnetic not magic, but Alessandra pipes up first. "It's a desk thing. You wouldn't understand."

"Yeah, it's a desk thing," Edie says. She beams at Alessandra so earnestly that Alessandra cringes. Edie is desperate to bond, but no, sorry, Alessandra can't let that happen.

A couple enter the hotel, loaded down with luggage and baby paraphernalia—a stroller, a car seat, a bulging diaper bag.

"Gotta go," Zeke says. "It's a bell thing."

Is it Alessandra's imagination or has Zeke been lingering around the desk an awful lot? Before she can stop herself, she turns to Edie. "I think he likes you."

Edie's eyes widen. "What?"

"He's always hanging at the desk, asking questions," Alessandra says. "Have you noticed?"

"Yeah, he asked you why you wear your name tag upside down and he asked you how to say *checkout* in Italian and he asked you the strangest place you've ever had sex," Edie says. "He likes *you*."

"I think he does that to make you jealous," Alessandra says, and she believes this. She's too much woman for Zeke, and he knows it. "I'm old enough to be his grandmother."

Edie laughs and grabs her bag. "I'm taking lunch."

She's leaving Alessandra with the onerous task of checking in the couple with the baby. They'll need a crib; they'll ask about laundry facilities and a babysitter, preferably someone with six references and four grown children of her own, so that they can have a nice quiet dinner at Galley Beach or the Chanticleer. Alessandra's phone, which she keeps stashed at the back of the shelf under her computer, buzzes with a text. That would be Dr. Romano. Alessandra is so pleased that she's able to give the approaching couple a nearly genuine smile. "Checking in?"

The woman, who is wearing a clingy green knit dress that shows off her breastfeeding boobs as well as her impossibly flat stomach, gasps. "Ali *Powell?*" she says.

Alessandra freezes like an animal in the wilderness confronted with a predator—because anyone who uses Alessandra's childhood nickname is an existential threat. She focuses on the woman's face.

Oh God, she thinks. It's Duffy Beecham from high school, the friend whose father she seduced, Stanford professor Dr. Andrew Beecham.

To Alessandra's knowledge, Duffy never found out about the affair. The reason why Dr. Beecham— Drew—was so eager to buy Alessandra a one-way plane ticket to Rome was that at some point, he realized Alessandra had the power to destroy his life. By the time Alessandra landed in Rome, Duffy was a sophomore at Pepperdine, lounging on the beaches of Malibu, dating aspiring movie execs. Their friendship had been winnowed down to the occasional text (when one or the other of them was drunk and heard the Dave Matthews Band).

Every so often, Alessandra stalked Duffy on Facebook and Instagram (Alessandra had nominal profiles on both but never posted). Duffy had married a Silicon Valley executive. (Alessandra's invitation to the wedding was delivered to her mother's home, but Alessandra, who was then living in Ibiza, told her mother to decline; she realizes only now that she never sent a present, which was maybe forgivable, since she was overseas.) Alessandra doesn't know the husband's name (though she'll find out in a few short moments!). Duffy went to grad school to pursue a master's in social work. She had always been a do-gooder; her senior service project was distributing blankets to the homeless in Oakland. There was a way, too, in which Duffy's do-gooding extended to her friendship with Alessandra—Duffy saw Alessandra as a project, a girl with no father and a shabby excuse for a mother.

On her social media platforms, Duffy posted the predictable photos of apple picking with her husband (they wore matching sweaters; it was almost laughable), waiting in line at Swan Oyster Depot, a picturesque fog lying beneath the Golden Gate, a pork-belly banh mi in the stands at a 49ers game captioned *Only in San Francisco!* And then, later, she posted pics of their new apartment in Nob Hill, where she allowed her 537 followers to weigh in on decorating decisions. Wallpaper or paint for the powder room? Salvaged wood floors in the kitchen or chicer epoxy?

Alessandra hasn't heard about the baby, so it must have been well over a year since Duffy last surfaced in Alessandra's consciousness. If she had been keeping track more closely, she might have been prepared for Duffy's trip to Nantucket.

"Duffy!" Alessandra says, trying to tamp down all of these confusing thoughts. "I can't believe it! You're staying here?"

"Yes!" Duffy says. "For three nights. Are you...working here?"

"I am!" Alessandra says, brightly stating the absolutely obvious. She won't let this be awkward, she thinks, though it is—it *is!* Alessandra was the far superior student in high school, the original thinker with the uncanny ear for languages. She should be the bigger success, but as this situation painfully illustrates, she's just not. "I'm the front-desk manager."

Duffy pushes the stroller toward the desk and the

husband jogs over after he finishes loading all the crap onto the luggage trolley that Zeke is holding steady.

"I thought you were in...I don't know...St. Tropez or something, living on some rich guy's yacht."

That was the plan, Alessandra thinks. "I lived in Europe forever," Alessandra says. "Italy most recently, but also Spain and Monaco."

"Honey?" Duffy says to the husband. "This is Ali Powell, my BFF from high school."

Zeke is lingering over by the door with the trolley, listening to every word, Alessandra can tell. If Zeke tells Adam that she used to go by Ali, she'll never hear the end of it.

The husband reaches across the desk to give Alessandra a strong Silicon Valley handshake with intentional eye contact. "Jamie Chung," he says. "Nice to meet you, Ali."

Alessandra, she thinks, but she can't bear to correct him, because she doesn't want to seem pretentious. "I'll be checking you in," Alessandra says. "I'll just need an ID and a credit card."

Jamie Chung slides a California driver's license and a purple Reserve American Express card across the desk. "So you know Duff from high school?"

Duffy swats him. "We were *best* friends!" she says. "We were *inseparable*. Ali practically lived at my house. She was the one who held my hair that time I got so drunk on tequila—"

"Aha!" Jamie says. "You're the reason my wife can't drink margaritas."

I didn't give *her the tequila,* Alessandra thinks. *I held her hair!* But again, she keeps quiet.

"My parents *loved* Ali, my mother especially." Duffy lowers her voice. "She used to talk about *adopting* you. She wanted to give you a nice normal home."

Alessandra won't take the bait, won't mention that she had both a mother and a home, and she won't give in to her rogue impulse to lean across the desk and say to Jamie in a stage whisper, *I had an affair with Duffy's father the spring of our senior year.*

Instead, Alessandra says, "I'm going to comp your first night."

"Oh my God, thank you!" Duffy says. "Aren't you just the summer Santa!"

Ho-ho-ho! Alessandra thinks. "I never got you guys a wedding present, so…"

Duffy's brow wrinkles. "You didn't?"

Alessandra shakes her head. Of course Duffy wouldn't keep track of things like wedding presents; she might not even have set up a registry, she might have just asked guests to donate to Rosalie House. Though from the looks of her diamond ring, the whopper diamond studs in her ears, and her Cartier tank watch (probably a push present—oh, how Alessandra loathes this term), she might be more materialistic now than she was then.

"How about upgrading us to a suite as well?" Jamie asks. "If you have one available?"

They have seven suites available but Alessandra is so taken aback by Jamie's brazen request—it's a Taser to her sensibilities—that she says, "It looks like the suites are all spoken for."

"It's just, with the baby…" Jamie says.

"This is Cabot!" Duffy says, pulling a cherubic little baby in a sailor suit from the stroller.

Cabot Chung, Alessandra thinks. He's a beautiful kid, at that most photogenic age for babies—what is that, six months, seven? Alessandra waggles her fingers at him. She's so unmaternal that this feels campy, but she goes all in with her gushing while inwardly she fumes. She offered Jamie and Duffy a *free night* but Jamie asked for more, so it feels like she hasn't given them anything at all.

She makes a show of tapping on her keyboard. "I'm going to work some magic and slide you into a suite after all," she says. "I'll have Zeke set up a crib and babyproof the room."

"Thank you!" Duffy says. "You're amazing! Can we take you to dinner one night while we're here so we can catch up?"

Alessandra peeks at her phone; there are two texts from a number she knows is Dr. Romano.

"I'm tied up all three evenings that you're here," she says. She activates the keys for suite 216 and slides them across the desk. "But I'm sure we'll find time to chat."

"I can't wait to text my parents and tell them I saw you," Duffy says. "They won't believe it!"

"Please give them my best," Alessandra says.

Alessandra can't help but revisit the fraught months that she was sleeping with Duffy's father. Alessandra had been eighteen, which she thought was old enough, though now, nearly the same number of years later, Alessandra realizes it wasn't old enough at all. She had been a teenager and Drew a tenured professor in his mid-forties. However, Alessandra can't call herself a victim, even through the lens of 2022.

She had always loved Drew, crushed on him, *idolized* him, seeing him as somewhere between an un-attainable celebrity and a father figure. The Beechams owned an entire Victorian on Filbert Street that they'd inherited from Mary Lou's parents. Classical music always spilled from the tantalizing, slightly ajar door to Drew's study. NPR played on a radio in the kitchen, where Mary Lou made the girls crepes for breakfast; for a weeknight dinner, she'd whip up Dover sole and frisée salad with lardons. Both Beecham parents read copiously; they subscribed to *The Economist* and the *New York Review of Books;* they attended the symphony. Alice Waters knew the Beechams by name, and they were always taking trips to Lisbon or Granada, where Drew would lecture. They weren't wealthy but they were rich—with intellect, with ideas, with experiences.

Duffy, however, shared none of her parents' interests. She liked Britney Spears and *Buffy the Vampire Slayer* and she was as much of a troublemaker as Alessandra, if not more so. She was the one who became friends with HB, the guy who met them in the Presidio with a bottle of Don Julio that fateful night. Duffy matched HB shot for shot, but Alessandra tossed her shots over her shoulder because she didn't like the look of HB and didn't want to lose control.

When Duffy started vomiting, Alessandra held her hair away from her face. It was ten o'clock p.m. on a raw Friday in March and they were sitting on the damp ground of Crissy Field. Alessandra wanted to leave, but Duffy couldn't make it three steps without doubling over and retching. Alessandra had no choice but to call Drew.

The Beechams had been in the middle of hosting a dinner party; candles glowed in the dining room, bottles of excellent Napa cabernet sat empty on the table, but the conversation and the laughing quieted when Drew ushered the girls past the dining room and down the hall to the kitchen. Mary Lou stood up from the table, making a joke about teenagers: *We all remember those days, right, Barry?* But when she saw the state Duffy was in, she flamed with anger, which she aimed at Alessandra (the unparented bad influence) until she realized that Alessandra was sober. For some reason, this served to make her even more livid and she snapped at Drew to get Alessandra "out of my sight."

Drew drove Alessandra home. She was numb from Mary Lou's words; she felt like she'd been slapped—until that moment, she had been something of a pet to Mary Lou. Drew tried to apologize; he thanked Alessandra for being a good friend. "You're a special young woman, Ali," he said. "You have a savageness to you—I mean that as a compliment. You'll get what you want out of this life." The street in front of Alessandra's building was dark and quiet. Drew shut off the car, which Alessandra found strange.

"Don't you want to get back to the dinner party?" she asked.

Drew leaned his head back against the seat. "God, those people are so *dull!*" he said. "Barry Wilson was talking about annuities." He turned to Alessandra. "When did I become such an...*adult?*"

"Are you worried about Duff?" Alessandra asked.

"She'll be fine," Drew said. "Tequila is its own punishment."

Alessandra was about to reach for the car door and say, *Okay, thanks for the ride,* but something about Drew was different. He was staring at her front door. "Your mom's at work?" he asked.

They both knew the answer was yes. Alessandra nodded.

"Will you be okay by yourself?"

Alessandra had been staying by herself since she was seven years old. She got the crazy idea that he wanted her to invite him inside. She leaned over, rested her hand lightly on his (upper) thigh, and kissed him. The kiss lingered; it was, to this day, the most romantic kiss of Alessandra's life.

"This is a bad idea," Drew said, but the next second he was opening his car door and they were heading into her house.

As much as Alessandra wants to dislike Jamie for shaming her into giving them a room upgrade, she has to admit that he seems to be an excellent father, husband, and guest. Zeke let it be known that Jamie tipped him a hundred bucks for babyproofing the suite, and early on their first morning, Jamie comes down to the lobby with the baby so that Duffy can sleep in. Alessandra watches him chat with the other guests; Cabot falls asleep in his arms while Jamie plays Louie in chess. (Louie wins.)

Alessandra is on high alert every time the elevator dings, and the instant she sees Duffy step off, she bee-lines for the break room. She feeds a dollar to the jukebox and chooses Kiss, Ozzy Osbourne, and Metallica and then takes her angst—she can't believe Duffy Beecham is here, haunting her!—out on the pinball machine. She plays one game, then a second, then a third (high score)—and then she hears Adam's voice sing out. "Alessannnnnnnndra, are you in here?"

"Hello?" Alessandra says, tearing herself away from the machine, though she has already dropped a fourth quarter in.

"Girl, get back out there! Edie is three-deep."

Alessandra hurries back out, and sure enough, Edie has a line at the desk, the first ever since the hotel opened.

"Sorry about that," Alessandra says.

"It's fine," Edie says. "I understand."

You don't, though, Alessandra thinks.

*　*　*

Duffy stops by the desk a while later with Cabot, who's wearing a tiny bucket hat and a little bathing suit printed with sharks. "We're taking him to the family pool," Duffy says. "I'll put him down for a nap around one and then I'll come chat."

"Whatever works!" Alessandra says. She doesn't want to chat with Duffy. She doesn't want to talk about high school or hear about Drew and Mary Lou (from Duffy's Facebook, Alessandra knows that they've both put on forty pounds and turned gray) and she doesn't want to learn about Duffy's fabulous San Francisco life with her successful husband and adorable baby. But what she really doesn't want is to be asked questions about herself. What were her years abroad like? Well, some of them were better than others. Alessandra held a string of jobs in beautiful hotels and she'd dated different men, all of them wealthy, most of them married, one of them—the one Alessandra thought would be her husband—a financial criminal, none of them appropriate. And what is her life like here on Nantucket? Last night, she slipped into Dr. Romano's room; they ordered room service (Alessandra hid in the bathroom while it was delivered) and had (completely mediocre) sex, and Alessandra left at two in the morning, emotionally numb.

When Duffy swings by on her way back up to her room, she says, "I'll be back down in a little while. Jamie will stay in the room with Cabot so that we can talk."

"Great!" Alessandra says.

Once Duffy is on the elevator, Alessandra releases a low moan and Edie says, "Why don't you take lunch now? You can go for as long as you want, it's okay with me."

Alessandra blinks. "Why are you being so nice to me?"

"I grew up on this island," she says. "I check the cars in the parking lot of the Stop and Shop before I go inside. There are old friends I would do anything to avoid."

Oh my God, Alessandra thinks. Edie *does* understand.

She takes one of the hotel bikes, goes to Something Natural, and sits at a picnic table for two hours, reading the new Elena Ferrante novel. When she arrives back at the hotel, Edie says, "You're safe. They went to the Oystercatcher for a late lunch and they're staying through sunset."

"Thank you," Alessandra says.

Once Alessandra learns Cabot's schedule, she's able to avoid a conversation with Duffy on day two and day three as well. She owes Edie big-time because she takes some seriously long-ass lunches, telling Duffy she has a doctor's appointment and then a Zoom meeting she can't miss. She blows Dr. Romano off on night two—she needs sleep—but she visits him late on night three, and after they've had more mediocre sex, Alessandra finds herself weeping uncontrollably. Dr. Romano—his name is Mark—thinks she's crying because she's become emotionally attached and he's leaving in the morning. Gently, he wipes her tears away with the pad of his thumb. He has lovely hands and even lovelier fingers; he's a surgeon.

"Please don't cry," he says. "We had a nice time together and that's what matters, right?"

Yes, of course Alessandra will never see him again—he has a wife and two little girls in Kansas City—but that's not why she's crying. She shrugs.

"Is there anything I can do to make you feel better?"

"Just hold me," she says, snuggling into him. "And if you could write a review on TravelTattler and mention me by name, that really helps. Just say I was exceptional on the desk or whatever."

He tickles her ribs. "You *were* exceptional on the desk." He reaches for the remote control and turns on the TV. *Caddyshack* has just started. "Have you ever seen this movie? It's a laugh riot."

Is there a man alive who doesn't think *Caddyshack* is a laugh riot? If so, Alessandra hasn't met him. "I've never seen it," she lies. "Is it about golf?"

"Oh, just wait, just wait," he says. "That's the judge…" Alessandra closes her eyes. "You're going to love it."

When Alessandra awakens, it's very late, nearly three a.m. The doctor is snoring beside her and Alessandra slips from the bed and gets dressed. She needs to get home. The good news is she can leave through the front doors rather than sneaking down to the lower level and going out the back because both Richie and Raoul will be gone. But when Alessandra enters the lobby, she sees Raoul just heading out. She comes to an immediate halt and ducks behind the corner but he must sense something because he turns and sees her. She's caught.

"Hey," he says. "What are you doing still here?"

She cocks an eyebrow. "What are *you* doing still here?"

He shakes his head. "There was a domestic issue in suite two sixteen. I had to call the police."

Alessandra says, "Suite two sixteen? Did someone complain about the baby crying?"

"The baby was fine, it was the parents. They had

dinner at the Galley tonight, then I guess they had drinks at Lola, whatever, they were all lit up, and they had a fight that got loud and suite two fourteen called down and I went up first but it was above my pay grade, so then Richie came up. The wife was crying and calling the husband a bastard, and he was calling her a psycho, and she said she didn't want him in their room…it was a mess. They pulled it together a bit when the cops showed up. It's fine now and they're checking out in the morning, thank God."

"You're sure the wife is okay?" Alessandra says. "He wasn't *hitting* her, was he?"

"The husband took me aside and said she's not really supposed to be drinking since she's nursing, but she made an exception because she's on vacation, and then she bumped into an old friend who really triggered her."

"'Triggered' her?"

"That's what he said, yeah. And don't ask me to clarify. I'm forty-two years old, I don't even know what that word means." Raoul musses Alessandra's hair, which she's sure is already pretty mussed. Raoul is the only person on planet Earth she would allow to do this. "What are you doing here again?" he asks.

"Oh, you know me," Alessandra says. "I can't get enough of this place."

Later that morning, Alessandra places the folio for the Chung family in an envelope and hands it over with a smile. *Sorry we didn't get a chance to catch up…Me too, so busy…The baby…This stupid thing called work, only get a day off every two weeks…So much fun, thank you for hooking us up with the suite, here's my number, call if you ever get back to San Fran, and hey, friend me on Facebook!*

"I will!" Alessandra says. She won't. "Bye!" Jamie and Duffy stroll cute baby Cabot right out the door. *And that,* Alessandra thinks, *is that.*

Except it's not. A few days later, Alessandra and Edie are powering up their computers and getting ready to start the day when Richie suddenly pops out of the back office, terrifying them both.

"Whoa!" Edie says. "I thought there really was a ghost!"

Richie doesn't seem amused, which is strange because normally he's happy-go-lucky and always has a dad joke ready. But he's clearly been here all night. Alessandra worked the graveyard shift her first few months in Lake Como; she understands how it splinters your nerves.

He shakes a piece of paper at Alessandra. "You comped a night in a suite for a guest named Chung? No code, no explanation, and no sign-off!"

"I…did," Alessandra says. She was so happy to have the Chungs gone (Duffy was "triggered"—Alessandra still hasn't processed that one; if either of them should have been triggered, it was Alessandra, and what was that crack about the nice normal home?) that she completely spaced on the fact that she would have to explain the comped night. The desk staff are allowed to comp a night if something goes wrong—if guests have an unusually bad experience or if they can't check in until after five o'clock—but staffers are not allowed to do what Alessandra did and comp at will. Every single comp must be run past Lizbet. Still, Alessandra had expected Richie to let it slide. He has never said a word about her taking five or ten bucks every few days from petty cash to pay for her lunch, though it's possible he doesn't know she does this. "Is it really that big of a deal?"

"It was a six-hundred-and-forty-five-dollar room rate," Richie says. "That needs to be paid. By you. You made a unilateral decision to comp the room."

"Okay?" Alessandra says. "I'll point out that Edie upgraded the Marsh family *for the summer* without anyone's permission. That adds up to a lot more lost revenue than six hundred and forty-five dollars, and no one is making *her* pay."

Both Richie and Edie are silent.

Richie huffs. "Fine. I'll let this go but don't do it again, either of you." He disappears back into Lizbet's office.

Alessandra turns to Edie. "I should have just gotten them a toaster," she says.

Edie gives Alessandra a withering look.

"I'm sorry, Edie," Alessandra says. She pauses. "Is it a desk thing to throw your helpful, kind coworker under the bus?"

"*Your* desk thing," Edie says, and Alessandra is more relieved than she can explain when Edie lets the tiniest smile slip.

15. Behind Closed Doors

Adam drags Raoul into the break room, and Grace follows them because it looks like trouble!

"We need to speak to Lizbet about the schedule," Adam says. "It's not fair that she switched our shifts. You need to talk to her. She likes you better."

"I don't *want* to talk to her," Raoul says. "Because, believe it or not, I'm ready to stop working nights. I did it for an entire month. Now it's your turn."

"You just want to spend all day with Zeke," Adam says.

Raoul blinks. "Or *you* do, and that's why you're kerking."

"I hope you're not accusing me of anything," Adam says. "Because I don't need to remind you which one of us was caught making out with that busboy at Nikki Beach."

"That was before we were even together," Raoul says. "I've been faithful since our first date. And working with Zeke isn't going to make me unfaithful. If you think that, then you have trust issues."

"*I* have trust issues?"

"Do you have a thing for Zeke, Adam?"

At that moment the door to the break room swings open and Zeke steps in. "Adam, you're on tonight? I've gotta bounce."

"I'll be right there," Adam says. "Just chatting with my *husband* whom I never *see*."

Zeke looks from Adam to Raoul and must sense something because he steps back out and closes the door.

"Why can't we work together?" Adam says. "Zeke can work nights."

"You know why we can't work together," Raoul says. "George said he'd recommend to any future employer that we be scheduled opposite each other."

"Well, I'm lonely. I made dinner plans with Alessandra three times and she ditched me all three," Adam says. *Surprise, surprise,* Grace thinks. There was Mr. Brownlee in 309, Mr. Yamaguchi in suite 215, and Dr. Romano in room 107. "I miss you."

"I miss you too, boo."

Suddenly, Adam and Raoul embrace and start kissing. Grace is delighted the fight is over and the making up has begun. She heads over to the jukebox and plays "Take My Breath Away," by Berlin, and then she lights up the pinball machine.

The gentlemen don't even seem to notice.

Could Kimber Marsh be any more obvious? Grace wonders. She comes down to the lobby—*again* at quarter past one in the morning (coincidentally after Adam has left and the Blue Bar has closed), *again* wearing her shorty pajamas, cardigan, and the hotel slippers.

"Richie?" Kimber whispers—but Richie isn't at his usual post out front. Richie, Grace sees, is in Lizbet's office with the door not only closed but locked. He's on his cell phone (forbidden at work unless you need it to conduct hotel business), having a terse conversation. What can Grace think but that he's speaking to his ex-wife? Who else would he be talking to at one fifteen in the morning? Then Grace sees what Richie has on the desk in front of him and she hears what he's saying into the phone.

Oh, dear, she thinks. This is what he's up to. What a disappointment.

Grace blows the paperwork off the desk in an attempt to be disruptive but Richie doesn't seem to care. Then she tries to mess with the phone connection but it's too late, the conversation is over. When Richie hangs up, he slumps back in his chair and grabs his head.

There's a tap on the office door. "Richie?"

The inevitable has happened, Grace thinks. Kimber has grown so comfortable at the hotel that she has crossed the border between guest and staff. She's *behind* the front desk—and now she's knocking on the office door. If it weren't locked, Grace suspects she would have marched right in and caught Richie at his odious business.

Richie jumps to his feet, and Lizbet's desk chair shoots back into the wall. Richie stuffs the paperwork into his pants pocket. He inhales a breath and exhales with a smile. He once again looks like the charming, affable dad everyone thinks he is. "Kimber!" he says, opening the door. "What's up?"

"Can't sleep," Kimber says. She seems to realize she's crossed some kind of invisible line because she scurries out from behind the desk. She waves what looks like a piece of notebook paper. "Also, I wanted to show you something."

What Kimber wants to show Richie at one fifteen in the morning is an article Wanda wrote entitled "The Mystery of the Haunted Hotel."

Richie reads aloud: "'The Hotel Nantucket has been plaqued'—is this supposed to be *plagued*?—'with difficulties for nearly a century. Girl sleuth Wanda Marsh has uncovered the reason. There's a *ghost* who inhabits the hotel's fourth-floor storage closet.'" Richie stops. "Did Wanda write this herself?"

"Edie helped her a little."

"'The ghost is the spirit of Grace Hadley, a chambermaid who died in a fire in the summer of 1922 in that fourth-floor closet.'" Richie looks up. "Is this true?"

"Wanda insisted we go to the Atheneum to look it up. They had old issues of the *Nantucket Standard* on microfilm."

"Your kids are incredible," Richie says. "Louie is a chess prodigy and Wanda is a burgeoning detective and investigative reporter. My three spend all their time playing Fortnite and watching YouTube."

"Wanda told me that she asked the ghost to knock, and the ghost did."

"Well, that's exciting," Richie says. He subtly plucks his shirt away from his body. His extracurricular activity in the back office has made him perspire.

"The thing is, she really believes it," Kimber says. "Shall we go up and check out the fourth-floor storage closet?"

Richie frowns. "I shouldn't leave the desk."

"It'll only take a minute."

"I can't afford to lose my job," Richie says.

"I'm beginning to think you don't like me," Kimber says. "You practically ran away from me the other night."

"I do like you," Richie says. He reaches across the desk for Kimber's hand. Is he being patronizing? Grace wonders. "I have a lot going on in my personal life right now."

"You can tell me if you're not attracted to me," Kimber says. "I'll survive."

Richie lets go of Kimber's hand—he's *not* attracted to her, apparently—but then he comes out from behind the desk. "I'm not the person you think I am," he says. "I know I put on a good act of being nice-guy Richie—"

Kimber puts a finger to his lips. "I'm probably not the person you think I am either," she says. "But it doesn't matter. It's summertime and we're on an island thirty miles out to sea."

Richie gazes at Kimber. He seems to be deliberating, and Grace, quite frankly, is on the edge of her seat. Finally, Richie puts his arms around Kimber and pulls her close. Kimber raises her face, Richie takes his glasses off and sets them on the desk—a nice touch, Grace thinks; things are about to get steamy—and kisses her.

Grace cheers silently, even though she fears the relationship won't last. But who doesn't love a little summer romance? She just hopes they don't forget about that article. If they solve her murder case, she'll finally be able to get some much needed rest. It has been an exhausting century.

It's Friday, a day that used to mean only one thing for Chad: slightly more raucous partying than his usual weeknight partying. Chad hasn't heard from Bryce or Eric in weeks, though he did get a text from Jasper thanking him for being cool about me and Winston. Chad responded, Hey, man, I'm happy for you. If you ever want to grab a bite, hit me up. Jasper hasn't reached out yet, but he might somewhere down the road. Chad feels only relief at the disbanding of his group of friends; the solitude has turned out to be kind of nice.

However, Chad is still desperately hoping for an e-mail from Paddy.

When Chad logs into his Yahoo! account first thing in the morning, he sees an alert that someone has hacked into the operating software of both the Steamship Authority and Hy-Line Cruises. All ferry service to and from Nantucket is halted. When he goes downstairs, his mother has the local news on television.

"They'd better get this fixed, pronto," Whitney says. "Dad is coming tonight."

Chad snaps to attention. "He's coming *tonight*?"

"Yes, silly. His deal closed; he's driving up with the car for the rest of the summer," Whitney says. "Can I make you an English muffin? Or…would you like a peach? They're ripe."

"I have to get to work," Chad says. His mother still hasn't quite acknowledged the fact that Chad has a job. Whitney Winslow is an expert at ignoring the things that make her uncomfortable. She obviously *knows* that Chad works every day at the Hotel Nantucket, but that doesn't mean she has to talk about it. Chad wonders if she's told his father.

Chad picks a peach out of the two dozen peaches piled in the fruit bowl; his mother has over-shopped again, and half of these will rot. Chad grabs two more. He'll give them to Bibi, and she can take them home and make baby food or whatever.

But when Chad gets to work, Bibi isn't there, and neither are Octavia and Neves. Because...there is no ferry service.

Ms. English accepts Chad's offer of the two peaches with a bemused expression on her face and then pulls on a pair of rubber gloves. "It's just you and me today, Long Shot."

"*You're* going to clean the rooms?" Chad asks.

"Who else is going to do it?" she asks. "The cleaning fairies?"

Chad assumes that he and Ms. English will split the rooms, but when Ms. English follows him to room 209, he understands they're going to deal with all the rooms together. They'll inspect the check-ins first (these rooms are clean, but they need to fill the minibars and run through the hundred-point checklist anyway). Chad is nervous. What if he makes a mistake or forgets something and she fires him? He tries to pay extra attention and soon realizes that he has already been paying extra attention, because every single day, he not only does his own job but also keeps an eye on Bibi to make sure she doesn't steal anything. The work goes quickly. Ms. English sings softly—she has a beautiful voice—and sends Chad down to the Blue Bar kitchen to get the goodies for the minibars. Down there, Chad bumps into Yolanda, the super-hot wellness guru. She's leaning up against one of the prep tables, eating an acai bowl topped with perfect circles of banana and strawberries and talking to Beatriz, who's over by the ovens.

"Hey, Chad," Yolanda says, and Chad nearly drops to his knees. Hot Yolanda knows his name!

"Hey," Chad says as casually as he can. He goes to the walk-in for the bluefish pâté, then to the pantry for the crackers, then to a special fridge for the beer and wine. He has to write down exactly what he takes in the log, for obvious reasons. When he comes out with everything in his blue plastic handbasket (it's hard to be sexy while carrying a handbasket but Chad tries anyway), Beatriz is slicing into one of the baguettes that she just pulled out of the oven.

"Stick around," she says to Chad. "I'm going to blow your mind."

Yolanda giggles. "Don't tease him, Bea."

"Not teasing," Beatriz says. She slathers two slices of the warm bread with butter from a crock ("Churned this myself"), lays pieces of paper-thin watermelon radish ("These were picked this morning at Pumpkin Pond Farm") across the top, and sprinkles the radish with sea salt. Beatriz hands one piece to Chad and one to Yolanda.

"Thank you," Chad says, and he takes a bite. The bread with the crunchy crust and the sweet, creamy butter and the peppery zing of the radish combine in a way that nearly brings Chad to tears.

Yolanda makes a loud, uninhibited moaning noise that sounds sexual and Chad feels a stirring in his pants. They *are* teasing him, but Chad doesn't mind.

It's the first semi-normal response he's had to anything since May.

Chad and Ms. English make their way briskly through the check-ins, but the checkouts are another story. Chad and Bibi always rate the rooms on a scale of 1 to 10, with 1 being a room that looks like it's barely been occupied (Bibi is amused by people who go to the trouble of making the bed before they leave) and 10 being an apocalyptic disaster. Most rooms fall between a 4 and a 6, but naturally on the day that Chad and Ms. English work alone, all five checkouts are a 10.

When they walk into room 308, Chad nearly gags. Not only is the place a horrendous mess, but it reeks. Chad vaguely remembers a pleasant-looking young couple with infant twins being in this room. There are two cribs shoehorned into the far corner, and in one crib is a dirty diaper lying wide open. Chad hurries to roll it up and throw it away, but the trash can is overflowing with dirty diapers as well as empty bottles of formula that smell like rancid milk. This couple left food all over the desk and dresser—granola bars, scattered almonds, a container of tuna salad that has, unfortunately, been sitting in the sun. There are ants *everywhere*. Most of the bed linens are in a heap on the floor, and the fitted sheet is stained with something brown. Chad finds half a melted Mounds bar under a pillow (that the stain is probably chocolate comes as a relief). Someone must have showered with the door open because the bathroom floor is a lake, and two of the thick Turkish towels are floating in it like islands. The father shaved in the sink and didn't bother to clean out his whiskers, which for some reason is the thing that grosses out Chad the most.

He turns to Ms. English, aghast. He can't believe

people aren't more considerate. He has a hazy understanding that twins are a lot of work, but don't the parents realize someone has to clean this up? A human being? He feels like he should apologize to Ms. English, like the state of the room is somehow his fault. He realizes how much he misses working with Bibi. If she saw this, she would call the guests every profane word she knows (and she knows a bunch), and they would both feel better.

Ms. English merely snaps on a new pair of gloves. "Okay, Long Shot," she says. "Let's get to work."

Thirty minutes later, the room is sparkling clean. There are fresh sheets on the bed; the cribs have been broken down and stored; the rug has been vacuumed; the food remnants have been thrown away and the ants along with them; the puddle in the bathroom is mopped up; the towels have been replaced; the sink, tub, and toilet are scrubbed. The minibar has been emptied, cleaned, and restocked. The hangers have been counted, the robes placed on the back of the bathroom door, the blow-dryer checked, the bottles of shampoo, conditioner, and lotion refilled. It's so satisfying, Chad thinks, restoring this room to glory. He's almost glad he's no longer friends with Bryce and Eric, because they wouldn't understand this feeling.

Paddy might understand. In the summers, he ran a lawn-mowing business in his hometown of Grimesland, North Carolina. He kept a push mower in the back of his Ford Ranger and drove to his clients' homes—most of them ranches or saltboxes that would fit into Chad's living room—and cut the grass, fifteen bucks for front and back. He did five or six lawns a day and put all his money in the bank so he'd have it to spend at Bucknell, but even then he had to be careful and sometimes he stayed home rather than go out to Bull Run, although Chad always offered to spot him.

Chad closes his eyes. The best part about working with Bibi is that he never has time to think about Paddy or wonder if Paddy is healed enough to go back to mowing lawns and look over the grass, striped with diagonal lines, and feel proud of his handiwork.

Normally, Chad is done with work around five, but today he and Ms. English don't finish until after six. Lizbet has let them know that the boats are up and running again, and there are some pretty unhappy people waiting in the lobby for their rooms to be ready. From the five checkouts combined, there are sixty-five dollars in tips, which Ms. English presses into Chad's hand, despite his protests.

"I don't want it," he says. "You take it."

This makes Ms. English laugh. "Don't be ridiculous, Long Shot."

Chad stuffs the bills into the front pocket of his khakis. "I'll give it to Bibi tomorrow."

"To Bibi?" Ms. English says. "She didn't earn it. She got a day off."

But she needs it, Chad thinks.

"I hope you and Bibi aren't getting romantically involved," Ms. English says. "I don't want to have to worry about you two alone in the rooms."

Chad feels his face redden. The idea of fooling around with Bibi in one of the rooms makes him very uncomfortable. He wishes Ms. English hadn't said that; he's afraid it will be all he thinks about tomorrow, and if he's awkward around Bibi, she'll notice.

"No way," he says. "Nothing like that."

"But you brought her peaches," Ms. English says, and she winks.

Chad has no interest in going home to face his father, so he delays the inevitable with a drive through town. It's a summer evening on Nantucket and there are couples strolling into galleries for openings and a well-dressed mob crowding the hostess lectern at the Boarding House. Chad sees a group of—well, for lack of a better term—*Chads* walking right down the middle of the street, cutting off traffic without any consideration for the drivers, heading (he's certain) to drink at the Gazebo, where they will order their vodka sodas and talk trash about their father's boats, their golf handicaps, and girls.

Chad used to be one of those guys but he isn't any longer, and he's glad. He loops around and heads for home.

He's driving out Eel Point Road when something catches his eye. It's the gunmetal-gray Jeep Gladiator that Ms. English drives, parked in the driveway of number 133. The house is huge, even bigger than the Winslows' home, and it's closer to the water. Chad slows down. He's pretty sure his parents considered buying number 133 as an investment property and renting it out for fifty or sixty grand a week until they eventually gifted it to Leith or Chad.

He watches Ms. English climb out of the Gladiator.

He comes to a stop and nearly calls to her. His Range Rover is hidden by the tall decorative grasses around the mailbox. What is Ms. English doing at number 133?

A dude wearing a panama hat and a wheat-colored linen suit comes out of the house and shakes Ms. English's hand. He holds open the door and she steps inside.

Chad takes a beat to absorb this. Ms. English must be interviewing to clean number 133. A side hustle.

Chad drives off, feeling queasy—and the worst is yet to come.

When Chad pulls into his own driveway, he sees his father's Jaguar.

He finds Paul Winslow on the back porch in a rattan chair, sunglasses perched on top of his bald head, eyes closed, gin and tonic on the table next to him. He's dressed in shorts, a polo shirt, and Top-Siders, which is what he wears all summer long except when they go out for dinner; for that, Paul favors pants printed with whales, lobsters, or flamingos. Chad gets it— his father works in the pressure-cooker environment of venture capital, and these six weeks are his time to relax. If Paul lets off steam by wearing flamingo pants, fine. He deserves to enjoy the things his money has bought—the pool, their private beach, the view of Nantucket Sound.

Chad doesn't hear anyone else in the house and he realizes his mother's Lexus wasn't in the driveway. He takes a step backward and Paul's eyes open.

"Hey, hey, hey, son!" Paul says, rising to his feet and offering a hand as though Chad is a client. "I've been waiting for you. Where've you been?"

"Hey, Dad," Chad says. He feels like a bluefish gutted with a gaff. What he wouldn't give to wriggle free of this moment. "Where are Mom and Leith?"

"They're at the salon," Paul says, "getting gussied up for dinner."

Dinner, Chad thinks. In the garden at the Chanticleer, which is their tradition the first night Paul arrives on island. Chad completely spaced about it. He can't believe things in their family have just gone back to normal after what happened in May, but maybe enough time has passed that they all feel they can just move on—or his parents do. Leith will hate him forever, he's pretty sure.

"I was at work, actually," Chad says. "I got a job at the Hotel Nantucket, cleaning rooms."

His father's face shows no surprise, so Chad's mother must have prepped him. Paul sits and extends a hand to indicate that Chad should take the seat next to his. "Let's talk that through for a minute, shall we?" Paul's tone of voice has switched to executive mode, and seeing no option, Chad sits. "Can I get you a beer, son?"

"No, thank you."

Paul chuckles. "Don't tell me you're on the wagon. If your mother and I thought you needed rehab, we would have sent you to rehab."

"No," Chad says, though he hasn't had a drink since that fateful night. "But I'm all set for right now."

Paul sits in a pose of introspection, leaning forward in the chair, elbows on his knees, fingers tented, head bent. "So what I'm hearing you say is that you got a job."

"Yes," Chad says. "At the Hotel Nantucket, cleaning rooms. I work for the head of housekeeping, Ms. English, who's an extremely cool person. There are three girls—women, I mean—on the crew with me. They all live on the Cape and commute over and back every day, so, because the boats weren't running earlier today, it was just Ms. English and me, which is why I'm late. I usually finish around five."

Paul nods along to all this, a signal that he's listening. "I just closed a five-billion-dollar deal. Do you have any idea why I work so hard, Chadwick?"

Chad isn't sure how to answer. His father's not brokering peace in the Middle East or curing childhood cancer or teaching undergraduates the novels of Toni Morrison. He's betting on the success of ideas, technology, natural resources. Every once in a while, this does the world some good; his firm buys a pharmaceutical company that brings out an important drug or backs a fledgling company that does something to improve people's lives. But mostly, Chad understands, Paul is playing a game on an exclusive field, which results in a lot of winning. A lot of money. "Because you like it?" Chad says.

This elicits a patronizing laugh. "I do it to provide for you and your sister and your mother." Paul raises an arm theatrically. "I didn't grow up with any of this."

Right, Chad knows. His father comes from a regular background, though not one as impoverished as he might like people to believe. He grew up in a split-level house in Phoenixville, Pennsylvania, which is close to the Main Line but pointedly not *on* it. It was Chad's mother, Whitney, who had the sterling pedigree—an estate in St. David's, private school at Baldwin, a father who was a managing partner at Rawle and Henderson, the definition of a Philadelphia lawyer. Paul met Whitney at Smokey Joe's bar on Route 30 when she was at Bryn Mawr and Paul was a scholarship student at Haverford. It was Whitney's father who helped Paul get into the business school at Wharton and then introduced him to the gentlemen at the Brandywine Group.

"I know," Chad says.

"You have the rest of your life to work," Paul says. "I thought we agreed that you would take the summer off to enjoy yourself."

Chad feels a lump in his throat. "I don't deserve to enjoy myself."

"I thought we agreed, as a family, to put what happened behind us."

"I can't just put it behind me, Dad," Chad says. He seeks out Paul's eyes. His father is essentially a decent guy who knows the difference between right and wrong. The mandate to keep "what happened" a secret is coming from Chad's mother. She has her reputation to think of. It's bad enough that so many people at home know; Whitney Winslow doesn't want her social circle on Nantucket whispering about it as well. "Have you heard from the lawyers?" Chad swallows. "Or Paddy's family?"

"Yes," Paul says. He exhales like he's about to deadlift three hundred pounds. "The surgery was unsuccessful. Patrick lost sight in the eye permanently."

Paddy O'Connor, Chad's best friend from college, his best friend possibly ever in his life, is blind in his left eye. Permanently. Chad feels blinded himself. He bends over his knees.

"We're offering a generous settlement—paying all the medical bills in addition to compensation for the eye."

How much is an eye worth? Chad wonders. What is the value of a full field of vision when you meet the woman you want to marry or hold your newborn child for the first time? Or when you go to MOMA to see van Gogh's *Starry Night* or watch the sun set in the evening? Half of Paddy's eyesight is gone. He can still see, but—Chad looked this up right after the accident—he'll lose depth perception, and he'll have difficulty judging distance and tracking moving objects.

"I want to contribute," Chad says.

"That's very generous of you, son, but—"

Chad pulls the sixty-five dollars out of his pocket

and slaps it on the table next to Paul's gin and tonic. He has nearly forty-eight hundred dollars saved from his paychecks. He'll give everything he makes this summer to Paddy. The amount will be dwarfed by whatever Paul has offered, but Chad wants Paddy to know that he didn't just roll over on his beach towel, beer in his hand, joint between his lips, and let his parents handle this. He went out and got a job where he deals with other people's dirty diapers and forgotten late-night candy bars and bathroom swamps.

Paul eyes the money. "I'd like you to give your notice at the hotel tomorrow."

"No," Chad says.

"Your mother doesn't like how it looks," Paul says. "You working as a menial laborer—"

"Menial?" Chad says. "I have another word for it: *honest*. It's an honest job, cleaning rooms for people who work hard themselves and who come to Nantucket to relax and have a vacation. You haven't seen these rooms, Dad; they're every bit as nice as the rooms in this house. The hotel is a special place—"

"That isn't exactly what your mother has heard."

"It doesn't matter!" Chad says. He realizes now why his father works so hard. It has nothing to do with the pool or the Range Rover or a bowl filled with ripe peaches. It's so he can control people. "I could be working at a roadside motel on Route Triple Zero in Nowheresville and the work would still be noble. People's lives include messes, and I'm cleaning them up."

"You're to give your notice tomorrow, Chadwick," Paul says.

Chad stands up. "Or what? You'll ground me? Throw me out of the house? Disown me?"

"Don't be ridiculous."

"*You're* the one who's being ridiculous," Chad says. What kind of parents don't want a child to actually take responsibility for his actions? *His* parents. Which is why he made such careless, thoughtless mistakes in the first place. His mother and father raised him to believe that he was invincible. They raised him to believe that nothing bad could ever happen in his life. But it did.

"I won't quit," Chad says. "I'm not a quitter."

July 11, 2022
From: Xavier Darling (xd@darlingent.co.uk)
To: Employees of the Hotel Nantucket

Good morning! I think we can all agree the summer is now in full swing. Once again this week, the reviews reflect an exceptional job done by our front-desk manager, Alessandra Powell, and this week's bonus goes to her. I hope the rest of you will strive to follow Alessandra's excellent example of service.

Thank you for your continued hard work.

XD

Edie is in the break room with Zeke when the Venmo alert comes into her phone, so she ignores it. She and Zeke have become friendly and Edie isn't going to let anything interrupt their bonding time. She spent all of her awkward freshman year of high school and at least half of her slightly less awkward sophomore year stalking Zeke English both in person and online, so the fact that they are now sitting next to each other at the Formica counter eating ice cream with their thighs practically *touching* is nothing short of miraculous to Edie in a long-delayed-dream kind of way.

Zeke says exactly what Edie is thinking. "I can't believe Alessandra won the money *again* this week. It's starting to feel like a setup."

Edie makes a noncommittal murmuring noise, though what she wants to do is emphatically agree. Something *must* be up with Alessandra. She's good on the desk, no question, but she doesn't go the extra mile the way Edie does. If a guest requests an extra pillow or towel or a second container of the smoked bluefish pâté, Edie zips directly up to the room and hands it over with a bright (and sincere) smile. She has learned the first names of everyone who answers the phone at Cru in order to secure hotel guests what is, for most people, an impossible reservation. She even went so far as to buy the little boy staying in room 302 a lighthouse key chain from the Hub because he was obsessed with Brant Point Light. Edie used her own money (of which she has very little), not the hotel's petty cash, which is what Alessandra uses to buy herself lunch. (Petty cash is not to be used for their personal expenses, Lizbet has told them multiple times, and yet Edie says nothing to anyone because she loathes a tattletale.) Then there are the Marsh children. Edie helped Wanda write an article about the "ghost," and when Wanda grew emotional and asked why nobody had saved Grace Hadley, Edie gave her a hug and said that was a long time ago, before there were smoke detectors. Edie also found Louie a chess instructor—a housepainter named Rustam who had been a chess champion back in Uzbekistan.

Edie would like to ask Kimber to write a

TravelTattler review—Kimber would surely mention Edie—but she can't bring herself to campaign on her own behalf.

Alessandra has won the bonus three weeks in a row. This is a side stitch that stays with Edie through all her working hours. It's cathartic to hear that it bugs Zeke as well.

"Do Adam and Raoul ever tell you what it's like to live with her?" Edie asks.

Zeke rolls his eyes. "Adam says she hardly ever sleeps there."

"What?" Edie says.

"She rolls in at five or six in the morning when Raoul is getting up to exercise," Zeke says. "She's out on the prowl, I guess."

Edie isn't surprised to hear this—Alessandra exudes a discreet but undeniable sexuality—but she won't take part in any slut-shaming. If anything, Edie feels freshly hurt that Alessandra has chosen to confide exactly nothing in her even though they work side by side all day long. Alessandra is always civil but never friendly or warm. Why?

Beneath Alessandra's polished facade is something else, Edie thinks. A broken doll, a smashed mirror. Alessandra is damaged. Or maybe Edie is just making excuses for her. Graydon used to tell Edie she should stop giving other people so much credit.

Zeke finishes his ice cream and stands up. "I'm heading home." He gives Edie his slow, beautiful smile. "I think we should start spying on Alessandra to figure out how she's winning the money."

Start spying *on her?* Edie thinks. Are they back in middle school? The idea, however, is not without its appeal. Edie likes the thought of having a little conspiracy going with Zeke.

"I'll see what I can find out," Edie says, though she knows she will find out nothing. Alessandra is all zippered up.

"Here, take my number," Zeke says. He picks up Edie's phone. "Someone named Graydon has requested a five-hundred-dollar Venmo," he says. He grins at Edie. "Who's Graydon? Your bookie?"

Edie wants to snatch the phone from his hand, but she just laughs. "Something like that." She watches Zeke type his number into her phone, but the thrill that should accompany getting Zeke English's cell phone number is missing. When Zeke hands back her phone, Edie sees the Venmo request, and her face burns with shame. She has no right to judge Alessandra. "I'll see you tomorrow."

"See ya," Zeke says, and he leaves her sitting with what is now a bowl of cold chocolate soup.

Five hundred dollars. Edie checks the date. It's exactly three weeks since Graydon's last Venmo request, which came exactly three weeks after his first Venmo request. The regularity of the extortion gives Edie an odd comfort. Graydon isn't asking more frequently or asking for more money. Edie wonders if she can just think of this like a car payment or a stupidity tax.

But no, sorry, that's absurd! She has lost a thousand dollars of her hard-earned money already and she's not going to buckle this time. Graydon is angry about the breakup and maybe he's lonely out in Arizona, but even so, he would never send those videos out. They would embarrass him as much as her.

She deletes the Venmo request—but then, as though he's watching her somehow, a text comes in from him.

It's her mother's cell phone number and e-mail.

Edie stops breathing for a second. She sends him the money.

16. The Cobblestone Telegraph

Jordan Randolph, publisher of the *Nantucket Standard,* has been sitting on Jill Tananbaum's article about the Hotel Nantucket for well over a month, but he hasn't been inspired to run it. Part of the reason is his own prejudice about the hotel being owned by a renowned London billionaire who has never even set foot on the island—it feels so *wrong*—and part of it is that Jordan likes to cover the *real* issues facing Nantucket. There's the housing shortage, which causes overcrowded conditions for both seasonal and year-round workers. There's the traffic; in the summer, Jordan avoids the intersection by the high school altogether. There's environmental sustainability, the argument against short-term rentals, and issues with the landfill. Nantucket is, in Jordan's opinion, already too popular, so inundated with visitors that the people who live here can't enjoy it. Jordan realizes this makes him sound like a crochety old-timer. Really what he wishes is that there were a story to the hotel's renovation that didn't have to do with money, thread count, or Farrow and Ball paint.

And then, suddenly, that story lands on his desk.

Edie Robbins comes into the office with an article written by an eight-year-old girl, a guest at the hotel. This child, Wanda Marsh, claims to have heard from a ghost living in the hotel's fourth-floor storage closet. Jordan reads the piece and chuckles—it's not bad; maybe he should hire this Wanda Marsh— and then Edie hands over the supporting document, an article published in the *Standard* a hundred years ago.

"I never knew about this," Jordan admits. There are, of course, ghost stories all over downtown Nantucket, just as there are in any historic place with creaky old houses. But this one grabs Jordan's interest. It's the combination of the hundred-year-anniversary angle, the little girl, and Edie herself, a young woman Jordan has known since birth. Jordan was friends with Edie's father, Vance Robbins; they served on the Rotary Club scholarship committee together for years, and Jordan was saddened by his passing.

He gives the little girl's story and the old article to Jill and asks her to write a new piece about the hotel. "Describe the renovation from the point of view of the ghost who has lived there for the past hundred years," he says. "People will love it."

And they do! Jill Tananbaum's article "Hotel Nantucket Haunted by Hadley" appears in the Thursday, July 21, edition of the *Nantucket Standard* and garners more reader response than any other article they've run this year. Summer visitor Donna Fenton, who stayed in the hotel with her family in the 1980s, *knew* there was something spooky about the place. Blond Sharon is intrigued not by the ghost but by the Matouk linens, the oyster-shell-tiled showers, and the blue cashmere throws from Nantucket Looms. Also, Sharon (who likes to know everything) had no idea there was a new adult pool out back. How can she get an invitation? She decides to book a room at the end of August for her sister, Heather, who is a world traveler and *very* discerning.

It just so happens that Yeong-Ja Park, a writer for the Associated Press, is staying on the island at her parents' home in Shimmo, and after she reads the article in the *Standard,* she writes an article about the haunted hotel as well. She tracks down half a dozen people who have stayed at the hotel over the past three decades, three of whom claim to have heard and seen things they couldn't explain. Yeong-Ja's article gets picked up by forty-seven newspapers across the country, from the *Idaho Statesman* to the *St. Louis Post-Dispatch* to the *Tampa Bay Times*. Some of the papers run the article right away; some save it for a slow news day.

Here on Nantucket, the excitement about the haunted hotel lasts only a scant twenty-four hours— because we have other gossip to discuss.

Something *very* scandalous has transpired on Hulbert Avenue. Rumor has it that Michael Bick, husband of Heidi Bick and the father of four, had an affair with their next-door neighbor Lyric Layton, and Lyric is now pregnant. This story is so salacious that Blond Sharon will be able to dine out on it all summer long. Apparently, Heidi Bick found Lyric's eye shadow in her makeup drawer, Lyric's René Caovilla stilettos in her closet, and Lyric's positive pregnancy test inside the Jennifer Weiner novel *Good in Bed*. (Is there symbolism in this choice of book? There must be!) Heidi invited the Laytons over for dinner on the deck, faking normality, but as soon as the first cocktail was poured, she confronted Michael and Lyric. It was a surprise attack so they couldn't confer and get their stories straight. Whoa, did this cause an uproar—mostly from Ari Layton, who had been mentally keeping track of how many times Michael checked out his wife these past few years. Ari had always suspected a flirtation between his wife and Michael but he was enraged to find out it was something far more. Ari had been so happy about Lyric's pregnancy (he was hoping for a little girl after three boys), but what if it turned out it wasn't his baby? Ari stood up, fists at the ready.

Both Michael and Lyric vehemently denied the accusation. They had never been together in any capacity, nor would they ever. Lyric was *appalled* that Heidi thought so little of her. She wasn't sure what her eye shadow, shoes, and pregnancy test were doing in the Bicks' house, but for the record, if she *were* having an affair with Michael, she wouldn't be stupid enough to leave those things behind!

Here, we had to admit, she had a point.

Michael claimed he was being set up. It was probably someone from his office who had found out he and Rafe were starting their own company. They'd sent a spy into the house. The guy who came to fix the internet, perhaps?

Ari said, "But how would anyone from your company get into *our* house? How would he know to take the eye shadow, shoes, and pregnancy test, which he must have found in our trash?"

Right, we thought. It made no sense.

Lyric was, by all accounts, calm but emphatic. She was happy to have the paternity of the baby tested as soon as that was an option. Michael, however, kept spewing conspiracy theories and generally acting like a man with a guilty conscience.

This made us wonder.

There has also been a shake-up at the Deck, one so disruptive that the restaurant announces a temporary emergency closing on Sunday, July 17. The Deck hasn't closed on a summer Sunday in fifteen years of operation. What is going *on?*

Romeo down at the Steamship Authority reports that he saw Christina Cross driving her bright orange Jeep onto the ferry, her belongings packed to within inches of the roof. It's Romeo's job to regulate that kind of thing—drivers are supposed to have a foot of visual clearance out the back window—but when Romeo approaches the car, he sees Christina is sobbing, so he waves her on. He has been doing this job for decades and knows a heartbroken woman leaving the island for good when he sees one.

Christina has left the Deck. Is that why they closed? Yes and no. Christina could easily be replaced by Peyton as hostess and Goose as sommelier. But Goose, who is JJ's closest confidant, tells his sister Janice, the dental hygienist, that JJ closed the Deck so that he could take a "personal day"—which involved a case of Cisco beer, a couple of three-way sandwiches from Yezzi's food truck, and a ride with Goose out to Great Point to fish. He told Goose that Christina had left, but that wasn't the problem. The problem, JJ said, was that he had gotten mixed up with Christina in the first place.

"I had the best woman I could have asked for," JJ said. "Lizbet was my friend, my confidante, someone I knew I could spend the rest of my life with. And I blew it."

"You blew it," Goose agreed.

17. Hot-Girl Summer

Business at the Hotel Nantucket has picked up considerably! Grace notes this with delight, and although it feels immodest to say, she knows it's all thanks to her. By the end of July, every room at the hotel is booked. Word has gotten out that the hotel is haunted by the ghost of Grace Hadley and everyone wants to experience the phenomenon. This is Grace's fifteen minutes of fame, and she can't afford to squander it. She's very busy in the nighttime hours making benign room visits. She knocks on walls, flickers the lights, messes with the electric shades (this is so much fun), and plays the guests' favorite songs out of nowhere.

These shenanigans delight the guests, but Grace begins to worry that cheap stunts will dilute her brand. Can she put her powers to better use? Yes! For example, seventeen-year-old Juliana Plumb wants to come out to her parents. They're staying in suite 314 and they've just had a lovely dinner at the Languedoc Bistro. As they were walking down the hallway toward their suite, Mr. Plumb teased Juliana about the cute busboy who had been flirting with her at dinner. Juliana looked uncomfortable, and Grace knows exactly why.

She watches Juliana stare at herself for a long time in the bathroom mirror after brushing her teeth. Grace marvels at how wonderful it is that one can just state one's sexual orientation and preferences in 2022. Back in 1922, well…Grace had a feeling that the hotel's GM, Mr. Leroy Noonan, preferred gentlemen, but he could never have said it. He was more "closeted" than Grace was!

Grace follows Juliana as she knocks on her parents' bedroom door.

"Come in," Mrs. Plumb says.

Juliana and Grace enter. Grace hovers close to Juliana, providing as much warmth and support as she can muster.

"I'm gay," Juliana says.

The Plumbs seem…taken aback. Mr. Plumb clears his throat; he exchanges glances with Mrs. Plumb. Grace nudges Mr. Plumb toward his daughter, and Mr. Plumb gets the hint and holds out his arms. "Juliana," he says. "We love you, sweetie."

"Thank you for trusting us enough to tell us," Mrs. Plumb says. "We'll support you any way we can."

My work here is done, Grace thinks, leaving the Plumbs to a group hug.

Grace discovers that the Elpines in room 203 have been experiencing some problems in the bedroom and that they're taking this vacation to "spice things up" and "reignite the romance" in their marriage. But despite the mood lighting and the fine linens, Grace reads the room and senses the Elpines are headed for disappointment—and, very likely, some counseling.

She positions herself just so in front of the full-length mirror and within Mr. Elpine's line of vision. Is he supernaturally sensitive? Let's hope so, for Mrs. Elpine's sake. Grace blows cold air toward Mr. Elpine and opens her robe. He looks over Mrs. Elpine's shoulder, and his eyes widen. It turns out that being watched by a beautiful, young, and naked female ghost is just the thing to cure Mr. Elpine of his chronic issue. Grace slips out, leaving the Elpines to get down to business.

Kimber goes to the Darya Salon at the White Elephant and returns with her hair dyed flame orange. Richie loves it, Wanda and Louie are nonplussed, and Doug the dog barks so sharply when he sees her that Kimber has to put on his muzzle (Grace is not unhappy about this). Now, nearly every night after the Blue Bar closes and Adam heads home, Kimber slips down the hall to the lobby to visit Richie. Their fooling around has gotten too serious for them to stay out in the open in the lobby—what if a guest should appear or one of the children wander down?—so they are constantly looking for more private places to be together.

Kimber suggests the fourth-floor storage closet, but thankfully, Richie shoots this idea down. "It's spooky," he says. He thinks they should go out to the adult pool and get busy on one of the extra-wide chaise longues. They try this, but although the chaises are sturdy, they aren't *that* sturdy, and Kimber complains about the mosquitoes. Kimber tries to lure Richie down to her suite but Richie is concerned about the children. They finally consummate the relationship in the break room. When Richie plays Marvin Gaye on the jukebox, Grace knows what's coming and floats out.

The break room becomes the regular site of their sneaky links. Grace notices that after Kimber heads back to her suite, Richie often falls asleep on the sofa, then jolts awake like he's being chased (Grace has nothing to do with this; she suspects it's his conscience at work). Sometimes he sits for long periods with his head in his hands; sometimes he goes into Lizbet's office, opens the safe, and stares at the piles of Kimber's cash (though Grace is happy to report he doesn't take a single dollar). He stays at the hotel until the birds begin to sing, then he slithers out the side door like a cat burglar.

Kimber tells Richie that she has to go off-island overnight the following week to meet with her divorce attorney, and she doesn't want to take the children with her. She asks Richie if there's any way he can sleep in her suite after he's finished work and spend the two days that Kimber will be away with the children.

Yes, of course! Richie practically shouts. He'd love to!

Kimber tells Richie that the best way to acclimate the children to him staying over while she's away is for him to stay overnight in their suite on a regular basis while she's there.

"The children will be fine with it," Kimber says. She has spent so much time in the sun that her once-wan skin is now subtly golden, and her hair holds appealing beachy waves. She's also, Grace notes, glowing from within. "They won't blink an eye."

"Well, that may be so," Richie says. "But it's against the rules. Staff aren't allowed to sleep with the guests, Kimber."

"Let's go talk to Lizbet," Kimber says.

"We can't," Richie says. "I'll get fired."

Kimber laughs. "You work seven nights a week! You barely even go home! She's not going to fire you, because she'll never, ever find anyone to replace you. We're consenting adults. We'll ask permission. Lizbet will understand."

Mmm, Grace thinks. This is a gamble. Lizbet has been known to stretch some rules, but to blatantly break one like a stick over her knee? Grace watches as Kimber leads Richie by the hand to the door of Lizbet's office. They enter together, Richie hanging back slightly, like a delinquent child.

"Good morning, Lizbet," Kimber says. "Just so you know, Richie and I are having a summer romance and some nights he'll be sleeping with me in the suite. We know this is technically against the rules."

"More than technically," Lizbet says, and Grace thinks she's going to nip it in the bud, but then Lizbet gazes at Richie and Kimber, and her face softens. "But at this point, you're more family than guest…"

"Ahh! That's so sweet of you to say." Kimber beams. "That's how the children and I feel too."

Richie clears his throat. "I promise to put work first, as always."

"Absolutely," Lizbet says. "So no bothering Richie at night anymore, Kimber, okay? He can come to your suite when he's off the clock. Richie, just please be discreet."

"Of course," Richie says.

Lizbet clears her throat. "I would never want anything inappropriate happening in, for example, the break room," she says.

MARIO'S PLAYLIST FOR LIZBET

"Love Walks In"—Van Halen
"Strange Currencies"—R.E.M.
"Kiss"—Prince
"Next to You"—The Police
"OMG"—Usher
"Girlfriend"—Matthew Sweet
"Can't Feel My Face"—The Weeknd
"Dreaming"—Blondie
"In a Little While"—U2

"Killing Me Softly"—The Fugees
"Soulshine"—Martin Deschamps
"The Guy That Says Goodbye to You Is
Out of His Mind"—Griffin House
"Nothin' on You"—B.o.B.
"Loving Cup"—The Rolling Stones and
Jack White
"Are You Gonna Be My Girl"—Jet
"Sister Golden Hair"—America
"Never Been in Love"—Cobra Starship
"Sleep Alright"—Gingersol
"Here Comes the Sun"—The Beatles
"Sexual Healing"—Marvin Gaye
"Summertime"—Kenny Chesney

Lizbet feels like a bubble in a flute of champagne; her outlook is golden and effervescent. It's as though all of her inspirational memes have come true at once.

First of all, the hotel is *thriving*. The article written by Wanda Marsh—an eight-year-old kid; you just can't make this stuff up—started a chain reaction that led to stories about Grace Hadley's ghost being printed in newspapers *across the country!* The phone rang nonstop and the website *crashed* from all the traffic. (Lizbet was tickled by this development, inconvenient though it was. The Hotel Nantucket had *broken the internet!*) Having a busy hotel feels joyous; it feels like a celebration. Every day when Lizbet walks into the lobby, she's entering the buzziest, most interesting room on the island.

Guests gather in the lobby for the percolated coffee (the richness of the coffee is mentioned time and again by guests on TravelTattler) and the almond croissants (ditto). They read the paper, start conversations, ad-mire the James Ogilvy photograph, and watch Louie play chess (Louie shows up every morning at seven o'clock sharp, hair combed, glasses polished, little polo shirt buttoned to the top). The chaises by the pool are claimed by ten a.m.; the complimentary shuttles that run to the south shore's beaches are full. Lizbet has had the piano tuned and every night before his shift, Adam comes in and plays show tunes while the guests enjoy the wine and cheese hour; people make requests, sing along, and slip Adam tips. After dinner, many guests forgo the lines at the Chicken Box and the Gaslight and instead choose to sit on the front porch of the hotel. They light up the fireplace tables, buy s'mores kits from the front desk, and indulge in their gooiest marshmallow dreams.

Lizbet would like to believe the hotel has finally hit its stride, but she knows the reason for the renaissance is…the ghost. But once potential guests have their interest piqued by the story of Grace Hadley, they check out the website and see the driftwood-and-rope canopy beds with the dreamy white sheers, the lavish bouquets of lilies and Dutch hydrangeas, the slipper tubs, the adult pool with the wall of climbing roses, the free minibar, and the carved teak ceiling in the yoga studio, and they think: *I'd like to stay here*.

The influx of guests includes the poet laureate of New Mexico, a family of ranchers from Montana, a mushroom grower from Kennett Square, Pennsylvania, a neurosurgeon from Nashville, the owners of an NHL expansion team, a renowned hip-hop producer, a YouTube phenom, and a prominent editor from one of the Big Five publishing houses in New York City. This editor reads Lizbet's Blue Book and says she'll pitch it. She gets Lizbet's e-mail address.

The secret of change is to focus all your energy not on fighting the old, but on building the new.

Lizbet is so busy that hours and even days go by when she forgets to be on the lookout for Shelly Carpenter. *Now* is when Shelly Carpenter will show up; Lizbet is sure of it—and Lizbet is also sure that if Shelly slipped in under the radar in the past couple of weeks, she was met with exceptional service. Edie, Alessandra, Richie, Zeke, Adam, and Raoul are all at the top of their games.

The only thing going better than Lizbet's professional life is her love life. Every day Lizbet goes to Mario's cottage on her lunch hour. They make love and then he cooks for her—composed salads with grilled shrimp and creamy chunks of avocado and a side of the homemade cheddar crackers that they used to serve at the Blue Bistro or, on a rare day of rain, clam chowder and giant popovers pulled straight from the funny little oven. Sometimes Lizbet brings a bathing suit and they swim off of Mario's front porch, and then she showers and braids her damp hair. When Mario comes in to work at four o'clock, he swings by her office with a double espresso—he figured out that the way to her heart is caffeine—and he often brings her a little gift: a cluster of roses, a perfect quahog shell, a grape Popsicle. He makes her a playlist to replace her breakup playlist. Lizbet closes her office door and they kiss like a couple of teenagers for a few stolen minutes before Lizbet straightens her skirt and Mario his chef's jacket and they get back to work. When Mario gets home from the bar at night, he sends Lizbet a text: I'm home, Heartbreaker. Or Sweetest dreams, Heartbreaker. He has her in his phone as *HB. Breaker, not broken!* she thinks. She's healed. She's *so* healed that when she hears that Christina left JJ, she feels only a pang of pity for JJ; she could have told him that relationship would end badly. She considers calling to see if he's okay but decides it's best not to. She's consumed with her romance with JJ's idol, the man whose picture she gazed at on the wall of JJ's office for fifteen years. It's the kind of crazy plot twist that happens only in novels and movies—but she's living it. She can't believe how happy she is.

But then.

Then a night comes when Mario doesn't text when he gets home from work. Lizbet wakes up at three in the morning to use the bathroom, checks her phone, finds nothing. *What?* she thinks. She can't fall back to sleep. The room is too hot; her mind is aswirl. Did something happen? Is Mario okay? Should Lizbet call him? Should she go to his cottage? She somehow knows she should do neither. She wonders then why Mario never asks to spend the night at her cottage. She lies awake until the birds start to sing, thinking that *this* was why Mario said they should be careful. (What he'd meant, of course, was that *she* should be careful.)

He was probably tired, she thinks. He forgot to text. So what?

The next day, Monday, Lizbet goes to the cottage for lunch as usual and everything is fine. The Blue Bar is closed on Tuesdays, and Mario asks if Lizbet can take the day or even just the afternoon off so they can spend it together.

It's exactly what she's craving, but the hotel has seventeen checkouts and seventeen check-ins, and Yolanda long ago requested every Tuesday off and Lizbet needs to be around to manage Warren, the fitness instructor who fills in, because he can be a little ditzy.

On Tuesday evening, the Blue Bar has a softball game against the Garden Group. After Lizbet finishes work, she drives out the long stretch of Milestone Road to the Tom Nevers Field to catch the last couple of innings. It's a close game even though the landscapers are young and in shape and play like real athletes. Mario is wearing an old Ramones T-shirt and his White Sox cap and when he gets up to bat with the bases loaded, he winks at Lizbet. She flushes, feeling like she felt when she was sixteen and watching her boyfriend, Danny LaMott, play for the Minnetonka Skippers football team.

Mario strikes out swinging and Lizbet is almost relieved that he didn't hit a home run and win the game, because she realizes she's dangerously close to falling in love with him.

Yolanda is up next. As Lizbet is wondering why Yolanda is on the Blue Bar softball team—and then if the hotel should field its own team, and then who would work if they did field a team—Yolanda wallops a pitch over the centerfielder's head and everyone on base scores. Lizbet is on her feet cheering along with the rest of the crowd when Yolanda crosses the plate, jumps into Mario's arms, and gives him a kiss on the lips. Suddenly, Lizbet feels not only like an outsider but also really freaking jealous.

From that moment on, Lizbet becomes *hyperaware* of Mario and Yolanda. Yolanda has always made frequent visits to the Blue Bar kitchen, and Lizbet assumed that Yolanda needed frequent snacks to fuel her exercise. Yolanda often walked past the desk holding an acai bowl or chia pudding, neither of which was on the menu. The Wednesday after the softball game, Yolanda emerges from the Blue Bar holding a tiny pavlova on the flat of her palm like it's a baby bird. She shows it off to Lizbet and Edie. It's filled with rose-scented pastry cream and topped with candied rose petals. "Is this not the most exquisite thing you've ever seen? Mario made it for me."

"Did he?" Lizbet says.

Yolanda strolls away, taking a lusty bite of the pavlova; she can eat whatever she wants and still maintain that slender, supple yoga body, which is reason enough to envy her. Zeke joins Lizbet and Edie in watching Yolanda descend the stairs to the wellness center.

"You know why she spends so much time in the kitchen, right?" he says.

"Why?" Lizbet and Edie say together. Lizbet gets the distinct feeling the bubble she has been living in is about to pop.

Zeke arches his eyebrows and takes a breath to say—what? But then a large party enters the lobby and Zeke, Edie, and Lizbet snap into guest-service mode.

A couple of days later, Lizbet is at Mario's cottage for lunch. It's too hot to cook, so Mario slices up a ripe, juicy melon and serves it with burrata and some salty prosciutto. They go for a swim and shower together afterward. Lizbet is delirious with happiness, thinking, *Yolanda who? Yolanda what?* Poor Yolanda has been mistakenly cast as the villainess in Lizbet's mind. She's going to let the Yolanda thing *go*.

While Mario is in his bedroom getting dressed, his cell phone on the kitchen counter, right next to where Lizbet is winding the last strip of prosciutto around the last crescent of pale green melon, dings with a text. The screen says Yolo. The text is printed in the alert: Hey, can you help me with a thing later? Followed by the winking-tongue-out emoji.

Lizbet feels the prosciutto repeat on her. She has to fight the urge to pick up the phone and check the text stream—Mario has no passcode, so she could easily do this, and then at least she'll know what's going on rather than stumbling around in a dark uncertainty— but at that moment, Mario calls out, "You getting ready to leave, HB? It's ten of two."

Lizbet doesn't respond. Mario pokes his head out of the bedroom and says, "Everything okay?"

"Yes," Lizbet says. "You got a text."

Mario takes his time ambling across the room. He scoops up his phone, checks the text. There's no change in his expression; he just slips the phone into the pocket of his houndstooth pants and heads for the door. He always walks her out the creaky dock back to her car. Lizbet tries to keep her panic on a very short leash. *Hey, can you help me with a thing later?* What kind of thing? Lizbet wonders. What kind of help? How much later? What about that emoji? It's the lewd face, the wink and lolling tongue. It can only mean something naughty. And what's up with "Yolo"? Has Lizbet ever heard *anyone* call Yolanda this? No. Lizbet is so consumed with these thoughts that she doesn't speak, and when Mario squeezes her hand and asks again if everything is okay, she lies and says yes.

The following Tuesday, Lizbet can't take off because the plumber is coming to fix a leak in the laundry room, and the water throughout the hotel has to be shut off for ninety minutes. Lizbet needs to be there to field the inevitable complaints.

Mario goes to Nobadeer Beach with his staff and when he comes to pick Lizbet up for their dinner date that night—they're going to the Pearl—he's not only deeply tan, he's a little drunk.

Lizbet teases him about it and he says, "I played beer die on the beach with some of the kids from the kitchen. It was a good day. And man, Yolanda can really surf."

"Oh," Lizbet says. "Yolanda was there?"

"She was shredding like Alana Blanchard."

"I don't know who that is," Lizbet snaps.

Mario doesn't notice her tone because they have entered the tranquil garden setting of the Pearl chef's table. It seats ten but Mario has reserved it for just the two of them, a lavish gesture. Lizbet has sat at this table before with JJ and some of the staff of the Deck and she's eager to replace those memories. Mario pulls out her chair. He's here with *her,* she reminds herself. Not Yolanda. She orders a passion-fruit cosmo.

The magic of the chef's table is that dishes just *appear*—lobster rangoons, tuna martinis with wasabi crème fraîche, the sixty-second steak topped with a quail egg, the wok-fried salt-and-pepper lobster. Because Mario is, in this world, Super Mario, each course comes with a pitch-perfect wine pairing. Lizbet drinks a little more robustly than she probably should, but who can blame her? Yolanda made it clear when the hotel opened that she wanted Tuesdays off. Is that merely a coincidence? Yolanda is only twenty-nine years old, nearly ten years younger than Lizbet, nearly twenty years younger than Mario. She's not only beautiful with a perfect body but she has the kind of luminous personality that draws people in. Why *wouldn't* Mario be attracted to Yolanda?

When dessert is set down—glistening chunks of fresh mango served with coconut sticky rice, Lizbet's absolute favorite—she can only stare at it and think, *Don't say it.* But she has held the topic at bay throughout dinner and the wine has done nothing but nourish her fears.

"You know what I was thinking?" Mario says.

"You should add caramels to your s'mores kits. Take it up a notch."

Don't say it, she thinks.

"I don't mean to overstep. I know the hotel amenities aren't mine to tweak, but you have to admit, a caramel s'more? That sounds pretty damn good."

"Mario?" she says. "Are you dating other people?"

Mario's eyes jump up from the dessert plate to meet hers. "Why are you asking me that?"

She holds his gaze. Their relationship is still so new that she's made a little dizzy by how attractive he is— those bedroom eyes, the sly smile—but she realizes she doesn't know him well enough to tell if he's been hiding something.

She shakes her head. "Never mind. I'm drunk, I think."

"Okay," Mario says. "I'll get the check." He turns around, the check appears; Lizbet tries to give him her credit card but he hands it back without saying anything. Is he upset? Has she ruined the evening? There's no way Yolanda's myriad daily visits to the kitchen and her presence with the Blue Bar staff on their day off is a coincidence. *Something* is going on. Hey, the text said, indicating a previous conversation, a context, can you help me with a thing later? The help is sexual, the thing is Yolanda's desire for him, and later is after service at the restaurant. The smutty emoji speaks for itself. Why doesn't Mario ever ask to come to Lizbet's cottage after work? *Because he's dating Yolanda as well.* He has Lizbet for lunch and Yolanda for a midnight snack. *Why are you asking me that?* That answer isn't a firm no—it isn't any kind of no. Lizbet wants to press him, but she's not sure she'll believe him if he says he's not seeing anyone else and she won't be able to bear it if he says yes, he is dating other people, because they never explicitly stated that they were exclusive.

Mario warned Lizbet to be careful but she dove headlong into a new relationship. As if her previous relationship hadn't hurt her badly enough. She's such an idiot. She hasn't learned a thing. And she hasn't changed.

Lizbet makes it out of the restaurant and down to Mario's pickup. Once they're both sitting in the dark truck, he looks at her. "What's going on, Heartbreaker?"

"Don't call me that," she says, though she loves the nickname.

"Do you want to come back to my place so we can talk this through? Or would you like me to take you home?"

Lizbet stares into her lap. *Talk this through.* That seems to indicate there's something to talk through. Of course there is. All Lizbet can see when she closes her eyes is Yolanda jumping into Mario's arms at home plate, Yolanda kissing him right on the lips. And the blasted text: Hey, can you help me with a thing later? That hideous emoji face (it's the emoji that bothers her the most). "Home, please."

They drive in silence to Bear Street and Lizbet can feel the cab of the truck filling with his confusion, but he says nothing and she's grateful. When they pull into her driveway, she knows she can still salvage things—invite him in, hope he stays the night. But instead she says, "I haven't been careful. I let myself feel too much too soon. And because of what happened with JJ, I need to take a step back. It's for my own mental well-being."

Mario covers her hand with his. "I'm feeling a lot of things too, Lizbet."

Lizbet shakes her head. "You're not feeling the same things I'm feeling."

Mario laughs. "You don't know that. Why did you ask if I was seeing other people?"

Lizbet shrugs. She can't say Yolanda's name. "It's just a sense I get."

"Your sense is wrong."

Maybe it is, maybe it isn't, Lizbet thinks. "I can't get hurt again, Mario."

"Lizbet, come on. How about a little faith?"

She glares out the windshield at her tiny shingled cottage, a cottage she bought with someone else. She had faith once upon a time. It didn't work out.

Mario sighs. "Is it okay if I walk you to the door?"

She doesn't answer but he does it anyway, giving Lizbet one last chance to change course. Why can't she just treat this relationship like an easygoing summer romance with great sex, water views, and delicious meals? It started out that way...but then there were the roses he brought her in the *Tom and Jerry* jelly jar and the lunch when he cried telling Lizbet about his cousin Hector who died of liver cancer. At another lunch, Lizbet was so tired that she skipped sex and skipped eating and just fell asleep on Mario's bed, and she woke up an hour later to him kissing her eyelids, and he handed her a brown paper bag with a home-made *pan bagnat* for her to take back to the hotel. She thinks about how he called Christina "Tina" and how he never starts the car unless she has her seat belt fastened and how he holds her face when he kisses her, his fingertips always grazing her earlobes. All of these things accumulated and now, suddenly, Lizbet finds herself losing her grip on her good sense. *Something* secret is going on with Yolanda; maybe it's unspoken or unpursued, but there's a fondness, a flirtation, and

Lizbet is both jealous and disappointed in herself for being jealous. She has to get out. Now.

Mario gives her a kiss that is tender enough to make her change her mind—and she nearly relents. How can she give this up? But in the end, she pulls away. "Good night, Mario."

"Good night, Heartbreaker," he says.

July 25, 2022
From: Xavier Darling (xd@darlingent.co.uk)
To: Employees of the Hotel Nantucket

Good morning! I just want to let you know how encouraging it is that the world has discovered the hotel and that reservations are where they should be: at 100 percent occupancy. The reviews on the TravelTattler website are a testament to everyone's hard work and dedication. But this week, one staff member was mentioned above all others, and once again that was Alessandra Powell. Keep up the good work, everyone!

XD

Every time Grace sees Alessandra enter a gentleman guest's room at night, she steers clear. Alessandra is sleeping with the guests—Mr. Brownlee, Mr. Yamaguchi, Dr. Romano—in exchange for them writing TravelTattler reviews that specifically mention her, a ploy that has so far earned her four thousand dollars in bonus money.

However, when Grace sees Alessandra go up the side stairs with a man named Bone Williams, she gets a dreadful feeling. She's annoyed by this—the last person she wants to rescue is the little witchy-witch Alessandra—but her foreboding is too strong to ignore.

When Bone Williams checked in, Grace saw flashing red lights and heard an obnoxious alarm sounding, but she chalked this up to toxic masculinity. (*Bone, what a name,* she thought. *Another man referencing his penis!*) He arrived on the first car ferry of the day, stormed into the lobby at half past nine, and asked Edie *why the hell* there was no valet parking and what was he supposed to do with his *Corvette Stingray* because he couldn't just *leave it on the street!*

Edie was the model of calm patience. She told Mr. Williams that the hotel had only twelve parking spots and those were reserved for people staying in the suites. Bone then told Edie with a barely concealed snarl that he had *tried* to get a suite but *they were all booked!*

"You can't penalize me for that!" Bone Williams was on the short side but very muscular (he probably "lifted"). Grace would put him at thirty-five or so, which felt young for his level of entitlement. "My room had better be ready."

"It's nine thirty," Edie said. "Our guaranteed check-in time is three p.m. But we'll do our best to get you in long before that, Mr. Williams."

"*Three o'clock!*" Bone shouted. "You have *got* to be"—he swallowed a word—"*kidding me!*"

"We have a complimentary continental breakfast, which you can enjoy on the porch, or I can have it delivered to you at the adult pool," Edie said. "Or, if you'd like to stroll into town for breakfast, we *highly* recommend the Lemon Press on Main Street."

"I'm not 'strolling' anywhere," Bone said. "I want to check into my room, not wander the property like a hobo when I've paid good money to stay here. And I need a secure spot for my Stingray."

"I'll contact you as soon as your room has been cleaned," Edie said. "Unfortunately, the guests in that room haven't checked out yet."

"Don't give me that crap," Bone said. "Let me speak to your manager."

At this point, Edie smiled. "Certainly." She turned to Alessandra. "Mr. Williams, this is Alessandra Powell, our front-desk manager."

Alessandra said, "You drive a Corvette Stingray? Wasn't that the pace car for last year's Indy Five Hundred?"

Bone's demeanor instantly changed. "It was, yes." He slid over to Alessandra's position at the desk and drank in her appearance. Her hair was braided with a hydrangea-blue scarf woven through, and she was wearing the white eyeliner and eye crystals that seemed to mesmerize every man she spoke to, including Bone Williams. "Hey, your name tag is upside down." He did the unfunny shtick of craning his neck, trying to read it. "Alessandra."

Grace gave a ghostly eye roll. *Every single man Alessandra has checked in this summer has said exactly the same thing.*

Alessandra jotted something down on a yellow sticky note and Grace read it over her shoulder: *Yes,* followed by a phone number.

"I'm fairly certain that the couple staying in suite two seventeen have come with bicycles only," Alessandra says. "So let me see if you might be able to use *their* parking spot."

"Oh, man," Bone said. "That would be…amazing." He plunked down his Centurion card and his driver's license, which gave a Park Avenue address in New York City.

Humph, Grace thought.

"I'm afraid Edie was correct about your check-in," Alessandra said. "But a Bloody Mary by our pool is a very pleasant way to start your Nantucket vacation, and I can pop out in a little while to check on you." Alessandra ran the Centurion card and matched the picture on his license to his face with a wink.

Bone softened like a butter statue in the sun (Grace had learned about butter statues from listening to Lizbet; it was a Minnesota thing). "I don't care about the room. Just please tell me you'll have dinner with me tomorrow night at Topper's. I'll take you up there in the Ray, but I can't promise I'll stick to the speed limit."

Alessandra pressed the sticky note to Bone's license before handing it back. "I'm afraid dating the guests is against our rules. I wish I could. I love Topper's, and who *wouldn't* want a ride in that car?"

Bone read the sticky note and grinned. "My loss, then," he said. "Figured it couldn't hurt to ask."

Alessandra secured suite 217's parking spot for Bone Williams's Corvette, and Grace assumes they did go for dinner at Topper's. Now Grace watches Bone and Alessandra going up the side stairs—most likely, Alessandra wants to avoid Richie and Adam, who are working in the lobby. When they reach room 310, Bone shoves her inside.

Grudgingly, Grace follows them.

Bone Williams is drunk. (Topper's is almost ten miles away along the curving Polpis Road, and Grace shudders to think about him driving home in that sports car in this state; Alessandra, frankly, is lucky to be alive.) Bone pushes Alessandra onto the bed and reaches under her dress, a vintage Diane von

Furstenberg wrap in a gorgeous print (Alessandra has impeccable taste, Grace has to give her that). Alessandra deftly knocks his hand away and says, "Hey, now, play nice."

"You ordered a five-hundred-dollar Barolo at dinner," he says. "You owe me."

"You asked me to pick the wine," Alessandra says. "You told me you wanted something extraordinary. And, as I'm sure a man like you knows, extraordinary comes at a price. If I was on a budget, you should have told me."

"Budget?" Bone says like it's a dirty word. He pulls Alessandra across the bed toward him as she tries to scoot to the other side. "You little whore." He rips open the front of her dress and Grace winces but doesn't intervene. Some people like rough sex; she has been haunting the hotel long enough to know this.

When Bone unzips his pants, Alessandra says, "No. I'm saying no. I'm leaving, Bone."

"You're not going anywhere," Bone says. He grabs Alessandra's wrists and pins them over her head. Despite Alessandra's thrashing—she isn't screaming, so she must be worried about getting caught—Bone holds her tight. He reaches up her skirt. This is such a drastic situation that Grace knows lights and music and the shades won't stop him. She coils all of her energy until it's as dangerous as a packed snowball with an icy core and hits Bone Williams in the jaw. Bone staggers back, giving Alessandra a chance to scramble off the bed. When he grabs her shin, she kicks him in the face, bloodying his nose. She runs out the door and down the hall to the third-floor storage closet, where she catches her breath and assesses the damage. She has bracelets of red fingerprints around her wrists; her dress is in shreds; she has lost a shoe. Alessandra strips down and puts on one of the hotel robes and a pair of slippers. Tears are streaming down her face, and when she wipes them away, she stares at her fingers as though she can't figure out why they're wet.

She peeks out the closet door. She wisely decides not to go past room 310, instead sneaking down the stairs at the opposite end of the building and, from there, out into the night.

You owe me one, missy, Grace thinks. She feels depleted. She's getting too old for this.

But even so, Grace can't resist the urge to mess with Bone Williams's lights, play Tiffany's "I Think We're Alone Now" at top volume, raise and lower his shades, and blow arctic air into the space where his heart is supposed to be.

18. Last Friday of the Month: July

The first shot of Shelly Carpenter's July Instagram post is of a mannequin bust sitting on an antique trunk in slanting rays of sunlight—and Lizbet wonders if maybe she has the wrong account. But then she double-checks the header and reads the caption. *Ahh,* she thinks. She clicks on the link in the bio just as Adam (who has come to the hotel specifically so he can dish with them) and Edie step into her office.

Together, they read.

Hotel Confidential by Shelly Carpenter
July 29, 2022

Sea Castle Bed-and-Breakfast, Hyannis Port, Massachusetts—3 KEYS 🔑

Hello again, friends!

There are bed-and-breakfast people...and then there is yours truly. However, in the spirit of reviewing every kind of lodging, I bring to you my thoughts on the Sea Castle B and B in the bustling hamlet of Hyannis Port, Massachusetts, on storied old Cape Cod.

Sea Castle is a Victorian mansion that was restored by its owners to meticulous period detail in 2015. It has eight guest rooms and a first-floor living-and-dining common area that offers a breakfast of champions each morning between eight and nine.

My room, on the second floor, had a king-size canopy bed that was so high off the ground, an actual wooden step was provided. There were, in my humble opinion, too many layers of bed linens for summertime—a top sheet, a velveteen blanket, a duvet, and a heavy brocade coverlet. The other furnishings were straight out of Grandmother's house in a fairy tale—an Eastlake dresser covered with a faintly stained doily, a rocking chair, and a trunk at the foot of the bed. When I opened the trunk, I found a bald, featureless bust that startled me so badly, I dropped the lid of the trunk and smashed a finger. What was a bust doing in the trunk of my room? When I asked the proprietress, she told me the original owner of the house had been a milliner, and that was her hatmaker's dummy.

This, friends, is my number-one issue with a B and B: you're living in someone else's home.

I felt churlish asking that the head-and-shoulders be removed; however, ask I did.

The bathroom was tiny with no surface for toiletries, so I placed mine on the back of the toilet, a decision that landed my moisturizer in the bowl. The bathroom had a fuzzy pink rug, and, friends, you know how I feel about rugs or carpeting of any kind in bathrooms. The sink's drain was sluggish, and the shower, while giving decent pressure, was subject to sudden drastic changes in temperature (probably due to the Hubertsons, on the same floor, flushing their toilet).

Although I bristled at the strict timetable for breakfast, I was in my seat promptly at eight. The proprietress brought out freshly squeezed orange juice and a fruit salad that included blueberries, raspberries, blackberries, sliced peaches, and fresh figs. (She won me over with the figs.) The "main course" was a mushroom, herb, and gooey Brie frittata with a side of crisp bacon and a golden hash-brown patty. Also on offer were banana pecan muffins and cheddar scones. The breakfast was the most delicious I've eaten in my life—yes, friends, better than the croissant with butter and apricot jam at the Shangri-La in Paris, better than the congee at the Raffles in Singapore—but my infatuation with the food was mitigated by the need to chat with the proprietress and the Hubertsons about which shop in town had the best penuche fudge and how much of a rip-off the whale-watching trips were. By the end of the meal, I was longing for the freedom and anonymity of a proper hotel.

In the end, I balanced the mediocrity of the Sea Castle accommodations (the sluggish drain, the unsettling contents of the trunk) against the extraordinary breakfast, and I arrived at three keys. Those of you who love quilts, stained glass, oak sideboards, cross-stitch, green-apple-scented candles, "country charm," and good-hearted chitchat may have arrived at four keys, but on this point we'll have to differ.

Stay well, friends. And do good.

—SC

"I can't believe she went to a *bed-and-breakfast*," Adam says. "Has she ever done that before? Next thing you know, she'll be reviewing Airbnbs."

"I thought she was harsh," Edie says. "My mom wanted to buy the Winter Street Inn a few years ago when Mitzi Quinn put it up for sale, but my dad talked her out of it. It's a lot of work, running those places. I like bed-and-breakfasts. I think they're quaint and cozy."

Adam groans. "Death by cross-stitch."

Lizbet happens to agree with Adam but she won't weigh in; she has something bigger on her mind. "Hyannis Port," she says. "Shelly Carpenter is getting closer."

19. The Blanket, the Belt, the Burglary

August 1, 2022
From: Xavier Darling (xd@darlingent.co.uk)
To: Employees of the Hotel Nantucket

Happy August, team! I'm pleased to offer this week's thousand-dollar bonus to a different staff member: Raoul Wasserman-Ramirez. Raoul's excellent service at the bell stand was extolled by a large family who recently stayed with us. He went above and beyond the call of duty to meet their needs and always had a smile. That's what I like to hear!

I'll be seeing you all in just a few weeks!

XD

August is the least favorite month of most people who work in the summer service industry—and Lizbet is no exception. July is merely a dress rehearsal for the flat-out theater-of-the-absurd production that is August. That was true at the Deck—every table every night was booked with a VIP. Lizbet once had to say no to Blake Shelton and Gwen Stefani requesting a table for eight because she simply couldn't bump one of her regulars (but it killed her to do it).

At the hotel, August is just as full as July—you can't get any fuller than full—but the clientele is more demanding. A woman named Diane Brickley *insists* that Edie rent her "the room you keep vacant for VIP walk-ins." Edie comes to Lizbet and says, "I need your help. Alessandra is on lunch."

"Still?" Lizbet says. Alessandra has been pushing the envelope where lunch is concerned—the day before, she was gone for ninety minutes, and when Lizbet spoke to her about it, Alessandra shrugged and said, "Fire me."

Which, of course, Lizbet couldn't do. Not in August.

Lizbet pokes her head out her office door. Diane Brickley is, Lizbet would guess, nearly eighty years old. She looks like one of the ladies who eat lunch every day on the patio of the Field and Oar Club. She's wearing a knee-length Nantucket-red skirt that she probably bought at Murray's Toggery back in the 1960s—it's faded to pale pink—a yellow slicker, and a rain bonnet (the forecast did call for thunderstorms, but out the front doors of the hotel Lizbet sees golden sunshine). There's an antique Nantucket Lightship basket hanging from Diane Brickley's forearm. Lizbet realizes that Diane Brickley *is* one of the Field and Oar ladies, and she sits on the board of directors at the Nantucket Lightship Basket Museum. She lives at 388 Main Street.

"Hello, Mrs. Brickley, it's Lizbet Keaton."

Diane waves a hand. "At least somebody here knows me. I have my daughter visiting with her four teenage sons and I can't handle the noise, the smell, or the mess. Please put me in the room you save for visiting dignitaries."

Hotels do not keep rooms vacant for VIP walk-ins; that's a myth. "I'm sorry, Mrs. Brickley," Lizbet says. "We're full. We don't have a single room available."

"Full?" Mrs. Brickley says. "The White Elephant is full, the Beach Club is full, and the Wauwinet is full, but I thought for sure you'd have a room available. Isn't this place haunted?"

Guests have been posting their "visits" from the ghost of Grace Hadley all over social media. Nothing that Grace does shows up on anyone's camera, but these people get likes and follows and reposts anyway. Derek White, a fourth-grade teacher from Shaker Heights, reported seeing a ghost reflected in his dark bedroom window; he claimed she was wearing "one of the hotel bathrobes and a Minnesota Twins cap." A few days later, guest Elaine Backler was applying eyebrow pencil when she saw a "floating robe and navy baseball hat" in the mirror behind her. (Lizbet is certain Elaine must have heard about Derek's sighting and was corroborating it to stoke intrigue. The detail about the Twins cap, though, nags at Lizbet. She misplaced her own navy Minnesota Twins baseball cap sometime during her first week of work and it hasn't turned up.)

The *Washington Post* calls, then *USA Today,* but all Lizbet can tell them for sure is that a chambermaid was killed in a fire at the hotel a hundred years earlier. Is Grace Hadley now haunting the hotel? "It's anyone's guess," Lizbet says lightly. The phone rings nonstop; people have started booking rooms for the following summer.

Lizbet wants to tell Mario about this—tell him he was wrong that the hotel might be a flash in the pan; Lizbet is half full for next June already—but she has consciously avoided any situation in which she might see Mario. She hasn't texted or called. He called her once at midnight, waking her up; it took extreme willpower but she let the call go to voice mail, and he didn't leave a message. He also sent Beatriz to the front desk with a bakery box—the homemade pizza rolls, the gougères, the doughnuts—and Lizbet brought it directly to the break room for everyone else to enjoy.

She longs for him every second of every day.

Her new obsession is monitoring Yolanda's trips to and from the Blue Bar kitchen. Yolanda seems to go mostly in the morning and the afternoon, and Lizbet knows that Mario doesn't arrive until four (or, when he wanted to make out with Lizbet in her office, three thirty). Yolanda also visits the kitchen in the late afternoon right before service starts, so this is when Lizbet watches her most closely. Does she seem ravished? Not really. She's as serene as always, and she's never weird or tense around Lizbet. One day, she stops at the desk and gives Lizbet an appraising look, and Lizbet thinks, *Here it comes. She's going to say: I'm so sorry, I didn't realize, I hope you can forgive, I never meant to hurt...*

Yolanda says, "You look like a person in need of a yoga class. How about thirty minutes in savasana pose?"

Lizbet manages a smile. Although Yolanda is right, Lizbet can't imagine ever practicing with her again, not after all this. "I'm fine, thanks," she says. "It's just August."

Lizbet worries beads along a mental string: *Mario, Mario, Yolanda, Mario, Yolanda.*

But then something steals her full attention.

It's eleven o'clock on Thursday, August 4, and the lobby is popping. Louie is playing Mr. Tennant from room 201 in chess and the match is so close, there's a little crowd around them; it includes Richie and (an exasperated) Kimber Marsh, who are waiting for Louie to finish so they can all go to the 167 Raw food truck for tuna burgers and then to Cisco Beach. Edie is on the phone with the Galley, trying to secure a beachfront lunch reservation for room 110, and Alessandra is calling the Hy-Line to make a reservation for the Keenan family, who somehow neglected to arrange for their transport home.

Lizbet is about to head to the percolator—it will be her eighth cup of coffee, which is a lot, even for her—when she notices a woman enter the lobby. This woman is dressed in the best kind of casual way: cute jeans, a white blouse that's as crisp as paper, and gladiator sandals. She's rolling in a hunter-green Away carry-on, which is the exact same bag that Lizbet travels with. Her dark hair is cut in a bob at her jawline and she's wearing chic glasses. None of this is particularly remarkable, but Lizbet gets a feeling. The woman stops just inside the entrance to the lobby to look around. She whips out her phone and begins to take pictures and type notes. Lizbet hurries over.

"Welcome to the Hotel Nantucket," she says. (Adam always sings this; it's a fun touch, but Lizbet can't pull it off.) "May I help with your bag?"

"Thank you," the woman says. She follows Lizbet to the desk, where she pulls out her Washington, DC, driver's license and a Delta SkyMiles Platinum American Express, both in the name of Claire Underwood.

Claire Underwood. Washington, DC. *House of Cards*! Lizbet thinks. (Lizbet and JJ watched all six seasons.) Here's what Lizbet has been waiting for: an inside-joke alias. Lizbet tries to act natural. She wishes that she could let Edie and Alessandra and Raoul and Adam and Zeke know that *Shelly Carpenter is in the house!* They should have come up with a secret signal word, like *Amsterdam* or *unicycle*. Why did Lizbet not think to do that? They all knew this day would come. Shelly posted her review of the bed-and-breakfast in Hyannis Port only five days earlier. Maybe she popped over to the Vineyard to check out the Winnetu or the Charlotte Inn and now she's here on Nantucket. She's purposely arrived at eleven in the morning, which is the most frenetic time of the day because of guests checking out. Lizbet quickly reviews the reservation: three nights in a standard deluxe room, paid in full, booked on July 5 (the day of Lizbet's first date with Mario, she can't help thinking). "Claire Underwood" booked long before all the brouhaha about the ghost.

Lizbet says, "It's so wonderful to have you staying with us, Ms. Underwood. Are you visiting Nantucket for any special reason?"

Claire/Maybe-Shelly smiles. "Just a quick getaway," she says. "I was curious about the hotel."

Lizbet bites her lower lip to keep from giving Claire/Maybe-Shelly an unhinged grin. "There are a few things you should know about our property. Technically, check-in is at three—"

"I understand," Claire/Maybe-Shelly says.

"But I'll try to get you into your room as soon as possible." Lizbet goes on to tell Claire/Maybe-Shelly about the adult pool and the wellness center, and then she hands Claire/Maybe-Shelly a copy of the Blue Book. "This lists all of our recommendations for shopping, restaurants, beaches, galleries, bars, and nightlife. If you have any requests, please let me know." Lizbet realizes with horror that she has forgotten to introduce herself. "I'm Lizbet Keaton, the general manager."

"I do have some requests, actually," Claire/Maybe-Shelly says, pulling a piece of paper out of her cute woven clutch. "First off, would it be possible for me to get a room upgrade?"

A room upgrade? Lizbet thinks. The hotel is full! But she understands that Claire/Maybe-Shelly *has* to ask; it's what savvy travelers (and famous hotel bloggers) do. How will they ever get the fifth key if Lizbet can't accommodate this request? *They won't* is the answer.

Then Lizbet realizes that they do have one free room: Xavier's suite, which is awaiting his arrival on August 24. Richie has asked Lizbet why she doesn't rent the room out, since they know Xavier's dates, and Lizbet said she wouldn't feel right. Xavier asked her to hold it for him; he's been paying the nightly rate all summer. Lizbet is certain that the day she agrees to let someone take Xavier's suite, Xavier will appear out of the blue for a surprise visit.

But Shelly Carpenter is a special case. *I bought the hotel to impress two women.* If Lizbet *doesn't* offer Shelly the owner's suite, she reasons, Xavier will be furious.

"I can upgrade you to the owner's suite," Lizbet says, and she watches Claire/Maybe-Shelly's eyebrows lift.

"Excellent, thank you," Claire/Maybe-Shelly says. "I also have these requests." She slides the piece of paper across the desk.

Thursday 7:30 p.m. Pearl bar seat
Friday 7:00 p.m. Nautilus bar seat

Saturday 8:00 p.m. Blue Bar bar seat
Four-door Jeep Wrangler hardtop Satur-
day, please also arrange pickup of
charcuterie platter from Petrichor
Stand-up paddle lesson, Friday noon
Tour of Cisco Brewers, Friday 5:00 p.m.
Yoga class before 10:00 a.m. Friday
through Sunday

"I'll handle all this right away," Lizbet says. She's relieved the Deck isn't on Claire/Maybe-Shelly's list. "Do you have any other luggage? I'll have Zeke, our bellman, bring it up to you right away."

"No," Claire/Maybe-Shelly says. "Just this."

"Well, then, give me a few minutes to have house-keeping prepare your room and I'll walk you up myself. We have complimentary Jamaica Blue Moun-tain coffee in the percolator."

"Fantastic!" Claire/Maybe-Shelly says. "I missed my coffee this morning. And I love percolated coffee. It's such a nice touch." A cheer goes up from the chess match. Louie has beaten Mr. Tennant. Lizbet takes this as a good omen. The hotel will win Claire/Maybe-Shelly over. They will get the fifth key.

What's not a good omen is the icy silence on the other end of the telephone line when Lizbet calls Magda to tell her to prepare the owner's suite, 317, for a guest checking in.

"That's Xavier's suite," Magda says.

"Mr. Darling's, yes," Lizbet says. "But since he's not here…"

"I would strongly advise against putting anyone in Xavier's suite," Magda says. "He's paying to keep it empty."

"Shelly Carpenter is here," Lizbet whispers. "She asked for an upgrade."

Magda clears her throat. "You're sure it's her? Beyond a shadow of a doubt?"

"No one is ever *sure*. But there's been more than one indication."

"Fine. Give us fifteen minutes to stock the minibar, dust, and plump the pillows for Ms. Carpenter."

"You need to do more than that," Lizbet says. "You need to run through the checklist. What if there are cobwebs? What if the windows stick? What if the sound system is doing that funny stuttering thing? And make sure the pens work and that the sink drains properly."

"Perhaps you'd like to come up and do my job for me?" Magda asks, and Lizbet presses her lips together. Lizbet suspects that although she is Magda's boss, Magda sees it as the other way around.

"Not at all, Magda," Lizbet says. "Thank you."

She has quietly informed the staff that the woman posing as Claire Underwood who is staying in suite 317 might very well be Shelly Carpenter. Lizbet has also told the staff not to overdo it. The last thing they want is for Claire/Maybe-Shelly to think her cover is blown and figure out she's receiving special service. If that happens, she won't write the review at all.

From the looks of things, Claire/Maybe-Shelly is having a wonderful time. She drinks the percolated coffee in the morning, takes an interest in Louie's chess matches, raves about her yoga class with Yolanda, rides one of the free bikes into town to shop and get lunch at the Beet; she lounges by the adult pool, takes her tours and lessons, and heads out for her solo dinners stylishly dressed (Lizbet's favorite look is white jeans, a sleeveless black bodysuit, and leopard-print wedges).

Late on Saturday afternoon, Claire/Maybe-Shelly stops by the front desk and says, "Where did you source those blue cashmere blankets? I'd like to get one to take home."

"Nantucket Looms," Lizbet says. She checks the time. "They're closed now but they open tomorrow at ten."

"Darn," Claire/Maybe-Shelly says. "My flight leaves at ten."

"Let me see what I can do," Lizbet says. She goes to the second-floor housekeeping storage, where they keep half a dozen extra blue blankets. Lizbet wraps one up in hydrangea-blue tissue. Is she being too obvious, too heavy-handed? Will Claire/Maybe-Shelly see the blanket for what it is—a bribe?

Lizbet takes the risk and presents Claire/Maybe-Shelly with the blanket the next morning when she checks out. Claire/Maybe-Shelly seems genuinely overcome by the gesture—so thoughtful, thank you, her stay at the hotel has been an utter delight.

"I'm a pretty tough customer," Claire/Maybe-Shelly says. "But I've never been as won over by a hotel stay as I have by this one."

Yes! Lizbet thinks. *Yes-yes-yes-yes-yes-yes!*

After Claire/Maybe-Shelly walks out the front door, trailing her Away carry-on behind her, Lizbet wants to high-five her staff, but she exercises restraint. They can all celebrate on the last Friday of the month when the Hotel Nantucket becomes the only property to ever receive five keys. For now, Lizbet will remain…cautiously optimistic.

The next morning, Edie knocks on Lizbet's office

door. Claire Underwood is on the phone and has asked for Lizbet personally. Something's up.

In the housekeeping office, Magda assigns Octavia and Neves the first-floor checkouts, but instead of sending Chad and Bibi to the second floor, she closes the office door.

"The two of you were responsible for the checkout of suite three seventeen yesterday, were you not?" Magda asks.

"We were," Chad says. He was, frankly, amazed that Magda assigned him and Bibi, rather than Octavia and Neves, to the owner's suite, but he took it as a vote of confidence. They've been doing good work— but yesterday, only Chad did good work. Bibi was in a foul mood, and when Chad asked her what was wrong, she said that her "baby-daddy," some dude named Johnny Quarter, had left the state without a trace, and with him went the five-hundred-dollar-a-month child-support payments. She had her aunt report Johnny Quarter to domestic relations, who issued a summons.

"But doing that doesn't get me my money," Bibi said.

She spent most of the time in suite 317 working like a person underwater. The owner's suite was bigger and grander than the other suites in the hotel. The Nantucket-night-sky mural was painted in finer detail; the library had brass rails and a sliding ladder to reach the upper shelves. There was a separate dressing room, and the second bedroom was an elegant study complete with a built-in desk; on the walls hung prints of the hotel in the early twentieth century. There were cream-and-blue Persian carpets instead of rainbow-hued Annie Selke rugs throughout, and the bathroom included a steam sauna. It was very extra.

"Why did they rent out this room?" Bibi asked. "The owner isn't here."

"I guess they thought Shelly Carpenter showed up," Chad said.

"I have no idea who that is," Bibi said.

"She has this Instagram account and blog called *Hotel Confidential,*" he said. "Don't you follow her?"

"Why would I follow something called *Hotel Confidential*?" Bibi asked, and Chad thought, *Because you work in a hotel?* But he had to admit, he'd never heard of the *Hotel Confidential* blog. Chad checked it out and fell down the rabbit hole, scrolling through a bunch of Shelly's past posts and clicking on her bio to read the reviews. Shelly Carpenter had been *everywhere*—to the Angama Mara safari camp in Kenya and the Malliouhana in Anguilla and Las Ventanas al Paraiso in Cabo—but she also reviewed more modest places, like motels on Route 66 and beach bungalows in Koh Samui, Thailand. The way she described these places was so detailed and precise that Chad felt like he'd been there too. It was exciting to think that she'd been to their hotel (maybe, no one could be sure). He wondered what she was going to write about the place.

"Well, it's a thing, she's internet-famous, and Lizbet offered her this suite as an upgrade."

"Internet-famous?" Bibi said. She paused. "Why don't you do the bathroom, Long Shot. I'll finish the bed."

Ms. English says, "The guest called to say she left behind a black suede Gucci belt. I went through the suite myself but didn't find it." Ms. English gives them both a death stare. "Did either of you see it?"

"I didn't see a Gucci belt," Bibi says. "Or any belt. Have you checked the laundry?"

"Yes, Barbara," Ms. English says and both Chad and Bibi stiffen. Has Ms. English ever used Bibi's real name before? No. They're in trouble, Chad thinks. Bibi is in trouble. Bibi took the Gucci belt, of course—just like she lifted Mrs. Daley's Fendi scarf. At some point when Chad was cleaning the bathroom of the owner's suite, he noticed the door had been closed behind him. He heard the vacuum running and he'd nearly poked his head out to check on Bibi. The reason he *hadn't* checked on Bibi, he admits to himself now, was that he hadn't wanted to know if she was actually vacuuming or just using the noise as a cover. She was upset about money, the loss of five hundred dollars a month, the specter of having to pay a private investigator to track down the baby-daddy. The guest in the room, Claire/Maybe-Shelly, had left a sixty-dollar tip, and as always, Chad told Bibi to just take the whole thing, which she did with her usual attitude of entitlement even though half of it was rightfully his.

But apparently that hadn't been enough. She had taken Claire/Maybe-Shelly's Gucci belt.

"What did the belt look like?" Chad asks.

"Black suede with a rose-gold double-G buckle," Ms. English says.

Bibi probably already has it up on eBay or Craigslist, Chad thinks. *She'll get six hundred bucks because those belts cost close to eight hundred.* Chad knows this because his mother has a Gucci belt and it's an egregious habit of hers to fake-complain about exactly how much her wardrobe costs.

"This is the second incident I've had with you two where something has gone missing."

Bibi glowers at Ms. English, her eyes like two cold, clear marbles. "I bet you haven't asked Octavia and Neves about it, have you?"

"They didn't clean the room," Ms. English says.

"But they have a master key!" Bibi says. "I'm telling you, they're trying to frame me."

This is the same outrageous claim Bibi made last time; it feels like a little kid pointing a finger at the playground. But her face shines with such indignant anger that Chad entertains that possibility for a second. Octavia and Neves seem like nice girls, but what if they *are* plotting to get Bibi fired?

Because he fears that's exactly how this is going to end.

"If it doesn't turn up by tomorrow," Chad says, hitting these words hard so Bibi gets the message, "can we just replace it?"

"I've already looked online," Ms. English says. "That particular belt, with the rose-gold buckle, has been discontinued." She looks from Chad to Bibi and back. "I don't have to remind you that this was a VIP guest, nor do I have to remind you that if and when a guest accidentally leaves something behind, it does not belong to you. It goes directly to the lost and found."

Chad bobs his head while Bibi scowls. He can't believe she isn't more concerned. If she loses her job, she's sunk.

"I was crystal clear that this was never to happen again," Ms. English says.

"Maybe the ghost disappeared it," Bibi says. "Did you think of *that*?"

"If the belt doesn't turn up by tomorrow, there will be consequences," Ms. English says. "Do you hear me, Barbara?"

As Chad and Bibi head up to the second floor with their cleaning cart, Bibi says, "Why do you think she said only *my* name?"

"Bring it back tomorrow, Bibi," Chad says. "We can hide it down in the laundry."

"You think I took it too?" Bibi says. "Really, Long Shot?" She looks so wounded that Chad again wonders if maybe he's wrong. Maybe Bibi didn't take it. Maybe it was Octavia and Neves. Or possibly Claire/Maybe-Shelly put it in a side pouch of her luggage and she'll find it next week when she flies to Dubai or Cartagena and she'll call the hotel to apologize. Or maybe the person pilfering the luxury goods is...Ms. English.

Ha! he thinks. *No, it's Bibi.*

When Chad gets home from work, he finds the driveway of his house lined with cars and, parked in Chad's usual spot, a van from the Nantucket Catering Company. He tries to recall the date and realizes it's Monday, August 8. Are his parents having their annual 8/8 cocktail party despite what happened? The answer is obviously yes—but the fact that neither Paul nor Whitney mentioned it to Chad (did they?) means his presence might not be expected, which is a relief. It also makes what Chad has to do far easier.

He enters the house and hears conversation, laughter, strains of Christopher Cross (his mother is having a moment with yacht rock) coming from the deck out back. Chad takes a second to see who's in attendance—Bryce's parents from Greenwich, Jasper's parents from Fisher Island, Paul Winslow's business partner Holden Miller from the Brandywine Group, and Leith and her friend Divinity, who are wearing matching LoveShackFancy dresses. Chad again racks his brain, but he has no recollection of hearing about this party. He's offended that his parents are having it. He understands they want to proceed as though nothing has happened, but a *party? Really?*

Chad hurries up the stairs. He might tell his parents he skipped the party in protest or that he didn't feel like he deserved to celebrate the eighth of August, considering what he'd done. He heads into his parents' room, the master suite, which is a universe unto itself. There's the actual bedroom, then there's his mother's sitting room, his father's upstairs study, the palatial marble bathroom complete with Jacuzzi tub for two, and his-and-her walk-in closets. Chad goes to his mother's closet—he hasn't set foot in here since he was eight years old, when they moved in—and tries to guess where Whitney keeps her belts. Her hanging clothes take up three walls of the room, and the fourth wall is floor-to-ceiling cubbies for shoes. There are…*sixty-four* pairs of shoes, *here,* on *Nantucket,* where a woman could make it through the summer with sneakers, flip-flops, and one pair of sandals.

He tries not to think about Paddy.

In the center of the walk-in is a free-form structure of drawers and shelves where Whitney keeps folded things—light sweaters, pashminas, T-shirts, her yoga clothes. There's also a tall, slender dresser by the door. Chad avoids the two top drawers, assuming they hold his mother's underwear, and opens the third drawer. It's socks and stockings. The fourth drawer holds clutch purses; there are half a dozen. Chad gets on his knees and opens the fifth drawer, which holds—bingo!—belts. They're coiled up like sleeping snakes and Chad pulls them out, one by one: Hermès, Tiffany, Louis Vuitton, and—yes, he just can't believe his luck, he really can't believe it—a black suede Gucci belt with a rose-gold double-G buckle. He doesn't have to think twice; he takes it.

On his way out, he gazes down at the party from his parents' picture window. The sun is setting, making all of the vivacious, well-dressed guests look like *they've* been dipped in rose gold. He thinks about how easy it would be for him to change into madras shorts and a pink oxford and slip through the crowd, shaking hands, making eye contact, saying, *Yes, sir, good to see you, sir, definitely looking forward to working with my father in September. I can't wait to dive into the world of venture capital.*

Chad knows he could quit his job tomorrow and be finished with Bibi's kleptomania and her complaining; he would never have to scrub another toilet, fold another towel, or see another hair wrapped around a bar of soap. He could golf all day, then drink a Mount Gay and tonic and eat mini–crab cakes with people who talk only about Wimbledon and their stock portfolios. But he can't pretend May 22 never happened. He has to do penance. That's what his job at the hotel is all about—it's an atonement. Maybe Paddy will never learn about Chad's job, or if he does, maybe he won't care. But Chad is going to keep at it anyway. He *likes* living a life of purpose.

He wraps his mother's belt around his fingers like brass knuckles and heads down the hall to hide in his room.

The next morning, Chad leaves for work an hour early. No one notices; his parents and Leith are all still asleep. (They were rocking out to Bob Seger and Madonna until almost midnight, and when his mother inevitably knocked on his bedroom door and asked him to "come down and make an appearance, please, Chaddy, people are *asking* about you," he said he'd be down in a minute, knowing his mother would forget—and she did.)

Chad arrives at the hotel at seven and uses the

service entrance, the belt inside an old L. L. Bean backpack of Leith's that he found in the mudroom. He waits until Joseph, who runs the laundry, goes on a cigarette break, then he buries the belt in one of the big rolling baskets of dirty linens.

Not all superheroes wear capes, he thinks. He's always wanted to say that about himself, but of course, he never had a reason. Until now.

At the start of his shift fifty-five minutes later, Ms. English announces that the Gucci belt has been located in the laundry.

"It *has?*" Bibi says.

"You sound surprised, Barbara," Ms. English says.

"Not surprised at all," Bibi says. She's a liar and a thief, Chad thinks. But he admires her audacity and he hopes she got a good price for Claire/Maybe-Shelly's belt. "I knew it would turn up."

Lizbet finally connects with Heidi Bick, who suggests they go to the Blue Bar for dinner. Lizbet says, "I will eat literally anywhere else. I have to get out of this building."

"But not the Deck?" Heidi says.

"Not the Deck either, I'm sorry." Lizbet *could* return to the Deck now that Christina is gone. In a weak moment, Lizbet texted JJ to ask how he was doing and he replied, I miss you. Lizbet had stared at that text long and hard but she didn't feel angry, she didn't feel sad, and she didn't miss him back.

She misses Mario.

Lizbet and Heidi meet at Bar Yoshi on Old South Wharf. They're seated at a high-top by the windows that overlook the harbor. The restaurant has a spare, chic vibe with lots of light wood, a floating glass-fronted cabinet that holds the liquor bottles, and excellent woven-basket light fixtures. Lizbet loves this place; she plans to completely overdo it on the sushi.

She feels good. She is out, finally, with a girlfriend.

Lizbet orders sake, Heidi a tequila cocktail, which is unusual for her—she's a devoted rosé drinker.

"Everything okay?" Lizbet asks.

Heidi's eyes widen. "You mean to tell me you haven't heard the rumors?"

"I have no one to hear rumors *from,*" Lizbet admits. "I'm always at work. I never see anyone from my old life."

"Well, *I* heard you were dating Mario Subiaco," Heidi says. "Someone saw the two of you at the Pearl."

Their drinks arrive and Lizbet raises her sake glass to Heidi's highball. "I'm glad we did this."

They touch glasses and drink. Heidi inhales nearly half her cocktail in one gulp.

"The thing with Mario didn't work out," Lizbet says.

"It was a good rebound, though, right?" Heidi says. "He's so *hot.* And such a legend."

Lizbet doesn't want to talk about how hot or legendary Mario is. "So tell me about the rumors," she says. "I'm ready."

But as it turns out, Lizbet is not ready.

"You remember how I told you Michael was up here all spring by himself working on a project? He and this guy from his office, Rafe, want to splinter off and start their own company."

Lizbet definitely remembers that Michael was here alone. Oh, does she.

"Well, when I showed up in June, I found an eye shadow in my makeup drawer that wasn't mine."

"Oh," Lizbet says. She already doesn't like where this story is going.

"Then I found a pair of René Caovilla stilettos in my closet. Size six."

What? Lizbet thinks. There's only one woman brave enough to wear René Caovilla stilettos here on Nantucket: Lyric Layton, Heidi's best friend. In her life before husband, children, and yoga, Lyric was a shoe model in New York.

"Lyric?" she says.

"And *then* I found a positive pregnancy test tucked into the pages of the book on my nightstand."

"You did *not*," Lizbet says.

"As I'm sure you've heard, Lyric is newly pregnant with her fourth."

Lizbet has *not* heard. The hotel really is a fortress. "So you think there was something going on between Michael and…Lyric?" This is smoking-hot scandalous news. No *wonder* Heidi is drinking tequila! Along with curiosity, Lizbet feels relief that the mistress wasn't Alessandra.

"That's what I *thought,* yes. That's how someone wanted to make it look."

"So it *wasn't* Lyric?"

"Lyric swears not. She said if she and Michael were having an affair, there would be no way she would leave those things behind for me to find."

Right, Lizbet thinks. *No way.*

Heidi throws back another healthy swallow of her drink. "We have a key to the Laytons' house labeled on a hook in our mudroom. Michael thinks someone from his company found out that he and Rafe were planning on leaving and set out to sabotage him."

Lizbet blinks.

"Michael thinks the guy he called to fix our Wi-Fi

was actually a spy who saw the key—because, you know, the router is *in our mudroom*—and this guy burgled the Layton house while they were out and then planted those things in our house."

"Michael thinks the cable guy did it?"

"Internet guy."

"Wow," Lizbet says. She brings her sake to her lips; her guard is back up. There's no chance a man would know to plant an eye shadow, shoes, and a pregnancy test. "Well, I guess you're relieved it has nothing to do with Lyric."

"Yes, definitely," Heidi says. "Though it did real damage to our friendship. She's angry that I suspected her." Heidi leans in. "But you have to admit, it's a hard story to swallow, that the internet guy set Michael up."

Lizbet nods. *Very hard to swallow,* she thinks. *Like, a handful-of-steel-screws hard to swallow.*

Heidi sighs. "But Michael is in the world of petroleum and you know how ruthless *that* is."

Is it the kind of ruthless that would stick someone else's pregnancy test inside a book on Heidi's nightstand? Lizbet wonders. Or plant a different brand of eye shadow, a different type of shoe?

No, Lizbet thinks. It wasn't the internet guy and it wasn't Lyric. It could have been some woman that Michael was sleeping with, a woman he met on the ferry and decided to let stay awhile because it was raw, chilly spring on Nantucket and he was always up for a little action with a beautiful woman and because Michael essentially gambled for a living and because this other woman was wily and had no morals. Alessandra saw the key to the Laytons' house and she'd probably gathered through eavesdropping or casual conversation that the Laytons next door were close friends, and *she* burgled the Laytons' house so that when she vacated the premises, Heidi would think Michael was sleeping with Lyric.

"I'm having the ramen," Heidi says. "What about you?"

"I haven't even looked. I want sushi." But Lizbet can't think about sushi. She isn't sure what to do. Should she tell Heidi what Alessandra said about meeting a "friend" on the Hy-Line back in April and staying with him on Hulbert Avenue? Should she describe following Alessandra by bike and being caught by Alessandra *right in front of Heidi's house?* Should she then mention how Alessandra is a casual liar who showed up with sketchy references (all of them European, like she's the Talented Ms. Ripley)? Should she tell Heidi how Alessandra is so startlingly beautiful that she's managed to overwhelm the hotel's male guests?

It's a proper quandary, one meant for an advice column. *If I suspect a friend's husband was cheating on her with someone I know, do I tell her? Or do I let her believe that it wasn't a mistress but rather a revenge plotted by her husband's nefarious work colleagues?*

The affair, Lizbet reasons, is over. Heidi and Michael are settling back into their summertime routine of beach and tennis and driving the kids to camp and going out to dinner. Who is Lizbet to disrupt their lives on a hunch? She has no actual proof it was Alessandra.

But one thing is for sure: Lizbet is going to start watching Alessandra more closely.

"The spicy tuna roll looks good," Lizbet says. "And let's get some sashimi."

August 8, 2022
From: Xavier Darling (xd@darlingent.co.uk)
To: Employees of the Hotel Nantucket

Good morning, all—

This week on TravelTattler I noted a lovely review of our hotel that expressly mentioned bellman Ezekiel English. This guest praised Ezekiel's intimate knowledge of the island, including the recommendation of Stubby's to satisfy our guest's late-night case of the "munchies." Outstanding job, Ezekiel!

XD

Edie and Zeke are, once again, eating ice cream together in the break room when Raoul pops his head in and says, "Congrats, Zeke. You won the bonus this week."

"I did?" Zeke says, and Edie thinks, *He did?*

They check their phones, and sure enough, there's the letter from Xavier.

Zeke laughs. "Those guests were plastered; they'd just gotten back from the Chicken Box and the dude was starving. I guess he assumed there would be chicken at the Chicken Box—"

Edie offers a lame smile that Zeke doesn't seem to notice.

"But since we all know there is not one piece of chicken at the Chicken Box, I sent them to Stubby's. And he wrote about it. Ha!"

Ha, Edie thinks. Her crush on Zeke has only grown more excruciating with each passing day, but that doesn't stop her from feeling bitter that he won the money for recommending Stubby's, which is essentially Nantucket's version of a McDonald's drive-through.

"Why were you even working night bell?" she asks. "Where was Adam?"

"It was the night he and Raoul went to the White Heron to see that play," Zeke says. "I covered Adam's shift."

He deserves the money, Edie thinks. He worked a double so Adam and Raoul could have a date night. She feels resentful that she can't even be properly resentful.

Zeke tosses his nearly full bowl of ice cream into the trash. "I'm going to run to Indian Summer and see about a new longboard," he says. He gives Edie's shoulders a squeeze. "Your boy is *hyped!*"

Edie would normally be glowing from the half-hug and the use of the term *your boy,* but once Zeke leaves, Edie feels bereft.

Then something on her phone catches her attention.

August 8, 2022
Abigail Rashishe—Cornell School of Hotel Administration Alumni Facebook Page

Warning to my fellow hotelies and especially to anyone who shares my obsession with Shelly Carpenter (I assume this means everyone): There's a woman at large who is imitating Shelly Carpenter. She shows up solo and presents IDs in various obvious aliases. When she checked into the Woodstock Inn (where I've recently been promoted to FDM!), her ID said Diana Spencer. She asked for a room upgrade, presented a written list of requests, and did that thing of trying to subtly take photos and type notes into her phone. I'm not ashamed to admit that I was completely fooled. I bent over backward to get "Diana Spencer" a room upgrade and I even gifted her a bathrobe after she asked where we sourced them. I was aghast when "Diana Spencer" called the next day to say that she'd left a Prada raffia tote behind. We couldn't find the tote—our house-keeping staff hadn't seen it—but nevertheless, we offered to replace it, which cost us over a thousand dollars. (Of course we replaced it—we were dealing with Shelly Carpenter, or so we thought!)

THEN a couple days later I heard from class-mate Chayci Peck ('21), who's the concierge at Round Pond in Kennebunkport, Maine. Chayci had a woman come in with an ID that said Miranda Priestly and who went through the same motions with room upgrade, list of requests, and sourcing questions in order to get free merch. A day after "Miranda Priestly" checked out, she called Round Pond claiming to have left behind a gold Tiffany-T bangle, and when the housekeeping staff couldn't find it, they too replaced it, free of charge.

This woman is NOT SHELLY CARPENTER! She's a con artist! I'm posting this so that no other hotel falls for her ploy. Shelly Carpenter has the dubious distinction of becoming such a phenom that she now has an imitator.

Could this day get any worse? Edie wonders. She too tosses her ice cream and goes to knock on Lizbet's office door.

Lizbet reads the Facebook post and groans. "Are you *kidding* me?"

When Chad hears the news, he can't wait to tell Bibi: Claire/Maybe-Shelly, the woman who stayed in the owner's suite, was an impostor and *there was no missing Gucci belt, it was a scam.*

"So *now* you believe I didn't take it?" Bibi says.

"I'm sorry," Chad says. "I just couldn't figure out...and I know you like nice things..."

"I'm not a thief, Long Shot," Bibi says. "I have a *daughter*. I need to set an *example*."

"I thought maybe you did it because you needed the money."

"I do need the money," Bibi says. She narrows her eyes at him. "If it was a scam, then where did the belt that Ms. English found in the laundry come from?"

Chad is tempted to say, *Must have belonged to someone else,* but instead, he blurts out the truth. "That belt was my mom's. I took it from her and planted it in the laundry because I didn't want you to get in trouble."

Chad isn't sure what kind of response he's expecting—maybe a thank-you, maybe "Aren't you sweet"—but Bibi just barks out a hard, one-syllable laugh. "Who's the thief now?" she says.

20. Here Comes Trouble

Edie sends out ten résumés to other hotels, including the Little Nell in Aspen (Edie's mother, Love, worked there in the nineties) and the Breakers in Palm Beach. Edie has decided to work somewhere else only for the winter season because she wants to come back to the Hotel Nantucket next summer. Lizbet has told her they're already full for certain weeks in June and July. Zeke said he's coming back next year as well—he's going to spend the winter surfing in Costa Rica—and Adam and Raoul are returning.

The only person who hasn't committed to coming

back is Alessandra. Maybe she'll turn tail and run back to Italy, Edie thinks—although she has to admit, Alessandra has mellowed a bit recently. Adam told Zeke that Alessandra has been staying in every night, eating dinner in her room with the door closed.

"Something happened with her, I think," Adam said. "But she won't tell us what."

Edie is on the desk one gloriously hot and sunny afternoon by herself. Alessandra is at lunch and everyone else is at the beach or the pool or biking to Sconset for ice cream or hiding from the sun at the Whaling Museum. Edie has a moment to check her phone just to see if all ten of her cover letters and résumés went through on her e-mail—and that's when she sees the Venmo request from Graydon for a thousand dollars.

Edie huffs out a short, indignant laugh. The nerve of him. No, really, the nerve! Edie isn't sure why—maybe because she now has a plan for her future, maybe because working the desk has made her more confident, maybe because she has Lizbet as a role model—but she decides in that moment that she has *had* it. She will be bullied no longer! She deletes the Venmo request and sends Graydon a text: We're finished. Leave me alone.

Three dots surface on the text stream immediately and Edie gets a hot, prickly feeling as she imagines Graydon typing.

His response: Pay me or I'll send the videos to all of your prospective employers.

Edie gasps softly and looks around the lobby. It's cool and serene; Jack Johnson is singing about turning the whole thing upside down. Edie hears splashing from the family pool and a moped going by out on Easton Street. She starts to shake. *How* does Graydon know about her résumés going out?

Well, he must have access to her e-mails and maybe her texts as well, maybe her entire cloud. Did she ever give him the password? No, but it wouldn't be difficult to guess: Nantucketgirl127 (her birthday).

She's tempted to call him but that will end one of two ways: with her screaming or with her crying and begging. He *knows* she has student-loan payments. He *knows* Edie and Love's financial future is uncertain. Love actually asked Lizbet if she could use one more person on the desk (Love did it under the pretense of "offering help," but she needs the money), and Lizbet snapped her up, so now Edie's mother is going to be working one night shift a week to give Richie a break. Graydon also knows that Edie's shame about what she did, what she *agreed to,* is deep and painful and that she'll do anything to conceal it.

Through the blur of tears, Edie takes inventory of the lobby. No one needs her; the phones are quiet. Zeke is stationed by the door in case of emergency.

Edie runs to the break room, and as soon as the door closes behind her, tears fall.

"Edie?" a voice says. "Are you okay?"

Alessandra is sitting at the counter with…some kind of craft project in front of her. Both this and the unexpected concern in Alessandra's voice stop Edie from going into a full-blown meltdown.

"Fine," Edie says, wiping quick fingertips under her eyes. She approaches Alessandra as she would a venomous snake and peers at the project before her. It's an eighteen-inch frame, the inside of which is spread with some kind of adhesive. Alessandra is pressing in broken pieces of pottery and colored glass. She has only half the square completed, but from where Edie is standing, it looks kind of like…

Alessandra says, "I'm making a mosaic."

"I didn't know you were crafty," Edie says, and this makes Alessandra laugh.

"I'm not, particularly," Alessandra says. "I just wanted to try my hand at this. It's harder than it looks. You have to lay down the pieces and hope that when you step back, it makes the whole you're looking for."

"It's a woman's face," Edie says. "It looks like you. Is it you?"

Alessandra shrugs. "I've always thought of mosaic as this big metaphor for my life," she says. "All these jagged, incongruous pieces…" She holds up a small shard of milky jade-green glass. "These are like the things that happen to you. But if it's laid out a certain way and if you take a step back from it, it makes sense."

Edie thinks about her own life: growing up the beloved child of two wonderful parents on an island where she felt safe and nurtured and championed, where she was such a success academically that she was accepted to an Ivy League college. Cornell was its own dreamscape. Edie loved the hotel school, her classes, her professors, the guest lecturers from New York City and Zurich and Singapore, and the natural beauty surrounding the campus. There was nowhere prettier than Cascadilla Gorge in the autumn.

But then, in January of her junior year, Edie returned from her facilities-management lecture to find Love and the dean of students sitting together on the bench in front of her dorm. When they saw Edie approaching, they both stood up, and Edie nearly turned and ran. She knew her mother hated to drive on the mainland, especially in winter—Edie's father was the one who always brought her back and forth; he had dropped her off just a few weeks earlier. Love never would have made the seven-hour trip from Hyannis to Ithaca under anything but urgent circumstances. There was also an unfamiliar expression on Love's face: a mixture of grief and dread. Edie dropped her backpack on the path and raced into her mother's arms, knowing before Love even said the words that her father was dead.

Edie took ten days off from school, and when she returned, she had acquired the questionable mystique and celebrity of someone who had undergone a tragic loss. Students whom Edie knew only tangentially, including Graydon Spires, the most popular and successful student in the hotel school, offered condolences. Everyone talked about Graydon's poise, his charm, his silver tongue, his social savvy. Edie's best friend, Charisse, once remarked, "It's almost freakish the way he *always says the right thing*." And not only did he say the right thing, Edie learned as she got to know him, he also always struck the right emotional note. He wasn't a conversational skater, he didn't speak simply to fill silence, he didn't do small talk. He listened and responded in a genuine and intelligent way. When he turned his light on Edie—asking her out for a midnight snack of burgers and coffee at Jack's ("I'm guessing you're not sleeping much these days")—she fell in love.

They grew close very quickly. ("Too quickly," Charisse said. She was offended by Edie's sudden abandonment—within days of the date at Jack's, Edie was *always* with Graydon.) When junior year ended, they both accepted summer jobs at Castle Hill in Newport, Rhode Island. They worked at the hotel's front desk and found they were *dynamic* together. The atmosphere in the lobby all summer was electrifying; the air crackled with the barely sublimated sexual and romantic energy between Edie and Graydon. They tried to outdo each other in customer service in a good-natured way, and the guests (and management) ate it up. They scheduled Wednesdays off together, when they did all the Newport-y things: went to Annie's for lunch, hung out on Thames Street, did the Cliff Walk, sailed on the hotel's Sunfish, biked around Fort Adams. Edie couldn't believe how Graydon had appeared just when she needed him most. She imagined the life they would have after they graduated—they would work together in hotels in Alaska, Australia, the Azores. They would climb their way up the corporate ladder at a major hotel chain—or they would start their *own* hotel chain. They would get married and have babies.

When they returned to Ithaca for their senior year, Edie was tapped to be the student director of the Statler Hotel—a very, very big deal. When Edie told Graydon, she expected him to pick her up and swing her around like it was the end of the war in a movie; she thought he'd take a selfie with her and post it on his Instagram with the caption *#girlboss*. But right away, she could see...he was jealous and resentful.

It was right after this that Graydon started asking for things in bed, things Edie wasn't entirely comfortable with—and eventually was mortified by—but she consented because she felt she had to *apologize* for her success. Graydon recorded everything they did—he told her that made it "way hotter"—and Edie, who wanted only to please him, did what he wanted and recited her lines.

As Edie stands before Alessandra and her half-finished mosaic, she gets a text from Graydon. It's a picture of a box of Pocky, the long chocolate-covered cookie sticks from Japan, and Edie feels a wave of nausea roll over her. She rushes into the one-person bathroom and can't decide whether to cry or throw up. She does a weird hybrid of both, desperately hoping that Alessandra will be gone when she emerges. *Please,* Edie thinks, *pack up your mosaic and leave.* The mosaic of Edie's life would be cute around the edges—bits of rose-colored glass and hand-painted bone china—but in the middle would be a chunk of tarry asphalt, black and oozing.

When Edie steps out, Alessandra hands her a bowl of vanilla soft-serve ice cream topped with M&M's, which is Edie's go-to snack. Edie didn't realize Alessandra even knew her go-to.

"Sit," Alessandra says. "Tell me what's wrong. I want to help."

For two months, Edie and Alessandra have worked side by side, and Alessandra has only been a hostile nation, the Axis to Edie's Allies. Alessandra's unyielding coldness has caused Edie hours of anxiety and, she's not afraid to say it, a little heartache. It's not fair for Alessandra to be nice *now,* when Edie has finally grown immune to her being not nice.

But Edie wants to tell someone, and who else does she have? She no longer speaks to Charisse (thanks to Graydon), she can't tell her mother, she couldn't possibly confide in Lizbet, and she can't tell Zeke.

Edie picks up the spoon just so she'll have something to do with her hands. "My ex-boyfriend is blackmailing me with videos I let him take of us when we were still together," Edie says. "He sent me a Venmo request for a thousand dollars and told me if I don't pay him, he'll send the videos to my prospective employers. Before that, he threatened to send them to my mother."

Alessandra nods ever so slightly. "Ah." She doesn't

seem shocked or appalled—but then, she hasn't seen the videos. She hasn't heard the things Edie said into the camera; she hasn't watched the acts. *No one can see those things,* Edie thinks. *No one!* She has to pay him the thousand dollars, even though that's forty hours of work. "I have to pay him."

Alessandra scoffs. "You do *not* have to pay him. You realize that posting revenge porn is a *crime,* right? A class-four felony? You can call the police."

Edie thinks about calling the Nantucket Police and speaking to Chief Kapenash. There is no way. And that's why women don't turn in their abusers, she thinks. It's humiliating—and the possibility of victim-shaming is very real.

"I can't call the police," Edie whispers. "He's out in Arizona."

"Phoenix?"

"Marana," Edie says.

Alessandra's eyebrows shoot up. "He works at Dove Mountain? I know the property. I'm sure the GM there would find his behavior very problematic."

"I don't want to…I'm not going to call his GM."

"He's threatening to post videos without your consent, is that right?"

Edie nods.

"And he's *blackmailing* you. How much money have you sent him so far?"

Edie bows her head.

"Edie?"

"Fifteen hundred," she says.

"What?" Alessandra jumps to her feet. "We're getting that money back. Just give me his phone number and let me take care of it."

"I can't," Edie says.

"Edie," Alessandra says. "I'm going to scare the hell

out of him. I'm going to pretend to be someone else. Now, I know I've given you no reason to trust me. But surely you have faith that I can be a convincing bitch on the phone and I can get this guy…what's his name?"

"Graydon Spires."

"I can get Graydon Spires to do exactly what I say. You believe that, right?"

Edie considers this. Can Alessandra be a total bitch? Yes. Can she get men to do whatever she wants? Also yes. She gives Alessandra the number, then squeezes her eyes shut. She overhears fragments of the conversation:

Mr. Spires, this is Alessandra Powell with the Pima County Sheriff's Department…Report of threats against…class-four felony before you even get to the blackmail…understand you work at Dove…We can either come round you up…Venmo the amount of fifteen hundred dollars back to the victim…internet fraud, identity theft…prosecute to full…

There's a pause. Edie can hear Graydon's voice on the other end of the line. Does he have just the right words for Alessandra now? Is he hitting the correct emotional note—contrite but charming? He was only kidding…he would never dream of posting…

Alessandra says, "I don't want to hear your bullshit, Mr. Spires. Venmo Ms. Robbins what you owe her immediately and leave her alone, otherwise we will file an electronic restraining order. If you ever threaten to post those videos again, we'll arrest you immediately. Am I understood?" The crystal under Alessandra's right eye seems to wink at Edie. "Am. I. Understood?" She pauses. "Well, I hope so. I won't trumpet my own accolades, Mr. Spires, but I've created quite a reputation wiping the floor with little men like you."

She ends the call and tells Edie, "If he doesn't

Venmo you what he owes you immediately, I'm going to fly out to Arizona and put his balls in a vise grip until he turns it over. But you are getting that money back."

Edie looks at Alessandra. "Thank you."

Alessandra smiles—not the cold, plastic smile Edie has grown used to but a warm, genuine one that illuminates her face and makes her look like a completely different person. "You're welcome, Edie," she says.

Edie's phone dings. A Venmo payment has just come in from Graydon Spires for fifteen hundred dollars.

Richie and Kimber are having the kind of summer romance that people write songs about—songs like "Summertime," by Cole Porter, "A Summer Song," by Chad and Jeremy, "Summer," by Calvin Harris—and Grace isn't sure how she feels about it. On the one hand, she can tell it won't end well—they aren't being honest with each other!—but on the other hand, they both seem so...*happy,* and how can that be a bad thing? Now that they've—Grace will say it, even though they haven't—*fallen in love,* Kimber's insomnia has disappeared and she lets Richie work the night desk undisturbed. She goes to bed after tucking in the children and doesn't stir until Richie joins her at two a.m. Then there is some spirited adult time. Kimber and Richie sleep intertwined (always in pajamas because of the children) until seven o'clock, which is when Louie heads out to the lobby to play chess and Wanda asks the hotel guests if they've heard the "Mystery of the Haunted Hotel." (Wanda is Grace's own little PR person.) Kimber goes down with them and then brings two cups of coffee—light and sweet for her, splash of milk for Richie—back to the suite.

The children eat the complimentary breakfast in the lobby—they're both partial to the croissants filled with almond marzipan that Beatriz makes—and Richie and Kimber skip breakfast for more alone time. Then they shower and embark on their day. Kimber seems to have abandoned writing her memoirs for the time being; she hasn't been on her computer in nearly two weeks.

Richie and Kimber deliver Louie to his chess lesson with Rustam and Wanda to the Atheneum so that she can read quietly for an hour and check out the next Nancy Drew mystery (she's up to number twenty-six, *The Clue of the Leaning Chimney*). Then they return to the hotel, put Doug on a leash, and disappear out the side door to go for a walk. The afternoons are adventures, ones Kimber selects from Lizbet's Blue Book and that Grace gets to live vicariously through the photos on Kimber's phone. Grace sees pictures of the big-enough-for-two sandwiches they get from Something Natural (turkey, Swiss, and tomato with sprouts and mustard on the famous herb bread) and watches the videos Kimber took of their trip up to Great Point. The long arm of golden sand in the afternoon sun is so *appealing* that Grace yearns to be able to leave the hotel, if only for the afternoon. She hasn't been to Great Point since before her brother died; George used to take her up in his fishing boat. There are pictures of Richie surf-casting with a rod Grace knows he borrowed from Raoul and then some photos of the children frolicking in the water with seals. (Doesn't Kimber know that seals mean sharks? Doesn't *Richie* know? What kind of outdoorsman is he, anyway?)

Another day they ride the hotel bikes out to Madaket and have lunch at Millie's (there's a picture of a seared-scallop taco with purple cabbage slaw), and over the weekend they head out to Sconset to do the bluff walk. (Grace remembers that bluff before a single one of those homes was built. She used to pay a nickel to take the *train* to Sconset!) There's a sweet photo of Richie and Wanda holding hands while Richie walks Doug and a funny one of Louie appearing to hold the Sankaty Head Lighthouse in the palm of his hand.

The late afternoons are always bittersweet because Richie has to be at work by six. He showers and changes in the suite, kisses Kimber long and deep, then heads down the hall to the front desk. He still makes phone calls in the middle of the night in Lizbet's office with the door closed, Grace notes. She finds this disappointing and blows cold air down the neck of Richie's dress shirt, but that doesn't stop him.

Then there's a happy development for Richie and Kimber. Edie's mother, Love Robbins, is willing to work one night shift per week, giving Richie the night off!

Because of the children, there's only one place Richie and Kimber can go for dinner alone, and fortunately, it's the only place either of them wants to go: the Blue Bar.

"I'll just charge it to my room!" Kimber says, and Grace notes the relief that washes over Richie's face.

Grace peeks in on the two lovebirds on their date. They order a cocktail called Here Comes Trouble and start feasting on yummy bites and spreads and dips and crunchy snacks; after their second Here Comes Trouble, Kimber orders the decadent caviar sandwiches. Eventually Beatriz, the whipped cream concierge, comes out with shot glasses of chocolate-mint-flavored whipped cream, and Kimber and Richie feed each other with the tiny spoons, then start kissing, and Grace can sense the bartender, a real pistol named Petey, thinking: *Get a room!* At exactly nine o'clock, Petey flips a switch under the bar and one of the panels in the coffered ceiling slides open and the copper disco ball drops. "White Wedding" starts playing and Richie takes Kimber's hand and leads her to the small dance floor in front of the penny-sheathed wall. They dance to "Burning Down the House" and "Hit Me with Your Best Shot" and "You May Be Right" as brilliant copper spots of light spin around them. Kimber throws her head back and windshield-wipers her arms in the air while Richie does moves he calls "the lawn mower" and "the shopping cart." Kimber is laughing; Richie is hamming it up. Then "Faithfully" by Journey comes on and they press their sweaty bodies together and shuffle in a tight circle (some dancing lessons should be in their future, Grace thinks), and when the song ends, Richie leads Kimber back to the bar, where she signs the bill, leaving Petey a huge tip.

Kimber throws back what's left of her Here Comes Trouble and, in the spirit of the greatest decade of the twentieth century, cries out, "Take me to bed or lose me forever!"

It's five thirty in the afternoon a few days later; Richie is in the bathroom shaving before he has to go to work. Kimber is sitting on the bed, still in her bikini, sandy from the beach, her skin golden from the sun, her hair newly dyed flamingo pink, which is actually quite flattering. Kimber watches Richie swipe clean strokes through the shaving cream with his chin lifted just so and she blurts it out.

"I love you."

Richie's head jerks a bit—he's lucky he doesn't cut himself—and his eyes meet hers in the mirror. *Uh-oh,* Grace thinks. Is it too much too soon? Kimber is always pushing the envelope. But then Richie sets down his razor and, with half a face of shaving cream, kisses Kimber. "I'm so in love with you," he says. "Maybe more in love than I've ever been in my life."

Way to double-down, Richie! Grace thinks.

That night, very late, when Richie comes to bed, Kimber says, "You know what I think we should do tomorrow? Go see your place. The children have been asking where you live when you're not here." She scratches her fingernails lightly down Richie's chest. "And I have to admit, I'm curious too."

Richie seizes up. "My place is really small," he says. "A dump, actually. I wouldn't want the kids to see it, because I don't want them to feel sorry for me."

Kimber waves a hand. "They won't care—they're kids. We'll just swing by and poke our heads in before we go to Fortieth Pole tomorrow. You said Cliff Road? That's on our way."

"Not a good idea," Richie says. "My landlady, Mrs. Felix, said no visitors."

"We won't even set foot inside, and we'll stay two minutes," Kimber says. "The children just want to see—"

"Kimber, no." Richie's voice is sharp. Kimber waits a beat, then sits up in bed.

"I just think it's weird that we're in love and I've never seen where you live. It's…suspicious. And after what I've been through with Craig, I just have to ask—is there something going on between you and Mrs. Felix? Or was there?"

"No!" Richie says.

"Then I guess I don't understand why—"

"Because I don't *have* a place to live," Richie says. "There is no Mrs. Felix. I made her up. I lied to you because I didn't want you to think I was pathetic and I lied to Lizbet so I could get this job, which I desperately need."

"What?" Kimber says. "Where were you living, then, before you moved in here?"

"The break room," Richie says. "And my car."

"Your *car?*" Kimber says. The look on her face is one of naked horror and Grace can't blame her. Who lives in his car? A hobo? *This is it,* Grace thinks. *This is the end of the cute romance.*

"I need to save money," Richie says. "I'm in so much debt, Kimber. The divorce carpet-bombed me financially. And I thought if you knew I didn't have a place to live, you would think I was using you so I could live in the suite."

Kimber's eyes shut for a moment, then fly open. "I asked you to stay overnight in the suite and you said no. I practically had to beg you."

"I would never want you to think I had ulterior motives," Richie says. "That's why I was so hesitant to start this relationship. It wasn't you—you're beautiful and fun and spontaneous and a terrific mother, bringing your kids here for the summer instead of shipping them off to camp or keeping them holed up in the city. It was that I'm homeless—my ex-wife took the house in Connecticut and I gave up my apartment when I moved here. You can do so much better than me, Kimber."

This is probably not untrue, Grace thinks.

"I don't want to do better," Kimber says. "I don't need a rich man. I had one of those and he ditched me for the nanny! I need a man who loves me and who won't leave me."

"I won't leave you," Richie says. "Someone would have to physically drag me away from you at gunpoint."

This is probably not untrue either, Grace thinks. *Nor unlikely.*

August 15, 2022
From: Xavier Darling (xd@darlingent.co.uk)
To: Employees of the Hotel Nantucket

Good morning, team—

I'm pleased to be spreading the wealth again this week and awarding the thousand-dollar bonus to Adam Wasserman-Ramirez. A guest of the hotel sang (wink-wink) Adam's praises for his showmanship at the piano during the wine-and-cheese hour. He indulged the guest's wishes with a rendition of "Let It Go" that the guest said "gave me goose bumps."

Well done, Adam! Here's hoping you don't leave us for the Great White Way!

XD

Adam deserves the bonus, Lizbet thinks. He plays the piano for the guests after his shift is over, purely for the joy of it. But the thing is, every member of her staff deserves the bonus. Every week. She hopes Xavier will see that once he comes to visit.

Her phone dings with a text and she has the same Pavlovian response to the sound that she's had for weeks: *Mario?*

But the text isn't from Mario. It's from JJ. I'm taking tomorrow night off. Can we talk?

Lizbet inhales, exhales, takes a sip of her coffee. Fine, she says. I'll meet you at the spot at 8.

Lizbet and JJ's spot is the Proprietors on India Street. On Saturday nights in the off-season, the bartender, Tenacious Leigh, would save them the two stools at the end of the bar. Lizbet hasn't set foot in Proprietors in months, and although she's ambivalent about meeting JJ (it's a meeting, not a date, she tells herself), she feels only joy when she strolls down the brick sidewalk to the white clapboard house, built in 1800, and opens the lipstick-red door.

Hello, old friend, she thinks. The restaurant's interior is one of her very favorites. There are refurbished wide-plank floors, exposed brick, Edison pendant lights, and a long, white-oak bar with a pressed-tin front. On the walls hang displays of mismatched china and a collection of antique door escutcheons; on the tables are mason jars filled with Nantucket wildflowers and flour-sack napkins with sage-green stripes. Lizbet almost left the Proprietors out of the Blue Book because she never wants the bar to become a place that's three-deep with tourists ordering Cape Codders. In the end, she tucked it into the fine-dining section, calling it "eclectic," a place for people who want a "thoughtful dining experience and the most creative cocktails on the island."

Lizbet has arrived before JJ on purpose. She waves at Leigh, embraces her across the bar, then orders her usual, a cocktail called Celery, Man, which is made with mescal joven (Lizbet has, quite intentionally, not touched tequila in months either) and celery syrup with a white-peppercorn rim. It's a savory cocktail, which she prefers to sweet (sorry, Heartbreaker). Lizbet relishes the first ice-cold sip. She has missed this place.

"Are you waiting for someone?" Leigh asks.

Lizbet shrugs. "Maybe."

Leigh cocks an eyebrow—and the very next second she breaks into a smile. "Look what the cat dragged in! It's just like old times. Can I get you the usual, Chef?"

"Please," JJ says.

Lizbet stands and greets him with a hug as though he's an old friend from high school. He takes the opportunity to squeeze Lizbet tight and she inhales his scent—boy fresh from the shower, Ivory soap, wintergreen aftershave, a lingering hint of the cigarette he smoked on his way here.

When she pulls away, he says, "You look gorgeous, Libby. I don't think I've seen that dress before."

"You haven't." Lizbet is wearing a red crinkled-cotton sundress—short, to show off her legs—and her nude wedges.

They take their stools, the same ones they've sat on a hundred times before. When JJ's drink arrives, they touch glasses. Lizbet has unwittingly slipped right back into her former life. This is a *meeting,* she reminds herself. Not a date. She knows Leigh is not only tenacious but discreet; anyone else would be sending an all-caps text around the island: LIZBET AND JJ REUNITING AT PROPS BAR!!!!

Lizbet isn't sure what to say to the person she knows better than anyone on earth. Should she ask him about Christina? (No.) Should she launch into the story about the impostor Shelly Carpenter? (No, he won't get it.) He seems *nervous.* His hand shakes as he holds up the dinner menu.

To put him at ease (she can't believe she's falling into the same old habit of worrying about his comfort), she asks about the restaurant.

"Worst summer ever," he says.

"We said that every August."

"I'm serious, Libby. Everything sucks. The place has no soul. My cooking is technically sound and the staff know what they're doing but there's no love, no magic."

Well, Lizbet thinks.

"My TravelTattler reviews are atrocious. Everyone calls the dining 'disappointing.' It's like we're being punished for being great in the past. Any idea how frustrating that is? People hear, 'Oh, the Deck is the best,' and they come in with unreasonable expectations. We're human beings running a restaurant. Things happen."

"They certainly do."

"I need you to come back, Libby."

Lizbet scream-laughs and Leigh glances over. Lizbet flags her. "We're ready to order."

There's no conflict or confusion where the menu is concerned because Lizbet and JJ always get the same thing. They start with one order of fried green tomatoes with pimiento cheese and black-pepper honey and one order of the bone marrow. Then Lizbet gets the chicken-fried trout and JJ the Korean short ribs with kimchi grits.

"Would you like another drink?" Leigh asks Lizbet.

"I'm going to stick with one," Lizbet says. "I have an early day tomorrow." She has an early day every day now and can't afford to stumble out of here the way she used to.

When Leigh leaves, Lizbet says, "I'm not coming back, JJ. You blew it."

He swivels toward her so that his knees are kissing her leg. He puts his hand on the back of her barstool, leans in, and speaks very softly. Lizbet can't make out everything he says, but she gets the gist of it: *I was such an idiot, a fool, a creep, I hate myself for what I did, I would do anything to go back to how it was, I was so unhappy with Christina, she's shallow and mean-spirited and insecure and so jealous of you, she almost ruined the restaurant, the staff hated her, she let some underage kids in on a Sunday and sold them the wineglasses even though a blind man could have seen their IDs were fake, I would do anything to get you back, if you don't come back, I'm not sure what I'll do.*

"You'll do what we all do, JJ," she says. "You'll keep on keepin' on."

"I'll sell the restaurant to Goose," he says. "Walk away."

"You would never."

"Watch me."

"It sounds like you're trying to threaten me," Lizbet says. "But I don't care if you sell the Deck. Why would I care? It's yours."

"So you're telling me you don't care about the Deck?"

Lizbet reaches for what's left of her Celery, Man and finishes it. "I cared so much. That restaurant was my…our…home. The staff was our family. But I wasn't the one who torched it, JJ. This is your arson, not mine."

Leigh arrives with their appetizers. "Here we go, guys, one fried green tomatoes, one marrow. Anything else I can bring you?"

Earplugs, Lizbet thinks. *A Valium. A graceful exit.*

She puts a tomato on a side plate for JJ, just like she always has. He spreads the luscious marrow on a thick golden slice of grilled bread for her.

"*Bon appétit,*" they say together. Lizbet can't get the first bite of tomato to her mouth fast enough. This is

Nantucket in a nutshell. She's in emotional hell but at least the surroundings are charming, the service impeccable, and the food maddeningly delicious.

Between the appetizer and the entrée, Lizbet goes to the bathroom, where the walls are papered with pages from a vintage copy of *June Platt's Party Cookbook*, which provides menus for each day of the calendar year. *March 24: pea soup, dressed crab, bishop's pudding*. The wallpaper improves Lizbet's mood— imagine, every day a party!—and when she gets back to the table, she decides to tell JJ the Heidi Bick/Lyric Layton drama. He becomes engrossed in the story— holy shit, he can't believe it; no, he hasn't heard about any of this, though, come to think of it, he hasn't seen the Bicks all summer and he's seen the Laytons only once.

"Yes, that was the night I was there," Lizbet says. "I saw Lyric at table three. She was crying."

JJ clears his throat. "Speaking of that night, what's up with you and Mario?"

Lizbet would love to say that things with her and Mario are hot and steamy but she just shrugs. "I ended it."

JJ fiddles with the strap of Lizbet's sundress, and she falls prey to memories of JJ zipping her dresses, clasping the hooks and eyes, fastening her necklaces. He could look at any outfit and tell her where they went the last time she wore it, what they ate, what they talked about, who they saw. His memory is his superpower, and it always made Lizbet feel like he was paying attention. He had *loved* her, that was the thing. She knew he loved her. So how the hell did Christina get to him?

"What happened?" JJ says.

"I wasn't ready." She waves at Leigh and points to

her glass. (She's like a woman in the throes of child-birth: *I will take the epidural after all!*) But this thought leads her exactly where she doesn't want to go: her brief pregnancy, the unprecedented joy, the intimacy she felt with JJ when the (three!) of them were nestled in bed. She acknowledges that she wasn't the same after she miscarried. She stopped having sex with JJ; she kept him at arm's length, pushed him away. She'd felt so confused—she was mourning something she hadn't realized she'd even wanted.

The drink arrives, delivering icy numbness. After a sip, she says, "I couldn't let myself trust anyone again."

JJ takes her face in his large, warm hands, pulls her in close like he's going to kiss her, and starts talking, his voice nearly a chant, the words coming out in an almost unintelligible rush: *I made a huge mistake, I messed up, it won't happen again, I swear to God, Libby, I love you and only you and I always have and I always will. We both love a good comeback story, right, and I want to be the best comeback of all, I will do anything on earth if you just please, please marry me, be my wife, we will try again for children or we will adopt or we'll do both, life is a crazy adventure, it's a road trip, I don't want any other woman in the passenger seat or in my bed but you, Lizbet Keaton. Please. Please listen to me. I love you.*

The words *road trip* remind Lizbet of how, when they were driving to upstate New York to see JJ's parents or halfway across the country to Minnetonka to see hers and JJ was at the wheel, he would turn the radio down so Lizbet could sleep (she, meanwhile, always kept the radio blaring while she was driving). She hears the words *in my bed* and thinks about how JJ liked to leave a bed unmade—the pillows askew, the comforter spiraled into a double helix—but Lizbet couldn't stand it and so, for fifteen years, JJ made the bed properly, covers drawn tight, pillows stacked.

He loved her. Where is she ever going to find someone who loves her like that again?

She draws the breath of surrender, ready to say, *Okay, fine, I give up, you win, I'll come back.* But then, over JJ's shoulder, she sees the front door to the restaurant open and a woman walk in. Lizbet blinks. It's Yolanda. Lizbet won't be able to handle it if Mario follows Yolanda in. But the person who comes in behind Yolanda is another woman. It's Beatriz.

Huh, Lizbet thinks.

They're at the lectern, talking with Orla, the proprietor of Proprietors. They're all laughing. Beatriz puts an arm around Yolanda and kisses her cheek. Orla plucks two menus off the lectern and leads Yolanda and Beatriz upstairs to the second-floor dining room, and as they ascend the stairs, Yolanda and Beatriz are holding hands.

Holding hands? And then it clicks.

You know why Yolanda is always in the kitchen, right? Zeke said.

And why she was always with the Blue Bar staff on Tuesdays and why she asked for Tuesdays off in the first place and why Mario was so openly affectionate with Yolanda. It occurs to Lizbet that maybe the "thing" Yolanda needed Mario's help with was the surprise the kitchen staff arranged for Beatriz's birthday: they all chipped in and flew Beatriz's mother from Mexico City to Nantucket.

"Are you okay?" JJ asks, following Lizbet's gaze over his shoulder.

The reason Yolanda is always hanging out in

the kitchen isn't Mario; it's Beatriz. "Take my trout home," she says. "I have to go."

She hurries down the brick sidewalks of India to Water Street, moving as fast as she can in her wedges, thinking, *It's Tuesday, his day off, he'll be out somewhere or entertaining another woman; he's Mario freaking Subiaco, for God's sake.* But Lizbet keeps going. She takes a left down the white-shell path behind Old North Wharf and sees Mario's silver truck.

He's home.

This nearly propels Lizbet back to Proprietors, back to JJ and safety. (It's ludicrous that she considers JJ *safe* after what he did to her; *familiar* might be a better word.) But every inspirational meme that Lizbet has stuffed inside her hollow places like a girl desperately padding her bra tells her to move forward.

Not on fighting the old.

But on building the new.

She strides out the long dock without wobbling or faltering and when she reaches the door, she takes a breath and acknowledges that this could be a very awkward moment.

But she knocks anyway.

There are footsteps, then a pause, and then Mario opens the door. He's wearing gym shorts, a gray T-shirt, his White Sox cap on backward. He's so handsome that Lizbet steadies herself against the shingled wall of the cottage. She peers over his shoulder. There's a beer on the table, an open pizza box, one plate.

Does he seem surprised to see her? Not really. He leans into the door frame and gives her his slow half-smile.

"Hey, Heartbreaker," he says.

"Hey," she whispers.

21. The Cobblestone Telegraph

When deep August arrives, a certain melancholy sets in, the kind people get on a Sunday afternoon. The summer, which seemed so endless back in June, will be over in a few short weeks.

Some of us are already saying goodbye. One of our local authors cries into the front of her son's T-shirt as she hugs him at the ferry; he's headed back to the University of South Carolina (a school that has been popular with kids from Nantucket High School ever since Link Dooley went there). Later that night, the local author is seen at the Blue Bar with her entourage, drinking a Heartbreaker. "Why do schools go back so early now?" she asks. "When we were kids, the first day of school was the Tuesday after Labor Day."

Yes, certain among us remember our parents rushing us into Murray's Toggery on the Saturday of Labor Day weekend so that we could get new school shoes. Then it was off to Joe the barber or Claire at the beauty salon, who would give us fresh haircuts and sweep our sun-bleached locks up off the floor. Blond Sharon holds dear the memory of her parents, who always booked the last ferry off the island on Labor Day itself—then Sharon's father would drive through the dark hours back to Connecticut. Sharon and her sister, Heather, would start school in the morning, often with sand still trapped in the whorls of their ears.

"We were tired but we never complained," Sharon says. "Because we wanted to squeeze every second out of the summer."

Nearly all Nantucketers agree with this sentiment and we bristle when people try to jump the season. Jill Tananbaum sees an Instagram post of a pumpkin-spice latte in her feed on August 18—and she immediately unfollows.

A rumor goes around that Lizbet Keaton and JJ O'Malley were seen eating together at the bar at Proprietors. They were huddled close, according to sources, and appeared to be having *a very intense conversation*. Were they reuniting? Some of us hoped yes—Lizbet was needed back at the Deck pronto; the quality of the experience had slipped significantly—but a day or two later, these hopes were dashed when we heard that Lizbet and Mario Subiaco were dating again. Tracy Toland and Karl Grabowski, two of our favorite summer visitors (and newlyweds to boot!), were eating dinner on the deck at the Straight Wharf and, in the moonlight, they caught sight of Lizbet and Mario kissing on the front porch of the little cottage that sat by itself out in the harbor.

The reuniting of Lizbet and Chef Subiaco is confirmed on the third Saturday of August when they attend our favorite charity benefit of the season together: the Summer Groove, which raises money for the Nantucket Boys and Girls Club. Lizbet is wearing a lilac silk dress, and her blond hair is styled in a braid crown; Mario wears a navy blazer and a matching lilac tie. They hold hands all night; they drift over to the raw bar, where Mario doctors cherrystone clams with lemon and cocktail sauce and oysters with mignonette before handing them to Lizbet. They accept hors d'oeuvres from silver trays even though the offerings at this party aren't quite as ambrosial as what we've been eating all summer at the Blue Bar. (The bakery box has spoiled us.) It turns out that Lizbet and Chef Subiaco have donated one of the auction items for the event—a three-night stay at the Hotel Nantucket for the following summer, plus a "chef's tasting" for two (with cocktails!) at the Blue Bar.

There are *numerous* competing bidders, all of them seemingly relentless, and the item goes for *thirty-five thousand dollars*. People in the tent go crazy!

It is, however, a bit awkward when the next auction item is announced: Dinner for ten at the Deck, including signature stemless wineglasses for the rosé fountain. In years past, this item garnered the highest bid, but tonight, only one hand is raised; it belongs to Janice, the dental hygienist whose brother, Goose, is the Deck's sommelier. Janice accidentally bids against herself (she's had a lot of wine), but even so, she wins the package for twenty-five hundred dollars, which is *less than the package is actually worth*.

Discreetly, we look around the tent, searching for JJ, and are relieved to discover he's not in attendance.

The Summer Groove is not only the best charity event of the summer, it's also the final one. When we wake up the next morning, our spirits sag. All we have to look forward to now are the "lasts." The last great beach days, the last lobster omelet–and–Whispering Angel lunch at the Galley, the last stroll over the sundial bridge in Sconset, the last chance to surf-cast in Miacomet, the last long afternoon drinking Gripah at Cisco Brewers, the last of the zucchini and corn at Bartlett's Farm (tomatoes will go strong into September and—eek!—are those pumpkins we see?).

We can squeeze in one more boat ride up the harbor to watch the kiteboarders, check out one more juicy summer novel from the Atheneum, and eat one more fish sandwich at the Oystercatcher while the sun sets over the water and guitarist Sean Lee sings that it's hard to get by just upon a smile.

But then Romeo at the Steamship Authority reports that *some really rich dude* is sending a Bentley over on the ferry with a chauffeur, and not only that but this same dude is flying in from London on his G5.

"He'll be here Wednesday," Romeo says.

Who could it be? we wonder. And then we realize: It's Xavier Darling.

22. Cedar and Salt

August 22, 2022
From: Xavier Darling (xd@darlingent.co.uk)
To: Employees of the Hotel Nantucket

Greetings, all, good morning—
   Although I am busy preparing for my trip across the pond, I have not forgotten about this week's bonus. I'm pleased to announce Edith Robbins as our winner. One heartfelt letter described the myriad ways that Edith went above and beyond during a family's extended stay. Wonderful job, Edith!

I will arrive Wednesday afternoon at 2:00.

Please prepare the footmen and the trumpeters! (Joking, of course.)

XD

Lizbet has known for months that Xavier would be arriving on August 24, but the date seemed impossibly far in the future, and then, as it drew closer, Lizbet was consumed with other things. However, time did what it always does: it passed.

Xavier arrives tomorrow.

Lizbet waits until there's a break between fitness classes, then enters the yoga studio, which is pleasantly dark. She sets one of the thick mats in the middle of the room and considers turning on some gamelan music but decides that the sound of gurgling water over river stones in the fountain is pleasing enough. She assumes a savasana pose and tries not to think.

Half an hour later, just as her eyes naturally flutter open—this room must have supernatural powers because she actually *slept*—there's a light tap on the door. The door cracks open. "Heartbreaker?"

It's Mario. Lizbet loves the sound of his voice. She lies back down. "Hey." She nearly tells him to lock the door behind him so they can christen the yoga studio—but really, what is she thinking?

Mario stands over her, holding her espresso. "Edie told me you were down here and I almost didn't believe her. What's going on?"

"I needed to reset." She stands up and kisses him. "And I did!"

"Well," he says, handing her the coffee, "that makes one of us."

"Are you nervous about Xavier?"

"He's my boss too," Mario says. "You noticed I tossed and turned last night?"

"You did?" Since they've been back together, Mario has spent every night at Lizbet's cottage. Lizbet climbs into bed at a reasonable hour, wakes up when Mario comes in, then dozes right back off. "What are you nervous about?"

"I'm not sure."

"The bar is amazing, Mario," Lizbet says. "It's packed every night, and it has an absurdly high rating on every restaurant-review app. It's positioned to become every bit as iconic as the Blue Bistro, if not more so."

Mario smiles but she can tell he's not feeling it.

"I'm serious," she says.

"I know," Mario says. "But men like Xavier…"

"I'm the one who should be nervous," Lizbet says. "I have a whole hotel to present—twelve suites, thirty-six rooms, the lobby, the pools, the gym and sauna, this studio. But I'm confident in what we built." She wraps her arms around Mario's neck and presses the length of her body against him. "I know you're anxious because you've lost a restaurant on this island before, but Xavier is going to love us. We have absolutely nothing to worry about."

That evening at change of shift, Lizbet calls a meeting in the break room. She asks Love to watch the desk so that Richie can come to the meeting along with Edie, Alessandra, Adam, Raoul, Zeke, Magda, and Yolanda. Lizbet thinks about the staff meeting she called back on opening day, when the hotel was like a fawn wobbling on new legs. She had barely known these people and they'd barely known one another.

Richie has shed thirty pounds, gotten a tan, and

is smiling far more genuinely than the night Lizbet interviewed him. He's in love with Kimber Marsh, their long-term guest; it's the stuff rom-coms are made of! (Lizbet will not mention this romance to Xavier, however, in case he disapproves.) Edie has been consistently thoughtful and kind, the perfect foil for Alessandra, with her fierce beauty and blinding confidence. But even Alessandra has softened a bit lately, so much so that Lizbet noticed Edie and Alessandra *laughing* together. (Lizbet did a double take. Was it genuine? Yes, it seemed so.) Zeke has grown into the bellman job beautifully; if his mother could see him now, she would be so proud. Yolanda is as serene as a hidden pond in an enchanted wood, and Lizbet is so glad she didn't tell Mario about her suspicions, because once that genie was out of the bottle, it could never have been put back: Lizbet would feel awkward, and so would Yolanda and Mario *and* Beatriz.

Magda sits with perfect posture on the edge of the sofa, legs crossed at the ankles. She remains unreadable, a sphinx. Has she ever let her guard down, shared a candid moment or personal revelation? She has not. She is the ultimate professional; Lizbet hasn't worried for one second about housekeeping. There hasn't been a single complaint about the cleanliness of the rooms. There were the two missing items, but Magda handled these incidents herself with the guests and her staff. Housekeeping is the bedrock of any hotel—if the hotel isn't *clean,* forget it—which makes Magda the most important person on the staff, maybe more important than Lizbet herself.

Lizbet remembers thinking that she didn't want to know her staff's secrets. But now that summer is nearly over, she decides that she would very much like to know Magda's secrets.

"Mr. Darling is arriving tomorrow," Lizbet says. "I want you all to do your jobs precisely the way you've been doing them. Mr. Darling will introduce himself to all of you over the course of his stay. We want to make sure he's comfortable and that his needs are met, just like any other guest. Does anyone have any questions?"

"How long will he be here?" Adam asks.

"Four nights," Lizbet says. "He's scheduled to leave on Sunday."

Alessandra raises her hand. "Does Mr. Darling have dinner reservations? If he wants to go to Cru or Nautilus…"

"Then he needed to make them thirty days ago," Edie says. "But Alessandra has an in at Nautilus and I've developed a nice rapport with the reservations people at Cru. So just let us know."

"Excellent question," Lizbet says. Xavier hasn't said a word about what he plans to do during his visit. It's his first time to Nantucket; he should read the Blue Book, or Lizbet can pull together some itineraries for him. She wonders if the chauffeur (who is staying at the Beach Club because their own hotel is full!) knows how to drive a Jeep on the beach. "I'll find out what Mr. Darling's plans are once I speak to him in person. If that's all the questions, then I'll end the meeting. Please, everyone, go home and get a good night's sleep. I'll see you bright and early tomorrow."

Xavier is coming! Grace thinks. *Xavier is coming!* She feels a surge in her energy levels. She wants to haunt the hotel—Mary Perkowski in room 205 came all the way from Broadview Heights, Ohio, in hopes of some spooky business—but Grace needs to reserve her energy so she can enjoy tomorrow's fanfare.

Grace isn't the only one who's all dialed up for Xavier's arrival. Zeke arrives at the hotel with a new haircut; Alessandra swaps out her clear eye crystals for ones that are sapphire blue. Edie's attention to guest services becomes so intense, like sunlight through a magnifying glass, that Lizbet gently reminds her that some guests prefer to figure things out on their own.

Richie surprises Kimber while she's on her laptop and sees that she's ordering school supplies from Staples to be delivered to her apartment in New York City. "Do you have to think about back-to-school already?"

Kimber snaps her laptop shut. "It can't be avoided. The teachers at PS Six like the children to be prepared on day one, pencils sharpened. And have you met my daughter, Wanda? She was bugging me to order this stuff weeks ago."

Richie flops in the window seat and gazes out at Easton Street as a couple on a bicycle built for two pedal by. "I have to mentally prepare myself. All of this is coming to an end. I'll stay at the hotel until Columbus Day, I promised Lizbet that much, but it won't be the same without you and the children here. We only have a few days left."

Kimber settles between Richie's legs and leans her head back against his chest. Doug the dog lies on the floor at their feet. He lifts his head when Grace hovers over him and starts to whine. He's still not used to her.

"Why don't you come to New York after Columbus Day," Kimber says. "Live with us."

"I couldn't do that."

"Why not? There are plenty of jobs in the city. My divorce will be final, or nearly."

"You wanted a *summer* romance," Richie says.

"Well, maybe now I want a *romance*-romance," Kimber says. She wraps Richie's arms around her. "I don't want this to end."

Grace sighs. So sweet! She would like to think of Kimber and Richie ending up together when they leave here. She wants to believe that the hotel is more than just cedar and salt. It's a place that can create at least one happily-ever-after.

On the morning of the twenty-fourth, Chad gets to work early at Ms. English's request. He figures this is because of Mr. Darling's arrival. The hotel has to be even more immaculate than its usual immaculate self.

When he gets to the housekeeping office, he sees an unfamiliar older woman in uniform—khakis and hydrangea-blue polo shirt—running through the hundred-point checklist with Ms. English. This woman has bright red hair that looks spun over her scalp like cotton candy. Her face is plump and wrinkled and kind-seeming. She must be a reinforcement for Mr. Darling's visit.

"Chadwick," Ms. English says. "Please meet Doris Mulvaney, your new cleaning partner."

"My…"

"You'll be showing Doris the ropes today. I told her you were one of our best cleaners!"

One of the best on a staff of four isn't much of an accomplishment but Chad feels a swell of pride nonetheless. He offers Doris a hand. "Pleasure to meet you, Ms. Mulvaney."

She giggles and her blue eyes twinkle. "Call me Doris, please, lad." She has an Irish accent, which is cool, Chad thinks.

Chad looks at Ms. English. "Where's Bibi?"

"You and Doris will start with third-floor checkouts. We need to get the entire third floor cleaned before Mr. Darling arrives."

"No problem, but—"

"Thank you, Chadwick. If you stop by here at the end of the day, we can chat then. But not now—we have too much work in front of us."

Chad and Doris take the service elevator to the third floor.

"How old are you, lad?" Doris asks.

"Twenty-two," he says flatly. Bibi was fired, he thinks. *Ms. English gave her the ax.* But she didn't steal the Gucci belt! That was a ruse cooked up by the fake Shelly Carpenter! Bibi probably didn't take Mrs. Daley's Fendi scarf either. Mrs. Daley must have left it at Ventuno.

"In university?" Doris asks.

"I graduated in May," he says. "From Bucknell University in central Pennsylvania."

"And now you're working here?"

"Uh-huh," Chad says. He wants to be polite, but he also doesn't want to encourage chatting. "My parents have a home here and this is my summer job." He wonders if maybe something else is going on. Maybe Bibi's daughter, Smoky, was diagnosed with some kind of awful cancer or maybe there was a domestic issue with the baby-daddy, Johnny Quarter. Maybe Bibi and Smoky got in the car and went looking for Johnny Quarter or maybe Octavia and Neves were mean to Bibi on the ferry and that made her quit.

"My son is the plumber for the hotel," Doris says. "And when I heard you were shorthanded in the housekeeping department, I offered to jump in and help. I cleaned rooms at the Balsams resort in Colebrook, New Hampshire, for years and at Ballyseede Castle back in Ireland when I was your age." She pats his arm. "So I know what I'm doing."

"When did you hear we were shorthanded?" Chad asks.

Doris shrugs. "Top of last week, I believe."

Top of last week? But Bibi has been at work every day. Just yesterday she informed Chad that they were tripling the floral arrangements in every suite because of Xavier Darling's arrival. There would be bouquets in the living room and both bedrooms. Chad and Bibi had groaned about this together—triple the lily stamens to trim, triple the hydrangea dust!—but there had been no indication that Bibi wouldn't be around to pluck the wilting snapdragon blossoms. When they'd parted ways the day before, Bibi had slung her backpack over her shoulder and said, "See ya, Long Shot." Just like usual.

He wants to text and ask her what happened. Is she okay? But Chad doesn't have Bibi's number. There were times when he'd wanted to ask for it, but he'd always stopped himself because…why? He obviously thought about Bibi when he wasn't at work—never in a sexual way, just in a friendship way. There were Tik-Toks he'd wanted to send her and news bulletins about fin sightings on the south shore (Bibi was a devoted fan of Shark Week), stuff they could talk about the next day at work. But he never wanted to seem weird or eager and he certainly didn't want to give her the wrong idea. Now, however, he has no way to reach her.

Chad knows Xavier Darling is supposed to arrive between two and three p.m., but at that hour, Chad and Doris are cleaning room 111 on the pool side of the hotel, so he can't watch for him out the window. Doris is a brisk and efficient cleaner and she doesn't mind tackling the bathrooms. "The loo," she says, "is my particular specialty." Chad is then left to handle

Bibi's particular specialty, which is the bed; it has been weeks, maybe even months, since Chad was charged with making a bed, but he does a textbook, if robotic, job. His mind is elsewhere—on Bibi, of course, but also on Xavier Darling's arrival. Chad expects to feel a shift in the hotel—a crackle in the air, a rumbling of the floors, alarms ringing or an alert on his phone.

Out the window, Chad hears only children laughing and splashing in the family pool. At a quarter to four, he and Doris move down to room 108, which has a fine view of Easton Street, but the street is quiet.

At five o'clock, Chad and Doris finish their last room of the day and Chad rolls the cleaning cart to the storage closet and restocks it for tomorrow. A hundred and twenty dollars have been left as tips and he and Doris split the money. He tries not to seem like he's rushing, though he is, a bit, and he says to Doris, "Nice meeting you, see you tomorrow!" in a falsely cheerful voice before he hightails it to the housekeeping office.

But Ms. English isn't there. Chad can't believe it. It's a quarter past five, his usual time of departure, and she had said he could come see her when he was finished for the day.

He waits for a few minutes, pointlessly checking his phone—nobody snaps or texts him anymore—and when he finally turns to leave, he nearly collides with a woman walking into the office.

"Oh," the woman says. "Long Shot. I forgot all about you."

Chad blinks. The woman is Ms. English, but instead of being regular workday Ms. English, in her hydrangea-blue blouse, the matching cardigan she often wears because she finds the hotel rooms chilly, and her hair pinned back in a sensible bun—this Ms.

English is wearing a hot-pink silk one-shouldered top and a pair of snug white pants. Her hair is piled on her head and wrapped in a bright floral scarf, and pretty curls hang down on either side of her face. This Ms. English is also wearing cat's-eye glasses bedazzled with rhinestones and a pair of platform stiletto sandals instead of the loafers that Zeke calls her "auntie shoes."

Chad manages to find his voice. "You look nice."

"Thank you," she says. She considers him for a moment. "I have plans tonight, as you can probably guess, but my dinner's not until eight o'clock, so let's you and I go for a drink now, shall we?"

Again, Chad is rendered speechless. Go for a drink with Ms. English? "Okay?" he says. He feels himself flush. Because Ms. English is not looking like herself but rather like some hot older woman, Chad kind of feels like she's asking him on a date.

"We'll go to the Brant Point Grill and sit at the bar," Ms. English says. "It's high time you and I had a talk."

On the morning of August 24, Alessandra receives an e-mail from Xavier Darling addressed to her alone. Very much looking forward to meeting you later today, Alessandra, it says. One of our front desk's shining stars! XD

Eccezionale! Alessandra thinks. She still has money in the bank, though not nearly as much as she'd hoped—her rent was expensive, the impractical vehicle she bought needs a new transmission to the tune of four grand, and she still has seventeen thousand in credit card debt to pay off from her previous life. She wants a permanent situation. Is it crazy to think that maybe she and Xavier Darling…

None of the men that Alessandra has slept with here at the hotel was wealthy or extravagant enough for her tastes—except David Yamaguchi, who, sadly, had a beautiful wife at home to whom he was very "devoted." That douche-canoe Bone Williams actually managed, for one second, to scare Alessandra, sending her into a period of reflection. What is she *doing?* She has always aspired to be different from and better than her mother; however, Alessandra admits to herself that despite the glamorous trappings of her lifestyle— living first in Europe and now Nantucket, the champagne, the pricey dinners out, the luxury goods—she's exactly the same, only she doesn't have a daughter to show for it. Alessandra has never wanted a husband or children or a house in the suburbs or (shudder) Disney vacations. But some stability would be nice. Xavier Darling is worth eleventy billion dollars. He has homes in London, Gstaad, and St. Barth's and apartments in New York and Singapore. He's not tall or strapping the way Alessandra likes her men (sigh— Michael Bick), but he has good posture, a kind smile, and a thick head of silver hair. Alessandra remembers reading that Xavier Darling had sunk thirty million into the hotel; it was what made her choose Nantucket over the Vineyard and Newport. At the time, she was thinking only of the wealthy clientele, though maybe subconsciously, she'd been thinking of Xavier himself.

He's a little older than her usual targets…but that might be what she needs. Someone older.

At a quarter past two, Lizbet comes flying out of the back office. She's wearing one of her cutest dresses, Alessandra notes with approval, a white linen Cartolina shift with a scalloped hem—but she's chosen her two-braid style, which makes her look like she's about to yodel.

"Xavier just landed!" Lizbet says. "He'll be here in twenty minutes!" She makes zero effort to maintain any chill, but isn't that the thing that draws people to Lizbet—that she wears her heart on her sleeve? At least Edie is calm. Ever since Alessandra scared away Edie's predator (the one accomplishment this summer that Alessandra is proud of), Edie has focused her warmth and light on Alessandra—"You're such a boss! How can I ever thank you?"—and Alessandra basks in it. Alessandra enjoyed nailing that jerk Graydon so much that she has even considered training to work on some kind of special victims unit—but of course, she would never pass the background check.

Lizbet poses in the entrance of the hotel like the hostess in a game show, Zeke and Raoul flanking her. Louie is playing chess in the lobby with the teenage girl staying in room 210 (this girl has just finished watching *The Queen's Gambit* on Netflix and swears she can beat Louie, though she's lost three games in a row quite speedily). There's a fresh pot of coffee brewing, and Sheryl Crow is singing that all she wants to do is have a little fun before she dies.

Lizbet whips around and squeals, "He's here!" Alessandra feels her heart hop a little. She glances at Edie, who is on the phone with the R. J. Miller Salon, trying to secure a pedicure appointment for Mrs. Baskin in room 304. Alessandra taps Edie's back and tells her Xavier's here, and Edie whispers, "I'm on hold. I can't hang up, she wants this for the morning." Alessandra thinks that Edie is far more professional than she is; she would have hung up immediately.

Alessandra is jealous that Edie has something to

occupy her. Alessandra just smiles at the door, then checks her computer for no reason. Xavier doesn't have a reservation like other guests, and Lizbet made his key cards hours ago.

Then Alessandra hears voices—Zeke's and Lizbet's; they both sound like stage actors—and an instant later, the man himself steps into the lobby.

Well, Alessandra thinks. He's taller than Alessandra expected—good—and he exudes a confidence that comes naturally to the very wealthy. He's wearing a cream-colored suit and a coral-pink shirt open at the collar, a belt with a brushed-silver buckle (nothing flashy, also good), and leather driving moccasins with woven uppers that Alessandra immediately identifies as Fratelli Rossetti. Xavier Darling's look is plucked straight from Capri. Alessandra experiences a pang for the summers of her recent past. She misses the turquoise water, diving off the bow of Giacomo's yacht, long lunches of grilled langoustines and crusty bread with fresh-pressed olive oil and salty, craggy chunks of Parmigiano. Xavier is deeply tanned, so she supposes his has been a summer well spent at the helm of his ship or in a private cabana on the beach at Il Riccio.

"This is nothing short of magnificent, Elizabeth," he says, raising his arms to the antique beams, taking in the whaling-boat chandelier, the James Ogilvy photograph, the beachy elegance of the lobby. "What an appealing space."

Beatriz from the service kitchen appears with a deep red cocktail—it's the Heartbreaker; Alessandra has heard all about it—and a tiny basket of gougères from the Blue Bar bakery box. The gougères are golden and fragrant, fresh from the oven but no doubt cooled to the perfect temperature so that Xavier doesn't burn his tongue. When Alessandra and Xavier are together, her life will be blessed with exquisite welcomes like this.

Xavier accepts the cocktail and raises his glass to the front desk. "Here's to you!" he says, and he drinks. Lizbet leads him over to meet Edie, who has just hung up the phone; she steps out from behind the desk, faces Xavier, and curtsies. Alessandra wants to cringe but Xavier throws his head back and laughs. He and Edie shake hands and while Lizbet brags to Xavier ("Edie was a Statler Fellow at Cornell!"), Alessandra steps out from behind the desk and waits a respectful distance behind Edie until it's her turn to be introduced. Xavier takes a deeper interest in Edie once she mentions that she grew up on the island, and Edie draws Zeke into the conversation because Zeke was raised on Nantucket as well, then Lizbet tells Xavier that Zeke is an accomplished surfer and also the nephew of Magda English, head of housekeeping, and *that* gets Xavier's attention. He's known Magda for over thirty years, he says. Alessandra is starting to feel awkward, like a literal lady-in-waiting; however, Raoul is in a mirrored position to Alessandra behind Xavier and his expression radiates good-natured interest in this conversation that has nothing to do with him. Alessandra takes a sustaining breath and reminds herself that she will stand on deck for as long as it takes, and when she gets into the batter's box, she will hit a grand slam.

The hotel phone rings, and although Alessandra is closest, she makes no move to answer it. She hasn't met Xavier yet! She wills Edie to hear the phone and sense that *she* should be the one to answer it, but Edie is still deep in conversation and Alessandra catches a pointed look from Lizbet (she doesn't like to hear the

phone ring more than twice). She goes back behind
the desk to answer the phone.

It's the secretary of a Mr. Ianucci, who will be checking in later that afternoon. The secretary is confirming
the reservation in a pool-view room for two nights.

Yes, yes, confirmed, didn't Mr. Ianucci receive the
e-mail? Alessandra knows he did but he was probably
too busy to even open it.

"We look forward to welcoming Mr. Ianucci this
afternoon," Alessandra says, her voice maybe a touch
louder than it needs to be so that Xavier will hear
her superlative phone skills and realize that at least
someone is working while everyone else grovels.

Alessandra hangs up just as Lizbet says, "Let me
show you the break room."

Edie returns to the desk, and Zeke and Raoul head
back out to the entrance. "Lovely to meet you all!"
Xavier says. Except he hasn't met Alessandra yet and
he sent that e-mail expressly to her, so she waits a
moment and then, in a rare act of desperation, follows
Xavier and Lizbet into the break room.

Xavier is standing at the pinball machine. "Hokus
Pokus! I played this during my one American summer
back in the seventies. I lived with my aunt and uncle
in Casper, Wyoming, of all places. My uncle owned
a ranch there, and the local watering hole had this
game." He presses the buttons on either side and the
flippers *clickety-clack*. Xavier turns to Lizbet. "You
don't happen to have a quarter, do you?"

Alessandra clears her throat. "I have one, sir."

Both Xavier and Lizbet turn around. Alessandra
thinks that Lizbet might be irked that she trailed them
into the break room but Lizbet just smiles and in her
new cheerleader voice says, "Xavier, this is Alessandra
Powell, our front-desk manager!"

Alessandra makes eye contact and shakes Xavier's hand, then pulls a quarter from behind her ear like a magician, but only Lizbet seems impressed. Alessandra has played a lot of pinball this summer. It has given her a chance to relive her own adolescence— there was a Hokus Pokus at the pizza parlor in Haight-Ashbury where she used to go with Duffy. (Alessandra can't think about Duffy now, though she has a friend request rotting in her Facebook account.) "Here you go, Mr. Darling. It's lovely to meet you."

Xavier accepts the quarter and Alessandra waits for him to say something about her remarkable performance on the desk this summer, at which point she'll mention her previous work experience in Europe. Surely they could have an excellent conversation about Italy or Ibiza or St. Tropez, but Xavier simply says, "Thank you very much," and turns to the pinball machine, inserts the coin, pulls back the springy lever, and lets the first silver ball fly. The machine comes to life, all dinging bells and flashing lights. It's clear Lizbet is going to stay and watch Xavier play but Alessandra senses she would be pushing her luck to stay as well. She returns to the desk.

Xavier and Lizbet emerge and head out the back door to the pools. After that, Alessandra supposes, it will be down to the wellness center, over to the Blue Bar, then up to the owner's suite.

She sees Zeke wheeling in the cart with Xavier's luggage—a garment bag, a suitcase, a weekender duffel—and she nearly offers to take it up, but how weird (and obvious) would *that* be? She'll have to think of another reason to visit Xavier's suite. She needs to have a conversation with him one-on-one. That's all it will take, Alessandra thinks. She'll dip her chin and gaze up at him. She'll touch his wrist between the cuff of his shirt and his watch. That's all it ever takes.

When Lizbet returns to the desk, she's flushed and panting as if she's just completed an obstacle course. "He's settled in," she says. "He loved everything. He was *so* complimentary and he noticed every detail. I'm not sure what I was worried about. This place is pretty perfect." Alessandra resists the urge to roll her eyes.

Edie says, "I feel like I just met royalty. He's so…elegant."

Elegant is the right word, Alessandra thinks. She should have been pursuing elegance—manners, breeding, experience, generosity—all along but she'd been distracted by looks and surface charm and that's why she hasn't landed in the right situation. Now that Alessandra has met Xavier Darling in person, she can see their future together more clearly. It will be the jet and the chauffeured Bentley, of course, but also private islands, hunting lodges in the wilds of Scotland, quiet evenings at home in Belgravia, Xavier smoking a pipe and checking the markets, Alessandra curled up on the sofa by the fire, reading a leather-bound edition of Dante. She'll lose her eye crystals and the white eyeliner; she'll start wearing her hair in a chignon. She'll call him X. He'll go from infatuated to besotted to deeply in love. He'll be captivated by Alessandra's intelligence, her ease with languages, her business savvy. He'll insist that she accompany him to Davos, where she'll draw the attention of the other moguls, and this sense of competition for her attention will prompt Xavier to propose. Or if marriage frightens him, which is what Alessandra suspects, he'll appease her by changing his will—and by buying her an extraordinary diamond that proves his commitment without requiring a church ceremony.

All she has to do is get up to his room.

Lizbet gasps. "I forgot to give him a copy of the Blue Book!"

Well, isn't that like the sky opening up and raining gold coins? Alessandra snaps up a copy of the Blue Book. "I'll take this up to him right now," she says. "I have to drop off tickets for the drive-in to suite three fifteen anyway." Alessandra waves the envelope that does, in fact, contain four drive-in movie tickets for the Hearn family in suite 315. Alessandra has been holding on to them all day, just in case.

An unfamiliar feeling comes over Alessandra as she approaches the door of the owner's suite. She has *butterflies*.

She is always the pursued, never the pursuer.

After she knocks, she quickly tousles her hair and arranges her face into an open, innocent smile. Xavier Darling opens the door. He has shed his jacket but not (thankfully) his shoes, and he's holding a glass of rosé. (Alessandra knows they stocked his minibar with Domaines Ott at his request.)

He gives her a look of vague recognition, like he's seen her somewhere before, but where...

"Mr. Darling, sorry to interrupt. I'm Alessandra Powell, the front-desk manager?" *You sent me a personal e-mail telling me how much you were looking forward to meeting me?* She then realizes, with no small amount of horror, that Xavier must have sent those e-mails to everyone. Or, even worse, his secretary sent them on his behalf!

"Yes?" he says crisply, maybe even a bit impatiently.

Alessandra clears her throat. She has been here ten seconds and she's already blowing it. "I wanted to hand-deliver the Blue Book, sir. It's our recommendation guide to the island—museums, beaches, restaurants, and the like. I say *our,* but this is Lizbet's brainchild. She wrote it, and our guests have *raved* about it. It's something that sets us apart from the island's other luxury hotels." Alessandra tries to radiate virtue: *See how I prop other women up and polish their crowns?*

"She's mentioned it, yes. Thank you." Xavier reaches for the book, and Alessandra instinctively holds on tight. *Come to me!* she thinks. "If you'd like me to set up any dinner reservations or arrange for any excursions, please let me know. I'm all yours." Ever so reluctantly, she allows him to tug the book from her. Xavier riffles through the pages. "I'll take a look when I have a moment."

"I'm at your disposal if you need dinner—"

"I had everything booked for me weeks ago." Xavier steps back and takes hold of the door; he seems like he's about to close it in her face. "Thank you, Alexandra."

That's it, she thinks. He didn't show the slightest interest. He didn't flirt, didn't wink, didn't smile; his eyes didn't linger. He wasn't intrigued, wasn't attracted. He didn't even get her *name* right.

When Alessandra gets back to the desk, she isn't thinking straight. Edie is on the phone, so there's no immediate follow-up questioning about how it went, although Alessandra is tempted to confide in Edie because she needs a friend. But what would she say? *I've been trying to find a suitable man all summer, someone who will make my life easier.* Edie would be *appalled!* Edie is idealistic, not only about marrying for love but also about women making their own way in the world. What kind of dinosaur pursues a sugar daddy? *I can't meet a regular guy and lead a normal middle-class life, I'm not programmed that way. I need someone of Xavier's caliber and there are only a certain number of straight, unattached billionaire men, Edie.*

Just as she is about to admit defeat—she'll be a hotel desk clerk forever; her beauty will wash out like an Old Masters painting left in direct sunlight; she'll die alone with her broken dreams—she remembers that she has a rip cord. She slips into the break room and pulls out her phone. She feels a sharp stab of guilt because she's standing at the very counter where she and Edie fought back against *exactly the kind of blackmail* that Alessandra is about to initiate.

But, sorry, she's desperate.

She finds the pictures of herself in the Bicks' house on Hulbert Avenue and sends them in separate text messages to Michael Bick.

I need fifty thousand more, she types. Otherwise, these go to your wife.

She'd like to claim cramps and go home, but there's only an hour left in her shift and she's dependent on Raoul for a ride because of her Jeep's crapped-out transmission, so she decides to show some grit and finish the day. She feels she's made the right decision and is, perhaps, being rewarded when a good-looking, broad-shouldered gentleman pulling a roller bag and carrying an attaché case steps into the lobby. He glances from Edie to Alessandra, and although Alessandra has stopped treating the front desk like a beauty pageant or a popularity contest, she smiles at the gentleman and he grins and strolls right over to her.

Good boy, Alessandra thinks. In seconds, he'll be eating out of her hand. "Good afternoon, welcome to the Hotel Nantucket," she says. "Checking in?" *Screw you, Xavier Darling,* she thinks. *You lost out.*

The gentleman pulls out his driver's license—

Robert Ianucci from Holliston, Massachusetts—and a gold American Express.

"Bob Ianucci," he says. "Here for two nights." He winks at her. "Your name tag is upside down."

"Ah, you noticed! I'm Alessandra, the front-desk manager. What a pleasure to meet you."

Bob Ianucci—Italian; she likes it—isn't wearing a wedding ring. Alessandra gets him checked in, thinking, *Gold card, not platinum card, a room, not a suite, and Holliston is a Boston suburb—a nice suburb, but a suburb just the same.* Bob Ianucci isn't worth going after but Alessandra needs an ego boost—oh, does she—and so when she slides Bob Ianucci his key cards, she attaches a yellow sticky note with her number on it and says, "If you need any help with dinner reservations, just let me know. That's my personal cell phone. I'm here for *whatever* you need."

Bob Ianucci peels the sticky note off the key-card envelope and regards it with a bemused expression. "Are you *soliciting* me?" he asks.

Alessandra runs her gaze over Bob Ianucci and notices things she overlooked in her haste: His blandly corporate look—gray suit pants, white shirt, navy striped tie, Seiko watch—his tight, military-style haircut, his close shave, his square jaw, and his direct gaze and she thinks, *Oh God.* She can't believe she didn't notice it right off the bat. This guy is a cop. Or, worse, a detective.

"What?" she says. "No!" She laughs and Bob Ianucci laughs and says, "Oh, too bad," and the whole thing becomes a joke and Bob Ianucci rolls his bag onto the elevator, and when the doors close, Alessandra turns to Edie and says, "I feel like the green-puke emoji, I'm sorry."

Edie says, "Go home, girl, I got this."

Alessandra wants to hug Edie, she is so grateful, but she "doesn't want to get Edie sick," and so she just collects her bag and scoots out the doors into the bright and newly confusing world.

23. Full Send

The Brant Point Grill is the restaurant at the White Elephant Hotel and Resort, the Hotel Nantucket's *rival,* so it seems like an odd choice for drinks—but Ms. English picked it and who is Chad to argue? The spacious bar has a lot of dark wood and big mirrors and the clientele is older and more sophisticated than in the places Chad frequents (or frequented, in his past life). There's a jazz combo playing in the corner—piano, drums, stand-up bass. Past the bar, Chad can see the elegant dining room, where enormous windows offer a vista of the flat blue sheet of Nantucket harbor, dotted with boats.

Chad has been to the restaurant before with his parents, an Easter brunch one year when Paul and Whitney thought it would be "fun" to visit the island in the off-season, but Chad remembers that he and Leith had been disenchanted by the whole experience—it was cold enough for them to need winter parkas on April 9 and everything was still closed downtown, including the Juice Bar and their yacht club, which was how they'd ended up at the Brant Point Grill.

Ms. English leads Chad to two seats at the long bar, ones that are in front of a mirror, which means that Chad is confronted with the reflection of himself sitting next to his now-fancy boss in a bar.

"What would you like, Long Shot?" Ms. English asks. "Drinks are on me."

"I can pay," Chad says.

Ms. English laughs. She motions for the bartender, who hurries over to take their order. "The usual, neat, for me, Brian."

"Appleton Estate Twenty-One, Magda, you got it," Brian says with a wink.

They know each other, Chad thinks. Ms. English comes here, to the rival hotel's restaurant. He supposes it's better than getting a drink at the Blue Bar, where Ms. English is still sort of at work and where everyone knows her. Another good thing about the Brant Point Grill, he realizes, is that they're anonymous, surrounded by another hotel's guests.

"I'll have a…" Chad is hesitant to order his usual, a vodka soda, because that's the stereotypical Chad drink. At the long-ago brunch, his parents ordered Bloody Marys, which came extravagantly garnished— one with a lobster tail on a skewer and one with a cheeseburger slider—but Chad doesn't want to inflate Ms. English's bar tab with an expensive drink. "A beer," he says. "Whale's Tale, if you have it on draft?"

"We do," Brian says. He sidles away to make the drinks. Although Chad is dying to ask Ms. English the question that's reverberating through his mind, he knows enough to wait until their drinks have been set before them and they've raised their glasses to each other.

"Thank you for inviting me," Chad says.

"Thank you for coming, Long Shot. This is way overdue."

Is it? Chad thinks. There's no time to consider how long Ms. English has been wanting to invite him for drinks, because the urge to know what happened to Bibi is overwhelming.

"So, what…"

"Barbara gave her notice at the beginning of last week," Ms. English says. "She was accepted at UMass Dartmouth with a scholarship and she's going to pursue a degree in criminal justice."

"What?" Chad says. "She *is?*"

"Yes, how about that! She forwarded me her acceptance e-mail—I fear because she thought I wouldn't believe her. Her first day of classes was today."

Bibi wasn't fired. She didn't go on the lam looking for Johnny Quarter. She wasn't bullied by Octavia and Neves (that was a crazy theory). She was going to college on a scholarship! Chad is embarrassed to find tears gathering in his eyes—he's so proud of her!

"Why didn't she tell me?" Chad says. Mixed in with his emotions is the sting of betrayal. Bibi just walked off the day before like everything was normal. *See ya, Long Shot.*

"She wanted me to tell you," Ms. English says. "She was afraid of a messy goodbye, I think. Some people are like that." Ms. English nudges Chad with her elbow. "And the two of you grew so close this summer!"

"It wasn't like that," Chad says. He drinks deeply from his beer. It's the first drink he's had since May 22, and it gives him an instant buzz. "We were friends."

"You were more than *friends,*" Ms. English says. "You planted that belt in the laundry in order to protect her."

No, I didn't, Chad wants to say—but he can't lie, so he shrugs.

"I take it that belt belonged to your mother?" Ms. English says. "Has she missed it?"

Ha! No. The last thing Chad is worried about is Whitney missing her belt. "I thought Bibi might have taken the belt and I didn't want her to get in trouble."

"All of my cleaners are extremely honest people," Ms. English says. "With squeaky-clean résumés. I see to that."

"What about me?" Chad asks. He finishes his beer; he probably drank it more quickly than he should have. Without his even asking, another one arrives in its place. "Did you do any background research on me?"

"No," Ms. English says. "You, I hired out of desperation." She laughs, and Chad has to smile. "I had a feeling about you, but it was a gamble. That's why I call you Long Shot."

Yes, Chad gets it. Preppy dudes from wealthy families don't clean hotel rooms— except this summer one did, and he did it well, he thinks. "Thank you for taking the chance," he says. "This summer helped me."

"Helped you?" Ms. English says.

Chad stares into his beer, then takes a long swallow. "Remember at my interview, I told you I messed up?"

"Yes, Long Shot, I do. I'll admit, I've wondered about that statement periodically over the summer. You're such a hard worker, conscientious, respectful, prompt, responsible, and, as I noticed in regard to your relationship with Barbara, thoughtful and kind. I can't imagine you being otherwise."

"Oh, but I was," Chad says. "I was otherwise."

Ms. English pats his back lightly. "You don't have to share," she says. "Unless you want to, in which case I will listen with rapt interest."

Chad thinks it over. He has done everything right this summer but he hasn't taken the most important step in moving on: He hasn't talked about what happened with anyone. *Share,* the word Ms. English used, makes him feel like she'll accept part of the burden he's been carrying around.

"Something happened this spring," Chad says. "On May twenty-second."

On the morning of May 22, Chad woke up freshly graduated from Bucknell University with gentleman's Cs, looking at a delicious, responsibility-free summer on Nantucket with his parents and his sister, Leith, before he joined his father's company, the Brandywine Group, in September. Chad's parents were driving to Deerfield Academy to pick up Leith, who had just finished her junior year. Paul and Whitney Winslow were making an overnight trip of it because they liked to include a romantic stay at the Mayflower Inn. (Chad didn't like to dwell on this, obviously; they were his *parents*.) All he cared about was having the house in Radnor to himself so he could throw a little graduation party.

Before his parents left, his mother kissed his cheek and said, "Please be good, Chaddy. And remember to take Lulu out every two hours. She can't make it to the door by herself anymore, so you'll have to carry her."

"I will," Chad said. Lulu was their fifteen-year-old dachshund whom Chad loved like another sibling. He would be good to the dog—but TBH, he couldn't wait for his parents to leave.

He'd invited everyone he'd ever known to the party, including a bunch of guys from Bucknell, some of whom had road-tripped for hours to get to the

Winslow home. Chad wanted the event to be a step up from the parties he'd thrown in high school, so he bought steaks to throw on the grill, and a bunch of the girls he invited showed up with potato salad and guacamole. Tindley Akers, whom Chad had known since nursery school, brought pot brownies. Chad sampled one as an appetizer—and it sent him flying! After dinner, Chad started a bonfire in the firepit while a bunch of kids splashed around in the pool. Things got wilder from there; honestly, Chad couldn't remember all the details. He knelt for the Full Send beer funnel multiple times; he did shots of Jägermeister and hoovered cocaine off the vanity in the downstairs powder room (that became a joke—"Meet me in the powder room"—though Chad felt guilty when he looked at his mother's little embroidered towels and fancy soaps).

Thinking about his mother made Chad remember the dog. He was supposed to take her out every two hours, and how long had it been? He found Lulu on her bed on the screened-in porch. Chad dutifully carried her outside, let her whiz, and then set her back on her plaid Orvis bed. She looked so old and forlorn that Chad almost wanted to tell everyone to go home while he and Lulu snuggled on the sectional in the rec room to watch *Family Guy*—that was their thing; Chad was certain that Lulu understood the show because it always held her rapt attention—but what was he, nuts? It was a party! His friends were here!

Still, he couldn't just leave Lulu to wallow in her old-dog misery, so he went in search of a rawhide or a treat, which required a trip to the basement—where Chad's attention was snagged by his parents' wine cave. (They pronounced it "kahv," which made Chad and Leith cringe.) He snatched a bottle of champagne off the rack, and upstairs, he grabbed a ten-inch chef's knife from the kitchen. In Chad's final week of school, his professor of French culture had shown the class how to saber the top off a bottle of champagne.

Chad ran outside to the deck, but the party was so out of control, there was no way to get anyone's attention. Everyone was in or around the pool— swimming, drinking, smoking, making out, dancing. The outdoor speaker blasted Pop Smoke's "What You Know 'Bout Love."

Chad ran the blade of the knife along the throat of the champagne bottle, just as Professor Legris had shown them, then hit the bottle with the blade, and— *whoosh*—the top of the bottle sliced off, neat and clean. Bubbles spewed over Chad's fingers. He enjoyed one split second of blissful satisfaction—the sabering worked! This was a party trick he could use for the rest of his life!—before he saw his college roommate and best friend, Paddy, hunched over, holding his face.

Somehow without even knowing, Chad knew.

He ran over to Paddy. "You okay, man?"

There was blood spurting out of the fingers that Paddy was holding over his left eye. The cork and the top of the bottle with its thick glass edge had hit Paddy in the face.

"Call nine-one-one!" Chad shouted, but nobody heard him and Chad's phone was over by the outdoor speaker, controlling the music. He grabbed the nearest person—Tindley, as it turned out—and called the ambulance from her phone.

Paddy wasn't making any noise, and he was as white as a sheet. Tindley had the presence of mind to bring Paddy a damp towel for his eye. Chad held Paddy's arm, the one that wasn't pressed to his face, and wished like hell the cork had hit anyone *but*

Paddy. Paddy Farrell was not only Chad's best friend; he was a genuinely good and smart person. He'd been a scholarship student at Bucknell. His dad was a long-haul trucker and his mom worked as a legal secretary; they lived in a town of four hundred called Grimesland, North Carolina.

"I'm so sorry, man," Chad said, wondering why the hell he had sabered the champagne when there were *people* around? How irresponsible was that? He hadn't noticed Paddy sitting on the deck; that was the thing. Paddy must have been alone in the dark, which made Chad feel even worse. Paddy didn't know anyone at the party besides the three other Bucknell guys, and he was quiet by nature. Paddy had driven up from Grimesland at Chad's insistence. *You have to come, man! There are going to be so many girls!*

When the ambulance arrived, some people scattered, thinking it was the police. Chad grabbed his phone but left the music playing and climbed into the back of the ambulance with Paddy, who kept insisting he didn't need to go to the hospital and *shouldn't* go because his parents didn't have that kind of health insurance.

"I'll pay for it, man. It was my fault," Chad said.

The paramedic, a woman named Kristy who was actually kind of hot, managed to pry Paddy's hand away from his eye. She said, matter-of-factly, "That's going to need surgery."

"I can't," Paddy said. "Afford it."

"I'll pay for it," Chad said again and he thought about how what he meant was that his parents— who at that very moment were probably gazing across a candlelit table at each other, splitting a chocolate mousse—would pay for it. They would find out about the party unless Chad got everyone out of there pronto. He wondered how bad it would be if he didn't go to the hospital with Paddy and instead stayed home and did damage control.

Bad, he thought. And for the first time in a long time, maybe ever, said a prayer.

When they got to the hospital, Paddy was rushed away; Chad heard someone mention an eye specialist. He was buzzing from the cocaine but also drunk and high and teetering on the edge of paranoia. A nurse gave him a form to fill out but he knew only some of the answers. He needed to call Paddy's parents—or his own—but he was waiting to see what the doctors said. He was hoping it would turn out to be just stitches and a shiner.

When he handed the clipboard back to the nurse, he said, "Whatever this costs, I'll pay for it, just make sure he gets the best care."

They were at Bryn Mawr Hospital, which was where Chad had been born. He hadn't had a reason to return here in twenty-two years and neither had anyone else in his family. They were just that fortunate, so fortunate that Chad almost broke down crying, but instead he stumbled over to the water fountain and tried to suck it dry.

His phone rang. It was Raj, which was not unexpected. After Paddy, Raj was the nicest guy that Chad knew. Raj was from Potomac, Maryland, and he was supersmart and driven; his parents were doctors. He was probably calling to see how Paddy was, but Chad couldn't talk to him yet. He didn't want to talk to anyone until he knew Paddy was going to be okay.

He declined the call. Raj immediately called back, and when Chad declined again, Raj texted: Pick up, bruh, it's urgent.

I can't talk, Chad texted back. Waiting room.

Raj sent a fire emoji, which Chad ignored. Then Raj called again and Chad whispered into the phone, "What?"

Raj said, "Someone set your house on fire."

Chad hung up. Raj was drunk, stoned, high, and he thought he was being funny, great. A man in blue scrubs entered the waiting room. "Chadwick Winslow?" he said.

Chad raised his hand like he was in fourth grade. The man approached and said, "Dr. Harding, nice to meet you. You're here with Patrick?"

Chad nodded.

"He's gone into surgery. The cornea appears to have been sliced. We're going to try to save the eye but there's a better-than-not chance Patrick will have partial to full vision loss."

Chad gagged, but no, he couldn't yuke here in the waiting room. He breathed in through his nose. "I want to pay for it."

Chad's phone rang; it was Raj again. Dr. Harding clapped Chad on the shoulder and said, "We're keeping him overnight. Why don't you go home and get some rest. One of our nurses has contacted Patrick's family."

No, Chad thought. He'd met Mr. and Mrs. Farrell a handful of times. They weren't fancy or sophisticated like Chad's parents, but they were kind, decent people. Paddy had an older brother, Griffin, who was in the U.S. Navy, stationed in Honolulu; they FaceTimed once a week.

The doctor disappeared back down the hall and when Chad pulled his phone out to call an Uber, he saw another text from Raj.

Your house caught on fire. The fire department put it out but the deck and the screened-in porch are torched.

You need to come home right now. Your neighbors are here. Also, man, I hate to say this in a text, but your dog is dead.

Lulu! Chad thought, and for a second he couldn't breathe.

Chad's phone rang again. The screen said DAD.

"I burned down part of my house," Chad says to Ms. English. "That was the least awful thing I did. I killed my dog, whom I loved so much, whom my whole family loved, and my sister still won't speak to me. She *hates* me." He gets an aching lump in his throat. "All I can think about is Lulu's fur catching on fire or her coughing from the smoke." He stops. It was so *terrible* and it was all his fault! He pushes his beer away. He thought he'd be okay to drink again, but now his stomach is churning just like it did that night at the hospital. "And my best friend, a guy I loved like a brother and always wanted to protect, a guy who was kind of like Bibi, because he didn't come from a background like mine, lost his vision in his left eye. Forever. And we're not friends anymore. I haven't heard from him since he went back home."

Chad had stayed at the hospital until his parents and Paddy's parents had shown up. Paddy underwent surgery and was released two days later. When the nurse wheeled him out with a patch over one eye, Chad started apologizing, insisting it was an accident, he hadn't *seen* Paddy sitting there, but he could hear his voice ricocheting off a new steeliness encapsulating Paddy that Chad hoped was just the painkillers but that turned out to be anger. *You're shallow, thoughtless, and oblivious to your own privilege. You didn't check to see who was sitting around you when you sliced the top off a glass bottle with a ten-inch chef's knife, because you didn't* care, *anyone sitting in your direct line of fire would have been* in your way, spoiling your fun, *and we both know nothing and no one means more to Chad Winslow than fun. Your whole existence is filled with empty, meaningless pleasure and this will continue to be true because no one is ever going to hold you accountable. You'll never develop character and you won't go to heaven or hell because you don't have a soul.*

Paddy had been at least partially right: Nobody held Chad accountable. His parents did extreme damage control, calling in a favor at the *Philadelphia Inquirer* so the incident didn't make the papers and personally phoning the parents of every kid who attended the party and promising favors in exchange for their kids' silence or threatening lawsuits because someone— Chad still doesn't know who—threw a can of lighter fluid into the firepit. The can exploded, and burning fragments sliced through the screen of the porch and instantly ignited the sisal rug and the drapes…and the dog bed. Chad overheard his mother lying to people on the phone, saying they'd "put Lulu down." *She was so old and feeble, poor thing.* Paddy didn't tell anyone anything; he returned to Grimesland, which was far, far away from the gossip channels of the Main Line.

"I didn't get in any trouble," Chad says. "My parents were angry, of course, and they were disappointed. But mostly, they were worried about how the incident would reflect on *them*. They thought everyone would say they were bad parents, and so they did what they could to sweep it under the rug. They bought me a brand-new Range Rover as a graduation present and it was delivered to my house the day after Paddy went home, so it felt like I had done all these heinous things and was *rewarded*." Chad shakes his head and his eyes flood with hot tears as he thinks, *What the actual f—*

Ms. English lays a cool hand on his arm. "But you corrected course on your own," she says. "You came to me and I put you to work in a place where we don't sweep *anything* under the rug."

Chad wipes his eyes with the back of his hand. "You told me that you believed even the biggest messes could be cleaned up."

"And that's what you did," she says. "I'm sure your parents are very proud of you."

"They're not, though," Chad says. "Neither one of them has praised me for getting this job. My father told me to quit!"

"But you didn't quit," Ms. English says. "Because you do have character, Long Shot."

"I don't want to work at my father's company," Chad says. "I want to stay at the hotel until it closes for the season."

Ms. English tsks. "You have to get on with your life."

"But I don't want—"

They're interrupted by a silver-haired gentleman in a pink shirt who puts a hand on Ms. English's back and says, "Hello, Magda."

Ms. English rises from her stool and offers the gentleman her hand. He kisses it like someone in the movies, and Chad thinks, *Who is this dude*? The guy is gazing at Ms. English like she's a Victoria's Secret Angel, and Chad feels uncomfortable—like he's the one interrupting them, not the other way around—and protective too. He gets to his feet.

"Hi," he says. "I work for Ms. English."

The gentleman turns to Chad, then looks at Ms. English. "This is your long shot?"

Ms. English chuckles. "It is indeed. Xavier, please meet Chadwick Winslow. Chadwick, this is Xavier Darling."

MARIO'S "I LOVE YOU" PLAYLIST FOR LIZBET

"XO"—Beyoncé
"Let My Love Open the Door"—Pete
Townshend
"Whatever It Is"—Zac Brown Band
"Never Tear Us Apart"—INXS
"Come to Me"—Goo Goo Dolls
"Everlong"—Foo Fighters
"Head Over Feet"—Alanis Morissette
"Never Let You Go"—Third Eye Blind
"Wonderful Tonight"—Eric Clapton
"Swing Life Away"—Rise Against
"Something"—The Beatles
"You're My Home"—Billy Joel
"I Believe"—Stevie Wonder
"Better Together"—Luke Combs
"You and Me"—Lifehouse
"All I Want Is You"—U2
"In My Feelings"—Drake
"Lay Me Down"—Dirty Heads
"Sunshine"—World Party
"Crazy Love"—Van Morrison
"Stand by My Woman"—Lenny Kravitz

It's late on the night of the twenty-fourth, so late it's the twenty-fifth, and Mario slips between the sheets of Lizbet's bed and starts the ritual of unbraiding her hair. He likes the way it looks all kinked and long, so she indulges him. Lizbet isn't fully awake but her desire stirs at the feel of his hands in her hair, his front pressed against her back. Because she's in that liminal state between waking and sleeping, her animal instincts emerge, and she loses all inhibition. Their lovemaking is a storm—and this night, she hears the tapping of rain on her cottage's roof, then the tree branches swiping at her windows, then a sharp crack followed by a grumble of thunder. Lizbet's and Mario's bodies move over the bed in a darkness that's briefly illuminated by flashes of lightning. It's cinematic, she thinks; how beautiful they are in those split seconds when their bodies are silvered by the electrical charge in the air.

Afterward, they lie flat on the bottom sheet, the duvet kicked to the floor, and Lizbet wonders if she's ever been this happy. She has focused all of her energy not on fighting the old, but on building the new, just as the sign at the end of her bed has been urging her to do for nearly an entire calendar year. She wishes that back on September 30, she could have somehow known that one day she would be lying in bed next to *Mario freaking Subiaco* after having impressed the hell out of the new owner of the Hotel Nantucket, where she was the general manager. Would she have believed it?

Mario expels a breath. "I love you," he says.

The rain has stopped, the wind has died down, the lightning and thunder have rolled past.

"What?" Lizbet says, though of course she heard him perfectly.

Mario faces her. "I love you," he says. "I'm in love with you." He starts laughing. "I honestly can't believe it. I'm...what? Forty-six, almost forty-seven, and in all those years, I've told only three other women I loved them. One was Allie Taylor in sixth grade, and yes, that was real love, the purest kind, awkward and unrequited. One was my mother, of course. And the third was Fiona. I loved Fee, but that was different because, although I would have lain down in traffic for her, we weren't romantically involved."

Lizbet's heart feels like an exploding star in her chest. She realizes it's time for her to say it back, but she wants to hear more.

"How can you be so sure with me?" she says. "Explain yourself."

"Working backward?" Mario says. "When you ended things a few weeks ago, I thought, *Okay, she's not ready, no problem.* Things had gotten serious pretty quickly and I knew you were coming off this other relationship, so I told myself I understood. But I was hurt by it, which was a new feeling for me, or new since sixth grade when Allie Taylor went to the Valentine's Day dance with Will Chandler instead of me." He grins.

Lizbet touches his face. He loves her.

"Before that? I wouldn't say it was *love at first sight,* but when I saw you in the parking lot that first day in those sexy heels telling JJ to leave you alone even though the dude was down on one knee proposing, I thought, *That poor guy blew it but I'm not going to.*"

"Stop," Lizbet says, though she's grinning.

"Before *that* ..." Mario says.

"There was no 'before that,'" Lizbet says. "That was the day we met."

"Before that, Xavier told me that he'd hired a lioness named Elizabeth Keaton to manage the hotel. He said you used to run the Deck with your boyfriend but that you'd parted ways and you were looking for a fresh start."

"*Lioness?*" Lizbet says.

"Direct quote. You don't forget a description like that. I was so intrigued that I did some stalking. I saw the feature about you and JJ in *Coastal Living,* then

I checked out the Deck's website, and I developed a little crush on you."

"You did not!"

"I did," Mario says. "You reminded me of Allie Taylor."

Lizbet swats him and he says, "I'm serious. She had blond hair like yours and pale blue eyes and that sweet-but-tough thing going that I haven't encountered in any other woman until I met you. I always said I was going to find Allie Taylor someday and marry her."

Lizbet is starting to feel a little jealous of Allie Taylor.

"But when I checked Facebook, I saw she was married with four kids at private schools in Manhattan and I also realized I was happy for her in that life. The magic was gone. But when I look at you..." Here, Mario traces his finger from Lizbet's shoulder down her arm. "I feel like I'm twelve years old again and everything is shiny and new and colorful and full of wonder. And that's how I know that I love you."

"I love you too," Lizbet says.

"There's a reason why I'm telling you tonight," Mario says, "even though I've been in love with you for most of the summer."

"What's the reason?" she says.

"Xavier was crazy about the bar, our numbers are good, and you said he was happy with the hotel."

"He raved," Lizbet says.

"So today it finally felt real," Mario says. "It felt *sustainable,* like I can dig in here. I can stay here and do my thing with the bar and you can run the hotel, and in the off-season we can go wherever the spirit moves us. I still own a place in LA. It's a bungalow with a little pool out back and an avocado tree."

"An avocado tree?" Lizbet says. She kisses Mario and pulls the duvet onto the bed. All she wants is to go to sleep dreaming of swimming pools and movie stars, an avocado tree and some Craftsman furniture in Mario's bungalow. Tomorrow, she will still have to charm Xavier, still have to make sure everything is beyond the beyond for him; a hotel experience isn't made in one afternoon or even one night. Lizbet closes her eyes and Mario starts breathing deeply but Lizbet can't settle. She's in a happy bubble, insulated and safe, but isn't there the teeniest tear, threatening to deflate it?

Well, she thinks.

The last Friday of the month is only two days away—which means a new *Hotel Confidential* post. Either Shelly Carpenter has stayed with them or she hasn't. If she has and she gives them less than five keys, or if she hasn't and doesn't review them at all...what will happen?

24. Heartbreaker

Xavier Darling is out to dinner and so Grace spends the evening doing a few minor hauntings. She's able to delight Mary Perkowski from Ohio by flickering the lights, then playing Mary's favorite song, "Thunder Road," spontaneously over the sound system, then by making the sheers of the canopy bed sway like the dress in the song. Next, it's off to suite 114, where

Grace peeks in on the Marsh children, who will be leaving in the morning. Today marked Louie's last chess lesson with Rustam, and Wanda returned her Nancy Drew books to the library. (She made it all the way to number forty-five, *The Spider Sapphire Mystery*.) Kimber isn't exactly an organized packer; she has been stuffing things in bags indiscriminately, a process that was interrupted by moments of her sitting on the bed with her face in her hands or writing her "memoirs" on her laptop with tears streaming down her face.

Grace has grown attached to Kimber—and Wanda and Louie, and even Doug. She can't imagine the hotel without them, but it's the very nature of a hotel to be impermanent. Hello, then goodbye; that's how it goes. If people stayed forever, it would be a home.

Grace moves in close to Wanda, the only supernaturally sensitive person in the past hundred years who has wanted to understand her. Grace kisses her cheek, leaving behind a cool damp spot.

Wanda's eyes flutter open. "Grace?"

I'm here, sweet child, Grace thinks. Then Doug growls—he's *such* a crank with her, though Grace likes knowing he'll protect Wanda—and Grace leaves the room.

Nighty-night.

She floats up two floors and across the hall to the owner's suite, a place she has consciously avoided all summer long—and sure enough, it triggers her right away. Despite the fact that it's bright and white and beachy modern now, Grace can picture her nineteen-year-old self crouched on the ground, trying to coax the damn cat, Mittens, out from under the bed. She's thinking that a woman who would throw a silver candlestick at her own pet is a woman with a turd for a heart. Grace hears the door open. In her mind, it's

Jackson Benedict, come to sweet-talk Grace, kiss her and press her hand to his crotch, and she will, in that instant, know she's ruined. But she will not yet know that she's doomed.

It's not Jackson Benedict who steps into the suite— obviously not; Jack has been dead for decades—but Xavier Darling with none other than Magda English.

Well! Grace thinks. This is something of a reprise— the owner of the hotel with the housekeeping staff. Except Magda isn't merely "housekeeping staff"; she is, in modern parlance, a "girl boss." No one pushes Magda around or tells her what to do, not even a man with as much money as Xavier Darling.

Xavier turns on the lights in the living area; they're on dimmers and cast a romantic, honeyed glow. He raises the room-darkening shades on the picture window so they can see over Easton Street to Nantucket harbor and the ruby beacon of Brant Point Light.

"Champagne?" Xavier says. There's a bottle of Pol Roger relaxing in an ice bath on the burled-walnut coffee table, and Magda says, "You know I never turn down champagne, Xavier."

Xavier opens the bottle with a flourish. He pours two flutes, then he and Magda settle on the sofa together and raise their glasses.

"To the hotel," Magda says. They drink.

"I bought it for you, you know," Xavier says.

This makes Magda hoot with laughter.

"I'm serious," Xavier says. "When you worked on my ships, I knew where to find you."

"You were always so subtle about it," Magda says. "Landing your helicopter on the bow or hotdogging in your cigarette boat. I'll never forget you pulling up to the docks in that devil-when I went ashore in Ischia." She caresses his face. "You used to be so dashing."

Xavier sighs. "I'm still pretty dashing, no? As soon as you told me you were retiring and moving to Nantucket, I did some research and found the hotel. I wanted to make it grand for you." He sips his champagne. "Another woman might be flattered."

"Another woman might think you were trying to control her."

"No one can control you," Xavier says. "Of all the women I've known in my life, you are the one who has haunted me."

Ha-ha-ha! Grace thinks. *Now, there's a choice of words.*

"You're so independent. So…elusive."

Magda puts a finger to Xavier's lips. He takes her hand and pulls her in for a kiss. The flutes of champagne are set down. Magda and Xavier move for each other in such haste that Xavier's knee jostles the table; his flute topples and champagne spills across the burled surface of the table and drips down onto the Persian rug, but neither Xavier nor Magda, with her eagle eye for cleanliness, seems to notice.

Downstairs at the front desk, the phone rings…but Richie isn't at his post. No, he's in Lizbet's office on his cell phone. *Again?* Grace thinks. This must be a response to Kimber and the children leaving. She feels both sad and disappointed. Richie's actions were so wholesome while he was in thrall to the romance; these calls had completely stopped.

Richie doesn't answer the hotel phone the first time it rings, nor does he answer it when the same people call back. (Richie can see from checking the phone on Lizbet's desk that it's the Sparacinos in suite 316.) When the Sparacinos call back a third time, Richie abruptly finishes the call on his cell phone and picks up.

"Good evening, front desk," he says as smoothly as a late-night DJ.

Mrs. Sparacino huffs. "There's a couple making quite a lot of...*noise* in suite three seventeen. My husband has tried knocking on the wall but they don't seem to get the hint. Would you call them, please? Ask them to be a little quieter?"

Richie assures Mrs. Sparacino that he will...but then it dawns on him that the guest in suite 317 is Xavier Darling.

Grace waits what she hopes is a sufficient amount of time for the passion to play out before returning to suite 317. Thankfully, Magda and Xavier are now tucked neatly under the covers, snuggled in among the pillows, enjoying their afterglow.

"I realize you love your work here," Xavier says.

"I certainly do," Magda says. "I loved it on the ships and I enjoy it even more here on land."

"But Magda, you have so much money. You've seen the latest statements? We're well past the twenty-million mark." He tickles her under the covers and she giggles like a girl before swatting him away. "You've come a long way from the night we met."

"I won nearly a quarter million that night," Magda says. "I put down my own hard-earned money, I placed the bets, I rolled the dice."

"But you invested it with my people..."

"Yes, you helped me build the fortune. It's possible that I've never really felt entitled to the money for that reason, although, don't get me wrong, it's nice knowing it's there."

"I'd like to see you enjoy it," Xavier says.

Magda sits up straighter and checks her hair; strands have fallen out of her bun, and she tucks them back in. "We're a lot alike. You have billions and you won't stop working until you're dead."

"I'll retire immediately if you agree to marry me," Xavier says.

Magda squawks. "What kind of foolish thing is that to say?"

"I've been in love with you since the second I met you on that ship. I know you want to be close to Zeke and William, but it's been nearly a year. I'm sure they only want you to be happy. Marry me, Magda. Come to London."

Eeeeee! Grace thinks. She's swirling around the room like a funnel cloud. Xavier loves Magda! He's proposing—and unlike Jack, who promised Grace every time he visited the storage closet that he would divorce Dahlia and marry her, Xavier means it. He probably already has a ring picked out.

Xavier reaches over to his nightstand, opens the little curved drawer, and produces a box from Harry Winston.

He sits up in bed, the covers still (thankfully) smooth across his lap, and presents the box to Magda.

"What have you done, Xavier?" she says.

"I went all in," Xavier says. "Open it."

Magda opens the box to reveal a movie-star engagement ring. It's a light pink oval diamond—Grace doesn't know carats from carrots but it's *big*—in a setting of pavé diamonds and rose gold.

"Well," Magda says.

"Try it on."

Magda snaps the box closed. "Oh, Xavier, I can't try it on. I'm not going to marry you. I think you're a wonderful man and I'm very grateful for all you've done for me." She stares up at the exact spot where Grace is hovering; Grace holds her gaze, even though she knows that all Magda sees is the Nantucket night sky painted on the ceiling. "I consider you a dear friend. You make me laugh; I enjoy your company and a little roll in the hay, because at my age, I'm happy I can still roll. But I don't love you. I do love this hotel and this job and being able to keep an eye on Zeke and William. I've been looking at some real estate on Eel Point Road, houses with ocean views and a pool and gardens. I haven't found the right one yet, but my plan, Xavier, is to stay here. I'm happy here."

"You're turning me down?" Xavier says.

Magda presses her palm to his cheek. "Yes," she says. "I'm turning you down, sweet man, I'm sorry."

Grace leaves the suite and spirits back up to the fourth-floor storage closet. If only she'd had the courage and self-assurance to say those words a hundred years earlier—*I'm turning you down, Mr. Benedict, I'm sorry*—she would have gone on to live a full life. But those words hadn't been available to Grace in 1922. She feels proud now, not only of Magda but of womankind. There's been progress made this century.

Grace chuckles. She suspects Wanda will be turning down men left and right.

Lizbet has arranged for Yolanda to take Xavier up to Great Point on Thursday. In Lizbet's opinion, Great Point is the ultimate Nantucket destination, and Yolanda's classic Bronco is as cool a vehicle as exists on this island. Lizbet asked Beatriz to prepare a picnic of chilled lobster rolls, yellow tomato gazpacho, corn salad, and some of Mario's church-picnic eggs in a proper hamper with a bottle or two of Domaines Ott, Xavier's favorite rosé. Lizbet wonders if Xavier will ask her to go along, since he barely knows Yolanda. She would love to say yes, she has been yearning to stretch out on the sand all summer, but of course she has to stay at the hotel and make sure things run smoothly. Maybe he'll invite Edie to go—they seemed to hit it off—or his old friend Magda. (Lizbet can't really spare Magda today or any day, though she'll have to if Xavier asks.) The only person Lizbet does *not* want to see go on a day trip with Xavier is Alessandra. The way she threw herself at him in the break room was embarrassing.

Lizbet gets to work early, but apparently not early enough, because when she walks into her office, there's a note on the desk from Xavier. He's gone.

"What?" Lizbet shouts. The note says simply: *Had to leave the island unexpectedly. So sorry. XD*

She bursts out to the desk, but no one is there. It's seven o'clock. Richie is spending his last morning with Kimber and the kids before they leave on the ferry. Edie and Alessandra won't arrive for another fifteen minutes, and neither will Adam and Zeke. The only person in the lobby is Louie. He's at his usual place at the chessboard by the front window, playing against himself. Even at this early hour, he's dressed in his little polo shirt with his blond hair combed and parted.

Lizbet approaches. Louie has been in the lobby every day since June 6—an eighty-one-day streak— and Lizbet hasn't found the time to play him in chess even once. She feels bad about this, but she can't dwell on it now.

"Louie?" she says. "Did you see an older gentleman with silver hair here in the lobby earlier?"

Louie blinks behind the thick lenses of his glasses. "You mean Mr. Darling?"

"Yes," Lizbet says. "You saw him?"

Louie moves a pawn. "I beat him in sixteen moves." He shrugs. "He wasn't bad."

"You played chess with him? This morning?"

"A while ago," Louie says. "Then his driver came in, and Mr. Darling asked the driver to take our picture because he said I'm going to be famous someday. Then he left."

He left.

Lizbet calls Xavier from her office.

"Xavier?" she says. "Is everything okay?" She's afraid something went wrong and Xavier is too much of a gentleman to tell her. Was the bed uncomfortable? Did he get frustrated with the automatic shades? Was he visited by the ghost? (Lizbet and Xavier have never discussed the ghost; she was too embarrassed to address it, though certainly he saw references to the ghost on their TravelTattler reviews.)

"Everything's fine." Xavier's voice sounds staticky and far away. She's on the speakerphone in his car, or maybe he's already in the air. "I have to fly home to tend to a business matter. I'm afraid it couldn't be helped, though God knows, I tried."

A business matter? Doesn't he have people for this? He's been on Nantucket for less than twenty-four hours!

"I'm so sorry to hear that, Xavier." If he hasn't actually boarded his plane, Lizbet might be able to lure him back. "I had a beach trip planned for you, a journey up to Great Point. We prepared a picnic."

"Sorry to miss it," Xavier says. "I'd like to say I'll do it next time, but I'm not sure there will be a next time."

Lizbet nearly drops the phone. What does he *mean,* he's not sure there'll be a next time? "Did something go wrong? Did something…happen?" She wonders if maybe Richie rubbed him the wrong way (impossible; Richie is an ace) or if maybe he found out about Doug the dog (wouldn't he have *said* something?).

"It's nothing to do with you or the hotel, don't worry." Xavier clears his throat. "You've done an outstanding job with everything. I'm proud of you, Lizbet."

Lizbet is struck dumb. He got her name right. She would count this as a victory, but something in his tone sounds so...final.

By the time she opens her mouth to speak—to say, *Thank you for giving me the opportunity, I look forward to next year when we actually know what we're doing, most of our staff is returning*—she hears a beeping noise. Xavier has hung up.

It was Edie who checked in the Marsh family back on June 6, and because Alessandra has taken lunch, it's Edie who checks them out.

Edie thinks back to the moment Kimber, Wanda, and Louie first walked in—Kimber with her peacock-dyed hair, Wanda and Louie in their little glasses—and then the surprise of Doug! If they'd checked in today instead of on day one, when Edie was so desperate to win the thousand-dollar bonus, would she have been as accommodating? Would she have booked them for eleven weeks *without a credit card*? Would she have *upgraded* them to a suite and *allowed a dog*? It's a moot point now. Edie can say—and the whole staff would agree—that they're happy to have had the Marsh family among them for the summer. The hotel will feel incomplete with them gone.

She presents Kimber with the final bill. "Your last night's stay is on us and last night's room service as well. We're really going to miss you."

Kimber waves a hand in front of her face. "Stop, you'll make me cry."

"I want to thank you," Edie says, "for mentioning me in the TravelTattler review."

"What are you talking about?" Kimber says. "I didn't write a TravelTattler review."

"You didn't?" Edie says. "I thought for sure…"

Kimber glances over at Wanda, and Edie gasps. "Did *Wanda* write it?"

Kimber grins. "No, it was me. You're one of a kind, Edie Robbins."

Richie comes down the hall with the luggage trolley. "Zeke is taking Doug out the side entrance." He looks at Edie. "And my stuff is packed up as well."

"Great," Edie says. "My mom says you can move in anytime." One of the other things that's changing with the Marshes' departure is that Richie is coming to live with Edie and Love until the hotel closes for the season. Kimber confessed to Edie that Richie had been living *in his car* before he moved into suite 114. When Edie told her mother this, Love offered Richie their spare bedroom for a very reasonable rent.

Lizbet appears from the back office as Kimber scans the list of charges. "This all looks good." She pays the balance in cash, then throws in an extra thousand dollars. "To split among the staff," she says. Her eyes glass over with tears. "Getting away this summer with the kids was the best decision I've made in my life. Thank you." She takes Richie's hand. "If we end up getting married, you're all invited."

"Come back and see us again," Lizbet says. She gives Kimber a hug and then, as they planned, Edie brings out two gifts from the back: Nancy Drew mysteries number forty-six through forty-eight for Wanda and the lobby chess set for Louie. Edie gives each of the children a tight squeeze; Louie squirms and Wanda starts to weep, saying, "I don't want to leave. What about Grace? She'll be lonely without me."

Kimber ushers Wanda to the door. "Let's go take a

picture of Adam and Zeke, honey." She gives Lizbet and Edie a weary smile. "It's going to be a long ride home."

"Be safe!" Edie says. She waves as the Marsh family steps out of the lobby into the sun, then turns to Lizbet. "This is the worst part of the job."

"By far," Lizbet says, running a finger under each eye. "You know I wanted to kill you when you told me you'd rented them a room without a functioning credit card. And then that you'd upgraded them to a suite for eleven weeks. And then that they had a pit bull. But that was the right call in the end, for so many reasons."

"Because Wanda wrote an article about the ghost," Edie says. "Which increased occupancy."

"More than doubled it."

"And Louie entertained people with his chess," Edie says. "So many people mentioned it in their TravelTattler reviews."

"And Richie was happy and had a place to stay," Lizbet says. "If he hadn't met Kimber, he might have quit, and I would have been stuck. He's such a team player. I haven't had to worry about billing; he's taken care of all the financials so that I could focus on the guests and the staff."

"It all worked out the way it was supposed to," Edie says.

"But you couldn't have predicted any of those circumstances. You made a decision based on your understanding of what hospitality means—saying yes rather than no." Lizbet leans in. "Next year, I want you to be our front-desk manager."

Edie perks up. "You do?" she says. "What about Alessandra?"

Lizbet shakes her head. "I doubt she'll come back next year. But if she does...she'll just have to deal."

* * *

The hotel feels empty in the aftermath of the Marshes' departure and Edie has to remind herself that they still have a full hotel. She calls Magda to let her know that suite 114 has checked out and is ready for a deep clean; fortunately, they built in a buffer night. No one will check into that room until Saturday.

Just then, Mr. Ianucci from room 307 steps in from the family pool in just his bathing suit with a hydrangea-blue towel draped over his shoulders like a cape. He lifts his sunglasses to the top of his head.

"I hate to bother you," he says.

Edie would beg to differ on this point. Mr. Ianucci seems to relish being high maintenance. Edie was the one who made the reservation with his secretary right after the ghost story broke. The secretary begged for a two-night stay when Lizbet had instituted a three-night minimum due to high demand. Fine, Edie granted a two-night stay. Yesterday he asked for a reservation at the bar at American Seasons less than an hour before he wanted to dine. Who does that? But Edie handled it. This morning, he showed up in the lobby in his pajama bottoms and a Hanes undershirt and typed on his laptop and drank coffee and ate two of Beatriz's almond croissants even though a sign encouraged the guests to take only one. He then asked Edie if she could arrange for a surfing lesson *for later that morning* and Edie smiled and said, "I'll try," though what she meant was *A little notice would have been nice.* However, Zeke was still friends with everyone at the surf school, so he arranged for a private lesson with Liam, the best instructor. Fine, great, Mr. Ianucci was so happy—not happy enough to tip either Edie or Zeke, but that's not why they do the job. Then Mr. Ianucci called down to the desk to say that the water temperature on the south shore was only 72 degrees. "That's a bit chilly for me," he said. "I'm going to stick to the pool."

Edie called to cancel the surfing lesson with her apologies but feared that the next time she asked for a last-minute favor, she would be turned down.

"What can I do for you, Mr. Ianucci?" Edie says now.

"The nice lady from the kitchen brought out the lemonade and the cookies," he says.

Edie's eyes widen. Lemonade and cookies? Is it three o'clock already?

"But the children at the pool snatched up the cookies before I could even get out of my chaise. Could I possibly get some more cookies?"

Edie will have to request another special favor, this time from Beatriz. "No problem. I'll ask the kitchen for another batch right away."

Mr. Ianucci holds up prayer hands, but does he actually say "Thank you"? He does not; he slips back through the pool door.

Edie calls the kitchen to ask for more cookies, and when she hangs up, Lizbet steps out of her office. "I'm going home early, Edie. This whole thing with Xavier…and the Marshes leaving…I'm schlumped. I need to recharge my batteries for tomorrow."

Tomorrow is the last Friday of the month, which means a new *Hotel Confidential* Instagram post. "No problem," Edie says. "I've got things covered here."

Lizbet's brow wrinkles. "Where's Alessandra?"

"At lunch," Edie says breezily, as if Alessandra hasn't been gone for over two hours.

A few minutes later, Beatriz appears with another platter of cookies. She shakes her head at Edie in mock disgust—asking for extra cookies is *no bueno* because Beatriz is prepping for evening service at the

Blue Bar—and Edie says, "You're going to make one guest in particular *very* happy."

"It better be Shelly Carpenter," Beatriz says, and Edie laughs, but when she steps out onto the patio of the family pool and sees Mr. Ianucci under an umbrella with his laptop out, she thinks, *Is Mr. Ianucci actually Shelly Carpenter?* He *has* asked for a lot of special favors, starting with the two-night stay, which means he'll be checking out by eleven a.m. the following day, conveniently one hour before the post comes out.

"Here you go, Mr. Ianucci," Edie says, offering him the cookies. She's so hungry she could eat the entire platter herself. The fresh-from-the-oven cookies are studded with milk chocolate chips, white chocolate chips, and toffee bits; they're crisp at the edges but soft in the center.

"What service!" Mr. Ianucci says, helping himself to two. Again, not quite a "thank you," Edie thinks. She wants to peek at whatever Mr. Ianucci is writing on his laptop. Is Shelly Carpenter really Bob Ianucci? A man?

Oh, Edie hopes not. That would be such a disappointment.

Edie steps back into the lobby to see a woman heading for the front desk like a blond bullet. She looks at Edie, then at Alessandra's unmanned computer.

"Where is she?" the woman hisses.

"I'm sorry?" Edie says. "Where is who?" Though Edie fears she knows.

"The little Jolene!" the woman says.

Jolene? Edie thinks, and she relaxes a bit. She thought the woman was looking for Alessandra.

"Her!" the blonde says, holding up her phone. She starts scrolling through photos: Alessandra in someone's kitchen, Alessandra on a bathroom scale, Alessandra lying across a very nice king-size bed that Edie suspects is *not* her bed at Adam and Raoul's house. "She sent these to my husband and told him she'd forward them to me if he didn't pay her fifty thousand dollars."

Despite her empty stomach, Edie feels like she might vomit.

"She's blackmailing him!" the woman says. "Where is she?"

"At lunch," Edie whispers. What's that saying? It takes a thief to catch a thief. Alessandra is a blackmailer just like Graydon! She's a hypocrite! She had sex with this woman's husband and took pictures of herself in their home (they aren't nudes, thank God).

It's now a quarter past three; Alessandra left for lunch two and a half hours ago. Of course Alessandra would make an exit right before she had to face the music.

"Let me call her cell," Edie says. "What's your name?"

"Heidi Bick. She knows who I am."

Edie dials Alessandra's number, her eyes stinging with tears. She and Alessandra became *friends*. They *bonded*. Not only because Alessandra stood up to Graydon and got Edie's money back, but also because Alessandra is smart and funny, and she's the only person who understands the ins and outs of Edie's days. Graydon told Edie she gave people too much credit, and that's something Edie now cherishes about herself. But she was wrong this time. So, so wrong.

The call goes to voice mail. Edie looks at Heidi Bick in frustration. "She's not answering."

"She *slept* with my *husband*," Heidi says. "She *lived* in my *house*."

Edie closes her eyes. She thinks about how, in nature, insects and reptiles that are brightly colored or flagrantly marked are the most venomous. Alessandra had all the signs—the attention-grabbing hair, the eye crystals, the upside-down name tag. She lured in vulnerable people, trapped them, exploited them.

"And *then!*" Heidi says. "The pièce de résistance! She robbed my neighbor Lyric and planted her things in my house so I would think Michael was having an affair with Lyric!"

Good God, Edie thinks.

Heidi narrows her eyes. "It was so damn clever that if I weren't appalled, I might be impressed." She reels back. "But I'm appalled. She's a despicable human being." Heidi holds up the phone. "This is blackmail. Fifty grand? It's extortion. I'm pressing charges."

The door to the family pool opens and Mr. Ianucci steps in. "Pressing charges?" he says. "Sounds like things are getting hot in here."

Edie whips out her fake smile like a gun from a holster. "Can I help you, Mr. Ianucci?"

"Seems I've lost my room key," he says. "Can you make me another?"

Please, Edie thinks. *You mean, Can you* please *make me another?*

"Happy to!" she says in her fake cheerful voice. Mr. Ianucci won't know it's fake, but Alessandra would because it's a desk thing. Edie doesn't want to be angry at Alessandra; she doesn't want the accusations to be true. She burgled the neighbor's house and planted the neighbor's belongings!

Edie turns to the back counter to make Mr. Ianucci a new key for room 307 and sees a manila envelope with *Edie* scrawled across the front in Alessandra's handwriting.

Suddenly Edie feels like she's living in a Nancy Drew mystery. Where did *this* come from? It's obviously been there since Alessandra went to lunch and Edie hasn't noticed it, though Alessandra knew Edie would notice it eventually.

Does this mean Alessandra isn't coming back from lunch…*at all?* Edie is crushed by the thought; she wonders how she can feel so angry and simultaneously so dejected.

Edie hands Mr. Ianucci his key card, and only once he has slapped off in his flip-flops (again without a thank-you) does Edie turn back to Heidi Bick. "Alessandra is gone for the day."

"You're covering for her."

"I'm *not* covering for her, believe me," Edie says. "I think what she did is appalling…ghastly." She tries to come up with some other strong SAT words. "Odious. I'll make sure she contacts you to apologize."

"I don't *want* her to contact me!" Heidi says. "I didn't come here for a big dramatic *Real Housewives* moment. I sent her a text saying I knew what she'd done and that I was calling the police." Heidi slips her phone into her bag. "Then I decided that texting was cowardly, so I came down here. And the closer I got, the more pissed off I became." Heidi takes a breath and looks at Edie with imploring eyes. "Listen, I realize half of this mess is my husband's fault. I just want her to leave my family alone."

"I understand," Edie says. "I'll give her that message."

Heidi Bick reaches across the desk and grasps Edie's wrist. "Thank you. Lizbet has a real treasure in you."

"I didn't realize you knew Lizbet," Edie says. The plot thickens.

"We're friends," Heidi says. "I considered calling her first and getting the little Jolene *fired,* but Lizbet has enough going on and it's hard to find help, and I'm determined to fight my own battles."

Edie's spirit flags with "it's hard to find help" because, as incensed as Edie is, she doesn't want to see Alessandra fired. What will they do if Alessandra doesn't come back? The quick fix would be to put Edie's mother, Love, on the day desk—and sorry, but that's not an option. (And yet, how will Edie ever be able to express her opposition to this arrangement to either Lizbet or her mother?) "I understand."

Heidi backs up toward the door. "Tell her to go ruin someone *else's* life!"

The instant Heidi Bick disappears, Edie rips open the envelope. Inside is a note—*Edie, I'm sorry. This is rightfully yours*—and a stack of hundred-dollar bills. Edie counts it: four thousand dollars.

Alessandra's bonuses.

As soon as Edie's shift is over and Richie shows up—he wants to talk about how nice Edie and Love's home is and how grateful, yada-yada, but Edie cuts him off; she doesn't have time—she hops on one of the hotel bikes and books it over to Hooper Farm Road, where Adam, Raoul, and Alessandra live. Edie rehearses what she's going to say in her head. She's going to air her anger first: *How could you, you're a hypocrite, I believed in you!* Once that's out, she'll grant Alessandra forgiveness. But when Edie pulls into the driveway, she finds Raoul and Alessandra loading Alessandra's Louis Vuitton duffels into the trunk of Raoul's car, and Edie forgets the anger part.

"Wait!" she says, skidding to a stop.

Raoul and Alessandra both turn to stare, but neither one of them says a word. Finally, Raoul checks his watch. "I need to get to work. I'm already late and we all know I'll hear it from Adam." He looks at Alessandra. "Am I taking you to the boat?"

"I talked to Mrs. Bick," Edie says. "It's fine, you don't have to leave, she isn't going to say anything to Lizbet, she just wants you to…back off."

Raoul's expression remains impassive and Edie wonders if she's creating a big, dramatic *Real House-wives* moment, but even if she is, Raoul won't tell anyone. He's a vault.

Alessandra nods at Raoul. "You go to work. I'll stay and talk to Edie."

"Your boat…" Raoul says.

"I'll change it," Alessandra says.

Alessandra leaves her duffels on the front porch and leads Edie inside, which is its own kind of jackpot because who doesn't want to see the place where her coworkers live, especially when it's 23 Hooper Farm Road. According to Edie's mother, this house has been the rental for a colorful cast of Nantucket characters over the years. For a number of summers, servers from the Blue Bistro lived here, and after that, a group of pilots for Cape Air, and after that, girls who worked on a high-end landscaping crew, one of whom was dating the bassist for the Dropkick Murphys.

But if Edie is expecting holes punched in the walls by jealous boyfriends or scorch marks from a fondue party gone bad, she's disappointed. The living room is dominated by Raoul's workout equipment, the kitchen has a peeling linoleum floor, and there's a short, dim hallway that must lead to the bedrooms. Alessandra takes Edie out the back door to a secluded yard, where the kitchen table sits atop a lawn that has just been cut (probably by Raoul). There are white fairy lights strung through the overarching branches of a big shade tree.

Alessandra takes a seat at the table and Edie sits next to her, thinking, *I'm going to have to beg her to stay, and how twisted is that?*

"You blackmailed that woman's husband!" Edie says. She's proud of herself for not completely buckling.

"I did," Alessandra says. "In my defense—and, honestly, Edie, there is no defense for what I did— Michael told me he and his wife were taking time apart, so I thought it was open season." She shakes her head. "I figured out he was lying pretty much right away but that was his sin, not mine. And then, when his wife was about to arrive for the summer, I had...bargaining power, and I cashed in on it."

Edie blinks. "And then you planted stuff from the neighbors' house?"

Alessandra sighs. "I did. At that point, it was like a game. I took her eye shadow, her shoes...that was probably good enough. I knew Michael would never realize that his wife wore Bobbi Brown and the neighbor wore Chanel or that his wife wore a size eight and the neighbor a size six. But then I found a positive pregnancy test in their bathroom trash, so I threw that gasoline on the fire."

"Gah!"

Alessandra touches Edie's arm. "This is why I didn't want us to be friends. I'm a horrible person. I'm ruined and rotten straight through."

Now it makes sense. Edie should *not* be friends with Alessandra. She should not look up to her at *all*. But even now, at this low moment, Alessandra has effortless style. Her hair is back in a ponytail, her makeup from that morning has faded, the eye crystals have fallen off, but even so, she looks chic in a pair of faded jeans, an old Dave Matthews T-shirt (the Shoreline Amphitheater, 2000, before Edie was even born), and the one gold bangle Edie knows will never come off, the Cartier love bracelet. Someone had once cared enough about Alessandra to give her that.

"Then I started sleeping with guests at the hotel in exchange for them mentioning me in their reviews." Alessandra leans forward and slaps her palms on the table. "That's how I won the four grand. I prostituted myself for it. I was trying to get the money and I only stopped because..."

"Because you realized someone else should have a chance to win the money?"

Alessandra scoffs. "No! I stopped because of that douchebag with the Corvette Stingray in three ten—remember him?"

"Ugh," Edie says. "Yes."

"He took me to dinner at Topper's," Alessandra says. "Talked all about himself, but whatever, I wasn't there for the conversation. Then when we got back to the hotel, he shoved me onto the bed, ripped up my dress, and pinned me down. He would have raped me if I hadn't thrown him off."

"Oh my God," Edie says. "I can't believe you threw him off you. That dude was all muscle."

"As bad as that experience was, it was also a wake-up call. I stopped targeting men and just focused on doing my job." She pauses. "But then when Xavier showed up, I thought, *He's wealthy and single, why not go after him?*"

"Ew," Edie says. "He's, like, seventy years old."

"Didn't matter, he wasn't interested in me. So I

texted Michael those photos I'd been saving in case of emergency." She gives Edie a direct gaze. "I wouldn't blame you if you never spoke to me again. I knew you'd been on the other side of that, and I did it anyway."

"Yeah," Edie whispers.

"I didn't have parents like yours growing up," Alessandra says. "Parents who led by example and showed me how to do things correctly. I didn't grow up in a nurturing community where everyone called me 'Sweet Alessandra' and had my back. I mean, that's no excuse, I know right from wrong and I consistently choose wrong. Heidi Bick *should* press charges, she *should* want to see me fired—"

"She's not doing any of that," Edie says. "As long as you stay away from them."

"I will," Alessandra says. She gives Edie a weary smile. "Sometimes I wish men weren't so predictable."

It's this statement more than anything else that illustrates their age difference, Edie thinks. Men are predictable to Alessandra, but to Edie, they're still a mystery.

"I want you to stay," Edie says. "I'm upset about what you did, but I can't bear to think of finishing up the season without you. Who would I complain to about Mr. Ianucci?"

"Ianucci," Alessandra says. "I'm telling you, that guy's a cop."

Edie grins. "I thought he was Shelly Carpenter."

"The post comes out tomorrow."

"Another reason why you have to stay," Edie says. "You *have* to."

"Okay," Alessandra says. Her eyes mist up. "Thank you for… I don't know, showing up here, being tough but cool." The corners of her mouth lift a bit. "I raised you well."

Edie pulls the manila envelope out of her backpack. "I'm giving you your money back, by the way."

"No!" Alessandra says. "I cheated. It's yours."

"You're great on the desk," Edie says. "It's yours."

"I'm not taking it back, Edie. I don't deserve it."

Edie pulls the cash out and riffles the bills. "How about we split it, then?"

Alessandra releases a breath. "Fine."

Fine. Edie counts out two thousand dollars and slides it toward her friend. She thinks about her little spy club with Zeke and wonders if she has any obligation to tell him about this.

She decides not. It's a desk thing.

25. The Last Friday of the Month: August

Lizbet and Edie are in Lizbet's office at 11:58— and at 11:59, Lizbet taps on her Instagram icon. As soon as her phone says noon, she visits the *Hotel Confidential* account and refreshes, but all she sees is the review from the Sea Castle Bed-and-Breakfast in Hyannis Port.

"Come on, Shelly," Lizbet says. She turns to Edie. "Has she ever been late before?"

"Hit refresh again," Edie says.

Lizbet inhales, then hits the refresh button.

On her screen is a picture of Zeke and Adam, framed inside the grand front doors, both of them waving and smiling; Lizbet sees the potted flowers on the steps and one wide rocker and fireplace table on the front porch. She blinks. This is real? This is their hotel? Those are their bellmen? Because it feels like a figment of Lizbet's imagination. A manifestation.

Edie, who is holding her own phone, shrieks—and Lizbet reads the caption.

She leaps out of her chair and grabs Edie and the two of them dance around the office. Lizbet's eyes blur with tears; she can't believe it, and yet she knew, she *knew* they would do it. In her heart, she knew. She used to think that meeting JJ and running the Deck was her dream come true—but no, it's this. *This* is what she was meant to do.

"We did it!" Edie shouts. "We! Did! It!"

Adam and Zeke come running in; Adam is on the phone with Raoul, who has just seen the review at home. Alessandra slips in and Lizbet gives her a hug, because any way you look at it, they couldn't have gotten five keys without her. Lizbet texts Mario: FIVE KEYS!!!!

Adam says, "Has anyone read the actual review yet?"

"No!" Edie says. "Let's all do it at the same time. One, two, three—"

"Wait, I'm not ready," Adam says. He scrolls. "Okay, go!"

They click on the link.

Hotel Confidential by Shelly Carpenter
August 26, 2022
The Hotel Nantucket, Nantucket, Massachusetts
—5 KEYS 🔑

Hello, friends.

I've been reviewing hotel experiences for nearly fifteen years and never once have I been tempted to use the word *best*. It's not an appropriate qualifier for a hotel. How can one compare the Siam in Bangkok to Auberge du Soleil in Napa to the Dulini River Lodge in South Africa? The answer is, one can't; though all exquisite, they're different species.

However, after a recent visit to the Hotel Nantucket, I find myself struggling for a word other than *best*. I have, for the first time, awarded a property five keys, and there's no doubt in my mind that this coveted fifth key is well deserved.

The Hotel Nantucket, originally built in 1910, has survived a fire, financial difficulties, and owners with poor taste. It fell into severe disrepair and sat on the market for over ten years until it was purchased by London billionaire Xavier Darling.

As you know, friends, the most important quality for me in any hotel is a sense of place. Unlike the three other luxury properties on Nantucket—the White Elephant, the Nantucket Beach Club and Hotel, and the Wauwinet—the Hotel Nantucket isn't located on the water. It claims a full block of Easton Street, which is easy walking distance from the cobblestoned streets of Nantucket's downtown. The lobby is a large, airy room that blends historical elements (the building's original oak beams, an authentic whale boat that serves as a chandelier) with modern (comfy chairs, ottomans, tables laden with books and games). Unlike some other lobbies I've visited, the lobby of

the Hotel Nantucket is one people gravitate
to. The hotel's simple but extraordinary continental breakfast is served here every morning
between seven and ten thirty (don't miss the
percolated coffee or the almond croissants),
and while I was in residence, a young chess
prodigy played with any guest brave enough
to challenge him. Often, a crowd gathered.

The magnanimity that was extended to me
throughout my stay began at check-in: I was
upgraded to one of the hotel's exquisite suites
for the price of a standard street-view room.
The living area of the suite included a library
wall that was lined with books—a mixture of
current bestsellers (with a whole shelf dedicated to "beach reads") and classics. There
was a cushioned window seat wide and long
enough to actually accommodate a reclining
adult human (so often, I feel that window seats
are only for show). Also in the living area was
the complimentary minibar.

That's right, friends, I said complimentary.

The minibar was stocked with local beer,
wine, and spirits, smoked bluefish pâté and
guacamole from local fishmonger 167 Raw,
and packages of crackers and chips (gluten-
free crackers available upon request).

The master bedroom featured the largest
bed I have ever slept in (it's a custom size
called emperor). The bed was sheathed in
Matouk linens (my preferred brand, as you
know) and topped with a cashmere blanket
from local weaver Nantucket Looms. The ceiling of the room was hand-painted with the
Nantucket night sky by Tamela Cornejo, which

was a particularly appropriate touch since Nantucket is the birthplace of noted female astronomer Maria Mitchell.

The bathroom was the Platonic ideal: spacious, luxurious, well appointed. The shower was tiled with oyster shells, the lighting over the sink made my skin look as dewy as Anne Hathaway's in *The Princess Diaries* (am I aging myself?), and there was a separate water closet, which I always prefer.

The hotel featured a wellness center (which, I will not lie, friends, I did not visit after my initial inspection, though other guests gushed about the gym, the sauna, and the yoga studio) and two glorious pools, one a joyous hive of activity for families and one a serene refuge for adults only.

Friends, I am officially over my word limit—but I refuse to stop, because the best is yet to come!

The hotel's restaurant, the Blue Bar, was the brainchild of Chef Mario Subiaco (I don't have space to list his accolades; google him). The Blue Bar offered an experience unlike any other on Nantucket; it feels like walking into a swanky A-list party you can't believe you've been invited to. The cocktails were made with top-shelf liquor, the fare was fun-loving (pigs in a blanket), a little retro (church-picnic deviled eggs), and a little decadent (luscious caviar sandwiches). All meals end with a visit from the whipped cream concierge. (Vegan whipped cream available upon request.) A copper disco ball dropped at nine o'clock and the music switched to '80s dance hits.

The best part of the Hotel Nantucket wasn't the conviviality in the lobby or the expansive real estate of the bed or the festive atmosphere of the Blue Bar.

The best part of the Hotel Nantucket was the staff. It may have taken me fifteen years to realize this, friends, but realize it I have: Hotels aren't about rooms. They aren't about amenities. They're about people—and the people who work at the Hotel Nantucket are what earned the property its fifth key.

The front-desk clerks, the bellmen, the night auditor, the housekeeping crew, and the general manager, Lizbet Keaton, were attentive. They listened. They were friendly. They were helpful. They were knowledgeable. And above all, they were kind.

Some of you might be wondering if I'm going to address the elephant in the room: Is the Hotel Nantucket, as reported by the AP, the *Washington Post,* and *USA Today,* haunted by the ghost of Grace Hadley, a chambermaid who was killed in a fire in 1922? I don't believe in ghosts—or I didn't before my stay at the Hotel Nantucket. During my stay I heard tales of flickering lights, music blaring out of nowhere, the electric shades going haywire. None of those stories persuaded me. However, I did feel a watchful, even nurturing, presence throughout my stay. It's my unshakable opinion that Grace Hadley makes most of the hotel's guests (including yours truly) feel safe—and yes, even loved. (But, as with any strong woman, I wouldn't want to get on the wrong side of her.)

I'm sure some of you have already predicted what I'm going to say next: This will be my final *Hotel Confidential* post. Some of you might suspect that I'm stopping because I have finally found perfection, my Shangri-La, and there may be some truth to that. Any property I visited after such a transformative experience would no doubt be a letdown. But the bigger and more important reason I'm retiring from this particular endeavor is because I want more time to stay home and take care of my children. (Surprise! I have two children—and a dog as well!)

I'd like to thank you, friends, for accompanying me on my journeys around the world. While hotel reviewing can be lonely (traveling solo and undercover, unable to share my true identity or life's details with anyone I met), I always felt that you, my readers, were with me. And you haven't seen the last of Shelly Carpenter! I'm starting a new blog about finding love after a marriage falls apart. I'm calling it *The Second Story*.

Stay well, friends. And do good.

—SC

Lizbet chokes up when she reads the adjectives Shelly used to describe the staff. *Attentive. Friendly. Helpful. Knowledgeable. Kind.*

Edie sniffles and Zeke plucks a tissue for her from the box on Lizbet's desk. (*Attentive,* Lizbet thinks. *And kind.*)

Then she reads the section about the ghost, Grace Hadley, and while a part of Lizbet thinks, *Just what we need, more guests showing up expecting a haunting,* she realizes that what Shelly says is true. Grace Hadley has been looking out for them all.

Next, Lizbet reads the shocking news of Shelly's retirement.

"Whaaaaaa?" Edie says. "Shelly Carpenter is staying home with her two children and her dog?"

"And her *dog*?" Zeke says.

"Lots of people have two kids and a dog," Adam says. "The whole world has two kids and a dog."

Then Lizbet reads about Shelly Carpenter starting a new blog.

"'About finding love after a marriage falls apart,'" Adam reads over Lizbet's shoulder. He honks out a laugh. "It *is* Kimber. Kimber is Shelly Carpenter!"

At that second, the door to Lizbet's office opens and Richie steps in.

Edie says, "We got five keys, Richie, did you see?" Then she gasps. "Did you *know*? Did you know Kimber is Shelly Carpenter?"

"I found out the night before she left," Richie says. "Kimber didn't want to tell me until after the review was finished. She's a professional." At that second, there's a buzzing noise and Richie pulls his cell phone out of his pocket. "Hey, boo," he says. "Yep, they figured it out. We're all in Lizbet's office." He pauses. "Aw, okay, I'll tell them. Love you." Richie hangs up and gives them a sad smile. "She says she misses you already."

August 28, 2022
From: Xavier Darling (xd@darlingent.co.uk)
To: Employees of the Hotel Nantucket

It was a pleasure and a privilege to meet you

all in person this past week. I'm only sorry I couldn't stay longer.

Congratulations are in order for the fifth key from Shelly Carpenter of *Hotel Confidential*. Hear, hear! Shelly has been a formidable critic of hotels and resort properties across the globe, and it was my not-so-secret goal to win the fifth key, but ultimately it was you, the staff, who impressed Ms. Carpenter the most. I will be including a thousand-dollar bonus in everyone's check this week.

Unfortunately, I must follow this up with some rather somber news: I am putting the Hotel Nantucket on the market, effective tomorrow. I have already received an offer on the place from a friend and colleague who wants to use the building as a satellite office space. This means that, unless another buyer comes forward with a competitive offer, the Hotel Nantucket will no longer operate as a hotel.

I thank you all for your time, energy, expertise, and dedication this summer. Every one of you should feel free to call on me for a letter of recommendation as you move forward into your various futures.

All best,
XD

An e-mail from Xavier arrives in Lizbet's in-box at five o'clock on Sunday evening, and Lizbet nearly ignores it because she's exhausted from the excitement of the past week. She wants to pick up a pizza from Pi, draw a bath, and then climb into bed to watch

Ted Lasso until Mario gets finished with work. But it's Xavier, so she can't wait until the morning.

Putting the hotel on the market. Use the building as a satellite office space?

She feels like she's reading her own obituary.

Edie cracks open the door and says, "Lizbet? Did you see?"

"I…I…" Lizbet doesn't have words. For the past two days, she has been *floating*. Everyone on the island has reached out—calling, texting, messaging on Facebook and Instagram—to congratulate her and the rest of the staff on the fifth key from Shelly Carpenter. JJ sent a bouquet (the first flowers from him in a year that she hasn't sent back). Lizbet's parents called from Minnetonka. She has heard from countless news outlets, including the *New York Times, Travel and Leisure, CBS Sunday Morning, Afar,* the *Armchair Explorer* podcast—wanting to do interviews, articles, segments. But most meaningfully, Lizbet heard from her old dorm mate Elyse Perryvale, who was the reason Lizbet came to Nantucket in the first place. Elyse wrote that her family had, sadly, sold their house on the island but that she would like to book rooms at the Hotel Nantucket the following summer for two weeks.

Lizbet had wanted to talk to Xavier about raising their prices ever so slightly because the phone has been ringing nonstop the past two days; at this rate, the hotel would be completely booked with a waiting list for next summer by Labor Day. You don't sell a hotel when the entire next season is booked! Lizbet thinks. Did Xavier not even glance at the financials? The business is booming, and now that they have the fifth key and all this media attention, they should be moving full steam ahead. Lizbet dreams of refurbishing the fourth floor and adding more rooms and maybe also extending their season through Christmas Stroll. She'd love to create a sunset-viewing platform on the widow's walk, maybe hire Adam as their full-time lobby entertainment, creating a little competition for the Club Car piano bar. Their Instagram could use some beefing up; she could give Edie a side hustle of being their social media manager. There are so many things…they're just getting started!

"He's selling it," Edie says. "He already has a buyer."

Lizbet gives Edie a wink. "He must be cranky about something else," she says. "This isn't real. He won't sell."

"He won't?"

"Let me talk to him," Lizbet says. As Lizbet dials Xavier, she wonders again if something happened while he was here. He left so early, so quickly, without saying goodbye. Maybe it was business—but Lizbet's gut tells her it was something else.

The call goes straight to voice mail. It *is* eleven o'clock on a Sunday night in London, but Xavier sent the e-mail only ten minutes ago. Surely he's still awake. She calls again from her phone. Voice mail.

She sends him a text, something she has never done before. It has always seemed too casual, too familiar, but this is an emergency. Xavier, can we please talk about your e-mail tonight? I'm not sure I'll sleep otherwise.

She stares at her phone, trying to manifest a response. Sure enough, three dots rise on Xavier's side of the chat. What is he going to say? She needs to *talk* to him, ask him what *happened*. Wasn't any negative experience he might have had while at the hotel washed away by Shelly's five-key review?

The dots disappear but no text comes through. Lizbet checks her e-mail—nothing. He doesn't want to talk to her; it's this that fills her with a hot, loose, watery panic.

She runs into the Blue Bar kitchen, even though the bar is filling up with guests and Mario has started service. She catches a glimpse of him, gorgeous as ever in his white chef's jacket, houndstooth pants, and White Sox cap, at the pass inspecting the plates, and she fully expects him to tell her to leave—she's never interrupted him at work before—but instead he steps away and says, "Beatriz, cover for me, please. I need a minute."

He takes Lizbet by the hand and they step into the quieter service kitchen, where a huge bowl of dough is proofing. Beatriz's croissants for the next morning.

"You heard?" Lizbet says.

"He did just what I was afraid he'd do," Mario says. "Pulled the plug."

"But *why?*" Lizbet says. "Doesn't he realize how great everything is?"

"He got what he wanted," Mario says. "The fifth key. Guys like Xavier aren't in this for the money or the greater good—restoring an historic building, boosting the local economy, creating jobs—they're in it for the bragging rights. He probably bet some guy he met at Annabel's that he could buy a hotel and get the fifth key. And he did and now he has no use for it anymore."

Lizbet wants to feel angry but she's too tired, so what overcomes her is grief. She cries against the front of Mario's pristine white jacket and he holds her tight, rubbing her back. "It'll be okay. We'll go to California. You can work at a hotel there. I know the GM at Shutters, you'll like that, on the beach in Santa Monica."

"I don't want to work at someone else's hotel," Lizbet

says. Does she sound childish? Probably, but she can't imagine getting a job in Los Angeles. She also can't fathom finding another position here on the island. She made one monumental change—successfully!— but she can't turn around and do it again.

"We'll figure it out together, okay?" Mario says. He eases her off him so he can look her in the eye. "You aren't alone anymore. I'm here, and I'm out of a job too."

"We need to make Xavier change his mind."

Mario sighs. "He isn't going to change his mind, Lizbet."

Suddenly, Zeke comes charging into the kitchen, and his presence is so startling that Lizbet thinks Xavier must be on the phone. *He called back, he's willing to talk!*

Zeke says, "Lizbet, we need you in the lobby. Stuff is going down."

Stuff is going down: When Lizbet gets back to the lobby, she sees Richie with three gentlemen in suits, one of whom is handcuffing him!

"Wait!" Lizbet cries out. Her head feels like it's going to topple off her body. "What's going on?"

"Mr. Decameron is under arrest for wire fraud," one of the gentlemen who's not cuffing Richie says. He holds up a badge. "Agent Ianucci, FBI."

Lizbet blinks. Mr. Ianucci, formerly of room 307.

"Richie?" she says.

Richie hangs his head. "I'm sorry, Lizbet."

26. The Cobblestone Telegraph

On Sunday evening, Fast Eddie heads into his real estate office on Main Street to type up the listing sheet for the Hotel Nantucket. He received a call from Xavier Darling earlier that afternoon; Xavier wants to sell, pronto. He's already gotten an offer from a colleague in London who wants to convert the hotel into an office building, but this colleague is holding firm at sixteen million.

"List it at twenty-five," Xavier told Eddie. "But between us, I'll take twenty."

"You put thirty into it," Eddie said. "Thirty-two if you count what you paid for it."

"I need to take it as a loss this year," Xavier said. "Though not *too* much of a loss."

Eddie puts the listing on his website at seven p.m. Xavier informed Lizbet and the rest of the hotel staff of his intent to sell at five p.m.

Poor Lizbet, Eddie thinks. She poured her heart and soul into that place and turned it into a genuine phoenix-risen-from-the-ashes success story. She has such a magic touch that Eddie decides he'll offer her a job as a sales associate with Bayberry Properties and sponsor her classes.

Eddie then pops into Ventuno for a celebratory cocktail. He tells the bartender, Johnny B., that he's re-listing the Hotel Nantucket for twenty-five million.

Those of us who overhear this tidbit note the barely suppressed glee in Eddie's voice. He's looking at *quite* a commission, especially if he comes up with the buyer.

One of the people who are sitting at the Ventuno bar within earshot of Eddie is Charlene, the nurse from Our Island Home. Charlene is drowning her sorrows because her favorite resident, Mint Benedict, has contracted pneumonia and the doctors say he's not likely to make it through the week.

The next morning when Charlene goes to visit Mint at the Nantucket Cottage Hospital, Mint asks her to collect everything from his safety deposit box at Nantucket Bank.

"There's some of my mother's jewelry that I want you to have," Mint says, his voice broken and gravelly. "And there are papers I'd like you to go through—letters and my father's journal."

Charlene pats Mint's hand, which is burning up, despite the intravenous antibiotics. "I'll bring it all here and we can go through it together, how about that?" She considers telling Mint what she overheard about the Hotel Nantucket going on the market *again,* but she isn't sure if this will make him feel better (he was right, the place does seem to be cursed) or if it will send him into a downward spiral. She decides to keep the news to herself.

Jordan Randolph at the *Nantucket Standard* notices the new real estate listing right away. He calls Lizbet to find out what's going on, but Lizbet isn't available for comment.

Jordan then hears about an FBI sting at the hotel and he immediately contacts the Nantucket Police Department to see what Chief Ed Kapenash knows about it.

"Wire fraud," Ed says. Ed is a gruff fellow on a good day, but tonight he sounds particularly worn out. Jordan empathizes—it's the end of a long, hot summer and everyone on this island is in need of a three-day nap. "Their night auditor was selling people's credit card numbers, addresses, and driver's license information. He was doing a brisk business in stolen identities."

"Wow," Jordan says.

"Apparently the Feds have been watching him for a while. He did some small-time embezzling at an insurance company in Connecticut—wiring his child-support payments out of their payroll account. The company didn't press charges because he'd been there so long and the ex-wife had really stuck it to him in the divorce. Then he hooked up with one of those sneaker brokers and that guy got busted for tax evasion, and I guess Decameron knew about it and was accepting cash to keep quiet."

"And Lizbet gave him a job anyway?" Jordan says.

"I'm sure she was desperate for the help," the chief says. "She hired some guy who presented well but who ended up being in over his head." He pauses. "Some days I feel like that guy."

"Yeah," Jordan says. "Me too." And the conversation ends on a laugh.

Blond Sharon can't believe her good luck. The Hotel Nantucket is at the center of all this gossip at the same time that her sister, Heather, checks in for a weeklong stay. Sharon picks up Heather (who is brunette) from the airport, drives her to the hotel, and accompanies her inside under the guise of "getting her settled," but really Sharon wants to find out what, precisely, is going on. She passes Sweet Edie Robbins on the front

steps. Edie waves and says she's going to lunch but
that Alessandra will be happy to check Heather in.

Bingo! Sharon thinks. Alessandra is one of the people
Sharon wants to see, because *Alessandra* is reputedly
the woman who slept with Michael Bick, then made
everyone think it was Lyric Layton. Sharon is expecting a villainess from a James Bond film, and while
she's not disappointed by Alessandra's appearance—
she's a stunner, with wavy strawberry-blond hair and
stylish makeup (she's wearing white eyeliner, and
Sharon wonders if she could get away with that or
if she's twenty-five years too old, and what about eye
crystals?)—Alessandra isn't the evil bitch that Sharon
expects. She's warm and genuine as well as incredibly
helpful and organized. She prints a list of all of Heather
and Sharon's dinner reservations and she has somehow
managed to score the two of them a tee time for the next
day at Miacomet Golf Club (which is basically impossible, because everyone knows there's a top secret list of
preferred clients even though the course is public).

Well done, Alessandra! Sharon thinks. "Is Lizbet
around, by any chance?" Sharon asks.

"Let me see if she's available," Alessandra says.

A second later, Lizbet emerges from the back office
looking as fabulous as ever in a black linen sheath
with peekaboo cutouts at the waist and a cute belt.

"Is the black because you're in mourning?" Sharon
asks. "I hear the hotel is being sold."

"I'm optimistic that whoever buys it will keep it the
way it is so we'll all have our jobs next summer."

"Hmmm," Sharon says. "Not to be Gertie Gloom,
but I heard there was a buyer already who wants to
turn it into a corporate headquarters."

Lizbet purses her lips. "Sharon," she chides, "you
know better than to spread rumors."

"I have a good source."

"Well, then, I suppose I'll be moving to LA," Lizbet says.

Sharon is rendered temporarily speechless. Nobody on this island wants to see Lizbet move away.

"What happened to your night manager?" Sharon asks. "I heard the FBI arrested him."

Lizbet smiles without showing any teeth. Sharon isn't without self-awareness; she knows she's pushing it with this question.

"Richie is a very sweet man," Lizbet says. "However, Love Robbins will be on the night desk until we close."

Sharon reaches out a hand. "We're all wishing you well, sweetie pie."

And it's true, we all are. It's one of the few things we can agree on. After watching the unlikely blossoming of the Hotel Nantucket over the summer, we want to see it succeed.

But we have to admit, it's not looking good.

27. Long Shot

At eight o'clock Monday night, there's a knock on the front door. Chad is up in his room playing Madden NFL, though he's supposed to be getting a head start on his packing. His job at the Brandywine Group starts the Tuesday after Labor Day.

After his drinks date with Ms. English the previous

Wednesday, Chad marched into his house and invited his mother, father, and Leith into the formal living room. They complied, probably only because it was such an unusual request; they *never* used the formal living room.

Chad had some things he wanted to say.

"First of all, I'd like to apologize. I'm to blame for Paddy losing an eye, for Lulu's death, and for all of the damage done to our house."

"Chaddy," his mother said. "I thought we agreed to move on."

Chad ignores this predictable response. "I got a job at the Hotel Nantucket because I wanted a summer of honest work. I didn't want to teach little kids to chip and putt, I wanted to do something difficult— unpleasant, even." Chad paused. "I didn't take the job to make you proud of me, I did it for myself. But even so, I'm surprised that you don't seem to find my decision laudable."

"You're using some good SAT words there, bruh," Leith says.

"You seemed embarrassed that I was cleaning rooms," Chad said to his parents. "You never refer to my job, never talk about it, never ask how my day was."

"It isn't what Mom and I wanted for you," Paul Winslow said. "We wanted you to be able to recharge your batteries before coming to join me at the firm."

"About that," Chad said. "I won't be joining you at the firm."

Chad's mother shrieked as though she'd seen a rat hiding beneath her prized Edra sofa.

Leith said, "This is getting good."

"I like working at the hotel," Chad said. "I want to stay in hospitality, maybe go back to school and get into a management program."

Paul kept his cool because keeping his cool was his job. "Our administrative assistants make over two hundred thousand dollars a year," he said. "Which is more than double what you'll be making as a manager at the Holiday Inn."

"I don't care about money," Chad said.

"That's easy for you to say. You've always had it. You don't know the first thing about being poor or even middle class, Chadwick. You've never had to pay for a single thing in all your life."

"I know that money doesn't make you happy," Chad said. "I mean, look at the three of you." With that, Chad stomped upstairs to his room, high on his own righteousness. He would stay on Nantucket through Columbus Day and he would get into some kind of hotel-management program. He would work at the Hotel Nantucket the following year even if it meant cleaning rooms again, though he hoped he could secure a job on the desk. He wondered what Ms. English would think of this.

But now, only five days later, everything has changed. The first thing Chad heard was that Richie Decameron, the night auditor, got arrested for selling guests' credit card numbers. This had actually been sort of good news as far as Chad was concerned (though he'd never admit this to anyone) because the position of night auditor was one Chad might be able to fill the following year. Then Chad learned that Xavier Darling was putting the hotel on the market. He was going to *sell* it—and it might not be a hotel at all next year.

And so Chad is back to facing a future at his father's firm. He's playing video games because it's a way to avoid preparing for a life he doesn't want to live. When he hears the knock on the front door, he jumps to his feet. He fears it's one of his (former) friends, trying to lure him out just once before the summer ends. Because who else could it be?

Chad peers out the window and sees the gunmetal-gray Jeep Gladiator that Ms. English drives.

Whoa! Chad thinks. He runs down the stairs, opens the front door, and sure enough, there's Ms. English standing on his porch.

She smiles at him. "Hello there, Long Shot."

"Ms. English!" he says. Ms. English is *here,* on Eel Point Road? Chad then recalls seeing her down the street at number 133 back in the middle of the summer. He'd never mentioned seeing her because he didn't want her to know that he knew she cleaned other houses. A chilling thought comes to him: Ms. English is here tonight to see if she can clean for *his* family. Now that the hotel is closing, she must need a job.

Chad feels mortified by what Ms. English has already seen: the long white-shell driveway lined on either side by pruned boxwood, the hydrangea bushes showboating along the front porch, and the needlessly enormo waterfront home behind him.

"Is your father at home?" Ms. English asks.

"My father?"

"Yes," Ms. English says. Her outfit falls somewhere between what she normally wears to work and what she wore to drinks the other evening. She has on white pants and a navy tunic printed with white hibiscus. Her hair is in corkscrew curls to her shoulders and she's wearing pearl earrings. "He's expecting me."

"He *is?*" Chad says—and at that second, Paul Winslow strides out from the back of the house.

"Magda, hello!" he says—and Chad nearly falls through the floor. His father *knows* Ms. English? Chad experiences a moment of vertigo as he wonders if maybe this whole summer has been a setup. Has Paul Winslow been pulling the puppet strings all along? Did his father want him to be working at the hotel to teach him the lessons that he thought he'd learned on his own?

"I went out today and got a bottle of Appleton Estate Twenty-One," Paul says. "Just to have it on hand for you. Can I pour you a glass?"

"I'd love it, Paul, thank you," Magda says.

Paul claps Chad on the shoulder. "Show Magda to my study, please, bud. I'll be back in a second with the drinks."

Paul heads to the kitchen and Chad stares at Ms. English for a second. Is this another one of those moments, like when she told him what happened to Bibi, where nothing is what it seems? Maybe Paul *is* interviewing Magda—not for a job cleaning their house but for a job at the Brandywine Group. If Ms. English works there, will that make Chad's position there any more palatable?

No, Chad thinks. Not really.

"The study, Long Shot?" she says.

"Oh, right." Chad shows Ms. English into the study. She sits in one of the butterscotch suede club chairs and crosses her legs. She pulls her phone and a legal pad out of her bag.

"Okay," Chad says. "I'll see you tomorrow morning."

"Don't you want to stay?" Ms. English asks.

"Stay?" Chad says. "If you don't mind my asking, what's going on? Why are you here?"

Ms. English laughs. "Oh, Long Shot, you should see your face, it's priceless." She leans forward and whispers, "Your father and I are forming a partnership. We're going to buy the hotel."

28. The Cobblestone Telegraph

When we next see Fast Eddie, he's seated at the big front table at Cru, where he has ordered a magnum of Dom Pérignon, which is attended by two servers and three live sparklers.

Well, it's no wonder. It has taken a mere three days for him to secure a twenty-million-dollar offer on the Hotel Nantucket. The buyer is known only as the Long Shot Trust, but because Eddie can't keep his mouth shut (something his sister, Barbie, scolds him for nonstop), someone among us discovered that the property was purchased in equal parts by two entities. One was Paul Winslow, a principal at the Brandywine Group who owns a home on Eel Point Road, and the other was Magda English, the head of housekeeping at the Hotel Nantucket.

"I knew Magda was hiding something," Nancy Twine of the Summer Street Church said. "I used to wonder about her putting so much in the collection plate on Sundays and now I find out she could have put in ten times more. She has millions!"

Yes, Magda English's net worth hovers around twenty-four million dollars. The (unconfirmed) story is that she caught the eye of Xavier Darling thirty years earlier when she was working on one of his cruise ships. He wined and dined her in Monte Carlo and they ended up at a casino where she placed a five-hundred-dollar bet (her own money, she would be quick to point out) and rolled the dice at the craps table for nearly two hours, going all in each time and walking away with two hundred and fifteen thousand dollars. She invested this money with Xavier Darling's bankers, where it grew at a steady rate. Then, in 2012, Xavier approached Magda with a dark-horse opportunity: he was investing in a company that was developing a new kind of personal security software. After reading the company's prospectus, Magda told Xavier she wanted in. The company went public in July of 2021 and Magda's small fortune became a big fortune. The following month, her sister-in-law, Charlotte English, died suddenly in her sleep and Magda moved to Nantucket to be with her brother, William, and her nephew Zeke. She had been looking at property with Fast Eddie, including homes on Eel Point Road, but hadn't found anything to her liking. She took the job as head of housekeeping at the hotel because she was always happiest when she was busy.

"At least that's what I've gathered from our chats," said Brian, the bartender at the Brant Point Grill. Brian was the one who'd spilled the beans about Magda and Xavier. "They were definitely having a thing," he said. "She told me he was an 'old friend,' but I was getting a vibe of 'old friend with benefits.'"

This makes Magda's decision to buy the hotel even more intriguing. Apparently, when Eddie told her that Xavier already had a private offer of sixteen million, Magda said, "I'm going to call Xavier's bluff. His friend who wants to turn the hotel into a satellite office is probably only half serious—who puts a satellite office thirty miles out to sea?—but my partner and I will give Xavier the benefit of the doubt and offer eighteen million."

"He'll close at twenty."

"Done," Magda said.

As for Magda's partner, Paul Winslow, he was overheard saying, "I'm sure I'll be accused of buying the hotel for my son, but in reality, I was presented with a smart business proposition by Magda English. The Hotel Nantucket is a piece of Nantucket history but it's also poised to be the most gracious accommodations on this island for generations to come. Who wouldn't want to be a part of that, given the choice? As for my son, Chad, I hope this deal shows him firsthand what kind of positive opportunities my firm can create. I hope he ultimately decides to come work with me. But if he stays on at the hotel, I respect that decision. The important thing is that the Hotel Nantucket is back in business."

Charlene from Our Island Home senses an exuberance in the hotel staff the moment she steps into the lobby. The air is rich with the smell of good coffee and fresh-baked pastry; Aretha Franklin is asking for a little respect; the place is buzzing with conversation and laughter. Charlene feels like a bit of a bubble-burster; she has come to the hotel on a sobering mission. She approaches the desk where Sweet Edie Robbins is working—Charlene has known Edie since the days her father, Vance, used to carry her in the BabyBjörn at the Stop and Shop, though now Edie is all grown up, looking quite chic in her silky hydrangea-blue blouse.

Charlene says, "Good morning, Edie. I can see you're busy, but do you have a minute to talk?"

"Of course, Charlene!" Edie says. She turns to her coworker, a woman with lovely long gingery hair, and says, "I'll be back shortly."

Edie leads Charlene through a closed door into the employee break room. Charlene has heard rumors about this room, and it doesn't disappoint. There's a Formica bar counter with bright orange leather and chrome diner stools, a jukebox, a pinball machine, and a curvy midcentury sofa, where Edie leads them to sit.

"I only have a few minutes," Edie says.

"Yes!" Charlene says. "You must be wondering what I'm doing here." She pulls a plastic bag from her purse, and from the bag she removes an old, leather-bound journal with the initials JFB in gold leaf on the cover. "I'm sad to say that Mint Benedict passed away yesterday."

Edie blinks. "I'm sorry, I don't know who that is. He was one of your residents? He was elderly?"

"Ninety-four," Charlene says. "He was the only child of Jackson and Dahlia Benedict."

Edie smiles politely. "I'm still not sure..."

"They owned the hotel from 1910 to 1922," Charlene says. "Then there was a fire and a chambermaid was killed."

"Our ghost," Edie says.

"Your ghost." Charlene hands Edie the journal. "This is Jackson Benedict's diary from that year. Mint kept it in his safety-deposit box. Mint's mother, Dahlia, died of alcoholism when Mint was only ten years old and Jackson passed from cancer in 1943. There are also photographs and some small items from the hotel—a handbell, a few keys, some pieces of china from the ballroom. Mint is donating those to the Nantucket Historical Association. But he wants you here at the hotel to have Jackson's diary. He made it clear he would like someone to actually *read* it."

"I'll read it," Edie says. "But I can't do it right now. I have to get back to work."

"Just promise you'll—"

"Yes, of course!" Edie says. "I'm pumped about this." She opens the journal's cover and sees the first page is dated August 22, 1922. "This is the hotel's history."

"I have to admit, I read it myself," Charlene says. "It reveals some secrets about this place. The literal skeletons in the closet."

"You should probably read it first," Edie says to Lizbet, sliding Jackson Benedict's diary across Lizbet's desk.

"Charlene gave it to you," Lizbet says.

"I'm not sure I can get to it tonight," Edie says. "I'm going to dinner with Zeke."

"What?" Lizbet says. "Is this hotel responsible for *another* romance?"

Edie shrugs. "We're just going out to celebrate the hotel purchase." She lowers her voice. "Zeke had no idea his aunt had that much money. He and his dad were totally blown away."

"Thank God for Magda," Lizbet says. "Or I'd be working as the concierge at the Peninsula in Beverly Hills."

Alessandra steps into the office. "The concierge at the Peninsula in Beverly Hills?" she says. "That's the job *I'm* applying for."

"I know," Lizbet says. "They called me today for a reference."

"And?" Alessandra says.

"I predict that next summer, you'll be back on the West Coast."

"Where I belong," Alessandra says.

Yes, Edie thinks. She'll miss Alessandra, but she's excited about taking over as front-desk manager. "I hope the men in LA are ready for you," she says.

"They aren't," Alessandra and Lizbet say together.

"Sit down if you have a minute," Lizbet says. "Edie is going to read to us."

August 22, 1922

Here, for my descendants, should I be lucky enough to have any, and for the historians and the detective inspectors, is a real and true account of the events of August 19 and 20, 1922. I'm not a gifted writer, nor, up to this point in my life, have I been particularly introspective, but I feel I must put these words down, if only to exorcise them from my soot-stained mind.

My wife, Dahlia, and I held a dinner dance in the ballroom of my hotel this past Saturday. The evening started with turtle soup, followed by beef Wellington and lobster tails, and everyone enjoyed gin cocktails and champagne. Dahlia got quite tight, as always. She flirted shamelessly with Chase Yorkbridge and asked him to escort her up to our suite as a way to make me jealous—but I was not jealous at all, only relieved. I left the party directly after Dahlia and headed up to the attic storage closet to see Grace.

Grace Hadley, my mistress. I was in love with her. I am in love with her still.

Edie looks up. "This is why Mint Benedict wanted us to read it. Grace Hadley was Jackson Benedict's lover."

Alessandra shrugs. "I always assumed that."

"You did not," Lizbet says.

"A chambermaid shacking up in the fourth-floor storage closet?" Alessandra says. "What did you think she was doing up there?"

Lizbet waves a hand. "Keep going, Edie."

When I knocked, Grace cracked open the door, cautious as always. She was afraid that one night she would find Dahlia pointing a revolver at her forehead.

Grace knew Dahlia far better than I, as it turned out.

When I returned from Grace's room, Dahlia was snoring and didn't stir. I figured, as I did every night I spent with Grace, that I had gotten away with something.

I awoke in the middle of the night shrouded in a thick cloud of black smoke. The chintz armchair by the window was on fire, and fire was sprinting up the drapes. I called for Dahlia. I checked her dressing chamber; she was not to be found. I stepped into the hallway to find people shouting. Leroy Noonan, the hotel's general manager, was intent on rushing me out.

I was thinking only of Grace. "I have to make sure she's okay," I said. Noonan, naturally, thought I was referring to Dahlia. He said, "She's on the street, Mr. Benedict. Let's go now, please, sir." He hurried me toward the stairs but I fought him, saying, "I need to get to the fourth floor."

"The fourth floor is on fire, sir, you cannot go up there." Noonan is a big man, six foot four and nearly three hundred pounds; he could have thrown me over his shoulder and

carried me out of the building. And that was what he would have to do, I decided, because I was determined to rescue Grace. I fought my way through the panicked stream of guests in their nightclothes to the bottom of the back stairway. But the entire stairwell was a fiery inferno. There would be no going up.

When I reached the street, I found Dahlia looking perfectly calm amidst the pandemonium. She had her silk robe belted neatly over her dressing gown, she had on her slippers, her hair was curled, she wore lipstick, she was smoking, and…she held our cat, Mittens. Something registered in me then, something I couldn't bear to think. I searched through the mob for Grace. Was she here? Had she escaped? I didn't see her. I told myself she would, naturally, be hiding because she had no good reason to be at the hotel at night. I approached the fire marshal, who assured me the fire was under control and everyone got out safely.

"Everyone?" I said. "Even the people on the fourth floor?"

"There was no one on the fourth floor," he said. "We checked."

He'd checked the fourth floor. Grace had escaped and now, I suspected, was lurking in the shadows somewhere.

I returned to Dahlia's side. She said to me, "The girl didn't get out. I locked her in from the outside."

I grabbed Dahlia's arm. "What have you done?" I said. I saw the orange ember at the end of her cigarette as an evil, glowing eye. "Did you set this fire, Dahlia?"

The cat wriggled free of Dahlia's arms and jumped to the ground, despite its bad leg. "I wouldn't say that too loudly. The insurance, Jack. If there's no insurance, you'll be ruined." She put a finger across my lips. "Accidents happen."

I wanted to rage against her but it only took a moment for me to realize that she was right. She had set the fire and locked Grace's door—but I was the one who had set Grace up in the attic, kept her the same way that Dahlia kept the damn cat. If Grace had defied me, I would have had no choice but to fire her and make sure she didn't find a job anywhere else on the island. I am responsible for the death of my beloved mistress, Grace Hadley.

—*Jackson Floyd Benedict*

When Edie stops reading, a hush comes over Lizbet's office.

Finally, Alessandra speaks. "What a buzzkill."

"No wonder Grace haunts the hotel," Lizbet says. "I would too if I were her."

Edie turns the page and finds it blank. "This is the only entry in the diary," she says. Her eyebrows shoot up. "This is all he wanted us to know."

29. Mosaic

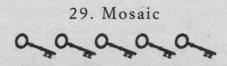

Grace was hanging—literally, *hanging*—on Edie, reading Jack's words, and it was even more cleansing and validating than she dreamed it might be. Dahlia set the fire, Dahlia locked the door so it wouldn't open, but Jack was correct—ultimately, Grace's presence in that room was his fault, and Dahlia's infernal jealousy also his fault.

It's a written confession, just like in the movies.

Lizbet puts the diary in the safe in her office. Tomorrow, she announces, she'll show it to Jordan Randolph at the *Nantucket Standard*. Grace can only hope that he'll write a follow-up article to the one published a century ago: "Crime Solved a Hundred Years Later! Grace Hadley Murdered by Hotel Owners!"

Grace feels lighter. There's no anger weighing her down, no indignation shackling her to the hotel, no leaden angst. She's free to go to her eternal rest. She's taking the robe with her—but she leaves Lizbet's Minnesota Twins cap on the Formica bar in the break room.

Let her wonder.

Grace finds the hatch to the widow's walk open and when she ascends to the fresh afternoon air, just tinged with salt, she catches Lizbet and Mario leaning against the railing, sneaking in some kissing. Grace tests out her new buoyancy, rising above them and gazing down. It's a whole new perspective. She can see the entire hotel. Edie and Alessandra are at the front desk. Alessandra is on the phone; Edie is checking in some guests. Zeke rolls a luggage trolley by and winks at Edie. Raoul is out front at the bell desk dealing with a guest who is checking in with an exotic bird, a hyacinth macaw. (Has word gotten out that although pets are technically forbidden at the hotel, exceptions will be made?) In the yoga studio, Grace watches Yolanda lead a class of perimenopausal women in a butterfly stretch. Over at the Blue Bar, Petey Casstevens is pressing fresh juices and refilling her garnishes. Beatriz is piping béchamel sauce into warm, airy gougères fresh from the oven. Octavia and Neves are cleaning room 108, and sure enough, Neves finds a pair of men's boxers draped over the telephone, which makes Neves grimace and Octavia giggle. Chad and the new cleaner, Doris, are wheeling their housekeeping cart down the second-floor corridor. They stop at the brass porthole windows because it's their day to be polished. Chad squirts solution onto a rag and starts buffing, and Grace thinks, *That's right, Long Shot, show her how it's done!* Doris isn't quite the cleaner she thinks she is.

Doris says, "So Mr. Darling put the hotel on the market because Magda turned down his proposal?"

"Yes," Chad says. "But that needs to stay our secret."

And mine, Grace thinks.

At that very minute, Magda is in the housekeeping office on the phone with her accountants. Edie's mother, Love, and Adam are walking up the front stairs; it's time for the shift change.

"Welcome to the Hotel Na-antucket!" Adam sings out when he steps through the doors.

Grace goes a little higher and finds she can check

in on other people she knows. Bibi Evans is sitting in her criminal justice class at UMass Dartmouth; she has her hair in a cute ponytail and tied around the elastic is what looks like…a black-and-gold Fendi scarf. (Grace gasps. It's either the scarf stolen from Mrs. Daley's suitcase or it's a knockoff Bibi bought from a vendor on Newbury Street. Grace chooses to believe the latter.)

Grace ascends a little higher, and New York City comes into view. What a hive of activity! But even with all the action, Grace easily homes in on the Upper East Side. She sees Louie in a classic-six prewar apartment on Park Avenue. He's taking a chess lesson from a grand master. Grace finds Wanda walking Doug around the Reservoir in Central Park. Doug is still sensitive to supernatural disturbances; he stops in his tracks and lifts his bucket head to the sky. Grace can almost read his mind: *You again? Here?* Kimber is strolling a few paces behind Wanda, talking on her phone, and Grace worries that Kimber has fallen back into her laissez-faire ways of parenting—but then Grace realizes that Kimber is trying to retain an attorney for Richie.

Standing by her man! Grace likes it.

All of these people, *her* people, glitter and sparkle on their own (*especially Wanda,* Grace thinks), but from this distance, they also become part of a bigger whole. It's a mosaic—maybe not as grand and celebrated as the ones Alessandra saw in Ravenna, but a work of art all the same.

Grace is about to go even higher up—into the heavens—when she notices a blank spot in the mosaic, a hole, an absence. It's *her* space, she realizes, and now that she's risen up here, she sees it as glaringly empty. How will the hotel continue without *her?* She feels a strong pull downward; it's a force she can't ignore.

It's love.

Grace can't leave yet! Magda and Mr. Winslow are buying the hotel and Lizbet has a list of improvements, including refurbishing the fourth floor. How about incorporating Grace's storage closet into one of the rooms? They can call it the Grace Hadley Suite.

Grace floats back down until she's hovering above the island of Nantucket, until she's directly over the hotel, until she's safely back inside.

Home.

Oh, fine, Grace thinks, whisking the Twins cap off the counter in the break room and fitting it snugly over her curls. *I'll stay.*

One more year couldn't hurt.

The Blue Book

Time and again I'm asked for recommendations of must-do's while visiting Nantucket. As Lizbet Keaton says in this novel, "The world needs a Nantucket guidebook written by an island insider." What follows is not a *guidebook*—because it is *not* comprehensive—but a *recommendation guide*. It is wholly personal, biased, and organic (I am not sponsored by any of the entities I will mention, nor given special treatment—at some of the restaurants, even I can't get a reservation in the middle of August!). But I feel this Blue Book will be helpful in enhancing any stay on the island, especially if you are an Elin Hilderbrand reader!

Two excellent resources for getting started on your trip planning:

Nantucket Chamber of Commerce, 508-228-1700. Website: nantucketchamber.org; Instagram: @ackchamber.

Town of Nantucket Culture and Tourism (known around town as "Nantucket Visitor Services"), 508-228-0925. Visitor Services keeps a list of available hotel rooms (and, yes, there were nights in the past few summers when the island was completely sold out!). They have a host of helpful practical information for your visit! Website: Nantucket-ma.gov.

GETTING HERE (AND BACK HOME) IS THE HARDEST PART

"How much is the toll for the bridge?"

There is no bridge! Nantucket Island is thirty miles out to sea and therefore is accessible only by boat or plane. There are direct flights from New York (JFK), Newark, Washington, DC, and certain other cities in the summer on JetBlue, United, American, and Delta. Cape Air runs a nine-seat Cessna from Boston and JFK year-round. (Warning: these Cessnas are not for the faint of heart, as per the scene in *Golden Girl*!)

We also have ferries, known on the island as "the fast boat" and "the slow boat." The slow boat is operated by the **Steamship Authority** and is the only way to bring a vehicle. If you want to bring your vehicle to Nantucket, you must get a reservation (and these sell out *way* in advance, starting in early January!).

My preferred mode of travel to and from the island is the fast ferry. From April through December, both the Steamship Authority and **Hy-Line Cruises** operate ferries throughout the day. The trip takes an hour, and round trip costs around eighty dollars.

Weather often affects travel to and from the island. If the wind is blowing twenty-five miles an hour or stronger, the ferries may cancel (each trip is at the discretion of the captain). If there is fog (which there often is in June and early July), planes are grounded. (Fun fact: Tom Nevers Field was used by the U.S. military in World War II to practice taking off and landing in the fog.)

Once on Nantucket, you can either rent a Jeep (**Nantucket Windmill Auto Rental, Nantucket Island Rent a Car**) or rent a bike (**Young's Bicycle Shop, Nantucket Bike Shop, Cooks Cycles,** and **Easy Riders**

Bicycle Rentals, who will deliver bikes to your lodging!). The island also has Uber, Lyft, and a host of taxis. My favorite taxi company is **Roger's Taxi,** 508-228-5779. **Cranberry Transportation** provides a proper "car service" and they also give private tours of the island.

WHERE SHOULD I STAY?

You just finished a novel called *The Hotel Nantucket,* so I'm going to start by recommending the inspiration for the main character in the book, which is **The Nantucket Hotel and Resort,** located at 77 Easton Street. Although the hotel in the book is a creation of my imagination, the Nantucket Hotel does have certain similarities: It has both rooms and suites, a family pool and an adult pool, a fabulous fitness center, a yoga studio, and a bar and restaurant. The staff is professional and friendly, and like the hotel in the book, the real hotel is located on the edge of town within easy walking distance of not only shopping, restaurants, museums, and galleries but also Children's Beach, Jetties Beach, and Brant Point Light. Website: Thenantuckethotel.com; Instagram: @thenantucket.

The only accommodation that is directly *on* the beach is the **Cliffside Beach Club,** which was the inspiration for my first novel, *The Beach Club.* Cliffside's lobby is one of the most spectacular spaces on the island. The hotel has twenty-three rooms (where you step out *into sand*), a pool and a fitness center, a small private café, and a private beach on Nantucket Sound. (The water is calm and good for swimming.) Cliffside is a splurge—if you can get in! Website: Cliffside beach.com; Instagram: @cliffsidebeachclub.

The **Greydon House** (not to be confused with Graydon, Edie's creepy ex-boyfriend) used to be a private home and dentist's office but it has been lavishly remodeled into a cozy boutique hotel with an unbelievably good restaurant, **Via Mare.** I have stayed at the Greydon House twice myself on a "stay-cation" and found the highlights to be the delicious breakfasts, the tiles in the showers, and the ideal in-town location. Website: Greydonhouse.com; Instagram: @greydonhouse.

When you *really* want to get away from it all, check out the **Wauwinet Inn.** It's nine miles out of town (this is very far by Nantucket standards), but the drive takes you along the beautiful, winding Polpis Road, where you'll pass farms, ponds, and the Nantucket Shipwreck and Lifesaving Museum. The Wauwinet is located on the harbor at the entry to Great Point. The hotel has an expansive deck lined with Adirondack chairs that overlook the harbor. There's a library, a charming tucked-away bar, and a fine-dining restaurant, Topper's (which is where Bone Williams takes Alessandra in this book and where Benji and Celeste have a rather emotional meal in *The Perfect Couple*). Website: Wauwinet.com; Instagram: @thewauwinet.

I Have a Place to Stay and a Way to Get Around; Now What Do I Do?

You're on an island, so let's start at the beach! Nantucket has fifty miles of coastline, most of it open to the public. Some of it has auto access but you'll need a four-wheel-drive vehicle with the proper sticker. For beaches such as **Fortieth Pole** and **Smith's Point,** you need a town beach sticker, yours for $100 (you procure one of these at the police station—and hey, maybe you'll see Chief Kapenash!). The sticker to access **Great Point** is purchased at the entry; it costs $160 (you can also get a day pass for $60). Most rental vehicles available on Nantucket come with these stickers. *Before you drive onto the beach,* you must let the air out of your tires down to 15 pounds (you can go lower for Great Point—there are two air hoses just past the guardhouse to refill them when you're heading back to civilization).

Here are my thoughts on drive-on beaches: I love them. This love intensified when I had children. Instead of schlepping all of our stuff from whatever parking spot I happened to find (*if* I found a parking spot—because when you have kids, it's challenging to get out of the house in a timely fashion), I just pulled onto the beach and all of their stuff was right there in the back of the car. There were years when the kids napped in the car, windows wide open. There were years when the kids climbed on the car (I had Jeeps; they were rugged vehicles). There were years when my kids climbed on my friends' cars (even better). Because you can drive onto it, Fortieth Pole is particularly good for evening beach barbecues with kids—the water is calm and warm, and you'll have a magnificent view of the sunset. Smith's Point is hands down my favorite beach because you can access both the waves of the ocean and the flat water of the sound. There's also a natural water slide (described in my novel *The Perfect Couple*). Smith's Point is open only during certain weeks of the summer, depending on the nesting of the endangered piping plover.

As Lizbet says in this novel, **Great Point** is Nantucket's ultimate destination. Great Point Light sits at the tippy-top of the long arm of sand that juts into the water to the north. Great Point is part of a nature preserve (hence the hefty sticker price for your vehicle) run by the Trustees of Reservations. It's a wild, windswept landscape with the ocean on your right and the harbor on your left as you drive out. There are almost always seals. There are sometimes sharks—you've been warned! It *is* "far away" (it takes nearly forty-five minutes to get there from town), but it's a Nantucket experience you'll never forget. There is a guardhouse just before the Wauwinet Inn where you purchase your sticker. On your way home, you can pop into the Wauwinet's super-cute tiny bar for a drink. (**Topper's,** the restaurant, is exquisite but expensive, even by Nantucket standards.)

There are some people who think driving on a beach is an abomination. I respect that—and so does Nantucket. Most beaches do not allow cars. Here are some of my favorite beaches that you can*not* drive on. North shore beaches front Nantucket Sound and have calm water without large waves. South shore beaches are ocean beaches and normally have waves. There are sometimes rip currents. Please be careful!

North Shore

Jetties Beach is walkable from town and has the added attraction of the **Sand Bar,** which I'll discuss in the restaurant section. **Steps Beach** has, quite possibly, the most beautiful approach of any beach in the world. You descend forty-three steps into sand dunes covered by rosa rugosa, which in the height of summer blooms with pink and white flowers. **Dionis Beach** is where Richie is found asleep in his car in this novel. In the book, I say that Dionis has public showers—this is fiction. It does *not* have showers. It does, however, have bathrooms.

South Shore

Surfside Beach was my beach of choice for my first three summers. In fact, I don't think I went anywhere else. It's *wide*. There's plenty of *space*. It also has the **Surfside Beach Shack.** It's not an exaggeration to say that if I could, I would eat lunch at the Surfside Shack every day of the summer, and so would my kids. The food is *delicious*. I get the "krabby patty" (crab, shrimp, and scallop patty) with avocado, bacon, lettuce, tomato, and their delicious sauce. My daughter gets acai bowls. The boys get the grilled chicken sandwich or burgers. It falls into my "can't miss" category if you're staying on Nantucket more than one day during the summer. However, there is often a line—you've been warned!

Nobadeer Beach: Party central. Are you twenty-five or younger? Go here. There is a walk-on section and a drive-on section. Both are filled with beautiful young people living their best lives. If you're walking on, please do not park on the road—you will get a ticket.

Cisco: Do you surf or like to watch other people surf? Go here. The beach is much narrower than at Surfside and Nobadeer and parking is often an issue.

None of these is my favorite. I have thought long and hard and decided not to name my preferred south shore beach, because what I love about it is it's not popular and never very crowded except by locals and summer residents. Because I feel guilty for holding back, I will say that if you want a terrific not-crowded beach, drive out to Miacomet Golf Course, but just before you reach the clubhouse, take a right onto the dirt road that leads past the big antenna. The road is what I have called in my books "the no-name road," and the beach is what I call **Antenna Beach.** There is a cottage to the left of the entrance to this beach that was the inspiration for Mallory's cottage in *28 Summers*.

WHAT IS THERE TO DO IF I DON'T LIKE THE BEACH?

Yes, I do realize there are people who don't like the beach. (I am merely grateful you like beach novels!)

Do you like to shop?

If the answer is yes, you're in luck! Unlike Martha's Vineyard, which has seven towns, Nantucket has only one town, called "town." (Locals say, "I'm going to town" or "I saw Elin in town.") Nantucket's central business district is four square blocks, chock-full of great shopping, all of it adjacent to the ferry docks. It's therefore possible to get off the ferry, shop, get something to eat, and get back on the ferry—and although you will not have seen nearly enough of the island, you also won't be disappointed. Town is just that great.

There are too many shops for me to mention, so I'm giving you only my very favorites.

Mitchell's Book Corner and **Nantucket Bookworks:** Hmm…why did I start with these? Well, because I believe independent bookstores are the cornerstones of civilization. Nantucket is lucky enough to have not one independent bookstore but two, and they're owned by the same person, my cherished friend Wendy Hudson. The good news about Wendy owning both stores is that instead of being competitors, they complement each other. Mitchell's is located at 54 Main Street and has two floors of books, including an outstanding selection of Nantucket-based books. From mid-June until mid-September I do a book signing outside Mitchell's every Wednesday at 11:00 a.m. for one hour. Mitchell's hosts signings all year round, including frequent signings with my fellow local authors Nancy Thayer and Nathaniel Philbrick. Website: Nantucket bookpartners.com; Instagram: @nantucketbooks.

Nantucket Bookworks can be found at 25 Broad Street. It's small and cozy and has an outstanding children's book section, a huge selection of toys, games, gifts, and chocolate!

The biggest celebrity at these bookstores is the events and marketing director, Tim Ehrenberg, who has a Bookstagram account @timtalksbooks where he gives outstanding recommendations. If Tim tells me to read it, I read it.

Flowers on Chestnut: If there is one store other than the bookstores that I would say you shouldn't miss, it's Flowers on Chestnut. Most visitors aren't in need of a florist, but you should stop into Flowers anyway just for the aesthetics. There's a sumptuous floral display in the middle of the first floor and a charming side garden. Beef up your Instagram— take pictures. Flowers on Chestnut also has a divine selection of candles, gifts, antiques, greeting cards, wrapping paper, cocktail napkins, and home furnishings. Website: Flowersonchestnut.com; Instagram: @flowersonchestnut.

Jessica Hicks Jewelry: I bought my first pair of Jessica Hicks earrings in 2008 and now, almost fifteen years later, I have well over a hundred pieces, including the silver thumb ring featured in *The Perfect*

Couple. Jessica's shop is tucked just off Main on Union Street—it's a must-visit for any Elin Hilderbrand reader. Her pieces have a wide price range, with something for every budget. Website: Jessicahicks.com; Instagram: @jessicahicksjewelry.

Hub of Nantucket: As the name suggests (just call it "the Hub"), this newsstand, which also has books, magazines, candy, souvenirs, gifts, coffee, and smoothies, is right smack in the middle of town, on the corner of Main Street and Federal. Website: Thehubof nantucket.com; Instagram: @thehubofnantucket.

Nantucket Looms: Oh, how I love the Looms. The hydrangea-blue cashmere blanket in *The Hotel Nantucket* is fictional, though Nantucket Looms does have an impressive selection of woven goods as well as furniture and art. They also sell two kinds of wildflower soap, which is a go-to gift of mine. Website: Nantucketlooms.com; Instagram: @nantucketlooms.

Blue Beetle: My favorite place for cashmere: ponchos, wraps, and sweaters, especially Nantucket sweaters. Possibly my favorite purchase of 2021 was the heather-gray sweater with a rainbow-striped ACK on the front. (ACK is the airport designation for Nantucket.) They also have sweaters with the island on the front (I have this in four colors!). Website: Bluebeetlenantucket.com; Instagram: @bluebeetlenantucket.

Erica Wilson: Erica Wilson was a pioneer in the world of needlepoint. This shop on Main Street is still partially dedicated to the art, but the other half is women's fashion. I nearly always find something wonderful here, and it features the jewelry of **Heidi Weddendorf** (Instagram: @heidiweddendorf). Website: Ericawilson.com; Instagram: @ericawilson nantucket.

Milly and Grace: Perhaps my favorite women's clothing boutique on the island, this shop, named for owner Emily Ott's grandmothers, also has home goods. This is where I first found the round towels by Beach People and bought my very first S'Well bottle. Website: Millyandgrace.com; Instagram: @shopmillyandgrace.

Hepburn: Another must when you're looking for women's fashion. Many of the dresses you see me wearing on Instagram came from Hepburn and this was where I bought my very first pair of Mystique sandals! Website: Hepburnnantucket.com; Instagram: @hepburnnantucket.

The Lovely: Owned by longtime Nantucketer Julie Biondi, this women's clothing boutique, which is located just past the **Lobster Trap** on Washington Street, shouldn't be missed. You're definitely going home with shopping bags! Website: Thelovely nantucket.com; Instagram: @thelovelynantucket.

28 Centre Pointe: Located at 28 Centre Street, this boutique is filled with unique kitchen, home, and table goods, as well as fashion. Owner Margaret Anne Nolen founded her own line, called Cartolina— and for those paying close attention, Lizbet is wearing a Cartolina dress when Xavier arrives! Website: 28centrepointe.com; Instagram: @28centrepointe.

Current Vintage: *Soup of the Day: champagne*. If this is your motto, Current Vintage is for you. This shop offers a joyful mix of old and new—vintage Lilly Pulitzer alongside cute slogan T-shirts alongside a great selection of wine, champagne, cheeses, and home goods. Website: Currentvintage.com; Instagram: @currentvintagenantucket.

Murray's Toggery: Murray's is the OG of Nantucket's shopping scene. It is the home of prep. It is the home of—wait for it—Nantucket red, the infamous red fabric that starts out a certain shade of brick and becomes, with each washing, more and more faded until it reaches its goal: a unique and unmistakable pale pink. The Murray family invented not only this color (and the Nantucket Reds clothing line) but also, in a sense, the social phenomenon that is so prevalent on Nantucket: the older and more loved an article of clothing (or a Jeep Wrangler or a lightship basket), the more authentic it is. To wear a brand-new pair of Nantucket-red shorts to dinner is considered gauche. Wash them thirty times first, then don them at every opportunity—when you're surf-casting at Smith's Point, when you're selecting tomatoes at Bartlett's Farm, when you're dancing in the front row at the Chicken Box. Spill your gin and tonic on them. Stand in the sea spray of the ferry. That's what they're made for. You can get Nantucket-red pants, skirts, children's overalls, and other assorted styles, but they *can only be properly purchased* at Murray's Toggery. (Note: Murray's also has other clothing. I spent many a panicked two-days-before-prom at Murray's with both of my boys as they tried on pants, shirts, ties, and jackets.) It's a family-owned and -run business that has a magical feel. Don't miss it. Website: Nantucketreds.com; Instagram: @ackreds.

Barnaby's Toy and Art Shack: Are you looking for someplace fun to take your young kids? Barnaby Bear's world expanded when children's book author and illustrator Wendy Rouillard opened Barnaby's Toy and Art Shack. Barnaby's is a whole experience— a curated toy store offering art classes such as beading, fairy-house building, and wood-slice art as well as a drop-in art studio where children can create any time of day. If you have little people, Barnaby's is a must. Also available for birthday parties and private events (once, when I walked in, a dude was teaching the kids magic!). They also sell great neon Nantucket lights. (I have one!) Website: barnabysnantucket.com; Instagram: @barnabybearbooks.

Force Five and **Indian Summer:** If your children are a bit older, say ten to seventeen, chances are they want to make a stop at the surf shop and clothier Force Five. Force Five has the added attraction of a hidden candy room in the back of the store. Indian Summer on the Strip is smaller but has everything to fulfill your dreams of becoming the next Alana Blanchard. Instagrams: @force5nantucket and @indiansummersurf.

Stephanie's: Stephanie Correia is a doyenne of Nantucket retail. Her eponymous shop on Main Street has women's clothing, footwear, bags and purses, and lots of nifty gifts. You can't miss it!

Remy: Come for the cashmere shark sweater, stay for Remy's bright, whimsical, and fun originals. Located on Old South Wharf, which is a charming place to stroll.

Are you in the market for art or photography?

Town is filled with galleries. The two I am fondest of are **Coe and Co** on Main Street—Nathan Coe's art photography is chic and sexy—and **Samuel Owen Gallery** (this is where I bought my "slushee wave" by photographer **Jonathan Nimerfroh** (Instagram: @jdn photography). Websites: Coeandcogallery.com and Samuelowen.com; Instagrams: @coeandcogallery and @samuelowen.

If you want to take home a piece of Nantucket, you should check out the surf landscapes by **Lauren Marttila** (website: Laurenmarttilaphotography.com;

Instagram: @laurenmarttilaphotography). I have these throughout my house. Another island artist whose work I both collect and write about is the landscape painter **Illya Kagan.** Website: Illyakagan.com; Instagram: @illyakagan.

Are you a history buff?

Perhaps the most robust nonprofit on Nantucket is the **Nantucket Historical Association.** The NHA's most popular site is the **Whaling Museum** on Broad Street, but the NHA also owns and operates the **Hadwen House** at the top of Main Street (across from the famous **Three Bricks**); the **Old Mill;** the **Oldest House;** and perhaps my favorite of the NHA properties: **Greater Light.** Built as a livestock barn in 1790, Greater Light was purchased and reimagined as an artists' oasis by two unmarried Quaker sisters, Gertrude and Hannah Monaghan. Greater Light and its exquisite gardens have been lovingly restored to their former glory by the NHA. To get updates on tour dates and times, visit NHA.org; Instagram: @ackhistory.

African Meeting House, Five Corners: On the corner of York and Pleasant, this post-and-beam cottage was built and occupied by Black Nantucketers in the 1800s. It is now a museum, offering cultural programs and interpretative exhibits. There is a Black Heritage Trail on Nantucket that leads one to sites such as the cemetery on Vestal Street; the Nantucket Atheneum, where Frederick Douglass gave his first public speech to a mixed-race audience in 1841; and abolitionist Anna Gardner's house. (I mention Anna Gardner and her pupil, Eunice Ross, in my novel *Golden Girl*!)

The **Nantucket Preservation Trust** operates walking

tours of downtown Nantucket during the summer months. Check at www.nantucketpreservation.org.

One great way to see all of Nantucket at once is to visit the **First Congregational Church** and climb up to the tower. (Anyone who has read my novel *Beautiful Day* knows that this is where Jenna and Margot have their heart-to-heart.) The tower has panoramic views across the island; it's Nantucket's answer to the Empire State Building.

Are you a movie buff?

Alas, there is only one official movie theater on Nantucket, but it's a beaut. The **Dreamland Theater** underwent a gut renovation in 2012 and is now, in my humble opinion, one of the most stunning (and energy-efficient) movie theaters in America. Open 364 days a year! I served as chairperson for the Dream Believer benefit in 2020, which was the year the Dreamland Drive-In movie theater was started, due to COVID. The drive-in operates in the summer months only. Website: Nantucketdreamland.org; Instagram: @nantucketdreamland.

WHAT IS SCONSET, ANYWAY?

Sconset is short for Siasconset (no one calls it Sia-sconset), which is the village on the eastern end of the island. Sconset has its own vibe (and the residents will no doubt bristle at my use of the word *vibe*). Sconset is understated; it's old-school and it despises pretension. Life in Sconset is slower; bumper stickers read TWENTY IS PLENTY IN SCONSET. (This refers to the speed limit.) In Sconset you're likely to see children on tricycles pedaling down the street and people in straw hats pruning roses; you'll see picket fences and 1988 Jeep Wagoneers with a rainbow stripe of beach stickers across the back bumpers. It's easy to be a tourist in Sconset but nearly impossible to become a bona fide Sconseter unless you were lucky enough to buy property there during the Ford administration.

There are two ways to get to Sconset. One is the Milestone Road, which is the only state-maintained road on Nantucket. It's seven miles long, relatively straight and flat, and fairly uneventful except for the stone markers at every mile (and at Pi, 3.14 miles from town). As you get out toward mile marker five, you'll have a nice vista so reminiscent of the African savanna that certain artistic pranksters built life-size elephants and lions that make appearances from time to time; look out for them as you drive or bicycle past. The other way to get to Sconset is on the long and winding Polpis Road. Polpis takes you past stone walls and wooden fences, a dramatic over-water view at the Nantucket Shipwreck and Lifesaving Museum, the turnoffs for the Wauwinet and Quidnet, and then past Sesachacha Pond, where you'll glimpse Sankaty Head Lighthouse in the distance before cruising past Sankaty Head golf course. The Polpis Road is nine miles long. Both Polpis Road and Milestone have bike paths, and the very fit and enthusiastic choose to do the "loop." You can also bike out to Sconset one way, then put your bike on the front of the **Wave,** Nantucket's public transportation, and get a ride home!

I made it to Sconset, now what do I do?

Sconset is famous for its colony of summer cottages, many of them tiny (like the one in my novel *Barefoot*), many of them old (some of the oldest houses on the island are in Sconset, including a house called Auld Lang Syne, part of which was constructed around 1675!), and many of them, for a limited time at the end of June and beginning of July, draped in cottage roses. There is no experience on Nantucket that is more storybook than wandering the quiet streets of Sconset when the roses are in bloom. I go every year— and every year, I am left breathless.

Along Baxter Road is Sconset's bluff walk, a path on the cliff above the Atlantic. You can walk out Baxter Road all the way to **Sankaty Head Lighthouse,** which looks like a peppermint stick.

You can also meander down Ocean Avenue to the **Summer House,** a hotel with a pool that fronts the ocean. There's a footbridge where you'll see a large sundial on the side of a private home. The bridge will lead you to the Sconset Rotary, where you'll find **Claudette's** sandwich shop (outstanding turkey salad), a package store, a tiny post office with irregular hours, the **Sconset Café** (home of the chocolate volcano cake), and finally, the Sconset Market. The market is the beating heart of town—it has not only groceries but ice cream and freshly baked baguettes every day!

Along New Street in Sconset are the **Sconset Casino,** the **Sconset Chapel,** and the **Chanticleer.** This little stretch shouldn't be missed. The Sconset Casino is now a tennis club, but it's also an event space used for weddings and benefits and it occasionally hosts movies in the summer. It was once used as a summer stage for the Broadway actors of the 1920s who chose to vacation on Nantucket. It's a building that evokes the days of old Nantucket.

Siasconset Union Chapel is an ecumenical chapel, used for services in the summer. (I was married in this church once upon a time…) The Sconset Chapel evokes a peaceful simplicity, and all of the kneelers were needlepointed by parishioners. One unusual feature is the Columbarium in the memorial gardens, where the ashes of Sconset residents (and *only* Sconset residents) are tucked into a tasteful wall.

The Chanticleer will be mentioned in the restaurant section, but even if you're not planning on eating there, you should be sure to snap a picture of the front garden with its iconic carousel horse.

IN A CATEGORY BY ITSELF: CISCO BREWERS

Dubbed by *Men's Health* magazine "the happiest place on earth," Cisco is, in modern parlance, a "whole thing." There are three barns, one housing a beer bar, one a wine bar, and one a spirits bar, all serving Cisco products, including their popular Whale's Tale Ale, Gripah, Triple Eight vodka, and my go-to, the sparkling cranberry pinot gris. However—and I do not say this lightly—alcohol is the least important thing about the place. This is a center of joy. There are food trucks—**167 Raw** for raw bar and guacamole, **Nantucket Poke** for bowls and tartare, and **Nantucket Lobster Trap** for swordfish sliders and lobster rolls. There is often live music. There are dogs and children and people relaxing at open-air picnic tables alongside the gardens that provide the produce and herbs for the mixed drinks. It is the *ultimate* après-beach scene, a must for any Sunday Funday, and just generally a destination you should not miss. For teetotalers, there are hand-crafted sodas as well. Cisco has proved so popular that satellite locations have popped up in places like Portsmouth, New Hampshire, and

Stamford, Connecticut. Website: Ciscobrewers.com; Instagram: @ciscobrewers.

To Market, to Market

If you're in search of a regular grocery store, the island has two **Stop and Shop**s. There's one downtown on the harbor, but this store is smaller than the newly renovated mid-island branch, which has the advantage of an attached family-run package store: **Nantucket Wine and Spirits.** Website: Nantucketwineandspirits .com; Instagram: @nantucketwines.

Bartlett's Farm has appeared in nearly every one of my novels. The farm itself is 160 acres of fields, including photogenic rows of flowers, like something out of a Renoir painting. It also has a nursery for all of your gardening and landscaping needs and a fabulous market. I go to the farm two to three times a week in the summer. Here are the things I love about Bartlett's: A selection of fresh flowers, including the lilies that grace my kitchen all summer long; homemade pies (I choose peach and blueberry); prepared foods (this is where I source my lobster salad and I also love their broccoli slaw). Produce! In mid-July the "corn crib" appears and then come the tomatoes (although Bartlett's also has outstanding hothouse tomatoes). I also adore their organic lettuces, which come washed in bags. In fall: pumpkins and gourds. Website: Bartlettsfarm.com; Instagram: @bartlettsfarm.

Moors End Farm: Some islanders insist that Moors End Farm, set along the Polpis Road, has even better corn than Bartlett's. (Quarrels have broken out on the topic.) And at the holidays, this is where *everyone,* including yours truly, sources their Christmas trees, wreaths, and garlands. Instagram: @moorsendfarm.

Nantucket Meat and Fish Market is a favorite not only of Magda English and Chad's mother but also of mine. I can't describe it any more lavishly than I did in the preceding pages ("swordfish steaks as thick as paperback books"); the meat and fish case is something to behold. Forgive me, vegans—I get the house-marinated steak tips and the gorgeous burgers with cheese and bacon already incorporated (I have hungry children at home!). This also has a Starbucks concession, so my daughter can get her "pink drink." Website: Nantucketmeatandfish.com; Instagram: @ack_meatandfish.

The place to get fish is **167 Raw.** The sign above the counter reads ANYONE WHO ASKS, "IS THE FISH FRESH?" MUST GO TO THE END OF THE LINE. I've been coming here since I bought my first house in 1998. Along with the freshest and most beautiful fish, the shop sells homemade smoked bluefish pâté and key lime pies. There's a food truck in the parking lot, but we'll get to that later! Website: 167raw.com; Instagram: @167raw_nantucket.

Hatch's, on Orange Street, across from Marine Home Center, is my liquor store. It has everything at the most reasonable prices. Period. Website: Ackhatchs.com; Instagram: @hatchsnantucket.

WHO'S HUNGRY?

Nantucket is an eaters' paradise. Once again, there are too many places to mention, so I'm going to give you my very favorites. I won't tell you what to order (yes, I will).

Sit-down lunch or dinner

Sandbar: If you're coming to Nantucket for a week or only for a day, I *highly* recommend Sandbar. It's located at Jetties Beach, which is less than a mile from town and can easily be walked (you'll work up an appetite!). Sandbar was the inspiration for the Oystercatcher in my novel *Golden Girl*. It's a true beach shack with open-air indoor seating and outdoor feet-in-the-sand seating. The menu is casual—fish tacos, burgers, an outstanding chicken sandwich—and there is often live music. The bar and raw-bar scene are lively, including a great buck-a-shuck in the midafternoon, but it's also very family-friendly. This is a must-do. Website: Jettiessandbar.com; Instagram: @sandbarjetties.

Galley Beach (aka the Blue Bistro): This is another on-the-beach setting, though one that is quite upscale. The Galley is quintessential Nantucket. In the late sixties, it was a burger shack (there's a scene set here in my novel *Summer of '69*), but over the decades, its atmosphere and food have become refined. It has unparalleled sunset views; by tradition, when the sun sets each night, everyone in the restaurant applauds. (There are dozens of times per summer when I'll see a breathtaking sunset and say out loud, "They're clapping at the Galley.") My controversial opinion is this: Go for lunch or cocktails, not dinner. Dinner is always crowded and a bit of a "scene." The cocktail hour can be a bit of a scene as well but one that is worth it because of the sunset. However, there is *no better place* on Nantucket to have an elegant sit-down lunch than the Galley. The food is fantastic. It's glamorous. It's the good life. The other perk to going to the Galley for lunch is the view of the green, yellow, and blue umbrellas lined up at the Cliffside Beach Club.

Trust me: go for lunch. Website: Galleybeach.net; Instagram: @galleybeach.

The Proprietors: This is the restaurant where Lizbet and JJ meet for dinner. In Lizbet's version of the Blue Book, she describes it as "eclectic," the place for "a thoughtful dining experience and the most creative cocktails on the island." The things I love about Props are the long bar (thirteen seats), the creative food (outrageously delicious), the shared high-top table behind the bar, the nook by the fireplace, and the wallpaper in the bathroom. Say hi to Tenacious Leigh for me! Website: Proprietorsnantucket.com; Instagram: @propsbar.

The Tap Room: The Tap Room at the historic Jared Coffin House has a "secret burger"—a Big Mac—esque patty melt—that isn't on the menu. It comes with outstanding French fries. Also, the popovers are a must. Website: Nantuckettaproom.com; Instagram: @theacktaproom.

The Nautilus: The only thing I don't love about Nautilus is that you need to be as wily, tireless, and determined as Indiana Jones to get a reservation. If you can meet the challenge of getting a table, everything will be delicious and the crowd will be lively and very attractive. My favorite dish is the blue-crab fried rice (I order it with two eggs), and this past year, I also really loved the Thai barbecue chicken. Website: Thenautilus.com; Instagram: @nautilusnantucket.

Cru: Another near-impossible reservation. Cru sits at the end of Straight Wharf and has a lot of fun outdoor seating that attracts an extremely beautiful crowd of bons vivants. Inside, there are three seating areas: front room, middle room, and back bar. I nearly always eat at the back bar. I nearly always order the lobster roll and fries with mayo (Chef Erin Zircher has been known to spoil me and send out an array of *flavored* mayos, which is my idea of heaven). Cru has the best raw-bar scene on the island, which is saying a *lot*. Cru has the appeal of see-and-be-seen with delicious, carefully prepared food, excellent service, and water views. There's a reason it's almost impossible to get in. Website: Crunantucket; Instagram: @crunantucket.

The Pearl and **The Boarding House:** As of this writing, my two favorite restaurants on the island, the Pearl and the Boarding House, have been sold to new owners. The Cobblestone Telegraph tells me the new owners are keeping not only the original feel to both restaurants but also the menus. In years past, I loved to sit at the bar at the Boho and order the crab dip, the lobster spaghetti, the chocolate cookies with mini-milkshake. Upstairs at the slightly fancier Pearl, I liked to get the tuna martini, the sixty-second steak topped with quail egg, and the lobster rangoons (limit two per customer). I can only hope that the excellence will be preserved. Website: Thepearl-nantucket.com; Instagram: @pearlnantucket.

Bar Yoshi: This is where Lizbet and Heidi Bick go for dinner in this novel. Bar Yoshi was new in 2021 and I ate there multiple times because the food is so light and fresh and the space so appealing. This is *the* place to go for sushi; I always opted for fried rice, dumplings, spring rolls. The restaurant is on Old South Wharf and has water views out the large open windows. Website: Bar-yoshi.com; Instagram: @baryoshinantucket.

Or, The Whale: Or, The Whale (which is the subtitle of *Moby-Dick*) occupies prime real estate on Main Street. It has a long bar and an adorable back garden. This past year, I discovered the best reason to go to OTW: the Korean pork butt. It's expensive but it will feed four people with leftovers to take home. This is a pork butt roasted for hours so that it is so tender and succulent, you can eat it with a spoon. And it's served with light, bright, and spicy sides—lettuce wraps, fresh mint, chili sauce. Website: Otwnantucket.com; Instagram: @orthewhalenantucket.

Ventuno: If dining out for you means Italian food, you want to go to Ventuno, located in the heart of downtown. During my first twenty years on the island, this was the beloved restaurant 21 Federal, which appears in many of my novels, including *The Blue Bistro* and *Golden Girl*. The antique building has remained the same but the cuisine has changed to upscale Italian, plus the best steak on the island. However, what I love most about Ventuno is the bar scene. Revelers might prefer the spirited back bar, but like Mint Benedict's nurse Charlene, I can be found at the inside bar with the legendary bartender Johnny B. Sometimes you want to go where everybody knows your name. Website: Ventunorestaurant.com; Instagram: @ventunorestaurant.

American Seasons: Great choice for a romantic night out. Chef Neil Ferguson's food is exquisite. The tiny bar is a hidden gem. Website: Americanseasons .com; Instagram: @americanseasons.

Straight Wharf: Straight Wharf has a split personality. There's the bar side, which attracts a young crowd and can get loud. But the restaurant side is some of the most elegant dining on the island. The dining room is stunning, and tables on the deck are the most coveted because you can watch the ferries coming and going and might be able to catch a glimpse of Lizbet headed into Mario's cottage! (It was while dining at Straight Wharf that I first noticed the cottages perched at the end of a dock and thought, *I'm going to have Mario* *live in one of those!*) Website: Straightwharfrestaurant; Instagram: @straightwharf.

Languedoc: The hits keep coming! Languedoc is a classic French bistro on Broad Street. I have set scenes in many books here—this is where Isabel's baby shower is held in *Winter Storms* and it's where Vivi and Willa go for a mother-daughter dinner in *Golden Girl*. The Languedoc is elegant yet relaxed; you can eat escargot in your Patagonia puffy vest (lots of people do this). I always order the cheeseburger with garlic fries; paired with the chopped salad as a starter and the sweet inspirations sundae for dessert, it's the perfect meal. The downstairs dining room and the bar, helmed by the great Jimmy Jaksic, are my preferred spots, although the upstairs dining rooms are cozy and charming. Website: Languedocbistro.com; Instagram: @languedocbistro.

Millie's: We've talked about Sconset on the east end of the island but we haven't yet talked about Madaket on the west end. Madaket is primarily residential—a drive out to Smith's Point will take you past the tiny summer cottages (such as Wee Bit in my novel *Golden Girl*). It is *the* place to watch the sunset, and the vistas over Madaket harbor will immediately improve your Instagram. The epicenter of fun in Madaket is the Millie's universe. Millie's is probably best described as a Tex-Mex-inspired restaurant with a heavy Nantucket influence. All of the menu items are named after places on Nantucket. I always start with the Altar Rock, chips with salsa, guac, and their incredible queso. Then I move on to either the Wauwinet, which is a luscious Caesar topped with grilled shrimp and served tossed in a creamy lime dressing, or the Esther Island, a seared-scallop taco with purple cabbage slaw. Millie's has a ton of outdoor seating as well as upstairs and downstairs indoor seating, but there is always a wait, which can be frustrating. I suggest going before you get too hungry! There's an ice cream stand for after your meal as well as a small market where you can provision for trips out to Smith's Point! Website: Milliesnantucket.com; Instagram: @milliesnantucket.

Chanticleer: The Chanticleer, out in Sconset, has a long-standing tradition of elegant French dining. I think it's fair to say that back in the day, it was a bit stuffy. (The original owner did not allow music in the dining room, for example.) However, since being bought by Nantucket restaurateur Susan Handy (of **Black-Eyed Susan's,** featured in my novel *Here's to Us*), it has achieved the perfect balance of classic and modern. The front garden, anchored by the iconic carousel horse, is one of the most delightful places to eat in the summer. There are also two indoor dining rooms as well as a sunporch. (I prefer the cozy, clubby dining room to the right.) In addition to more formal French fare, there's an outstanding burger on the menu (I'm not embarrassed to say this is what I usually order). The restaurant used to attract an older clientele, but that has completely changed—it is now popular with savvy millennials, and I am so here for it. Website: Chanticleernantucket.com; Instagram: @chanticleernantucket.

Petrichor: A hidden gem. This wine bar located in mid-island has outstanding food, including my favorite fried-chicken sandwich on the island, and it does a terrific business at brunch. Highly recommended, and after dinner and some thoughtfully curated wines, you can walk right over to Island Kitchen for dessert! Website: Petrichorwinebar.com; Instagram: @petrichorwinebar.

Island Kitchen: Also located in mid-island, Island

Kitchen is exactly that, a terrific and cozy local spot where the food is outstanding and the ice cream is even better. The ice cream flavors change with the season, but in years past, I have been a huge fan of the lemon soufflé and the peach and biscuits. There was a time a few years ago when my daughter was obsessed with their charcoal ice cream. (It was delicious.) Island Kitchen ice cream can also be found at the **Counter on Main Street** in Nantucket Pharmacy and at my beloved **Surfside Beach Shack.** Website: Nantucket islandkitchen.com; Instagram: @iknantucket.

Sea Grille: A classic, family-run seafood restaurant and islander favorite! The Sea Grille is my choice for best lobster roll and best lobster bisque. I like to sit in the fun front-bar area and order from the bar menu! The food is crazy good. Website: Theseagrille.com; Instagram: @theseagrille.

Get it to go!

Wicked Island Bakery: Home of the infamous morning buns. Full disclosure: In the summer of 2021, my daughter worked at Wicked Island Bakery, and therefore I heard endless sagas about the morning buns. (It might be a stretch to say I could write a novel about the morning buns, but this will definitely be the topic of my daughter's college essay.) When I dropped off my daughter, who was then age fifteen, at six a.m., there was already a line of people waiting for the bakery to open. Once, a man saw my daughter get out of the car and he hurried out of *his* car, because he thought she was there to get in line. It's that bad and worse. The morning buns are hand-crafted cinnamon rolls that are produced in batches of thirty, and they take forty-five minutes to make. The frenzy is caused by how delicious they are, yes, but it's also the law of supply and demand in action (there is a six-bun-per-customer limit in the summer). The stories I heard about Adults Behaving Badly in regard to the morning buns prompt me now to remind everyone that civility and kindness are always mandatory, especially when you're dealing with people in the service industry and especially when those people are teenagers working summer jobs. We adults must lead by example. Period. Wicked Island Bakery also has *outrageously delicious* ham-and-cheese croissants as well as the almond croissants that I used in this novel! And it's where you can procure **Amy's Cookies,** adorable sugar cookies decorated in any number of charming ways by #girlboss Dr. Amy Hinson. (Amy served as my forensics expert for *Golden Girl*.) Website: Wickedislandbakery.com; Instagram: @wickedislandbakery.

Born and Bread: This is where I get my sourdough. (They also have an addictive olive sourdough on certain days.) The bread is baked fresh and sliced right there. Terrific sandwiches as well, including Lizbet's favorite, the ABC grilled cheese! It's right downtown on Centre Street. Website: Bornandbreadnantucket.com; Instagram: @bornandbreadnantucket.

Lemon Press: Do you love fresh-pressed juices, kombucha, acai bowls, avocado toast? If so, then you must make a visit to Main Street superstar Lemon Press. It provides a breakfast or lunch of champions—fresh, healthy, delicious. And it's owned and operated by two women! The line can be quite long, since this place is super-popular for a reason, so bring a book (or buy one—Mitchell's Book Corner is right across the street!). Website: Lemonpressnantucket.com; Instagram: @lemonpressnantucket.

The Beet: While we're supporting women

entrepreneurs and eating delicious and healthy food, why not stop at the Beet? The menu is fun fusion; I know people who are devotees of the Kung Fu Fighter salad, and I adore the chicken burger. Website: The beetnantucket.com; Instagram: @thebeetnantucket.

Walter's and **Stubby's:** Both Walter's and Stubby's are on the Strip, which is the block between Easy Street and Water Street known for inexpensive, fast, and delicious eats. **Easy Street Cantina** is on the Strip, as are **Steamboat Pizza** and the **Juice Bar** (you'll know the Juice Bar by the hundreds of people waiting in line). My two favorite stops on the Strip are Walter's and Stubby's. Walter's has made-to-order hot and cold sandwiches, including the best Reuben on the island (you heard it here). Stubby's is, as Edie says in the novel, Nantucket's version of McDonald's. It's known for its waffle fries—they come highly recommended—and they also have excellent fast-food-type burgers and chicken sandwiches. Stubby's stays open until two a.m., making it *very* popular with a late-night crowd, and this past year, some marketing genius finally created a hoodie that says ENDED UP AT STUBBY'S. More than one of these hang in my own mudroom! Website: Stubbysnantucket.com; Instagram: @stubbysnantucket.

Lolaburger: There might not be words to describe how much I love Lolaburger. I love it so much, and it is the most requested dinner treat in my household (so much for Cringe Cooking!). It's a luxe burger joint with the best grilled-chicken sandwich on the island (it comes with Swiss, bacon, and avocado). They are also known for their truffle fries (*divine!*). And they have milkshakes. They do have indoor and outdoor dining with bar service but I prefer to call in my order and pick up. The wait can be up to an hour on busy evenings, so you've been warned! (But, oh, it's worth it.) Website: Lolaburger.com; Instagram: @lolaburger.restaurants.

167 Raw food truck: This is the food truck next to the fabulous fish market. It has the best tuna burger on the island. You can order online and pick it up on your way to the beach. Highly recommended! You can also get fish tacos, carnitas tacos, lobster rolls, and their famous ceviche and guacamole. Website to order in advance: 167rawtakeout.com.

Something Natural: An island institution. It was, perhaps, my discovery of Something Natural herb bread in my first summer, 1993, that made me want to move to Nantucket. The sandwiches at Something Natural are the stuff of legends; they're huge—a whole sandwich can easily feed two people. The cookies are also huge, also legendary. Something Natural has a garden setting with picnic tables if you want to bike up Cliff Road and eat there, or you can phone in an order to go and head to the beach. My usual order is the avocado, cheddar, and chutney on herb bread, which might sound weird, but it tastes like summertime to me. You can buy loaves of their breads at the Cliff Road location or at the Stop and Shop. My kids are partial to the Portuguese bread, which makes *the* best toast. Website: Somethingnatural.com; Instagram: @somethingnaturalack.

Thai House and **Siam to Go:** Takeout Thai food of the highest quality. I like the spring rolls better at the Thai House but the shrimp pad thai better at Siam to Go. Nantucket can sometimes feel wanting when it comes to authentic, inexpensive food from other cultures, so I am grateful for these two places. Websites: Ackthaihouse.com, siamtogonantucket.com; Instagram: @thaihouse_nantucket.

The Boathouse: There was a time when everyone who worked at the Boathouse knew my middle child by name, he ate there so often. In addition to burgers and fried-chicken sandwiches, it has outstanding tacos and burritos. Everything is fresh and reasonably priced. A lot of times, if I'm going out and I have hungry kids to feed, I'll order dinner for them here and everyone is thrilled. Website: Boathousenantucket.com; Instagram: @boat_house_nantucket.

Sophie T's: A classic, family-run pizza parlor that has long been our go-to for pizza and subs (for a stretch of maybe ten years, every sleepover party involved a run to Sophie T's). I love the ACK Mack pizza, a play on a Big Mac with ground beef, American cheese, onions, pickles, and a sesame crust, drizzled with special sauce. It's delicious! Website: Sophietspizza.com; Instagram: @sophietspizza.

I LOVE THE NIGHTLIFE, I'VE GOT TO BOOGIE!

The Chicken Box: And now, the moment you've all been waiting for: the Chicken Box! A few things you should know: It's best referred to as simply "The Box." If you say, "I closed the Box last night," you'll sound like a Nantucket local. Also: There is no chicken, *not one piece of chicken*. It's just a bar, the best dive bar in America, with beer-sticky floors and beautiful people three-deep at the bar and terrific bands, including headliners like G. Love, Grace Potter, and Donavon Frankenreiter, who come (I believe) because of their love of the venue. When I go, I don't mess around; I can be found in the front row, dancing. The trip to the Box is the most popular event during the Elin Hilderbrand Bucket List Weekend and it is the most visited place by people who come to the island looking for all the spots mentioned in my books. (It appears in *The Love Season, Beautiful Day, The Identicals, The Perfect Couple, 28 Summers,* and *Golden Girl,* among others.) Website: Thechickenbox.com; Instagram: @thebox nantucket.

The Gaslight: Want to hear live music but don't want to leave downtown? You're in luck! The building that used to house the Starlight movie theater was reimagined a few years ago to become the Gaslight, a bar, restaurant, and live-music venue. The food is nothing short of amazing—it comes to you from Liam Mackey, the chef of Nautilus—and at ten o'clock, the music kicks in. If you need one more reason to check it out, there's also a champagne vending machine! Website: Gaslightnantucket.com; Instagram: @gaslightnantucket.

The Club Car piano bar: The Club Car is a fine-dining restaurant that incorporates one of the train cars from the old Nantucket Railroad as its bar (hence the name). The food at the Club Car is fresh and inventive but the real star of the place is the sing-along piano bar. Plan to tip twenty bucks if you want to hear "Tiny Dancer," "Shallow," or "Piano Man." (Other songs—I like to request "Rich Girl," "Home Sweet Home," and the theme from *Welcome Back, Kotter*—are free.) Website: Theclubcar.com; Instagram: @nantucketclubcar.

SALONS

R. J. Miller Salon: This has been my salon for over fifteen years—hair, nails, facials—and I love it. There are scenes in this salon in my novels *Silver Girl* and

Beautiful Day, and of course, this is where Amy and Lorna work in *Golden Girl*. Website: Rjmiller salons.com; Instagram: @rjmillersalonspa.

Darya Salon and **Spa at the White Elephant:** I love Darya! And for those paying close attention, she's the one who dyes Kimber's hair orange in the novel. Her salon can now be found at the White Elephant, right down the street from the Hotel Nantucket! Website: Daryasalonspa.com; Instagram: @daryasalonspa.

Working Out

Forme Barre: Forme Barre can probably be called my home away from home. I go every day (assuming I'm not traveling). I have stated on my social media that the best way to see me on Nantucket is to attend the daily 9:30 a.m. barre class at Forme during the summer. We can plié together! In the summer, Forme also offers Beach Barre classes with the barre bus at Nobadeer Beach. I go to barre on the beach at least once per summer. (Forme also has virtual classes, which I take when I'm traveling.) Website: Formebarre.com; Instagram: @forme.nantucket.

Nantucket Cycling and Fitness: If you're looking for a spin class, this is the place! Before I bought my Peloton, this was where I would spin. The studio is tucked back off Old South Road and can be tricky to find, but once you know where it is, you'll be charmed. The space is appealing, the instructors are tough, and you will get your money's worth. Website: Nantucket fitness.com; Instagram: @nantucketcyclingfitness.

The Nantucket Hotel: The Nantucket Hotel has one of the best fitness centers on the island and they offer memberships to the public. They also have a magical yoga instructor in **Pat Dolloff.** Follow Pat on Instagram: @patricia_dolloff.

OTHER FUN STUFF!

Cooking classes at the **Nantucket Culinary Center:** On the corner of Broad and Federal is the Nantucket Culinary Center. The NCC offers cooking classes, many of them taught by my friend and culinary hero **Sarah Leah Chase.** (Sarah developed recipes for my novel *Here's to Us* and I used her *Nantucket Open House Cookbook* extensively throughout *28 Summers*.) On the lower level of the NCC is the **Corner Table Café.** Website: Cornertablenantucket.com; Instagram: @cornertablenantucket.

Nantucket Island Surf School: If the waves are good, give it a try! The instructors are young, many of them current or former Nantucket High School students who grew up surfing right there at Cisco Beach. Website: Nantucketsurfing.com; Instagram: @nantucketsurfing.

Endeavor Sailing: The *Endeavor* runs three sailing cruises per day plus a sunset cruise (weather permitting) on a thirty-one-foot Friendship Sloop that was built by Captain Jim Genthner. You can reserve spots on the boat with others or rent the entire thing for yourself. Perfect for groups—large families, bachelorette parties, girls' weekends, and so forth. You can bring your own food and drink. In *Winter Storms,* someone gets engaged aboard the *Endeavor*! Website: Endeavorsailing.com; Instagram: @endeavorsailing.

Miacomet Golf Course: As Blond Sharon points out in this book, it *can* be tricky getting a tee time at Miacomet Golf Course, because it's the only public eighteen-hole course on the island. Miacomet also has a very good and popular restaurant and bar, a driving range, and a putting green. Website: Miacomet golf.com; Instagram: @miacometgolfcourse.

Absolute Sports Fishing ACK and **Bill Fisher Outfitters:** For all my Angler Cupcakes out there! I know the captains involved in these two charter fishing businesses and you'll be in good hands. Charming and professional. Websites: Absolute sportsfishing.com, Billfishertackle.com; Instagrams: @absolutesportsfishingack, @billfishertackle.

HOLIDAYS AND FESTIVALS

Daffodil Weekend (the last weekend in April): Daffodil Weekend (aka "Daffy," as in "Are you coming for Daffy?") kicks off the unofficial season on Nantucket. The stores in town reopen, the ferries fill up with people wearing yellow and green, and you start seeing a lot of classic cars around. Daffodil Weekend began in the mid-1970s when the Nantucket Garden Club sponsored a flower show. Two years later, garden-club member Jean MacAusland started an initiative to plant one million daffodil bulbs across Nantucket. Today, there are over two million daffodils on Nantucket, and the island celebrates their blooming with not only a flower show but also an antique car parade that starts in town and travels out the Milestone Road to Sconset. The cars often have themes—"Renoir's Boating Party," for example—and once in Sconset, the cars park along Main Street and set up tailgate picnics. I have scenes set at Daffy in my novels *The Matchmaker* and *28 Summers*.

Figawi (Memorial Day weekend): Are you older

than thirty? Skip Figawi. Figawi (the name reportedly comes from sailors who were lost in the fog and shouted, "Where the f*ck are we?") is technically a sailing race between Hyannis and Nantucket, but over the years it has devolved into a weekend where people in their twenties come bearing thirty-packs of Bud Light with the intent of drinking as much as they can for as long as they can. (I describe Figawi in my novel *The Rumor.*) Figawi is such a blight on the island that every Memorial Day weekend, I hope for rain…and I am not alone in this.

Nantucket Book Festival (mid-June): I'm obviously not impartial, but as a person who has done many, many book festivals, I can say that the Nantucket Book Festival is the best. (It often falls when I'm on tour, so I don't always participate.) Website: Nantucketbook festival.org; Instagram: @nantucketbookfestival.

Nantucket Film Festival (mid-June, but after the book festival): The NFF was founded in 1997 and from the beginning has been focused on screenwriting. It is very low-key as far as film festivals go, though celebrities do come to Nantucket during this week. The films are screened at both the Dreamland and the Sconset Casino, and there are plenty of talks as well, some at glorious private homes around the island. Website: Nantucketfilmfestival.org; Instagram: @nantucketfilmfestival.

Fourth of July: The Fourth of July is undergoing something of a transformation after COVID. Traditionally, this included a bike parade up Main Street, pie-eating contests, and then an infamous water fight with the Nantucket Fire Department. On the evening of July 5, Visitor Services sponsors fireworks, and people crowd onto Jetties Beach. This was canceled in 2020 and 2021. Nobadeer is the beach of choice for revelry on the Fourth—again, if you're over twenty-five, you might want to check out one of the other beaches I've suggested in this guide!

The Pops (second Saturday in August): My personal favorite "holiday" on Nantucket. The Boston Pops at Jetties Beach began in the late nineties to benefit the Nantucket Cottage Hospital and usually raises upwards of two million dollars. People pack picnics (like Mallory in *28 Summers*) and sit in the sand while the Boston Pops perform. In recent years, they've included various special guests—we've had Carly Simon, Kenny Loggins, the Spinners. The show ends with a magnificent fireworks show. It's the best night of the summer.

Halloween: Nantucket does Halloween right—especially if you have kids! Main Street closes, all of the stores hand out candy (good candy!), and there's a costume parade. There's also a haunted house at the old fire station.

Thanksgiving: Thanksgiving on Nantucket has traditionally been celebrated by the Turkey Plunge at Children's Beach, which benefits the Nantucket Atheneum. Yes, people go into the water, no matter the weather. (Full disclosure: I have never done it.) The other Thanksgiving event happens on Friday. Everyone gathers downtown for the tree lighting. Nantucket's streets are lined with Christmas trees that will later be decorated by classes at the elementary school and the nonprofits. At five o'clock there is a little ceremony and then the switch is flipped and all the trees light up at once! We sometimes have visiting dignitaries for this!

Christmas Stroll: The biggest holiday in the off-season and possibly all year is the Nantucket Chamber of Commerce's Christmas Stroll (known simply as

"Stroll," as in "Elin is signing at four thirty the Saturday of Stroll"). We already know that the trees are lit, and as you might guess, the shop windows are festively decorated. The Killen family places a Christmas tree in a dory at the Easy Street Boat Basin. (Did you even *go* to Stroll if you didn't photograph the Killen dory?) Traditionally, the Nantucket Historical Association throws a benefit party to preview its "Festival of Trees" display in the Whaling Museum. This is my favorite party of the year (sadly, it was canceled in 2020 and 2021). I describe this party in, you guessed it, my novel *Winter Stroll.* However, the Festival of Trees exhibit is open to the public through the new year and should not be missed—businesses and creative islanders decorate trees that are displayed throughout the museum.

On the Saturday of Stroll, Main Street closes. Santa arrives on a Coast Guard vessel at noon, and children can visit with him in the Methodist church. There are Victorian carolers. There's a food tent in the Stop and Shop parking lot at the bottom of Main Street. In years of yore, you would see ladies from New York in magnificent fur coats. Now people tend to dress up as Buddy the Elf and the Grinch and naughty Mrs. Claus. There are book signings at Mitchell's throughout the day. There are live bands at Cisco Brewers. Not every restaurant is open, so it's very important to make dinner reservations way in advance—most restaurants start taking these reservations after Columbus Day.

One of my readers from Jacksonville, Florida, Jenna T., compiled a super-helpful list of Stroll tips. She mentions getting the Stroll Scarf—there's a new scarf created every year, and the official one can be purchased only at the Nantucket Boat Basin Shop. She recommends **B-ACK Yard BBQ** on Lower Main as a great place to get drinks as you watch for Santa's arrival. She and her crew had lunch at the **Corner Table Market,** a lovely spot for sandwiches, pastries, prepared foods, and coffee. Jenna loved the front porch of the **Nantucket Hotel** for drinks and the indoor **Breeze** restaurant for lunch or dinner. Jenna recommends booking your hotel early and reminded me that, as at the Hotel Nantucket, there is a three-night minimum over Stroll.

The proper greeting is "Happy Stroll!" Thanks, Jenna!

GIVING BACK

If you've visited Nantucket, you've already done your share by plumping the local economy with your hard-earned dollars. (And as you've learned, Nantucket is *not* cheap!) However, if you're inclined to give even more, I will share my favorites of the Nantucket-based nonprofits. The three places I'm suggesting are extremely beneficial to the year-round community, including the workforce who clean your rooms, wash your dishes, prune the hedges, and pick up the trash.

Nantucket Boys and Girls Club: I sat on the board of directors here for nine years and chaired their summer benefit for three. (Fodder for my novel *A Summer Affair*!) The club is my number-one nonprofit because without a safe place for people to send their children after school, the island would stop running. The club underwent a massive renovation and it is now a leader among its peers—not only the building itself but the programming. If you donate to the club, you will be directly helping all of working Nantucket. Website: Nantucket boysandgirlsclub.org; Instagram: @nantucketbgc.

Nantucket Booster Club: All of our student athletes (among them three of my own children) have to travel on the fast ferry to get to away games. This costs money, as does ground transportation on the other side. If you're a person who's passionate about youth sports, then donating to the Boosters might be for you. Website: Nantucketboosterclub.com.

Nantucket Food Pantry: The winter months on Nantucket can be tough, and we do have a vulnerable population once the summer visitors stop coming. The Food Pantry has long been addressing the needs of our islanders with food insecurity. Website: Assist nantucket.org.

On behalf of Nantucket, I thank you for reading this section!

That brings us to the end of this guide. Did I miss things? Yes. A more comprehensive guide may be in my future, but this will certainly get you started.

I want to say a few parting words about the island. I came to Nantucket in 1993 intending to stay just for the summer and "write my book." (This was a novel called *Girl Stuff,* which never saw the light of day.) I was living in New York City at the time, and when I returned to my apartment in Manhattan, I burst into tears. My roommate looked at me and said, "I take it you had a good summer?" I knew then that my future would be in Nantucket; I moved there the following June. I had fallen in love with the island—the dunes and the eelgrass and the sandy roads that cut through the moors; the houses with names and boot scrapers on the front steps and lavish flower boxes; the simple aesthetic of gray shingles with white trim; the days of fog and the days of bright sunshine; the singular pleasure of driving a Jeep onto the beach and watching the sun set over the water at Fortieth Pole; the smell of butter and garlic as I walked into 21 Federal; the taste of corn picked from the fields of Bartlett's Farm only an hour before; the sensation every night of going to bed with sand in the sheets. But more than all of that, I fell in love with the people. It's the people of Nantucket who have made the island my home and who have made raising three children here such a wonderful experience. The year-round community is diverse and vibrant. We are hardy folks, patient and tolerant, and there is no community that comes together to help one another like we do.

I owe Nantucket Island everything I have and everything I am. What a muse she has been!

XO, Elin

Acknowledgments

I had a lot of help in creating the Hotel Nantucket. My inspiration was the Nantucket Hotel and Resort, owned by Mark and Gwenn Snider. Mark and Gwenn lead by excellent example, and they have assembled an incredible team, many of whom have worked at the hotel since it opened in June of 2012. I would like to thank general manager Jamie Holmes for sitting down and talking with me. I also had an extremely informative conversation with LeighAnne McDonald of the hotel's front desk. In no particular order, thank you to Nicole Miller, Tim Benoit, Deb Ducas, Johnathan Rodriguez, Carlos and Fulya Castrello, John Vecchio, Sharon Quigley, Kate O'Connor, Matthew Miller and Rick James, Danilo Kozic, Patricia Dolloff, Frederick Clarke, Wayne Brown, and Amy Vanderwolk. As Shelly Carpenter says, "Hotels aren't about rooms. They aren't about amenities. They're about people." The people who work at the Nantucket Hotel and Resort are some of the very finest in the hospitality industry.

For design inspiration, I want to thank Elizabeth Georgantas, Erin Gates, and my brilliant sister-in-law Lisa Hilderbrand. I must give credit to Elizabeth Conlon for the penny-sheathed wall.

The books I found helpful were Jacob Tomsky's *Heads in Beds: A Reckless Memoir of Hotels, Hustles and So-Called Hospitality* and Micah Solomon's *The Heart of Hospitality: Great Hotel and Restaurant Leaders Share Their Secrets.* I stalked the websites of the Cornell University School of Hotel Administration and the Statler Hotel, but the versions of the hotel school I present in this novel are fictional.

For all things Minnesota/Minnetonka-related, thank you to friends of (gulp) thirty-seven years, Fletcher and Carolyn Chambers.

Thank you to Amy Finsilver and Pamela Blessing of XV Beacon in Boston for being the ultimate lifesavers.

Thanks to Ashley Lasota for the term *deep August.* I love it.

Thank you to the Instagram account @Chadtucket. (You know why!)

As many of you know, I do not have an assistant, but I do have a "work husband." His name is Tim Ehrenberg, and he's the marketing director for Nantucket Book Partners and the creator of the Bookstagram account @timtalksbooks. He is also the secret to my success. Tim and I work tirelessly in the scary basement of Mitchell's Book Corner, where I sign thousands of preorders that Tim then lovingly packages and ships out. He is the best companion, the strictest taskmaster, the savviest interviewer, the most generous reader, and one of my closest friends. I love you, Tim Ehrenberg! Never leave me!

Huge thank you to my editor, Judy Clain, who once again blessed my work with her intellect, her sharp sensibility, her humor, and something elusive that feels like magic.

Thank you to my agents, Michael Carlisle and David Forrer, for making every dream I had as a writer come true.

Thank you to the great Michael Pietsch, Terry

Acknowledgments

Adams, Craig Young, Ashley Marudas, Lauren Hesse, my publicist Katharine Myers, Brandon Kelly, Bruce Nichols, Jayne Yaffe Kemp, Tracy Roe, Anna de la Rosa, Mariah Dwyer, Karen Torres, and Sabrina Callahan. I appreciate every single brilliant thing you do on my behalf, which is a lot of things!

To my home team: Rebecca Bartlett, Debbie Briggs, Wendy Hudson, Wendy Rouillard, Liz and Beau Almodobar, Margie and Chuck Marino, Katie and Jim Norton, Sue and Frank Decoste, Linda Holliday, Melissa Long, Jeannie Esti, the fabulous Jane Deery, Julie Lancia, Deb Ramsdell, Deb Gfeller, Anne and Whitney Gifford, David Rattner and Andrew Law, Manda Riggs, Helaina Jones, Heidi Holdgate, Matthew and Evelyn MacEachern, Holly and Marty McGowan (Marty made the book!), Richard Congdon, Angela and Seth Raynor, Rocky Fox, Julie and Matt Lasota, and the talented Jessica Hicks. What would I do without you?

Thank you, Timothy Field, my sweetest friend, for loving me through the crazy.

Thank you to my family: my mother, Sally Hilderbrand, as well as Eric and Lisa, Rand and Steph, Todd, and Doug and Jen. The biggest hug of all goes to my sister, Heather Thorpe, for being my fiercest champion, my best friend, and the "woman who walks me home."

Finally, gratitude to and for my children: Maxwell, Dawson, Shelby, and, now, Alex. The greatest privilege of my life is watching you mature into adults. I love you all beyond the beyond—and every word I write is, as ever, for you.

About the Author

Elin Hilderbrand has lived year-round on Nantucket Island since 1994. In the summers, she has a house filled with young adult children, and she loves cooking, going to the beach in her Jeep, and riding her Peloton. *The Hotel Nantucket* is her twenty-eighth novel.

Turn the page to read an excerpt from Elin Hilderbrand's newest novel, *The Five-Star Weekend*.

Prologue: Nantucket

Another summer on the island is upon us and, as usual, we have a lot to talk about. Chef Mario Subiaco proposed to Lizbet Keaton on the widow's walk of the Hotel Nantucket; there's a camera crew filming out in Monomoy (Blond Sharon has it "on good authority" that it's a limited series for Netflix); police chief Ed Kapenash has been admitted to the Nantucket Cottage Hospital after complaining of chest pain — and there's a steamy debate about whether or not Nantucket should allow topless beaches. (We think of ourselves as progressive and sophisticated, but let's face it — we're not France.)

Then we hear a rumor that Hollis Shaw is hosting something she's calling the "Five-Star Weekend" at her house in Squam.

This, of course, captures our full attention.

Hollis Shaw is something of a unicorn.

She started out life as one of us. She was the daughter of Tom Shaw, Nantucket's busiest plumbing contractor, and Charlotte Shaw, a kindergarten teacher. When Hollis was a toddler, not quite two years old, Charlotte Shaw died of an aneurysm in the shower, and Tom Shaw was left to raise his daughter alone. But on this island, we pitch in — it takes a village! — and we all offered moral support as Hollis grew up. We watched her dance in ballet recitals, shoot free throws at the Boys and Girls Club, and cheer for her boyfriend, Jack Finigan, in the stands at the Nantucket Whalers football games. Hollis was a good student, an outstanding softball pitcher (the team won the state championship Hollis's junior year and came in second her senior year), and a hard worker. The cottage out in Squam where she lived with her father was modest (though the land it sat on was worth a fortune), and as soon as Hollis was old enough, she kept house and cooked every night. She got a job opening scallops on Old North Wharf after school, and in the summers, she and her best friend, Tatum, waited tables at the Rope Walk.

In her senior year of high school, Hollis wrote what her English teacher Ms. Fox called "the best college essay I've read in thirty-one years." It took the form of a letter to Hollis's deceased mother, Charlotte. *Dear Mom,* it started, *I think you would be proud of the way I turned out. Here are some of the reasons why.*

It was bittersweet when Hollis decided to go to the University of North Carolina at Chapel Hill. We were proud of our girl — she received a full academic scholarship — but once she left, we missed her.

After graduating from college, Hollis moved to Boston, where she worked as the assistant food editor at *Boston* magazine and got to eat, on the magazine's expense account, at all of the city's "Best New Restaurants." Eventually she met Harvard Medical School surgery resident Matthew Madden. They were married in Wellesley, bought a house in Wellesley, and raised their daughter, Caroline, in Wellesley.

When Hollis's father, Tom, died in 2007, Hollis inherited the Squam property. Over the winter, we watched as the tiny cottage where Hollis had grown up was moved to the edge of the lot, and a gracious post-and-beam home was built in its place.

It's official, we thought. *Hollis Shaw has become a summer person.* (But at least she was *our* summer person. After all, she could have immigrated to Martha's Vineyard.) She joined the Field and Oar Club, where she played tennis; she volunteered at the Nantucket Book Festival; and on Sunday afternoons, we saw her at the Deck, sitting at one of the best tables along the railing above the Monomoy creeks, drinking rosé, and laughing with people we didn't recognize.

Were we bothered that Hollis no longer acted or seemed like a local or that she came to the island only during the summer months and the Holiday Stroll, with the occasional Thanksgiving and Daffodil Festival weekend thrown in? The honest answer to these questions was this: Some of us were bothered, while others were just happy that she was happy.

We were all, however, quick to claim Hollis as our own when she became internet famous!

During the darkest days of the pandemic — when businesses closed and the stock market crashed and restaurants pivoted to takeout only and the death toll was rising, rising, rising — Hollis posted well-edited content on her then-modest food blog, *Hungry with Hollis* (at the time, it was a "food community" of 274 subscribers). Hollis calmed herself in her Wellesley kitchen making a meat-loaf sandwich with home-made refrigerator pickles on freshly baked Japanese milk bread. The video went viral. Just like the video of the Italian gentleman playing the violin for his neighbors on his balcony in Bologna, Hollis's video struck a chord. The sandwich was elevated: the meat loaf was flecked with onions and herbs and topped with a rosy "special sauce"; the pickles were crisp, bright, and tangy; the Japanese milk bread — that Instagram darling —- was pillowy but sturdy enough to maintain the integrity of the sandwich.

Was the sandwich time-intensive? Yes — but suddenly the world had nothing but time.

Was the sandwich cheap? Yes — four sandwiches could be made from merely seventeen dollars' worth of groceries. And an "impossible" version could be made for vegans.

It was what everyone needed: comfort food that was aspirational.

Hollis's modest food blog suddenly became immodest, flashy even. In a week's time, the blog's newsletter had over half a million subscribers. Hollis added her recipe for creamy yellow tomato gazpacho and a shatteringly crispy fried chicken. The blog's fans responded not only to the recipes but to Hollis herself. She became the best friend they all wished they had; she served up "everything is going to be okay" vibes. They loved that in her cooking videos, Hollis presented an unvarnished version of herself — wrinkles, freckles, a slight double chin. (The middle-aged women among them thought, *Better her than me; I would never allow a camera to zoom in that close;* the Millennials and Gen Zers thought, *If she doesn't want makeup, fine, but how about a polish-and-glow filter?*) Hollis's blond hair showed a touch of gray, and she styled it in a non-style: straight, parted down the middle, tucked behind her ears. Her neck always looked good. *(What does she use on it,* they wondered, *and will she link to the products somewhere?)* She always wore a crisp cotton blouse (she had the same one in a rainbow of colors, though everyone agreed Hollis looked prettiest in the sky blue) with the starched collar flipped up and a pair of gold hoops the diameter of a quarter. Someone asked about the earrings, and she confided that they were a present from her father when she graduated from high school in 1987. Hollis's fans lauded her for "keeping it real," though they couldn't help noticing her enormous diamond engagement ring (it must have been three carats!) and her diamond-and-sapphire wedding band.

After Hollis posted a video for a potato-and-white-cheddar tart with a crispy bacon crust, her blog's newsletter broke the one million-subscriber milestone. (Leave it to bacon!) With the help of her daughter, Caroline, who was a film student at NYU and extremely tech-savvy, Hollis started a website for the blog and added two features. The first, called Kitchen Lights, was an interactive map of the world. When someone was engaging with the website, a pinprick of light appeared on the map so that visitors to the site could imagine another cook in, say, Spokane, Washington, or Grand Island, Nebraska, standing in her or his kitchen mincing chives and parsley for Hollis's tortellini salad.

The second feature, called the Corkboard, allowed Hollis's faithful followers to leave messages, post recipes, review restaurants, critique cookbooks, and ask questions such as *Why does Planters still include Brazil nuts in its mixed-nuts can when no one eats them?* Hollis posted on the Corkboard herself once or twice a week, updating the community on her latest triumphs: She had been approached to design her own cookware, she had a book deal looming, there was talk of her own show, which would include not only cooking but lifestyle tips.

Yes, yes, yes! Hollis's millions of fans wanted it all. They couldn't get enough of our Hollis Shaw (we were thrilled she'd kept her maiden name). Her life was so neat, so tidy, so blessed, and their lives improved simply by being Hollis-adjacent. Hollis had 1,670 newsletter subscribers from Nantucket (including her former English teacher Ms. Fox, who "always knew she would do big things"). In the summer of 2022, Hungry with Hollis was as popular as Wordle and the Wicked Island Bakery's morning buns; we couldn't go to the RJ Miller Salon or for drinks at the Ships Inn without hearing about Hollis Shaw.

She had become a bona fide Nantucket celebrity.

On Thursday, December 15, Ms. Fox is on the website looking for the easy holiday hors d'oeuvre recipes that Hollis promised to post — Ms. Fox has a Yankee swap to attend — when a new Corkboard message from Hollis pops up on her screen.

> To the Hungry with Hollis community:
>
> My husband, Matthew, passed away this morning unexpectedly. I need to ask for privacy as I grapple with this devastating tragedy. I'll be stepping away from the website for a while, as I'm sure you'll all understand. I hope to return at some point, though right now, I can't imagine when. Hold your loved ones close.
>
> With gratitude, Hollis

Ms. Fox gasps. *Oh no! What happened?* She searches Matthew, husband of Hollis Shaw. She knows Hollis is married — those rings! — though she never mentions her husband. (Ms. Fox and some of the others wish he were more present, like Ina Garten's Jeffrey.)

Whenever Ms. Fox thinks of Hollis with someone, she pictures the high-school boyfriend, Jack Finigan, with his cute dimples.

The next morning in the *Nantucket Standard,* we all see the obituary: "Summer Resident Dr. Matthew Madden Killed in Car Accident." There are also notices in the *Boston Globe* ("Renowned MGH Surgeon and Harvard Med Professor Killed in One-Car Accident in Wellesley") and the *New York Times* ("Dr. Matthew Madden, Leading Cardiac Surgeon and International Lecturer, Dead at 55").

Ms. Fox wants to reach out, and she's not alone — within a matter of hours, there are 17,262 Corkboard messages offering thoughts and prayers, some posted by people who had themselves lost husbands, wives, parents, siblings, children. Hollis's followers find her note so raw and relatable that they can picture her trembling fingers as she typed; they can hear her ragged sobs. They all want to offer solace . . . but their motives aren't completely selfless. When will Hollis be back on the website? Valentine's Day? (No, too soon.) Easter, maybe?

Here on Nantucket, we think how unfair life can be: Hollis's mother died too young, and now her husband has as well. We wonder if Hollis will return to the island for the summer. Will she feel like playing tennis at the Field and Oar Club or drinking rosé at the Deck? Fast Eddie Pancik, our perennially thirsty real estate agent, asks his sister, Barbie, if it would be in bad taste to see if Hollis is planning on selling the house in Squam.

Yes, you idiot, Barbie says.

On June 21, the first day of summer, Romeo at the Steamship Authority reports that Hollis Shaw has just driven off the ferry in her trusty Volvo, which is packed with boxes, bags, and what looks through the window like a portable pizza oven; Hollis's Serbian sheepdog, Henrietta, is asleep in the back seat. *Good for Hollis!* we think. *She came home.*

For a few weeks, sightings of Hollis around the island are rare. She doesn't attend the Nantucket Book Festival or the annual Squam Road Homeowners Association meeting. Johnny Baylor, who drives for DoorDash, reports delivering sushi from Bar Yoshi to Hollis's house one night and a lobster roll from the Sea Grille another. Hollis's longtime neighbor Kerri Gasperson sees Hollis walking Henrietta at dusk, but Hollis has AirPods in, and Kerri doesn't want to bother her.

We understand that it takes time to process a sudden, unexpected loss. We assume Hollis will spend her summer alone, practicing self-care and privately mourning the man she was married to for twenty-four years.

But when we hear about the Five-Star Weekend — so creative! so unusual! — we all agree: This could be just the thing she needs.

Accident Report I

It's early morning on December 15; Hollis Shaw is in the kitchen of her Wellesley home prepping the dough for cheddar tartlets. Her husband, Dr. Matthew Madden, has a ten o'clock flight to Germany — he's presenting a paper at a cardiology conference in Leipzig and will be gone for five days.

This opening scene, should Hollis show a video of it, would seem to be one of domestic bliss. Hollis wears a pair of tailored red-plaid pajamas; her hair is held back in a clip. She has a footed bowl of café au lait steaming next to the slab of cool, gray-veined marble where she's rolling out her pastry dough. Carols play over the sound system; "The Holly and the Ivy" is Hollis's favorite and she sings along in a faux-operatic voice. Hollis's kitchen is all decked out for the holidays: spruce garlands encircle the weathered wooden beams, and her collection of copper pots gleams like new pennies on her open shelves. She's trimmed a "kitchen tree" with culinary ornaments: a tiny metal whisk, a wooden rolling pin, a bone-china box of doughnuts. Hollis has also hung miniature wreaths on all her glass-fronted cabinets. (Her daughter, Caroline, would probably declare the wreaths — as well as the apothecary jars filled with ribbon candy and gumdrops — "too much.") The picture window above the sink where Hollis does dishes looks over the mature oaks and evergreens of her side yard. The view offers a pleasant distraction, especially this morning as snowflakes as big and fluffy as cotton balls float to the ground. Hollis loves nothing more than snow during the holidays.

Her timer chimes, and Hollis pulls a tray of crispy bacon from the oven. Like magic, her Serbian sheepdog, Henrietta, jingles into the kitchen (Hollis has put bells on her collar) and raises her furry face.

"Fine," Hollis says, and she gives the old girl a piece. She drains the rest on a paper towel next to the red-pepper-and-smoked-Gouda quiche she made earlier that morning. She cuts a wedge of quiche and arranges it on a plate with a few slices of bacon and sections of a Cara Cara orange, which are a delightful and surprising pink.

When she hears Matthew's footsteps on the stairs, she closes her eyes and takes a sustaining breath.

Don't bring it up, she tells herself. *Let him go graciously.*

But the truth is, this trip to Leipzig bothers Hollis; she was up half the night fretting about it. Matthew will present his paper tomorrow morning, so he could easily leave Germany tomorrow afternoon and make it home in time for their annual holiday party on Saturday. Hollis and Matthew have hosted a holiday gathering every year since they moved to Wellesley, and it's always the third Saturday in December. Matthew claimed he "thought it was later," so he made plans to stay at the conference until the end and then travel to Berlin to visit his mentor Dr. Emanuel Schrader, who was just diagnosed with Parkinson's and can no longer practice surgery.

"But you can't miss our party!" Hollis said when he told her.

Matthew had chuckled. "We can both agree this is *your* party, sweet-love. With all the Swellesley glitterati in attendance, you won't even notice I'm not there."

His tone had been light, playful even — but Hollis was still hurt. She *did* throw the party pretty much single-handedly every year. She made all the food — the cheddar tartlets, the tenderloin sandwiches, the tiny potatoes topped with caviar — she buffed the champagne flutes, lined the luminaires along the driveway, stuffed gift bags with her homemade toffee for guests to take home. She sent the invitations, and her list *was* longer every December (except for the year when Hollis broke up with Electra Undergrove and her crew).

Despite this, Hollis can't imagine standing in the doorway to greet everyone without Matthew at her side. It's *literally* unthinkable.

But apparently not for him.

* * *

Now Matthew walks into the kitchen. He always wears a suit when he flies, and today he has on the red Vineyard Vines tie printed with Santas in speedboats — the very tie Hollis purchased for him to *wear to the party!* He hums along to the carol currently playing — "Once in Royal David's City" — and holds his right wrist out so that Hollis can help him with his cuff link, which is a silver reindeer. He's certainly in the holiday spirit.

Hollis inhales the scent of his Kiehl's shaving lotion. She loves the smell; it reminds her of date night and of the (increasingly rare) mornings when she wakes up in his arms.

She can't believe he's leaving.

She wills herself to say, *Here's breakfast,* or *Let me get your coffee* — Matthew takes his coffee black and scalding hot, and she doesn't pour it until he's standing right in front of her. But instead what comes out of her mouth is "I *really* wish you'd change your plans."

After Matthew leaves for the airport — far later than he wanted to — Hollis gathers the pastry dough into a ball, wraps it in plastic, and sets it in the fridge. She no longer feels like cooking. Matthew's breakfast is untouched, but instead of covering the plate with foil and saving it for later — she deplores waste, one product of being Tom Shaw's daughter — she scrapes the food into Henny's dog bowl. Then she rips a paper towel from the roll and wipes at her eyes. She can't believe how quickly their conversation escalated into a fight.

"Lately, you've been making anything but me a priority," she said. "Work, travel, and now Dr. Schrader."

"The man was my mentor, Hollis. Berlin is a two-hour drive from Leipzig. It would be egregious not to visit him, considering the circumstances."

Instead of conceding this point, Hollis launched into her graver concerns. She had felt them drifting apart ever since Caroline left for college. Hollis had always dreamed of a marriage just like Matthew's parents had — they were romantic and devoted to each other to the very end.

But when, Hollis wondered, was the last time their marriage had felt romantic? It would be romantic if Matthew canceled this trip, but that wasn't going to happen. She could tell simply by the set of his shoulders, his jaw; he was eager to get out the door.

"Sometimes it feels like we're nothing more than roommates," Hollis said. She was tempted to mention how long it had been since they'd had sex, but that was as much her fault as his. During the day, she was busy, busy, busy and she fell into bed exhausted every night.

Matthew did his doctor's trick of appearing to listen but not, which was how Hollis knew he wasn't engaged; he was just waiting for her to be done, which was equal parts infuriating and disheartening. Matthew cleared his throat and checked his watch. Hollis wiped away her gathering tears as he pulled on his trench coat and his leather driving gloves. Matthew crouched down to rub Henny's face, then gave Hollis a fierce squeeze — she felt something, at least, in his touch.

Just before he left, he turned around. "You've changed," he said, then sighed. "And we've changed." He stepped out into the snow, closing the door behind him.

* * *

Now the words ring in Hollis's ears. *You've changed. And we've changed.* She would like to say she has no idea what he means — but she fears she does. Since Hollis's website took off and the opportunities to exploit her new popularity arose, she's become a different person, one who has a hard time experiencing a moment without wanting to document it for her newsletter subscribers. She is always, now, on a screen — her phone, her laptop, or both. She has changed, and by extension, she supposes, they've changed. But surely Matthew understands that, after twenty years of being a wife and mother, Hollis is excited about building something of her own?

She picks up the phone and calls him, ready to apologize for being a bull in an emotional china shop, but she's shuttled to Matthew's voice mail. She calls right back — again, voice mail. She waits for the beep, then says, "My love for you hasn't changed."

In case Matthew doesn't listen to his voice mail (does anyone listen to voice mail anymore?), she sends a text: I love you, Dr. M. You're important to me. We are important to me.

She waits a few moments, but there's no response. It seems suddenly urgent that she convey this message to him, that he hear her say the words *I love you. You are important.* She tries calling again, and again, she gets voice mail.

Fine, she thinks. *He needs time to simmer down.* She'll try him again once she's sure he's settled in the Lufthansa lounge. But the phrase *And we've changed* concerns her. What was he trying to say?

She feels herself growing melodramatic, which is very unlike her. Everything will be fine. Matthew will miss their party, yes, but he'll be home in plenty of time for their family Christmas. Dr. Schrader has Parkinson's. Of course Matthew should visit him.

Hollis sits down at her laptop and decides to make a dinner reservation for two at Mistral on New Year's Eve. She and Matthew will Uber into the city so they can drink as much champagne as they want; Hollis will buy a new dress, something black and flirty. Next, Hollis intends to check her website — her followers are waiting for the cheddar-tartlet recipe — but instead, she logs onto Facebook. After a few pointless seconds of trying to resist her worst impulses, she ends up at the profile page of Jack Finigan, her high-school boyfriend. There are no new posts; Jack posts only two or three times a year. The last time was in the fall: a photo of Jack standing at the edge of a lake somewhere in Western Massachusetts, holding up a trout. He hasn't posted any pictures of Mindy, his longtime girlfriend, since the summer before last. Hollis has done the predictable thing and tried to look at Mindy's profile, but Mindy has privacy settings in place so all Hollis can see is her background photo, which is a quilt, presumably one she made herself. Hollis knows she's stalking, but it's innocent; she would never reach out to him. She wonders if Jack — or Mindy — has heard about the *Hungry with Hollis* blog.

The knock at the front door startles Hollis; she feels caught. She clicks out of Facebook and hurries down the hall. Blue and red lights reflect off the snow in her front yard.

"Mrs. Madden?" the police officer says. He's young, maybe only a few years older than Caroline, and Hollis can't imagine what he's doing there. It's so early; she's still in her pajamas. She nearly corrects him: Her last name is Shaw, not Madden. But in that instant, she realizes he must be here because of Matthew — something about Matthew?

"Yes?" she says.

The precise words are lost but somehow Hollis understands that there was an accident, something involving deer, a mama and baby, the officer says. Matthew's car spun out of control and flipped over on Dover Street.

Dover Street? Hollis thinks. They drive it all the time, every day; they've been doing that for years, decades. And yes, there are always deer running across Dover, especially during hunting season. "Is he hurt?" Hollis says, her voice still sort of normal-sounding despite the panic that enfolds her. She peeks around the officer's shoulder to his cruiser. Is Matthew in the back? Was he . . . taken to the hospital? Then she meets the officer's eyes. "Is he okay?"

"He's dead, ma'am," the officer says.

Suddenly Hollis is on the door, screaming, wailing; she doesn't care that a stranger is watching. Henny comes jingling in and starts licking Hollis's face. Hollis hears the strains of a song playing in the kitchen — "Ding Dong, Merrily on High" — and she covers her ears. The officer asks if there's anyone she would like him to call.

"My husband! Call my husband!" she screams. In that moment, this still seems like a possibility. Matthew is a doctor, a fixer; he'll make this better. He's the only one who can.